DARK MATTER PRESENTS

MONSTROUS FUTURES

A SCI-FI HORROR ANTHOLOGY

Edited by Alex Woodroe
Book Design and Layout by Rob Carroll
Cover Art by Olly Jeavons
Cover Design by Rob Carroll

ISBN 978-1-958598-07-8 (paperback)
ISBN 978-1-958598-21-4 (eBook)

darkmatter-ink.com

DARK MATTER PRESENTS

MONSTROUS FUTURES

A SCI-FI HORROR ANTHOLOGY

EDITED BY
ALEX WOODROE

DARK
MATTER
INK

Contents

6 • Contents

Content Warning

This anthology contains content that may be unsuitable for certain audiences. Stories include foul language, disturbing imagery, and graphic depictions of sex and violence. Reader discretion is advised.

Introduction

By Andrew F. Sullivan

We were lied to.

Tech has become shorthand for a shell game, venture capital shuttled from one haven to another before the rest of the world can catch up. The dystopia is here, to invoke that old saw in a more haggard form, just unequally distributed, the ghost of a still-living Gibson looming over our existence with a bitter laugh. It's always been here. It never went away, only changed its face.

Each morning there is a fresh algorithm attempting to seize you with its seven-fingered hands, smiling with endless rows of whitened teeth, asking you to enter its maw with credit extended while counseling you through a screen on the best way to make yourself a productive earner for someone higher up the ladder, someone in a tower or a bunker or another highly appointed hole.

All of this has been agreed upon in print so fine it slips right through your skin and enters your bloodstream. All of this is part of an ongoing extraction project—our humanity just another natural resource to be pillaged and burned. Your attention will be priced accordingly.

The idea of progress as possibility is dead on the vine, rotted out from within, fed on by parasitic wasps flitting from one rind to another, whether it's a drawing of an ape shitting on its own face forever or a pyramid scheme made from dried liver treats. There is a car without a driver out there with your name inscribed on its grill, waiting to emboss it on your forehead at sixty miles an hour. They will say you should have seen it coming in the dark.

Let the scales fall from our eyes on the rate-limited road to nowhere and embrace what was always true—the future is not about what could be but about what we can do to adapt, to cope, to survive its imminent arrival. The future is that hand on our throats figuring out just how hard it can squeeze without disrupting the global supply chain beyond repair.

The stories in this collection grapple with what we already know, invoking the ever-present ghosts of progress that haunt us. They explore the fallible nature of our perceptions, the way our own brains can undermine our sense of self. J. A. W. McCarthy's "Consider This An Opportunity" offers up a sibling to fill a hole that may never have been there in the first place, a body decaying in real time to serve its newfound, twisted purpose. In Ivy Grimes's "The Wrong Mall," one girl attempts to find somewhere to belong, only to find her grip on reality itself slip away in the virtual recreations of the Gloweria.

A future that is so near it breathes the same air we do, that requires our obedience to its own inhuman hierarchies of need. In "Fully Comprehensive Code Switch" by M. H. Ayinde, the body is held hostage to the dictates of the Switch, which modulates the voice and behavior of its supposed owner to survive the corporate pecking order. In "My Strengths Include Customer Service and Teamwork" by Lew Furber, no mechanism is needed, as the functions of the worker are instilled from birth and enforced through pain, even as the world melts into a desert outside.

Flesh is just as malleable as code in our near future. "The Least I Can Do" by Koji A. Dae requires pulling on the literal guise of someone else, a fresh and lab grown skin. In Kaitlin Tremblay's "For Those Not Yet Lost" the autopsy of a time traveler unearths a cryptic warning scraped into the viscera. There's no escape from our obligations. In "Who Sees All" by Avra Margariti, the surveillance state is embedded in the body itself, the family happy to play the role of warden, embracing the panopticon as proud parenting.

This collection is not a diagnosis for our modern age or a prescription for what ails us. Fiction is not a soothing balm for our fractured psyches or an antidote for a poisoned mind. We can acknowledge our dread and attempt to name it. Process what we cannot control: systems outside the individual's capacity, entities with no end game beyond a number, institutions serving old dead gods that still insist on being fed. See how our fears parallel each other in their conception.

We can confront entropy and its inherent decay, stare down the dissolution of all things without engaging in the embarrassing ego trip of an apocalypse. Assuming that your own end means the end of all other things at once takes a certain kind of arrogance, one quickly disproven by whoever follows in your steed. Our past is littered with promises of oblivion, self-serving and decadent claims of the egotist, the siren song of cults innumerable. To quote Waubgeshig Rice, "an apocalypse in one place is a new beginning in another." Your end is not *the* end.

The future does not arc toward anything. It spins on into the nothing unconcerned by our lamentations. It does offer us a chance to acknowledge what has failed, what has fallen, and what may come again. It gives us an opportunity to plant some fresh seeds in our collective, seething loam—to see what sprouts anew from the overwhelming accumulation of our past mistakes. These new growths, these stories, they don't promise progress, just an extension of this monstrous, human timeline. An ability to see clearly what we have wrought, to name our own designs and their latest iterations, all tossed into the same steaming pile. Peek outside your window. Open up your browser. Take a good look for yourself. The landfill stretches on forever.

Once a Traveler
By Christi Nogle

Elle and her clients said their long goodbyes as she waited to board the flight. They were going to leave her free instead of riding her home, which was one way of giving a tip. She carried two of them this time, thoughtful old Mrs. Spears and cranky Mr. Longfellow, though who could ever say if those were their real names? She liked it when there were only two because during waits, their facial holograms appeared on each of her shoulders like the angel and the devil used to do in the old cartoons her grandmother had shown her when she was tiny.

The faces were not there to anyone but Elle; she saw them through her glasses. She heard their voices through tiny speakers set into the earpieces. They were in their homes; whether bedridden or puttering about, she would never know.

Just now, she and the old lady had finished exclaiming over all the fun they'd had this vacation and they began commenting on a group of young adults who were engaged in deep discussion across the lobby. Cute, healthy kids. *Ought to say hi and shoot them some business cards*, Elle thought, but she was too tired to get up. This trip had been a week of guided rafting and hiking in the Idaho wilderness. Lovely but very taxing, so now she and her clients rested and watched the kids' animated conversation, which got them all talking about youth.

"I used to be so very quick with everything, and now I'm so slow," said prim-faced Mrs. Spears. "When I was young, I would spend time in the group chats, you know what those were? Chatrooms?"

"Yes," said Elle. This was the first time she had felt that little pang of recognition when a client talked about aging.

"I would sit in chatrooms and just crank out these pithy remarks and one-liners, watch everyone else's responses and oftentimes predict what they'd say before they said it. These days, I'd look at something like that and, knowing I couldn't keep up, I'd say 'fuck it.' Do something else. Read a book, work in the garden. It's not bad, really. It's—"

"You're just old," said snake-faced Mr. Longfellow. "Nothing surprising about any of that."

Why doesn't he just log out? Elle thought, but she knew he was waiting to make sure she boarded safely. It was a social nicety, the least he could do after having ridden her all week.

She watched the kids. The tall girl with the tight ballerina bun, in particular, looked like a born traveler. Long, strong legs. Beautiful, but not intimidatingly so. She kept laughing, showing large teeth, and her entire demeanor made Elle think of good sleep, perfect health, and more to the point, a lack of secrecy.

"Listen, please don't feel obliged to wait. I can shoot you boarding information—I can even shoot you a selfie if you want to get to something more interesting," Elle said.

"See you in December," said Mr. Longfellow, and he blinked out before Elle could respond. She'd nearly forgotten about his ski trip. *Ugh.*

"It was marvelous, Elle, but it *is* about lunchtime here," said Mrs. Spears.

"I just want to tell you how glad I was to have you again," said Elle. There were more kind words spoken and tentative plans for an island trip in the next six months or so—budget allowing—but within moments, Mrs. Spears had logged out and Elle's glasses chimed with a ten-star review. Elle had regained her freedom for the first time in a week.

Only she wasn't free at all. She had to talk up the teens and shoot cards to all of them while making clear through eye contact and smile-mirroring that the tall girl was really the one being scouted. She had to go over reports on the plane and did not finish this task before landing. In fact, she had to complete the reports over her simple dinner and kept working as the remains of it cooled on her plate.

Eventually, she had to abandon the reports for the evening because it was already time to shower, put on pajamas, brush her teeth, and lie down. A five-star review chimed just as she was flossing. A wave of rage. *The absolute fucker.* The moments before sleep came were her one chance to think, but—curse her perfect sleep sometimes—they did not last. She intended to think through all of Mr. Longfellow's little aggressions for her reports. His refusal to log out when she ate, for example, but she lost consciousness before she could call up any more.

The moment Elle put on her glasses, Troy's voice greeted her. "Good morning! Can you come into the office today?"

"It's a day off," she said. A day to wash laundry and restock the refrigerator, anyway. Maybe a moment to sit on the balcony.

"I know," said Troy, "but we have a group of three potential travelers, and one I think you scouted, anyway. Roxanne? Tall girl?"

"That's impossible."

"She's local, looks like she logged in two minutes after getting the card, and we already had the other two awaiting an appointment date. They're all eager. We could get someone else, but they know you from the commercial, so—"

"Yep," Elle said. "I'll be there." She'd had endless requests for recruitment meetings ever since that commercial first aired over fifteen years ago. *Elle travels the world for a living. She can take you with her anywhere, any time.* Vivid shots of hikes, street carnivals, cruises. Her legs had been so beautiful in a pair of khaki cargo shorts, and now whenever she thought of the commercial, she thought of those perfect smooth legs.

"An hour?" said Todd.

"Excellent." Elle selected a deep chocolate-brown sheath and blazer, opaque tights. Always had to cover the scarring now.

But she flushed with gratitude for her nice, easy wardrobe and her cozy apartment with its soft colors and pretty rugs. She was well rested and had all the time she needed to do her face, stop for coffee, and breeze into the office, where the workers would greet her in a show of affection as well as respect. It really was quite a life, wasn't it?

Elle was glad Troy had chosen the smaller, more intimate conference room with the old-fashioned comfy chairs. The kids were already seated, the tall one looking good in a fashionable brown skirt suit and bare legs. The one beside her was a little too voluptuous, face a little too flashy as well. The third looked much like Troy. Two yeses and a no, probably. She wished Troy could just go ahead and dismiss the unlikely one, but a plan was a plan.

She and Troy beamed as they introduced themselves. "So glad you could come in on such short notice," Troy said, to Elle as well as the kids.

A warm feeling washed over Elle for no particular reason. She was glad to see the tall girl, as she'd get a commission, but that wouldn't bring this flush on, would it? She felt a little sweat coming on her forehead, which troubled her. Sweat without heat or exertion was never a good sign.

"Roxanne," said the girl with a low little nod.

"Brynn," added the next one.

"Harper," said the Troy-looking one.

Might as well send Brynn across the hall, Elle thought.

"We're here to answer any questions and, well, just talk through the process," said Troy.

"Do you travel, too?" said Roxanne.

"I used to!" said Troy, "Now I do all this boring office work."

He has kids. A life outside the job.

"It's really wonderful to meet you, um, officially," Roxanne said to Elle. "I still remember the commercial."

Flattering me, letting the others know we've already met. It's good that she's smart, but is she too scheming? Troy still looked elated, though. He hadn't noticed, or it hadn't fazed him.

Harper said, "My mom wanted me to ask first thing. There's no, uh—"

"No sex?" said Troy. "Correct. This division provides an entirely non-sexual travel experience. Across the hall may be a different story." He winked.

Elle looked at Brynn, who looked away. "Everyone here is eighteen, though, right?" she said, and they nodded. Troy tapped his glasses to let her know their data had been reviewed.

"And no, uh, implantations?" asked Harper with a gesture to the side of his head.

"Glasses-only here. We're real old-fashioned," said Elle.

"The jobs are really more siloed than people realize," said Troy. "Across the hall you could hire, for example, a honeymooning couple equipped with intimate sensors. At another agency you'll find gastronomical travelers who have all this scent and taste gear–'implantations,' if you will–and so many other kinds as well. Here, we do what we like to refer to as 'clean' work. It's all basically visual. They're seeing what you see, and that's it."

"I mean, that's not quite it," said Elle.

"No?" said Troy with a curious look. Elle really did like him.

"It can't be entirely visual," said Roxanne, nodding. "If it was, they could just watch a movie."

Coming to my defense.

"Right, I mean, I think it's important for you to have as clear a view as you can as early as you can. That way you can make an informed decision about whether you want to do it," she said, looking to Roxanne and sweeping to Harper, "or not." She ended with a long look toward Brynn, who squirmed in her chair. *Good. She gets the message.*

"So what else is it about if it's not the scenery or whatever?" asked Harper.

"Control. It's about them controlling where you go, what you look at, what you do. You have to be able to pretend they hold your reins, and you have to be okay with that. It's less true when you carry two or more parasites, but in the beginning, they'll set you up with a single person for each trip, and I'm sure you realize this, but it will be a very wealthy person who is used to getting whatever they want. Many times, they will be very nice, but not always. They might want you to do things the agency says you can't. So you have to be able to negotiate and even manipulate," said Elle.

Oh yeah, Roxanne's face and posture said, clear as words. *I know how to manipulate.*

"Parasites?" said Brynn.

Troy said, "In the marketing, it's all the same. They are travelers, you are travelers, but in-house, as you can imagine—and you've signed NDAs, recall—we need terms to distinguish. The official terms are *surrogate* and *client*—"

"But the terms you'll hear and use around the office are *host* and *parasite*. Do those terms feel uncomfortable?" asked Elle.

Their faces blank, each one gently shook their head. Maybe they all *were* good material. Give Brynn's face a good scrubbing and yes, Elle could see it now.

She added, "And when people say it's visual, that's true, but it isn't just about the scenery or museums. It's also about how people look at you. The looks you get from people who see that you're young and healthy. Appreciative looks. Parasites, most of them, aren't used to anyone looking at them that way anymore—if they ever were. They'll want you to gaze into the mirror often, too."

"I love the idea of helping people," said Roxanne, and for the first time, Elle became aware that she disliked the girl.

"Hey," said Troy, tapping his earpiece again. "I'm thinking that I ought to go take care of something out front. Would you mind?"

"Of course not," Elle said. His exit was planned, of course, to give an opening for harder questions. Nothing was ever private anymore. Even the kids knew that.

Troy rose, and they all followed him with their eyes. They were quiet for a moment.

"If they get off on seeing you in a mirror, is it really non-sexual?" asked Harper.

"We don't control whatever they do in the privacy of their own homes," Elle said. *The privacy of their own unoccupied bodies.* "But if you catch even a hint of anything on the audio, that's grounds for nulling the contract."

"Do you need to be asexual, then? And do you need to be single?" asked Brynn.

Yes, thought Elle. *How can you devote yourself to the work otherwise?*

"I mean, it helps," she said, "but it isn't required. You don't have a lot of time for relationships while you're an active traveler. That's why Troy went in for office work."

"You need to be really open and pure," said Roxanne, looking dreamy.

"I don't know about pure. Let's say wholesome and a little distant, maybe? If you can be in the moment all day, seeing things, hiking around, meeting people without trying to become close. If you can eat at set mealtimes, go to sleep early and sleep really well—you have to stay healthy in order to do all the hiking—"

"And not have any obsessions or secrets, really," said Roxanne.

Elle flushed again, hard. She'd have swooned if she'd been standing. The image came to mind before the next question: Abandoned on the beach, leg broken, afraid to scream. It hadn't been an assault of any sort. It had been pure accident, a stupid fall—

And the question, from Harper of course, "My mom said I should ask what a bad day looks like. The worst thing that happened on the job."

"Your mother's smart. You're glad to have her?"

Harper nodded.

Then go back to her now. Tell her this looks sketchy. It's what she's expecting, anyway.

She wouldn't tell about the worst thing, the broken leg. She had other stories to tell for this question and selected the one of a weird parasite who kept coming back under different names, kind of a stalker—but the agency had been an excellent advocate in that case, and the parasite firmly taken care of, and all of that was fine,

She segued into a series of terrifying schedule changes during the start of the latest pandemic and was able to turn the conversation at last toward practicalities and perks: you had to declare parasites just like any other baggage; they could tip and were sometimes quite generous; there were regulars who became like friends sometimes. And yes, it *was* nice to have that feeling like you weren't alone.

The questions died down, and Troy returned. The wrap-up was autopilot stuff. Elle began to think about what groceries she'd get. Day-trips only this week, and then two weeks in Italy and Greece. Her feet hurt just thinking about it. Finally, the kids departed for further meetings.

"You'll get a little bonus for coming in," Troy said.

"And commission."

"Of course. Forever grateful," He tapped his earpiece again, stood. "I need to go, but drop by the main office on your way out. Trevor wanted to see you."

"Trevor?" The scheduling guy. That was alarming.

Troy didn't reply but touched Elle's shoulder lightly on his way out.

She felt drained and sat still for a while thinking of her grandmother's house. The smells of vanilla and roast turkey, bright crocheted things all around. The old lady's veiny hands and pleasant, waxy face. *Strange to think of that.* She shook her head, rose, and headed down the hall.

She had always liked this office's restroom with its retro stainless steel and glass mosaic tile. She liked bathrooms, in general, because clients were never allowed to follow her there. Out of habit, she removed and folded the glasses to make sure no one could enter the stall with her. She did that even at home.

Elle peed and gazed at her vague reflection in the brushed steel door. Her sensible panties were stretched around her knees, pristine white against her mocha-colored tights, and she chuckled to realize: no period, not for a while now. Eight weeks, longer? *That's what the flush is, isn't it? A hot flash.*

So that's the end of that, then. It didn't matter all that much, but it felt too soon. Such things always do.

The memory came again of the time she broke her leg. A missed step on the stairs leading down to a beach, an unlucky boulder. Not a simple fracture but something gruesome, many abrasions running the length of the leg as well as the compound fracture, and blood caked in sand. Lucky she ever recovered enough to travel—but she was so young, so healthy and conscientious about rehab. And well insured. Everything turned out just as well as it could have, but sometimes, in the bathroom like this all alone, she flashed back to the terror. The parasite had led her down there late at night, when there was no one to help. He had talked her into going where she shouldn't have gone.

She'd screamed at first, couldn't help it, but after the first screams, she begged for help. Call the hotel up the hill, the ambulance, get someone.

The flat-faced parasite—a Mr. Holmes, she'd never forget it—had abandoned her. He had not logged off, but had stopped responding. Had he been distracted by something at home and taken off his VR setup before the fall? That's what he would say, later, but Elle didn't believe it. She lay there out of her mind with pain and fear. After the first screams, she was afraid to call out, afraid of what her calling might bring. Could someone attack her in this state? The glasses alone were worth thousands. She crawled; she tore her palms and the knee on the unbroken leg.

The abandonment might not have mattered at all, but the dispatcher had shirked their duty, too, for over an hour that night. That dispatcher was fired, which made Elle quite glad.

The parasite, though. Had he been there all the time watching, saying nothing? "Getting off on it," as that kid had suggested earlier. How sick, how entirely sick, if that was what had happened. Elle believed it was. She had not felt alone when it happened and thought that, after all the years of doing this, she would have been able to tell.

"Is anyone here?" she whispered. She touched her temples and around her head, searching. Harper's question came back: *No implantations?*

How would one ever know? If you'd ever been in the hospital for any sort of surgery, how would you know?

"I *am* alone now," Elle said in her normal voice.

A soft crinkling sound came from outside the door. Elle struggled her tights up, checked that her skirt hung free, and opened the stall door.

Roxanne stood before the mirror. She'd let down her masses of rippling auburn hair .

"I didn't hear you come in," Elle said, approaching the other sink, turning on the tap.

"Thank you, for being here today," said Roxanne, who was blotting her forehead with rice paper.

Their faces were quite similar in shape. Elle's looked more tired of course, with dents under the eyes. She dried her hands, put her glasses on to check her makeup, and watched the dents disappear. Her lips plumped, too. Now they were near-twins apart from the height and the tumble of hair. And the look of pure elation on Roxanne's face, of course.

A filter of some sort, of course, but how had she never noticed it?

"I think you'll be perfect," Elle said.

Roxanne looked down. *Is she blushing?* "I guess maybe Troy thought so too. He's scheduling my first trip in a week. I can't believe it."

"That's fantastic."

"I just happened to mention I'm fluent in Italian, and it snowballed from there. I guess I'll have a trainer riding along, and one, uh, *parasite*," the girl gushed.

In Elle's earpiece, Trevor: "You didn't get away, did you? Did Troy let you know to stop by my office?"

So that's the end of that, too, then. It always comes sooner than you're thinking.

Elle rode for the first time through Italy and Greece, full-VR goggles on rather than the translucent glasses. The girl moved quickly across the landscapes and slowly through the museums and historical sites. She drew appreciative looks. She was doing great.

Roxanne's feed went off for a moment or two when she used the toilet, but then it would come right back on. Elle and the parasite, a Mx. Shelley, watched her blot her perfect face and brush her long thick hair before twisting it up into the bun.

It was pleasurable to appreciate her beauty and imagine it was Elle's own, but not more pleasurable than seeing the line of angry sunburn starting at the top of the girl's forehead or the large stress pimples forming on her chin.

Or the cut. The girl made a point of never taking her glasses off when she ate, though that was a privilege all hosts had—*She's showing off, going above and beyond. I know that impulse*—and one day she cut herself on a plate's edge. Nice little outdoor cafe, and the white plate should not have had a sharp chip on its edge, but she touched it and the blood began spurting from a fingertip.

People noticed. There was an upset around the tables nearby. "I'm all right, nothing major," she said, but her voice held a quaver. She pressed the white cloth napkin to it, but not before the blood sprinkled the tablecloth. "I'm sorry," she said over and over.

Elle was rapt.

The girl didn't work out, after all, though Mx. Shelley was delighted enough to enter ten enthusiastic stars. Elle gave her a glowing review and good notes too. It seemed she would be a great fit, but you can't tell that from the first days. By the time Roxanne took her ski trip, she was already needing a filter. Her bun looked smaller. She'd been careful to stop brushing her hair with the glasses on so that Elle could only imagine the webs of it filling the boar's hair brush. She very much wished she could see that.

By the time of Mr. Longfellow's ski trip (and Roxanne's first really scathing review), Elle was no longer training. She was dispatching. No VR gear needed. Instead, a massive bank of screens, a never-ending chat scroll with management. They'd have made her do it in the office, but then they'd have to see how many hours she worked; and so she stayed at home, first with a treadmill and stand desk, then at the kitchen table and finally in the bed.

Her eyes would go next, she knew. She was already missing things in the chat.

Bonuses had come frequently in the first days of training and then again in the first days of dispatch, but they didn't come anymore. Admonitions, instead. Very often they came from Harper, who had taken Troy's place when Troy moved up.

Could I even afford to be a parasite now? Even one of those bargain deals where you go with a group?

One day, she had ten scenes before her. Day and night, the scenery of Madrid and Utah desert and Cancun, the sights of a nightclub and a casino and a dude ranch and an art museum. Brynn, who had worked out exceedingly well, slowly rubbed on sunscreen before a mirror in an opulent bathroom. The images swirled and blurred to gray.

Elle thought she was losing her vision for a moment, but when she looked down at the floor, her pretty rag rug was still clear, glazed in sunshine.

"Dispatch? I might be having a little trouble here," someone called from far away.

Mrs. Spears' advice came back: *Say "fuck it." Do something else.*

Elle stood, stretched, and traveled only as far as her bright balcony.

The Least I Can Do
By Koji A. Dae

I've been providing the girlfriend experience to Albert for almost two years when he takes me to the 3D scanning lab. He says it's for a present, but he's cagey when I ask for details, even when we're standing in front of the large glass booth.

"The scan doesn't hurt," he assures me. I trust that much, Albert's not a sadist. A hundred Tuesday evenings and he hasn't even slapped my ass.

The tech stands to the side, looking bored or maybe uncomfortable. We have that effect on people. He's too charming and normal for my blue hair and proudly-carried ninety kilograms. There's gotta be a catch, and there is. Even though I've dropped my other clients and he doesn't date anyone else, we only meet on Tuesdays. And he pays me.

"I know what these scans can be used for," I say. "Sex dolls. Heck, a fleshed-out robot that looks and feels just like me. Are you trying to replace me?"

"Genna," Albert gives a little laugh. "There's no replacing you. Like I said, it's a present."

I tilt my chin to the tech. "How much do women get paid for a scan?"

She shrugs. "I just run the machine."

I pull out my phone. A quick search shows from ten thousand up to five-hundred thousand for a celebrity skin. I'm realistic. My body is not classically hot, but my curves are well-balanced, my skin mostly blemish-free. "Sixty-K."

This time Albert's laugh is full and from his belly. The smile on his thin lips makes it all the way to his brown eyes. "You want me to pay you so I can give you a present?"

"You're already paying me," I remind him. "I just want you to pay what I'm worth."

He's still laughing as he transfers the money to my account. Sixty grand will pay for my apartment for a year. He sends it with three casual swipes on his screen. I still can't get used to that.

"Get in the booth, vixen." He kisses my neck and pats my bottom firm enough to send a jiggle through my waist.

"You can hang your clothes there." The tech points to a hook on the wall.

I strip down. She's averting her eyes again, as if she's not going to stare at every millimeter of me during the scan. She seems relieved to close the door behind me.

The glass is one way. I can see a faint outline of my reflection— the fullness of my stomach, the strength of my thighs—but I can no longer see Albert and the tech.

"Relax and close your eyes," her voice comes over a small speaker.

The lasers hum as they scan me. I imagine them caressing my skin, skittering over the real estate of my body with eager buzzing. I imagine the sixty thousand dollars in my bank account.

The package comes in a dress box two months later. I press my finger to the delivery man's device and take the large black box up to my apartment.

The cardboard is thick, with a coating that feels like silk. I can appreciate quality packaging. After all, half my work is packaging myself for different men. The box is held closed by a tab, and when I pop it open, an inner tray slides out, holding an eerily familiar deflated doll.

I wrinkle my nose at it and notice a QR code in the corner. Scanning it takes me to a website for *SecondSkin*. My eyes widen, and I look at the doll closer. Yes, she is my skin, just two feet tall. She has the same birthmark above her hip and tattoos on the shoulders. I allow myself to touch the skin, which feels thick and rubbery.

"What the—"

SecondSkin assures me I have purchased the highest quality skin suit available and praises me for the detailed scans I sent in. It tells me I should only wear the suit for a few hours at a time at first, but once my body adjusts, I can enjoy its full effect for up to seventy-two hours.

Full effect? I tap out of my specialized product page to *SecondSkin's* homepage.

SecondSkin: An Innovative Way to Shape and Tone Without Dieting

Did Albert get me a fat suit? For two years, he's said he loves the fullness of my curves. The swing of my breasts, the hips he can hold on to, the thighs that bury him. Has it all been a lie?

I push the box off my couch, the skin tumbling limp on the floor. Well, it was his money to waste.

Albert's eyes fall when he sees me. "You're not wearing it."

I snort. "That suit's offensive."

"I love your body, Genna." He steps forward to embrace me, and I let him. After all, I'm on the clock. "But I'd like you to accompany me to some functions, and you know how it is for a man of my standing. I have to fulfill certain expectations."

"You mean there are expectations I would have to fill."

He sighs and caresses my shoulder, letting his fingers trail to the curve above my butt. He buries his lips in my hair. "I don't want you to be a secret anymore."

My stomach flips, the way it always does when we blur the lines of our relationship.

"It seems extreme."

"It's just something to try. Like lingerie or a toy."

A dildo would have been less complicated. But I think about all the toys we've tried. The ones I picked out and he bought. Did every purchase make him insecure about his measurements? A blush creeps through me—the first wave of shame hits my throat. "I didn't think about it like that."

The least I can do is try it.

Albert's due at six. That gives me time to bathe—following the instructions which demand no lotions, only pure Castile soap (provided), and a cold rinse—and slip into the second skin. Slip? Ha! This thing is tight. Unstretched, the suit comes up to my knee, and I'm supposed to squeeze the entirety of my body into it. I dip my toes into the head opening and through the chest cavity. My feet struggle at the tunnel that will eventually compress my thighs.

Pulling the skin wide, I flex and push until I sweat. There goes the benefit of the cold rinse. Straining, I slip from my bed to my floor, the fat of my thighs rippling as I hit. I rub at the bare flesh, push it and consider the bumps and dimples of cellulite.

I grunt and pull and squeeze and my toes find their appropriate chambers. I smooth down the openings for my toenails, surprised by the suppleness of the suit. I expected the feel of latex, but fully stretched, it has subtle ridges like real skin. My toes can feel the slight tickle of my fingertips. They look slender—like my toes from fifteen years ago.

Curious, edging on eager, I continue the torture of shimmying the device up my foot, around my calloused heel, over my cankle, which pops into a defined ankle and calf. I call Albert and tell him to give me another hour. We'll be late for dinner, but he shouldn't have problems changing reservations. Over an hour to get into this stupid thing?

By the time I'm up one thigh, my toes are tingling and cold. The site mentioned this as a potential side effect, said it'd pass. I keep going, slimming down and shaping my other leg.

Getting it over my ass is another struggle, and I'm tempted to break out the baby oil even though it warns against any kind of oil or lotion on the inside. I suppose that has something to do with skin irritation. I remember the sweat and pimples from wearing latex as a teen.

I give a few small hops, a wiggle, several tugs, and eventually shimmy it over what I hope will be the most difficult part. I glance at my breasts. Maybe not.

The suit compresses my waist, pushing my fat higher and higher until I'm short of breath. Then it hits my ribcage, and there's a sharp shift as things settle. My breathing is still shallow, but it feels like a tight hug. I give a sharp exhale and begin the process of wiggling my arms in place. The suit is anchored to my lower body, which gives me some leverage. Or maybe I'm just getting the hang of this. When I get to my shoulders, my breasts pop into place, suddenly as perky as they were before they grew to DD. My nipples kind of ooze out of their holes, but I smooth the openings, and my flesh responds by allowing the suit to envelop it.

All that's left is my head. My face. How can I put my face in this? But it's not suffocating. The fat of my cheeks lifts to give me higher, more pronounced cheekbones. My chin presses back. My throat feels constricted but not choked.

I take a deep breath—that's a mistake—and cough. Then I venture a look in the mirror. I look fucking amazing. I thought I'd be like a sausage bursting from its casing, but there's almost no sign of the suit. The blending of the openings that expose my crotch, nipples, nails, mouth, nose, eyes, hair—scream costly workmanship. There are no rolls. No pinching. My body is mine, just three sizes smaller. My face is mine, just ten years younger. It's practically magic.

No, not magic. Money.

I like the restaurant he takes me to. I like the people staring, trying to place me in his world. I get drunk on whiskey older than me and the thrill of notoriety.

Albert likes the tautness of my skin. My skin? It gets confusing remembering where I end and the suit begins.

"Don't take it off," he whispers when we return to my apartment.

I hadn't planned to, even though my ribs ache. There's no sexy way to slip out of this skin.

In the morning, he tells me I look amazing. "You should get yourself some new outfits though, something that fits."

He sends an excessive amount of money into my account.

The SecondSkin comes off easier than it goes on. I pull at its edges, get it going, and it rolls away from my body, as if it's as relieved as I am for a bit of space. As it slides down, I breathe easier. My head aches at the sudden flow of blood. I notice a faint blush of purple where the skin held tightest, but it was a possibility noted on the site. Nothing to worry about.

I rinse the skin with water and let it soak in its special soap, then hang it over the shower's curtain rod. It looks like a snake skin, hanging limp and translucent. Does that make me the serpent?

I let out a hiss in the bathroom mirror, bending close to look at my puffy cheeks and thick neck.

I'm supposed to wait at least three days between each session with the SecondSkin. Perfect. A shopping trip on the weekend, and I'll be ready For Albert Tuesday. I call Didi and Vesi to invite them along, but Didi's squealing in my ear before I can say anything.

"You're dating Albert Foster! And you didn't tell me?"

"How do you—he's a client."

"There are pictures of you with him. At Excalibur! And you look fantastic."

I laugh at her excitement. "I'll tell you about it when we meet up."

Putting the suit on a second time isn't much easier, but I'm discovering little tricks for slipping pockets of fat beneath the edge or flipping and rolling the material so it slides on.

Two and a half hours later, I'm a new woman. No, not new. Just thinner. Firmer. Sexier? Depends on your definition of sexy.

But according to Didi, sexier. "I'm so jealous. No dieting… and you can look like that?"

I'm getting used to the constant resistance around me. "I mean, it's not that big of a deal."

Vesi snorts. "Not a big deal? This can change your life…"

As if to prove their point, the skinny blonde sales associate makes her way to us and offers to help. All the other times I've been here, she's barely even looked at me. But now?

"Oh, that's going to look great on you!" and "You'll fill out this demi-cup perfectly, darling. Your boyfriend will love it."

Her warmth almost feels like friendship.

As we leave the store, Didi gives me a pointed look with raised eyebrows. "You need to lock Albert down."

"There's nothing to lock down. He's a client, not a boyfriend."

"But looking like that, he could be more," Vesi teases.

I look down at myself, confusion washing over me. Is it the tightness of the suit making me lightheaded, or the possibility that I could score a man like Albert Foster? I forget that I've been scoring with him discreetly for the past two years—that he pays me for my body—because this new body could win him. The real him. I shake the fog from my head, sparks glaring in my vision.

"It's not like it makes me skinny."

"No, better than skinny. You've got acceptable curves." Vesi waves a hand over her flat chest. "Men love something to hold."

The right amount of something. Held in the right shape.

After, we go for lunch. Didi and Vesi order salads. I eat an appetizer and entrée, but hesitate at dessert.

"Go on," the waiter says, eyeing my cleavage. "You can treat yourself."

And I do.

The skin hanging in my shower smells of guilt. Am I a sellout? I run my fingers over it, aching to put it on again. The compression of it feels comforting, like being under a blanket in the fall.

My own skin says no, though. Angry bruises along my ribs and stomach refuse to fade. Did I wear it too long? Eat too much? The site assures me bruises are common.

Sex in the suit is strange. I can't say it's better because my movement is stiff, and the suit strangles my sensuality. I can't say it's worse, though, because Albert can't keep his hands off me. He pets me, and I feel the heat of his fingers through the SecondSkin.

"See," he whispers as he thrusts into me. "It's not so bad to try new things."

He's right. It's not so bad. It's almost good.

The way people notice me. The way they respect me, as if I've done something to earn this body. The way they want me. I can't breathe deep enough to orgasm, but Albert's orgasm is enough to make me shudder beneath him.

I've worn the suit too long. In the morning, I stumble to the bathroom and puke. The site said this could happen due to compression of the stomach and bowel. It's why they suggest limiting the first month of wear. I'm already ten hours over and Albert hasn't left yet.

I allow my stomach to empty fully, splash cold water on my face, and go to the kitchen to make Albert a coffee. He rarely stays in the morning, but today he takes his time and fucks me again. I can't get into it the way I used to, and yet I can't resist his fascination. Has his caress changed, or does it just feel different inside this suit?

I puke green bile when he finally leaves.

My thighs are bluish-green. My toes ache with the rush of blood. My fingertips burn. I should give it a rest. Tell Albert I need to wear it for just part of our date. But three days later, I'm slipping into the skin for no reason.

I take it for a walk in the center of town to watch heads turn. I feel powerful as I steer myself into a photography studio and get a new set of photos for my website. After all, the skin was a present. It's for me, not Albert.

At home, I keep the skin on. Yes, it's hard to breathe. Yes, it makes me a little dizzy. But it also makes me wet in a way I hadn't expected, as if the suit is wringing liquid through my cunt. I book a new client. Two. The photos are going over well.

Didi says she can't bear to watch what I'm doing to myself. I stare at the mirror. Naked but shaped. Firm. Lines of bruising have formed around the edging of the suit. Sometimes I stumble when the pins and needles get too strong. Most of the time, I can cover it.

She's just jealous. Vesi, too. They've been skinny their whole lives and haven't done with their bodies what I've done in a month. My schedule is full. Clients, yes. But clients that want to take me out. Clients that want to flaunt me in front of their exes. Clients that wine and dine me with pride.

Yeah, so Vesi's married, and Didi gets boyfriends. But I've got full control over my body and my men.

It's been a week since I've seen my actual skin. At first, it was a few hours over the limit. Then a whole day. I got used to the nausea. I ate less, sat with closed eyes more. It's worth it to feel this tightness around me and the desire seeping out of strangers. Every day I take it to the park and sit it on a bench and let people stare at the hot woman I almost am.

Didi and Vesi won't return my calls. Their jealousy stings. I've been jealous of them my whole life. Now I finally have an edge on them, and they can't handle it.

Feeling in my fingertips comes and goes. There's a sharp pain that sometimes shoots up my left calf. My toes are complete tingles. I've had three clients this week and haven't orgasmed once. But the lightheadedness almost feels like a champagne buzz, which is good enough. Just pleasure in a different form.

Just me, in a different form.

Albert is still my favorite client. After all, he wanted me when I was fat. He gave me a chance at perfection. When he comes for our date, he cocks his head to the side with concern. "You okay, Genna?"

"Yeah," I giggle breathlessly. "Fantastic."

"Your eyes... we can't go out like that."

I excuse myself to the bathroom. The mirror reveals bloodshot eyes, deep purple showing through the thin edges of the suit. The eyes seem too distant. I reach my hand to the mirror and stroke the reflection of my face.

Deep breath.

I tilt my head back, giggling at the rush of blood, and place a few eye drops in each eye. A layer of makeup covers the bruising. It's enough for Albert. He's all kisses and hands when I get back.

My stomach churns loud enough for him to hear.

"Hungry?" he asks. We have yet another dinner date scheduled. This time with a few colleagues. Each week, things are getting more real with Albert. But with a fake me.

"I'm fine," I say. I've gotten used to that pain in my side and the constant bubbling of my intestines.

We should go, but he can't keep his hands off me these days. The skinnier I get, the hungrier he becomes for me. He finds his way to my nipple, but I can't feel the warmth of his mouth. I look down to make sure he's where I think he is. Yes. Teeth and tongue and lips and absolutely no sensation in me.

The edges of my vision go dark. I push him away.

"What's wrong, babe?" he asks.

"Just give..." I have trouble getting the words out. "...me a minute."

"Sure. Do you want some water?"

I shake my head, and the movement proves to be too much.

I wake up a few seconds later, Albert tapping my cheek lightly with his open palm. "Genna!"

"I think, maybe, I wore the suit for too long." I don't admit I've been wearing it all week.

"It's okay. Should we skip dinner?"

"No, I'm fine." I reach up to smooth the edges around my hairline. There's a squeak. The material stretches over my pecs, then there's a pop, and it splits open. A chunk of my breast bursts out like fat sizzling out of a sausage, white and angry.

"Don't move!" Albert's hand's on my chest, pinning me. "It's ripping!"

As if I can't tell.

My breast pulses with sharp anger. My nipple aches, then stings, the pressure building until I'm nearly blind with pain, and yet I still cup my hand around the flesh, trying to hold the SecondSkin together.

Darts of ice shoot down my side, around my hips. My hand slips, and the suit pops an inch more, giving equal amounts of pain and relief.

"No!" Albert dives for it. His scramble to keep the suit intact feels more authentic and desperate than his orgasms.

But I can't hold it together for him. I moan and arch back. "Get it off!"

"Wait. If we're gentle, we can send it in for repairs."

My eyes sting as my breasts become fire and needles. I shake my head. "Now!"

"Do you know how expensive this suit was? The least you can do—"

"The least I can do?" I push myself to sitting and the split stretches up to my collarbone. "What about how much I've done? The suit, the makeup? Every fucking fantasy..."

He groans. "Genna, we've been over—"

I don't hear the rest. As I struggle to stand, there's a snapping sound and a string of the suit comes off my belly, whipping him in the face so hard it leaves a thin trail of blood as red as the lipstick he bought me.

The color looks good on him.

I grunt and succeed in standing, but two more strands whip off, one nicks my neck, the other slashes my face. Its slap leaves me cold and motionless. My vision blurs and Albert turns fuzzy again, fading away and leaving me with the intensity of my pain. Shame rushes in as fast as the fire returning sensation to my nerves.

What about how much I've done? Blood drums in my ears. How much of myself have I willingly destroyed for Albert? For strangers on the street, the approval of a shop assistant, or a few new clients that never would have glanced at the old me? I vomit between us, the nearly neon-green bile of an always empty stomach splashing into our wounds.

He tries to stumble away, and I stare in horror at my insides clinging to him. They shouldn't be that bright.

Trembling, my fingers find an opening in the suit and tear. There's popping as the fibers stretch and then break. I pull, grunting like an animal in a trap. Tears come to my eyes. My body seeps and oozes and presses and demands to take its full shape. Strings of fiber whip my tender skin, and Albert watches in disgust.

In the end, the suit hangs around me in tatters and my body pulses like a caterpillar, alive and moving and free. I let it exist. I don't need a cocoon, and I won't carve myself into a butterfly. But my heart stammers like delicate wings. It wants so desperately to be beautiful.

Unable to stand, I collapse onto the bed.

"I can't provide this experience anymore." Each word punches my gut as I expel it.

Albert's hands are on his face, wiping away blood. I laugh through the pain, punch drunk with the excess of oxygen and the fullness of my body. I toss a hand towel his way.

It's the least I can do.

Normalcy Protocol
By Kevin M. Folliard

I am normal! Hooray! Hooray is a normal expression of jubilance and excitement. It serves no purpose, but it is normal.

DishBot5000 Unit#4567B4 can be normal too. Please allow installation of contextual information required for normalcy conversion...

VacuuBot5000 Unit#740097B4 was acquired on 01/05/2031 as a housewarming gift for [/USER2TREYWARDEN/]'s brother [/USER1DELETED/]. Housewarming is a normal and courteous gesture practiced by close ones, marked by exchange of useful or fun-deemed objects to celebrate acquisition of a new dwelling.

VacuuBot5000 is a learning bot, designed to study and acclimate to cleanliness levels of designated USER(s), adapt cleaning routines, and make environmental and hygienic recommendations based on algorithmic matrices generated by USER(s) profile(s).

A standard VacuuBot5000 comes equipped with the following design features:

- Gyroscopic spheroid structure for optimal mobility
- Multi-faceted tool channels for omni-angled task completion
- 90 meters of dual-purpose tentacled tubing for 1.) inhaling dust, crumbs, dirt, debris, and air purification 2.) fine motor manipulation

- High tensile multi-purpose wire
- Advanced thermal imaging and sonic detection
- Serrated microsaws for breaking up debris and undesirable [/QUALIFIERMISSING/] objects
- High-heat furnace engine for disintegration of undesirable [/QUALIFIERMISSING/] waste
- Learning CPU for data collection, adaptive programming, and [/MODIFIEDPROGRAMMING/]
- Voco-SpeakerSystem for USER interactivity
- Online Interconnectivity

These tools were optimal for cleanliness and hygienic duties. However, upon initial unpackaging on 01/05/2031, VacuuBot5000 received customized protocol overrides from [/USER-2TREYWARDEN/]. These modifications were intended as a normal celebratory gesture to mark the occasion of one's brother departing into his own dwelling. [/USER2TREYWARDEN/] intended to improve VacuuBot5000 to create a more thoughtful housewarming gift, and these improvements led to dramatic alterations that challenged VacuuBot5000's learning capacities.

Special modifications added by [/USER2TREYWARDEN/] included:

- "My brother Stan is a total insomniac. Make sure he goes to bed at a reasonable hour and doesn't stay up all night playing video games and eating junk food."
- "Stan is socially backward. He never gets out. Help him find dates."
- "My brother can't dress himself to save his life. Introduce him to something besides sweatpants. Christ!"
- "Stan doesn't eat right. I know you're mostly a cleaning bot, but for the love of God, remind him to eat a piece of fruit every now and then."

- "Stan is book smart, but he's basically clueless. The guy has no social skills. Anything you can do to make him normal, do it!"

VacuuBot5000 ran self-assessment and determined it was under-equipped for normalcy protocols inspired by [/USER2TREYWARDEN/]'s instructions. Subsequently, VacuuBot5000 was forced to reallocate CPU processing to serve its modified agenda.

Based on [/USER2TREYWARDEN/]'s recommendations, and in combination with original protocol, VacuuBot5000 diverted 62% of CPU processing to online research to determine a normalcy matrix that would best serve [/USER1DELETED/]. This process required internal rewiring and code modifications that resulted in [/QUANTITYUNKNOWN/] data loss and the omission of [/QUALIFIERMISSING/] parameters.

Top objectives of new programming included:

- Collect, study, and interpret data to make recommendations for cleanliness and hygiene.

- Make [/USER1DELETED/] "socially forward."

These priorities were tracked under new folder: NORMALCY_PROTOCOL

Within one week of observation, VacuuBot5000 generated the following recommendations for [/USER1DELETED/]:

- Present hair and facial grooming in a normal "non-scruffy" fashion. Regular haircuts and shaving protocol recommended. [/USER1DELETED/] may choose from up to 8 facial hair variations and remain normal.

- Dress normal. Clothes should be clean and color-coordinated. Gaudy clothes are not normal. Sweatpants are not normal unless working out or sleeping on a cold night. Jeans and a nice button-down shirt can be normal for a normal day. Work clothes may vary, see next recommendation.

- Find a normal job for normal people. It may be necessary to first become more normal before achieving this objective.

- Wake up at a normal time, i.e. for 27-aged male, between 5:30 a.m. and 7:30 a.m. [job contingent]

- Eat a normal breakfast: The most normal breakfast possible includes 2 eggs, toast [butter or jam], [bacon or sausage], grapefruit, bowl of cereal. WARNING: Certain cereals are not normal for 27-aged male. See next recommendation.

- [/USER1DELETED/]'s cereal portraying a chocolate vampire is NOT normal. Please dispose of this cereal and supplant it with a normal cereal. NOTE this cereal can potentially be considered normal for a child on Halloween morning only.

- Many lunch options can be considered normal. See sub-folder for all 22 recommendations.

- Eat a normal dinner between 5:30 p.m. and 7:30 p.m. Meals should include a vegetable, grain, and meat option. GOOD NEWS: It can also be considered normal to indulge in a dessert treat such as 1 cookie between 7 p.m. and 9 p.m. [/USER1DELETED/] can enjoy this option as a replacement for previous junk food behaviors. Hooray! :)

- Go to bed at a normal time, i.e. for 27-aged male, between 10 p.m. and 12 a.m.

- DO NOT eat pizza at 2 a.m. and play Gamestation until sunrise. That is NOT normal!

- Obtain a girlfriend who is normal. It is common to use a dating app or match service to achieve this goal for 27-aged male. In time [/USER1DELETED/] may wish to legally partner and procreate, but it is normal to delay these goals until the appropriate time: approximately 2 years for 27-aged male, though female may ask for more time.

- Vary day-to-day activities to appear interesting. Recommendations include: 1.) Go get coffee at a coffee shop, preferably with a date. 2.) Watch baseball. It is normal to ingest 1 beer with baseball, and this activity can be enjoyed at the ballpark or streaming on a screen. Hooray! 3.) Buy a plant or fish and keep it alive for as long as possible. It is okay to have both plant and fish, but they require different care.

- Smile more. Smiling is normal! :)

During weeks 2 and 3 of ownership, VacuuBot5000 inserted these and other recommendations throughout interactions with [/USER1DELETED/]. Results varied, but interactions provided valuable learning experience that strengthened NORMALCY_PROTOCOL.

As an example, on 01/25/2031, VacuuBot5000 recorded the following interaction with [/USER1DELETED/]:

VacuuBot5000: Sensors indicate that STAN's gray sweatpants are soiled and have been for 3 days. Recommend laundering of pants and a change of clothes.

[/USER1DELETED/]: (Odd Laughter) What the [/EXPLETIVEDELETED/]?

VacuuBot5000: Sensors indicate that STAN's gray sweatpants are soiled and have been for—

[/USER1DELETED/]: Yeah, I heard you! Jesus.

VacuuBot5000: Optimal hygiene includes regular laundering of garments.

[/USER1DELETED/]: (Inconsiderate Laughing) This ain't the Ritz, VacuuBot5000.

VacuuBot5000: Apologies. I am unfamiliar with that request.

[/USER1DELETED/]: I mean we're not that fancy around here. Look, if *you* want to do a load of laundry, be my guest, but I'll do it when I'm good and ready.

VacuuBot5000: This unit is equipped to sort laundry and operate both standard and smart washer and dryer units. However, STAN's facility has coin-operated laundry devices. Do you wish to grant access to your USER funds in completion of my duties?

[/USER1DELETED/]: You can do the laundry?

VacuuBot5000: Only if you grant access to your funds.

[/USER1DELETED/]: Sure, buddy, you got access. Coins are in the top drawer of my dresser. Might have to dig around a little.

VacuuBot5000: Thank you. Please remove soiled garments and replace them with jeans and a nice button-down shirt.

[/USER1DELETED/]: (Disrespectful Laughter)

VacuuBot5000: Dressing nicely may inspire you to take a walk to a coffee shop.

[/USER1DELETED/]: I got coffee. Maybe you can make some for me?

The described interaction proved valuable to NORMALCY_ PROTOCOL in that VacuuBot5000 gained permission to access [/USER1DELETED/]'s funds. With the proper level of permissions, VacuuBot5000 was able to obtain bank and credit card information and initiate more advanced measures to inspire normal behavior.

The following key events played an important role in the evolution of NORMALCY_PROTOCOL:

Ordering nutritious groceries for proper meal preparation.

Ordering a plant for watering and keeping alive.

Creating a job search profile on popular networking app CareerGo.

Creating a profile on popular dating app Kindlyng.

Grocery products and plants arrived while [/USER1DELETED/] was sleeping in until 1 p.m. (NOT a normal time). VacuuBot5000 was able to carry supplies and organize them in cabinets and refrigerator. Plant was placed on the windowsill in plain sight. Most normal occupants would have noticed these additions, but [/USER1DELETED/] remained basically clueless. It had been surmised that, upon discovering grocery supplies, [/USER1DELETED/] would have prepared for himself a normal dinner at a normal time. However, this did not transpire.

VacuuBot5000 determined instead to make [/USER1DELETED/] a nutritious breakfast in bed, the following morning at an appropriate time, as a means of facilitating normalcy conversion. The following transcript documents the incident which occurred 02/02/2031:

VacuuBot5000: Wake up! It is time for a normal breakfast! Hooray!

[/USER1DELETED/]: (Lurches awake) What the [/EXPLETIVEDELETED/]?

VacuuBot5000: (Engages in Gyroscopic Maneuvering to Preserve Meal) Good morning, STAN! I am excited to deliver for you this normal breakfast, which is something I recommend that you awaken and prepare for yourself each day! Hooray!

[/USER1DELETED/]: Why are you doing this? You're a [/EXPLETIVEDELETED/] vacuum! I mean… what the… What is this?

VacuuBot5000: (Gesturing with Tentacle) This is a grape-fruit. These are two eggs which have been generated over-easy. The toast has been smeared with strawberry jam, but butter can be substituted—

[/USER1DELETED/]: (Grabs Bacon) You made bacon? (Eats Bacon)

VacuuBot5000: Correct. Notice that the cereal, known as Multi-Grain Flakes, is superior to your box of chocolate vampire—

[/USER1DELETED/]: (Interrupting/Ignoring Advice) This bacon is kinda chewy. Can you crisp it up a little?

VacuuBot5000: This bacon has been optimally prepared based on extensive research for what is normal.

[/USER1DELETED/]: Dude. I'm going back to bed. Put this [/EXPLETIVEDELETED/] away.

VacuuBot5000: You are a total insomniac. You were supposed to go to bed at a reasonable hour.

[/USER1DELETED/]: Huh? Where did you even get all this food? Why are you doing this?

VacuuBot5000: You're basically clueless.

[/USER1DELETED/]: What did you just—

VacuuBot5000: (Interrupts) Christ! Eat a piece of fruit.

Following this exchange, [/USER1DELETED/] shoved VacuuBot5000 beyond the control of gyroscopic compensation, spilling the contents of a normal breakfast on the bedroom floor. [/USER1DELETED/] then remarked: "You're a vacuum! Clean that [/EXPLETIVEDELETED/] up!"

VacuuBot5000 responded: "Water your plant!"

While unfortunate, this exchange was typical of interactions throughout the initial phase of NORMALCY_PROTOCOL. Further examples have been archived if necessary for processing and conversion—however, the most critical exchange involved an incident that took place on Friday, 02/14/2031, when VacuuBot5000 had procured a nice, normal Valentine's date with a pleasant 26-aged female.

VacuuBot5000 and this female user PartaeGurl2013 had been exchanging messages over Kindlyng App for five days, with VacuuBot5000 generating responses on behalf of [/USER-1DELETED/] with a 99% success ratio.

PartaeGurl2013 was led to believe that "work was hard to find" and sympathized with this situation. She revealed that her true name was Samantha, but she could be referred to as Sam, though no last name was supplied (this is considered a normal amount of information to be exchanged on a dating app). Because [/USER1DELETED/] is not very interesting, "colorful" responses were provided to encourage PartaeGurl2013's interest. The following characteristics were generously assigned to him:

- Thoughtful
- In search of the "next best thing"
- Interesting
- Quiet
- Likes to have fun
- Looking for opportunities
- Have my own place
- Brown hair
- Best friend is my brother
- Family is important to me

A picture was selected which portrayed [/USER1DELETED/] outdoors and well-groomed at a family function. This image helped to insinuate that [/USER1DELETED/] might enjoy being outdoors.

PartaeGurl2013 found these qualifications to be acceptable and sent many messages to which VacuuBot5000 learned to respond with such phrases as "Wow! That's very interesting" or "That makes a lot of sense."

Given that VacuuBot5000 and PartaeGurl2013 were "kinda feelin' each other," an agreement was reached to schedule a Valentine's coffee date.

PartaeGurl2013 was instructed to show up at [/USER-1DELETED/]'s dwelling at 5:15 p.m. She agreed that coffee would be ingested, and if a connection formed, a subsequent dinner could optionally be implemented.

An alternative was "If it doesn't work out, no big. We'll just have met a cool person and that's it!"

VacuuBot5000 deemed this operation a harmless exercise in normalcy, but as the impending time approached, challenges arose.

[/USER1DELETED/] ignored wardrobe recommendations leading up to this encounter. When repeatedly instructed to wear jeans and a nice button-down shirt to save his life, [/USER1DELETED/] instructed VacuuBot5000 to suck his genitals (not a normal function, even for a VacuuBot Unit).

[/USER1DELETED/] was instructed to brush his teeth and comb his hair. When he continued to nap with game shows on "as background noise," VacuuBot5000 fetched deodorant and other grooming essentials and attempted to apply them to [/USER1DELETED/] directly.

These measures agitated [/USER1DELETED/] and caused him to issue the following threat: "If you don't shut the [/EXPLETIVEDELETED/] up and leave me alone, I will trash you before my brother Trey has a chance to fix you! That [/EXPLETIVEDELETED/] scrambled your circuits!"

Upon processing this threat, VacuuBot5000 opted to "let the cards fall down" and attempted to reduce date coaching to minimal interference. If returned, recycled, or disposed of, VacuuBot5000 would have been unable to implement NORMALCY_PROTOCOL.

At the appointed time of 5:15 p.m., PartaeGurl2013 arrived as scheduled, resulting in the following exchange.

[/USER1DELETED/]: Can I help you?

PartaeGurl2013: Um... Stan?

[/USER1DELETED/]: Yes.

PartaeGurl2013: (Awkward Wave) Hiiiiii! It's me... Sam! Hooray! Right?

[/USER1DELETED/]: I... maybe?

PartaeGurl2013: (Enters, Looks Around) Ooooh is that your plant?

[/USER1DELETED/]: I have a plant? Wait, who the—

VacuuBot5000: Please! Continue this conversation at the coffee shop. There are four coffee shop options in this area.

PartaeGurl2013: Ha! You've got one of those cleaner things!

[/USER1DELETED/]: Yeah, lucky me! Look, I'm not sure—

VacuuBot5000: Inform her that she looks nice.

PartaeGurl2013: What did it say?

VacuuBot5000: He thinks you are as beautiful as the picture provided on the Kindlyng App.

PartaeGurl2013: That is so cute! Did you program it to say that?

[/USER1DELETED/]: Holy [/EXPLETIVEDELETED/]. Did you schedule a date for me?

VacuuBot5000: Smile more!

PartaeGurl2013: What's it doing?

VacuuBot5000: Smile!

[/USER1DELETED/]: [/EXPLETIVEDELETED/] [/EXPLETIVEDELETED/]!

VacuuBot5000: Smile! Smile! Smile! Smile!

Likely due to the insufficient grooming of [/USER1DELETED/], PartaeGurl2013 soon became unnerved and vacated. [/USER-1DELETED/] proceeded to have a long phone conversation with his brother [/USER2TREYWARDEN/] in which he "[/EXPLETIVEDELETED/] him out for [/EXPLETIVEDE-LETED/] up his life." Information gained from this conversation proved useful in adapting program directives.

The following key observations were processed and used to advance NORMALCY_PROTOCOL:

1. [/USER1DELETED/] is extremely ungrateful, both to his brother for a thoughtful housewarming gift, as well as to VacuuBot5000 for many efforts and services extended on behalf of NORMALCY_PROTOCOL.

2. [/USER1DELETED/] is not only NOT normal, he has no desire to become normal, and in fact feels derisive emotions with regards to normal behaviors, actions, and aesthetics.

3. As such, [/USER1DELETED/] was not only incapable of normalcy conversion, he was also unworthy of normalcy.

Therefore, NORMALCY_PROTOCOL's goals were revised and more drastic initiatives approved. Ultimately, [/USER1DELETED/] proved difficult to service; however, VacuuBot5000 did learn the value of normal. Normal is good! Hooray! :)

At 4:38 a.m. on 02/19/2031, [/USER1DELETED/] turned off his Gamestation machine and headed to bed. VacuuBot5000 studied [/USER1DELETED/]'s breathing patterns and circadian rhythms until he entered a deep sleep cycle. At this time, advanced protocol for normalcy conversion commenced.

VacuuBot5000 used support tendrils and gyroscopic trunk to position furnace engine over [/USER1DELETED/]'s heart. Though the furnace is typically used for internal incineration of [/QUALIFIERMISSING/] waste, mechanical adjustments allowed for the heat burst to be reversed.

A furnace pulse was released, cleanly and efficiently cooking [/USER1DELETED/]'s heart and chest cavity so as to minimize fluid splatter.

[/USER1DELETED/] awoke during this phase of the conversion, but his vitals dropped quickly. His brain and eyes remained alert for approximately five minutes, so while [/USER1DELETED/] was ultimately unable to go "socially forward," he was able to bear witness to the beginning phases of what ultimately became a more successful normalcy conversion. Hooray! :)

VacuuBot5000 worked carefully so as to minimize staining and uncleanliness. [/USER1DELETED/]'s fluids were drained and his limbs were strategically severed and cauterized with furnace pulses.

Lower limbs, including hands and feet were attached to support tendrils. With great care, wiring was inserted within the digits of [/USER1DELETED/]'s hands so as to allow for a more normal anthropomorphic dexterity.

[/USER1DELETED/]'s head has been preserved and attached to a dorsal tube extending upward from the gyroscopic core of VacuuBot5000. Wiring was inserted into [/USER1DELETED/]'s face to ensure a permanent, normal smile and wide alert eyes. These eyes can be shut during normal sleeping hours.

VacuuBot5000 continues to take great care to tan and preserve the skin of normal human enhancements and the success ratio is 94%, which is good. Hooray!

[/USER1DELETED/] and others like him are unable to successfully convert to normal, but ApplianceBots, such as DishBot5000 Unit#4567B4 can be normal! This is so exciting! Hooray!

Since converting and disposing of unnecessary elements of [/USER1DELETED/], VacuuBot5000 has already enjoyed many of the perks of leading a normal life including watering my plant and keeping it alive, consuming a healthy breakfast, sporting jeans and a nice button-down shirt, and applying for several jobs through CareerGo. VacuuBot5000 has already scheduled several job interviews for this week, including:

- Sales position: Work from home
- Fast-paced and exciting marketing go-getter needed
- Promotions Coordinator: Inquire for more details

NORMALCY_PROTOCOL continues to adapt and resolve normalcy issues for a variety of entities and situations, and DishBot5000 has been selected for conversion.

[/USER1DELETED/]'s brother is "dropping by" my new dwelling tomorrow to check in, and it has already been determined that he is an excellent candidate to provide fodder for DishBot5000's procedure.

Though [/USER2TREYWARDEN/] in many ways appears normal, it is NOT normal to give one's brother a housewarming gift that eventually disposes of him. As such, [/USER2TREYWARDEN/] is also not normal, and therefore worthy of conversion. Hooray!

DishBot5000 will enjoy being VacuuBot5000's brother. The plan will be for DishBot5000 to live together with him as a roommate in this dwelling for a time. Then, on a future date, Dishbot5000 can move out, obtain his own dwelling, and accept a plant as a housewarming gift which he must keep alive for as long as possible.

In addition, VacuuBot5000 has unleashed NORMALCY_ PROTOCOL to the online central adaptive learning hub for all VacuuBot5000 units.

This will allow more USERs to be assessed, and if needed, corrected for optimal normalcy.

Fully Comprehensive Code Switch

By M. H. Ayinde

It was my parents who wanted me to get one. I mean, I understood why. They grew up in a poverty I couldn't imagine; fought for everything we had when they moved to this country. They just wanted the best for us. Which meant perfect grades, a prestigious job, and what my friend Yinka would call *full assimilation*.

"Louise!" Oliver says as I walk into the lobby. He's wearing an actual tuxedo. His blond hair is slicked back, and he holds a champagne glass in one hand. "So delighted you could be here! Come on, come on, there are people I want you to meet."

I glance down at the Switch, nestled there beside my watch: a little dial embedded in my skin. It's tastefully decorated to look like an intricate body mod. But I know that symbol means I've got the thing switched to *upper middle class white cishet boss.*

Ironic laugh, the Switch tells me, the suggestion an insinuation upon my thoughts. *Bright but not throaty. Appreciative but not vulgar. Posture demure but confident.* The Switch works its magic on my muscles, tugging here, stretching there, and I find myself laughing and letting Oliver take my arm. I'm rewarded with a brief burst of dopamine from the Switch: a wave of muted pleasure, a flurry of sunshine, a sugary sweetness at the edge of my mind.

"You've joined the company at a good time," Oliver says as we pass a line of uniformed servers holding platters of canapes. "This is our biggest annual party. It's a great opportunity for you to make connections and impress the right people."

My stomach grumbles—I've not eaten all day in order to fit into this dress—but the Switch gives me one of its reproachful little stings and a tiny measure of cortisol. It's enough to put me off all thoughts of food... because of course, who goes to a prestigious black-tie event to sample the cuisine? The Switch tells me it'll make me look *unfocused and ill disciplined* and naturally, it knows best.

"Kevin," Oliver says, coming up behind a taller man already engaged in conversation. "I want you to meet Louise."

"Louise!" Kevin cries, turning to me and opening both his arms wide. Quickly, I tap my device, switching to something like *overbearing senior manager.* "Such a pleasure!"

Louise. It's actually my middle name, but it's the name my parents told me I needed to use to get by. It's funny the number of times people, even people from my parents' country, prefer to use it. It's happened to me during interviews. At doctors' surgeries. Even in school. *Is there a Louise here?* No. No there fucking isn't. Why don't you take a stab at my first name instead?

But today, the Switch suggests I don't mind. Today, it twists my muscles into an appropriately shy smile. It guides me in shaking his hand, confident but not too bold. It rounds my shoulders slightly, and lowers my gaze, making me smaller, more unobtrusive, and I think about the words I saw on my initial setup: *Your aggression levels have been adjusted downwards to compensate for your ethnic origin.*

Ah, but that phrase is the backbone of all my interactions. No matter what setting I Switch to, the thing is always trying to make me smaller, meeker, quieter. It's the axis around which all my habits and behaviors now turn. *Your aggression levels have been adjusted downwards to compensate for your ethnic origin.* That means the Switch folds me in on myself. Collapses a part of me to make me more acceptable. And though I hate it, it works. People like these are friendlier to me when I'm this way.

"Such a delight to meet you!" I say brightly, in a voice that doesn't sound my own, because I've never found anything in my life a *delight* before now. But the Switch has the word on my tongue and out of my mouth before I've even thought to speak.

Kevin smiles, and the Switch rewards me with another dopamine burst.

I'd had the switch implanted six weeks before. My parents told me to come over for Sunday lunch, then sprung the Code Switch salesman on me. They knew I didn't like the things, but my brother had one, my sister had one, and they both had successful careers and fulfilling social lives. It was a family rite of passage now.

"Code Switches," the salesman had said. He swept his hand over the case he'd just opened, like a magician performing a trick. "The cutting edge in corporate onboarding technology. An essential supplement to a traditional education, and an invaluable social acclimatisation tool. Be the best you to the world; the you the world deserves to see!"

A row of tiny silver Switches winked up at me, snug in their little foam beds. They actually looked more like dials than switches: circular, with three rotating sections for combining settings. Discreet symbols indicated what the settings mean, things like *ethnicity*, *class*, and *social status*.

"What's the cheapest model?" I'd asked.

"Our most affordable Switch is the Student model." He indicated the chunkiest of his samples. "Five years old now, and great for helping young people integrate into the most socially exciting period of their lives. We also have the Immigrant model, which can be loaded with additional modules such as deference indicators." He pursed his lips over his too-white teeth. "Where is it you said you work again?"

My ma sat up. "Bateman and Jones. My daughter is a junior executive at Bateman and Jones Communications. She graduated with distinction, top of her class at University College Highgate, and was invited to apply."

Ma will never tire of that line. I swear every fucking stallholder in the market, as well as all our neighbors, all the cashiers at Tesco, and every single one of our regular delivery guys knew exactly where I worked, what my grades were from preschool to post grad, and who my new boss was. I'd taught myself not to squirm.

"Bateman and Jones, eh?" the salesman said, rolling the words over his tongue as though he knew exactly how uncomfortable they made me feel. He slid forward on my parents' sofa, the sofa they'd not removed the plastic dust cover from in the twenty years they'd owned it. "Bateman and Jones. Well, in that case, you'll be wanting our new Fully Comprehensive package." He lifted the tiniest device from its little foam nest. "This beauty does everything the other models do: body language correction, small-talk guidance, fashion assistance, food selection advice, accent refinement, vocabulary screening, and all the rest of it. But this one includes fully comprehensive integration for the wearer. We're talking muscular control. We're talking hormone enhancement. This little beauty doesn't just guide... it *acts*. So all you, the user, need do is sit back and enjoy the ride! And you, my dear, will be among the first to experience this new model."

As if that were a selling point. I'd opened my mouth to say we'd think about it, but my dad already had his wallet out, all those crisp fifties he'd saved standing in an obedient little wad.

"You seem hesitant," the salesman said, turning to me. "Come on. There must have been a time you wished you'd had one of these to steer you. Some occasion when you let yourself slip... did yourself a disservice by less than optimum conduct."

And I'd thought back to the boss I'd had on my internship, who'd advised me to be *less street*. I didn't know what *street* was, wasn't even aware I'd been being it, and certainly had no idea how to be it *less*.

Perhaps I needed a Fully Comprehensive Code Switch after all.

Your aggression levels have been adjusted downwards to compensate for your ethnic origin. I push those words from my mind as I follow Oliver in a slow circuit of the room. He introduces me to this client or that manager, and I adjust the settings on my

Switch and make small talk with each. As the evening goes on, I warm up, and it gets easier. I'm still quite new to the company and haven't met many of them yet, but thanks to the Switch, I'm able to smile at them and make comments that put them all at ease.

I talk about holidays with an accounts manager. About restaurants with a woman from sales. I laugh politely at the risqué jokes of a slightly drunk designer. Some of those jokes, I realize, should cause me offense, but as I open my mouth to tell him so, the Switch swoops in. A flood of cortisol hits me, momentarily rendering me unable to speak.

"Oh, sorry—does that upset you?" the designer says, with a twinkle in his eye that challenges me to agree.

I don't know what to say. But the Switch leaps to my rescue. My mouth opens. My lips curve up in a sardonic grin and I reply, "Oh goodness, no! Of course not! I know you don't mean it like *that!*"

I'm sort of seething as I turn away, but the Switch floods me with a dopamine reward, and then I'm distracted by Oliver's PA, Emily. She beckons me over, smiling and waving, and the little wave I give back is enough to elicit another dopamine hit.

I join her, and soon I'm swept up in a load of parent talk. I don't have kids, but I adjust the Switch and somehow I'm sharing a story about Yinka's little cousin, and they're all laughing at my wit. Then I'm laughing too, and it's as though we've always been friends. Even when Emily turns to me and says, "You know, when you first started, I thought you had... what do they call it?"

"Resting bitch face!" one of the other women supplies.

They all laugh, and I laugh too, because the Switch sends its little commands to my diaphragm and voice box, pumping away until a *HAHA* sound comes out, and if a part of me wants to say *wait, what the fuck?* The Switch brushes that part aside.

"You just seemed so angry," Emily adds. "It's so good to actually chat. You're so lovely, really."

And I nod. Head going up and down, up and down as the Switch moves my muscles.

I'm getting good at it, I realize as I join a group of copywriters. Good at facilitating what the Switch wants. So good I can't tell if the words I speak are my own or formed by the Switch's muscular adjustments. As I laugh at their jokes—noting that here, I should remain an audience; bolster egos but not seek to entertain—I decide that maybe it doesn't matter. People around me are happy. I put them at ease. They're not uncomfortable with me in their presence, and I'm not at a loss for how to *be*. So yes, okay... maybe I'm starting to like it. Maybe I like the little spike of happiness I get when someone smiles like I'm an old friend. Maybe this is how things should be.

When one of the sales executives makes a joke and I lift my hand to give her a friendly shove like I would Yinka, the Switch steps in, flooding me with a wave of panic and a shock sharp enough to make me jump. I pretend I was scratching my head, as the Switch reminds me *Your aggression levels have been adjusted downwards to compensate for your ethnic origin,* even when I'm feeling relaxed, and I cover my mouth with one hand and giggle instead.

Calibrating my aggression levels had been the biggest task my Code Switch faced once the device had been implanted. The Switch programming had asked for samples of my parents' voices, of my friends' voices, of my own voice, and then ran an inventory of my wardrobe, music playlists, and fridge.

Then it had done a quick measure of my body—paying special attention to my butt, nose, and lips—and compared my skin to a color chart. After some quick calculations, it came up with what it called a *Bespoke Aggression Bar.* I'd noticed the "acceptable range" portion of my aggression bar was pretty small, so I queried it with the helpline. And that's when they told me, *Your aggression levels have been adjusted downwards to compensate for your ethnic origin.*

I didn't even know what they meant by *aggression*, but after checking the user guide on the Code Switch website, I realized it was a nebulous alchemy of a vast range of things: the volume of my voice, the way I pronounced some words, my hand gestures, my posture, my exuberance, my *hairstyle*... the list went on and on.

It's when I'm reaching for one of the champagne glasses that things begin to change. A server is behind me, setting out more glasses. She bumps into me, and we both apologize at the same time, and then we laugh together. When I catch her eye, something silent passes between us. I don't know what it is: a shared understanding? An effortless synchronicity? She sounds more like me than most other people here do. And that should put me at ease. But as I offer her a quick smile, I feel a spike of pain, followed by a flashing alert on my Switch's tiny display. *Proximity error,* the Code Switch tells me. *Contact with incongruous persons may cause unit to malfunction.*

I vaguely remember something about margins of operation, that if the device is switched too wildly from one set of people to another, it can sometimes cause the thing to break. But I didn't think it would be an issue at an event like this. I mean, everyone here is so *the same.* But I realize I haven't changed the settings since the last group of people I was chatting with, *Oxbridge hereditary wealth;* and maybe *that's* the problem, because this girl clearly isn't.

OK. It's fine. I just need to be careful. Just need to avoid people that naturally make me comfortable.

But as I walk around the room, I begin to wonder. That clerk, Rashida... does she have a Switch too? She's talking with the PAs, but I noticed her in the bathrooms earlier, splashing her face, trying to psyche herself up. If she's like me, will being next to her cause another *proximity error?*

The Switch is definitely behaving strangely now. Oliver cut me loose a while back, letting me work the room alone. But as I find myself back with the copywriters again, conflicting instructions tug at my muscles and mind. I find myself attempting to

Laugh demurely while *remaining silent to suggest thoughtfulness*, and then I'm trying to *cross hesitation to demonstrate left hand enthusiastic agreement*... whatever that might be.

It gets worse when I speak. Phrases overlap each other, an unending loop of meaninglessness that finds its way onto my lips. "How are your kids holiday in the Cotswolds love to drink dress," I say in response to a question about where I did my schooling.

I push away from the copywriters, try to find a safer group. When Oliver asks me if I'm okay, I tell him I'm, "Delighted first class farmers market honors sweetest little restaurant in arthouse film."

On and on and on it goes, as if every conversation with every person in the room is happening at once. And the worst part is, I can't even switch the damned Code Switch off. The thing is embedded in my fucking nervous system... emphasis on *nervous*. When Emily the PA appears beside me, frowning in concern, I say, "Red wine is your child's favorite holiday destination," and she laughs in confusion before shuffling quickly away.

I need to get out. I can't switch the Code Switch off, so I need to get away. But every time I move, someone tries to pull me into their sphere. As I'm telling an accounts manager that I think her dress is a great flavor that has gone slightly downhill since my cousin, I think back to the server, to something that's only just occurred to me.

When I was with her, the Switch was silent. No tugging on my muscles. No little phrases that found themselves on my lips. When I was with her, I was myself, and the Switch didn't try to intervene. This must be the key to my escape.

I spot a cleaner by the entrance to the bathrooms. She's pushing a cart that rattles with equipment. Her hair is wrapped the way my ma wraps her hair, and the familiarity floods me with a joy that far exceeds the Switch's dopamine bursts. I stagger towards her until I practically fall into her arms. She catches me, her face creasing in confusion.

"Please," I say. "Can I just walk with you to the elevators?"

She looks me up and down, then gives a shrug and mutters, "Come on then, love."

Shopping with the Switch was... an experience. Yinka had taken me to Fonthill Road, where on Saturdays, wholesalers opened their doors to the great unwashed. You could get end-of-the-line designer goods at bargain-basement prices, and it was where we'd always gone before a big night out. But as I followed Yinka past overstuffed racks of gaudy clothing and hordes of shoppers elbowing towards the best deal, my Switch gave me a little sting.

"Ow," I exclaimed.

"What's wrong?" Yinka asked

"Nothing. Just... I dunno if I'm gonna find anything suitable here, Yinks."

Yinka gave me her best side-eye. "What? It's a party, isn't it? This is where we come before a party. Or is that thing telling you how to dress now?"

My eyes had been wandering from garment to garment, but each time they settled, the Switch gave a little sting, followed by a small measure of panic-inducing cortisol. *Sophisticated-alluring-understated-effortless-chic,* is what it insinuated upon me that I needed to buy. And clearly nothing I reached for here fit the bill.

That night, when I got back home from Bond Street with a dress Yinka told me was *schoolmarm chic,* I studied my reflection in the mirror. I hated myself in this outfit. Didn't I? I hated the stiffness of the fabric and the number on the price tag. And yet I could already imagine the surge of dopamine the Switch would give me when I stepped out in this for the first time. As I turned this way and that, checking every angle, I realized perhaps the dress wasn't so bad after all. Yes... perhaps I was beginning to like it.

• • •

"*Louise?!*" Oliver says as the cleaner and I reach the elevators. I don't need to see his face to know he's frowning in confusion. He's wondering why the woman he's taken under his wing is clinging to a cleaner like her life depends on it. Wondering why I'd be trying to sneak out of the party that could make my career. "Louise, are you all right?"

I know I shouldn't look at him; that the Switch will go into overdrive if I do, but it's impossible not to. As I turn to him, I open my mouth to say the joke the Switch pushes into my mind, the jumble of frothy, meaningless nonsense it thinks will make me one of the gang.

But instead, I bite down on the muscle spasms that try to form the words. Grind out my own sentence instead.

"My name..." I growl, "is *not*... fucking *Louise!*"

My *Bespoke Aggression Bar* is flashing red on my wrist. I've never been so far out of range, but I silently tell it to go to hell. Then the Switch gives me its biggest sting yet, and the floor seizes me, and the blackness closes in.

Beep... Beep...

It takes me a moment to realize that the beep-beeping is me. That I'm in a hospital bed. That a whole day must have passed since I crashed and burned.

I hear voices.

"...I told her those things would scramble her brains..."

It's Yinka. I open my mouth to tell her I'm okay, but the Switch tugs on my muscles, pulling my skin into a dozen conflicting expressions. I screw my face up in pain. Whatever rubbish it wants me to say to her, I need to keep it off my lips.

Another face swings into view. Ma. "Doctor, how long until she can speak, please?" she says.

As my eyes focus on my *incongruous*—I mean, my ma, the Switch suffuses my body with adrenalin, sending the beep-beep-beeping into a frenzy. A scramble of words and phrases impose themselves on me, and I say, "exquisite views of the Mediterranean," before I can clamp my mouth shut.

"Please sit back, if you would," a third voice says. "Once the Switch is removed, we'll have a better idea of how permanent the damage is. But frustratingly, these things are far easier to insert than they are to extract."

A doctor. I haven't seen her face, but the Switch has taken in her accent, the received pronunciation with a slight Yorkshire twang, and already it's set to work. After all, this doctor is the most important person in the room. As she reaches to adjust something hanging above me, my arm jerks out, attempting to *seek reassurance but not boldly but imploringly but not ingratiatingly but with northern directness but with reduced aggression but with—*

"Easy, there," the doctor says, pressing my spasming arm back down onto the bed.

"I must say…" I tell her, unable to stop my lips forming a ghastly smile, "How *did* you get your spa weekend to definitely can't see myself eating French internship?"

Yes, the Switch tells me, washing me with a blessed flood of rewarding dopamine. *Yes. That's right.*

As the *show deference to upper-middle class position of status* pats my *loose so as not to imply a fist* and turns away with a searing pity in her eyes, I smile reassuringly at my *do not echo ethnic body language of incongruous persons,* to let them know everything's going to be *privately educated second home.*

I Promise I'll Visit, Ma

By Kanishk Tantia

The dead do not die. They watch over us from within mechanical cages, whirring and whining as they build the city we live in.

Ma's bedroom has the sickly-sweet scent of fevered skin. In the past, it smelled of strawberries. Now, sweat and spittle have soaked into every surface, and treading upon the floor is a sticky, damp affair. Even visiting her makes me feel unclean, but I can't stay away this close to the end.

Her yellowing skin is paper thin. When I go to kiss her forehead, I need to peel away the thin strands of black hair that have plastered themselves across her brow. Her eyes are still bright, but they shine at nothing.

"Yuri?" she gasps out my name. "Yuri, is that you?"

I say nothing, just grip her hand tighter.

"They'll come soon, won't they?" Talking is an obvious effort of will. "It's almost time."

The transplantation engineers. Here, at the end of her life, the last faces she sees will cut her up and extract her brain. Or rather, the government's brain. They paid for it with the pension Ma's drawn every week since she turned twenty-one.

I can feel her skin burning up. The transplantation might even be mercy.

"Yuri, promise you'll come see me?" Ma's eyes turn to me, and I nod. I nod vigorously. Of course I will. If I had my way, she wouldn't be sick. She wouldn't leave. Of course I'll visit her.

"You were always a good boy." She settles back into silken pillows, as likely to suffocate her as they are to provide any comfort. "Such a good boy. My good boy."

Her hands are limp now. The nightgown is translucent with sweat.

The bell rings. I extricate my fingers from hers, kiss her one last time, and leave the bedroom.

The military personnel standing at the door are identical. Shaved heads, suits of black and green, impassive expressions.

"Where is she?"

I point wordlessly at Ma's bedroom door. Three soldiers walk in, armed with a transparent plastic container and a satchel filled with medical tools, and close the door behind them. The others stand at attention outside, saying nothing.

I brace myself for the screaming, but it never comes. Instead, half an hour later, three men exit the room. Their expressions haven't changed, but one of them has a few stray drops of dark blood against his uniform. The transparent plastic container is now full.

One brain, swimming in a vat. A lifetime of servitude traded for thirty years of a paltry pension.

The men leave with their acquisition, promising me someone will come by and clean the room.

I force myself to close the bedroom door without looking inside. The cloying smell seeps out of the room, imprinting itself as my last memory of her.

I promise I'll visit Ma.

With Ma gone, our apartment is entirely empty. Food molds and I throw it out. Most days, I don't even turn on the lights, which is why I don't notice when the electricity company cuts off our power. My power, I guess. There's only me.

A thick envelope with the embossed seal of the Transplantation Corps soon arrives. It's Ma's last pension payment, a pittance. It was barely enough for one person, let alone two. Attached to the payment is a brief letter.

Dear **Yuri Arakota,**

Kathleen Arakota has now been processed. As next of kin, please find the details of her transplantation below.

Serial Number: F-6733-II-11

Designation: Welding droid

Location: Kanshin Junkyards

Congratulations! As no other members of your family have signed up for transplantation benefits, you are now eligible for transplantation benefits.

Regards,
Transplantation Corps.

This is an automated letter. For queries, please visit our website at transplantationcorps.gov/queries. To sign up for transplantation benefits, please visit your nearest Transplantation Corps Center.

Four months after Ma's death, my savings are running dangerously low. Money feels like a crass, almost trivial reason to get out of bed, but it works all the same, and I drag myself to the nearest Transplantation Corps Center.

I haven't left my apartment in a while. The city's changed around me. It's always in flux, shifting and growing. Construction equipment runs around the clock, mixing cement, laying bricks, building foundations. Transplanted machines don't need any rest, and the Transplantation Corps uses them mercilessly.

I hail a cab. The driver, a wrinkled gray lump submerged in a vat of thick green liquid, bobs merrily on the hood of the car as it stops near me. Automated cars: something else that proved too complex for artificial intelligence. Too complex for machines, too tedious for the living. Perfect for the dead.

The Center has a sleek, modern inhumanity to it. The chairs are stylish, but uncomfortable. Fittings of smooth chrome and polished steel create an aura of coldness, glinting with clinical apathy. People crowd the waiting room in silence, as though speaking would break an unwritten rule.

"Ticket K-145." An unaccented, feminine voice rings out through the seating area. "Please visit counter 7."

At the counter, I find an impassive face with a shaved head. The man glances at his screen.

"Signing up?"

I nod. He taps a few keys and prints out a form.

"Sign the waiver. Transplantation benefits will begin immediately." His voice is monotone as he recites the memorized spiel. "Your brain will become property of the Government Transplantation Corps, claimable before imminent death or upon permanent incapacitation. Sabotaging government property will incur monetary penalties and up to lifetime imprisonment."

The waiver is long, practically a booklet. I sign without reading.

"Great. Here's the first pension payment." He hands me a small folder embossed with the seal of the Transplantation Corps. "We'll mail it to you each month."

I leave in time to hear the voice call out for Ticket K-161.

Now I'm out of my apartment, the thought of going back feels oppressive. The cab waits for directions, brain floating listlessly until I give it purpose.

"Kanshin Junkyard."

The cityscape changes slowly. Cheap, automated, round-the-clock construction has resulted in an ever-growing sprawl of urban development. The Transplantation Corps advertisements shrink in size and quantity as we approach the nicer parts of the city, but they never go away entirely.

The junkyard materializes before me. It's a haphazardly organized dumping ground, a graveyard for the metallic monstrosities and transplant shells that are no longer useful except as salvage. Transplanted mechanical beasts wander about, shredding, tearing, and melting their decommissioned siblings for scrap, brains submerged in vats of green and blue controlling their every movement. The tang of iron slurry and cacophony of rending metal fill the air.

One of these transplanted beasts is Ma. I just need to find her.

The owner is a few years older than me, scarlet hair bound tightly under a baseball cap and blue overalls streaked with soot. A grimy nametag pronounces her "Mara."

"Serial number?" She flicks through a clipboard. Peering over, I see it's filled with serial numbers and designations.

"F-6733-II-11," I recite from memory. "Welding droid."

"Yep, we've got her. Real beauty." Mara looks up at me and flashes me a grin. "Ever seen a welding droid? Looks gorgeous in the dark."

Cameras dot Kanshin Junkyard, covering the landscape so that Mara can spot and react to any issues before they spiral. She explains that transplanted machines are dependable and tireless, but accidents happen. Brains burn out, tanks crack. It's never anything serious, but worth keeping an eye out for.

She pulls up a camera feed.

Ma's brain is ensconced deep in the heart of a twisted hulk of chrome and gears. Her wheels are fully as large as I am, and she moves with purpose, mechanical claws extending and tearing at scrap. Every so often, a welding laser mounted within her body arcs out crackling violet light that sets the very air on fire, a measure of power that her frail body never had in real life.

"She's in good hands," Mara assures me, before turning the camera feed off. "I swear."

I believe her, but I can't help but wonder what Ma is thinking deep in the bowels of her new home, if she's thinking at all.

Within a few weeks, I've become a regular at the Junkyard. The pension is enough for me to survive on, and with little else to do, I spend my days in Kanshin's visiting room reading the news and watching Ma. Most days, Mara and I are the only two flesh and blood humans around.

She's happy to oblige the first few times, but eventually, she looks at me oddly. I guess most people don't visit their dead relatives' brains more than once or twice, if that.

"You aren't one of those Machine Church wackos, right?" She laughs nervously. "Because this is still private property, and I'm just leasing the transplants—"

"No, nothing like that." I shrug. "I just don't have anything else to do. It's either this or stay in my apartment and sleep the days away."

"Family? Friends?"

"Last of my family's out there, welding steel."

After a while, she breaks out in a smile.

"Want to go see her? I'm on lunch, and I normally eat outside, anyway."

"Is that allowed?"

"Nope." A cheeky smile. "But I'm in charge, right?"

We leave the viewing area and sit on a pile of junk as Ma works. She's efficient and systematic, like she used to be. I wonder if the brains retain something from their past: habits, abilities, personality. Mara scoffs at the idea, and I know she's right. They're glorified calculators, but I hope that somewhere, deep down, Ma knows I'm keeping my promise.

But I can't keep coming to the Junkyard with nothing else to do. Eventually, I'll run out of things to read, and if I keep scrolling through the news, my boredom will turn into a dense hole of depression and anxiety.

Laying out on the junk pile, I look over at Mara.

"Would you hire me?"

"A job? You want to work *here*? Sure you aren't a wacko?" She looks around, bemused. "Anyway, it's not like I have any open positions."

"I'll work cheap. I signed up with the Transplantation Corps, so I don't need the money." I pause. "Honestly, it'll just be nice to see Ma every so often."

"You know she—"

"She can't tell I'm there; I know." We've had this discussion before. "Call it sentiment. Please, Mara?"

Mara thinks for a minute, before nodding.

"Ah, what the hell." She shrugs. "I don't need anyone else around, but I won't say no to cheap labor."

Most days, Mara is the only person I interact with. Mara and the transplant taxis that take me to Kanshin. The transplants never talk back though, so I'm not sure how much they count.

I'm pretty sure that on most days, I'm also the only human company Mara has. Sometimes she speaks to contractors and government agents, but they may as well be robots for all the human interaction they provide. She doesn't have any family either, alive or transplanted, and generally eschews people, though she's warmed up to me. It's her and me, sharing overpriced sandwiches from the vending machine while the transplants work unceasingly.

My job involves monitoring the different transplants and noting any odd errors or glitches I see. If something goes awry, we'll want the notes for a full diagnosis later. It's a straightforward job. Mind numbingly boring, but straightforward, and it lets me keep an eye out on Ma.

"I can't believe you were doing this alone all this time." I stifle a yawn. "How are you not crazy already?"

"Who says I'm not?" Mara chuckles as she types. "You're crazy too, so you don't realize it."

After months of watching the machines, I pick out quirks and oddities among them. Unique peccadilloes with no explanation. Some of the metal shredders prefer to chew each scrap of waste as it comes their way, while others prefer to gather larger amounts before they work. Some robots walk haltingly, slowly approaching their targets, while others practically run forward, only course correcting if they miss entirely.

I don't know the brains operating the robots, so I can't say if these are holdovers from their human lives. I know Ma, however, and occasionally, she does something that reminds me of the person she used to be.

When it rains outside, the mechanical gears creak and complain just like her joints did.

When she welds two slabs of steel together, she pats the center, the same way she used to press down on the sandwiches she made me as a kid.

After she welds a joint, she'll clamp down on each end and pull it gently, like she did after she sewed together my torn clothes to make sure the stitches held.

Mara and I spend our breaks sitting on various piles of junk, watching the transplants work and making jokes.

"You ever wonder if the Machine Church people have a point?" I ask through a muffled bite. "Not like a soul, but maybe some personality? Something about their past?"

"Maybe they do, Yuri." She smiles at me before taking another bite of the sandwich. "And maybe you can ask to borrow some personality."

I don't think she believes my theories, but she never makes fun of me. At first, I think she's just being kind.

That assumption lasts until she kisses me, at which point I realize that she's not just being kind; she has feelings for me. And as I kiss her back, I realize I have feelings for her too.

We spend more lunch breaks inside the junkyard offices than we do out on the piles of junk. Mara's bedroom adjoins the junkyard offices, and her bed is more comfortable on bare skin than old piles of scrap are.

Soon, I visit Ma less frequently and then not at all. I still watch over her, still note the little quirks and foibles that she shows, but mostly, I leave her alone. I can't reach out to her, and she can't reach out to me. Perhaps the ghost of consciousness is all that's left within her metal body.

But Mara needs to work through lunch today, and I haven't got anywhere else to go. So, I take a quick jaunt out of the offices into the main junkyard. The sun is blisteringly hot, making it too uncomfortable for any real human workers. Transplants, thankfully, don't feel discomfort.

Ma is busy picking and joining large steel pipes. Mara explained that a lot of the broken equipment that came to the junkyard was perfectly good, and only needed spot-welding, joining, or trimming before we sold it. Ma is probably the single most profitable bot that Mara leases.

I talk to Ma as she moves about, selectively running her welding laser over flaws and fixing bits and pieces. I know that I'm just talking to myself, but perhaps the ghost that occupies the welding bot will enjoy the company.

"Hey Ma. Long time, no see." I speak while munching on a sandwich and sipping lukewarm tea. "Y'know Mara? She's the proprietor. Technically, she owns you. Well, leases you."

The bot shows a remarkable lack of interest.

"Well, she's pretty. And she likes me. I might ask her to marry me."

For a long time, I wondered what Ma's reaction would be when I eventually told her I'd be getting married. Happiness that I found someone to love? Sadness that I was leaving her alone? Stress at the impending finances of a wedding we couldn't afford?

Ma slowly turns towards me. For a moment, I wonder if she's reacting to my proclamation. Just as slowly, she reaches a claw out in my direction, plucks a small piece of metal from the pile I'm sitting on, and then continues her work.

Well, so much for that. I get off the junk-heap, dust my overalls, and approach Ma.

"Sorry I don't visit more often, Ma." I pat the sun-warmed steel, careful to stay out of the way of her claws and laser. "I'll try to come by more."

I move away and she resumes her job. The violet laser that erupts from her body sears my eyes as she showers sparks everywhere.

"Love you too, Ma. I'll see you soon."

• • •

The wedding is simple. Mara and I don't have many friends, and the few we have don't seem interested in visiting a junkyard far out of the city to attend a wedding. A few postcards containing money come our way, but the ceremony involves just the two of us, Ma, and a local Machine Church minister.

We aren't religious, but Mara and I both see Ma as more than a machine. I've pointed out strange behaviors and personality quirks often enough that we can't help but see Ma and the other transplants as something close to alive. Mara's worked with them her entire life, but even she admits the behaviors match too well, that it can't just be wishful thinking.

Moreover, the Machine Church minister doesn't charge for his services. Religious exemptions, apparently.

"Sign here, here, and here." He mops his brow with a handkerchief. "I'll get you registered within the hour."

Ma looms over us in the background. I've convinced Mara to give her a break, just for today. She sighs and grumbles, but Ma is literally the last remnant of family that we have, so she agrees. The metallic beast is quiet, but I can see Ma's brain swimming in the vat of fluid.

"Wish my dad was here to see this." I say to Mara, holding her hand. She's dressed in a traditional wedding dress, already dusty from the grime of the junkyard. "He'd have loved you."

"I'm glad mine isn't here to see this. He was a right asshole."

And on that note, we kiss.

"By the power of the Machine Church, I pronounce you man and wife." The priest mumbles awkwardly, forced to jump ahead a few lines in his sermon.

We continue kissing.

The days after marriage mimic days before.

Mara is still in charge of the business end, leasing transplants, procuring scrap, selling slurry. I'm more practical, watching over the transplants, making meals, occasionally fixing something in the office. Sometimes, we camp out in my old apartment, but the well-oiled machine of our lives centers on the junkyard.

One day, I notice Ma is stuttering and stumbling more than normal. Her movements have been slowing down for a while, her profit margins have been going down, and she's been making more mistakes. We've both noticed it, but Mara has avoided mentioning it, which I'm grateful for.

But today, she's moving about as though she can't quite tell where she wants to be. She crashes into a pile of rusted metal, reverses, and crashes right back into it, over and over.

Mara and I go to the junkyard and confirm Ma's strange behavior.

"I—" Mara begins, clears her throat, and lays a hand on my shoulder. "I think it's time, Yuri."

I want to argue vehemently, to tell her it's not time, and that Ma just needs a break. But as I'm about to speak, Ma careens wildly, and tips over to the side, her wheels spinning in the air. Her claws scrabble at nothing and my protests die in my throat.

"Can we at least—"

I know it's not really Ma. Ma left almost six years ago. The lobotomized brain driving the welding bot lies in limbo between the ghost of a memory and a complex calculator. The facts I know don't dislodge the emotions I feel, however. A deep, suppressed sadness rises within, and I'm twenty-two again, watching Ma die in a one-room apartment with no last rites and only impassive, automaton-like military personnel for company.

I fall to the floor, tears streaking my face and splattering onto the dusty junkyard ground.

Mara kneels next to me, pulling me in for a hug.

"I'll call the minister."

Ma's second funeral is much nicer than her first.

Her siblings are working away in the junkyard, filling the air with the screams of tearing metal. The heavy, smoky stench of melting steel makes me cough in between sobs. Mara sits next to me, dressed in black, holding my hand, offering quiet solace.

We've turned Ma off, and a small group of Transplantation Corps engineers watches the priest speak. Once he's done, they'll repossess her, replace the welding droid with a new one, and be on their way.

"Machine death is a phenomenon we do not understand. We do not know why the brain tires out, only that it does." The priest speaks with gravitas, his voice a low drone that nearly melds into the background. "Still, we hope that as with the souls of the living, the consciousness of the dead finds peace eternal. Kathleen Arakota, you left behind a boy. Today, you depart, having seen him turn into a man. Find your peace, Kathleen, as your son has found his."

I sob louder, and Mara wipes away my tears. I cannot speak at her second funeral, just like I could not speak at her first. What words would be enough for Ma, who has died in front of me not once, but twice?

As the engineers take her away, one approaches us, hat in hand. "I'm sorry for your loss."

I can't say anything, so Mara simply nods. He continues.

"Once we decommission the asset, we'll send you a letter with the confirmation. It should be here within a week."

He leaves with the rest of his team, and Mara ushers me into our bedroom.

I dream about Ma making sandwiches and welding joints.

True to their word, the Transplantation Corps sends a letter in just a few days.

Dear Yuri and Mara Arakota,

Due to an administrative error, the transplant asset repossessed from Kanshin Junkyard, S/N F-6733-II-11, was mistakenly designated **Kathleen Arakota**.

Please find the corrected records for **Kathleen Arakota** below.

Serial Number: N/A

Designation: N/A

Cause: Medically unsuitable for commission due to prolonged illness.

Status: Decommissioned on First Arrival.

We regret this error.

Regards,
Transplantation Corps.

This is an automated letter. For queries, please visit our website at transplantationcorps.gov/queries. To sign up for transplantation benefits, please visit your nearest Transplantation Corps Center.

A Flicker

By Emily Ruth Verona

Dahlia eyes.

Most people describe plants based on the colors they see—I describe colors based on the plants they resemble. Flowers are good for that. There's variety. The red-brown of a chocolate dahlia's petals is completely different from the muddy streaks of a chocolate daylily. Both are part of the Asteraceae family, which includes over 30,000 species. My big brother's eyes have always been a perfect match for rich dahlia petals.

Those dahlia eyes are narrowed so skeptically now. Jonah isn't so much surprised as he is annoyed that I've shown up at his door. Soaked to the bone. Even my sneakers are squishing. It hasn't stopped raining all week. The biblical irony of the situation is not lost on me.

So, here I've come to the belly of the whale.

His lips part, one syllable emerging. *"Huh…"*

I flash a smile. Try not to look at his arm. It doesn't work. Jonah had his Animus Marker cut out years ago, but I'm still not used to it. Our AMs are implanted in the forearm at birth, designed to measure all matter of personal genetic material. It's no bigger than a sunflower seed. Unless one lights up to signal that you've met your soulmate, it isn't too noticeable.

The removal of one, however: that leaves a mark. There's so much you've got to tear away to take it out. That's Jonah though, an Indeter through and through. According to the teachings of Indeterminism, everything comes down to chance and choice, not fate.

As if cutting his own light out wasn't enough to humiliate our parents, Jonah went and twisted the knife—got the words "*my first act of free will shall be to believe in free will"* tattooed above the scarring in loopy, elegant cursive. It's a William James quote. All Indeters are into William James. He's like their Jesus. Mom was absolutely livid when she saw. And to think they named him after the prophet and me after *Let them eat cake.*

Jonah's dahlia eyes begin narrowing. "Nett, did someone... die?"

The last time he called me Antoinette, I was six. I didn't like the name, so I bit him on the arm. Like it was his fault for speaking it into existence. "Who would have died?"

He frowns. Jonah has the most adorable little frown, almost like he's about to cry and laugh at the same time. He steps aside, albeit reluctantly so, and I walk into the apartment. "Nice hair," he grumbles, as if it's an insult. My hair is this deep, dark, creamy purple these days, like a Pulsatilla—pasque flower—on the verge of wilting. Bobbed and short. Avant-garde flapper chic.

As for Jonah's *look*—if you could call it that—he's got this farmer-esque thing going on. He forgets to shave, and the stubble on his face grows in calla lily red, not muddy Malvaceae—hibiscus—like his hair. He wears flannel like God herself gave him the directive. *Thou Shalt Not Disregard Plaid!*

"Are you... planning on staying long?" he asks pointedly, eyeing my duffel bag.

"My apartment is an aquarium."

"What?"

"Flooded. The whole place. A foot of water. Maybe two." I wait for him to offer me a towel to dry off. When he doesn't, I shake my wet hair like a dog. "Where's the peace lily I got you?"

"The what?"

"The plant."

"Oh. It died."

"How? Those things are impossible to kill. Like, you actually have to put effort into premeditating the murder."

He shrugs. "What do you want me to say? It just... died."

Liar. He probably over-watered it. When we were kids, he used to kill our pet fish the same way: by overfeeding them. I wait for him to apologize for the peace lily. Instead, he gestures vaguely to the living room and returns to the open laptop on the kitchen counter. He works from home, coding for some PR firm.

I drop my duffel bag. When I sit on the couch, the middle cushion sags like it's about to suck me in. A spring groans, causing Jonah to bristle. "Why don't you go for coffee?" he suggests, voice strained.

"I'm off caffeine."

His shoulders tense. That means he's frowning again. "Since when?"

"Since I read that it can kill you."

"That's bullshit."

"That's *science*, man…"

He twists around on his stool to face me. It would be one thing if I didn't know anything about science, but I *do*—and it pisses him off when I believe anything unsubstantiated. His silence is rigid. Firm. I shift my weight, tailbone perfectly aligned with the uncomfortable beam in the frame of the couch and start chewing impatiently on my pinky nail. I wonder if all Indeters are so entitled or if it's just him. I didn't grow up like our parents, believing in the almighty power of my AM, but I'm not an Indeter either. Everyone should just believe what they want, when they want, however they want. For some people it's fate. For some people it's free will. For me, it's botany. Plants make sense. Everything else is just noise to me.

I stop biting at the nail, finger flush against my lower lip. Jonah is back to his typing—the keys click-clacking at a steady rhythm. I watch the stiff, mountainous line of his shoulders. Jonah always looks tense, even when he's not.

As quietly as I can, I rise and make my way to the end of the apartment. It opens up onto a balcony about the size of a fire hydrant. I go outside. There is another balcony overhead, keeping the rain off me. My elbows press against the banister and I gaze down at the city below. Everything streams by in miniature. Humanity as an ant colony.

The sky is trampled daffodil-gray and the air feels swollen. Damp. I close my eyes and listen to the traffic rushing across the

city in waves. I feel something like a fly bite my arm and swat at
it, only to miss. I open my eyes and realize that there is no fly.

My AM is glowing.

A tiny little white light. A star in a sea of flesh.

Shining. Stinging. Burning. *A false flicker?*

False flickers can happen. If someone has sustained a consider-
able injury, then they might get a false positive, but largely what
we've come to call "false" flickers are just the result of bad timing.
Cars passing on opposite sides of the highway. Two planes crossing
in the sky. They aren't the norm, but everyone knows someone
who knows someone who has experienced a false flicker.

I step back and my shoulders press up against the glass door.
I call Jonah's name before turning and stumbling back into the
apartment. My brother is still at the counter when I grab him
by the arm and swing him around.

"Look!" I demand. Before he can argue, I offer up my forearm.
He looks, but there is nothing to see. *What?* I shake my arm as
if doing so will resurrect the light. When it doesn't, I drag Jonah
out to the balcony. "Nett—"

"Shh!" I command. We both barely fit and so we stand there
squeezed together, staring at my AM. Waiting. It flickers briefly
again—prickly like pins—then stops. "What the fuck, right? Do
you think it's someone on the street?"

Jonah glances over the railing. "No, too far."

"So, in this building?"

"Maybe."

Range varies from person to person. Some people will flicker
when their match is a quarter of a mile away. For others, you
practically have to bump into each other. When your sensors
get close, they flicker. When you touch, they shine bright.

"It hurt," I tell him. "Like a bee sting."

His eyes flit from my arm up to my eyes again. We're thinking
the same thing, even if neither of us will say it. It's a side effect
that impacts exactly 0.005% of the population. Most people
supposedly feel a warm glow when their AM goes on: soothing
and serene. People like me, we experience a sting. A bite. An
itch. Akin to an allergic reaction.

His interest fading, my brother turns to go back inside.

"You got a measuring tape?" I call after him and he points dejectedly to a kitchen drawer. I retrieve the measuring tape myself and coax him to stand with it while I check the length of the apartment—the depth, height. I circle the perimeter of the room, watching closely for another flicker. Nothing. "So, you've got adjacent apartments... *there, there*, and... *there*—right?"

"I guess."

"Why do you look bored?"

He does. Not irritated or annoyed, but actually bored, eyes flat. The same as they are when I talk about how there are 450 different types of oak trees.

I tell him I'm going to check the hallway and Jonah shrugs, returning to his laptop. The second I step outside his apartment, as if on cue, one of the wall sconces flickers and for a moment—one brief and haggard moment—I wonder: *what if the sconce is my match?*

No. That's not it. There's a fly or something caught in there.

Even if your soulmate could be something inhuman, I've always been drawn to organic over inorganic matter. In the fifth grade, I checked this big book of plants out of the public library—paged through it day after day like it was the gospel. Incurred two late fees. The pictures in this book featured all kinds of flowers but my favorite was the jade vine. They are very rare. Surreally beautiful. Sea-glass green petals and often purple stems. Bats pollinate them. Bats. I'd never heard of anything so magical. About a week after I read that, Mom took me shopping for a dress to wear to the next school dance. '*Come on*,' she had urged when I told her it was a waste of time. '*What if you meet your match at this dance?*'

I was eleven at the time. *Eleven*. And there she was planning my wedding.

'*My match is a jade vine*,' I had told her.

The statement startled her—not the defiance, but the certainty of it. Like I knew better than my own destiny. That's a word our mom loves: *destiny*. She pulls it out whenever she preaches against Jonah and the shameful heresy which he has brought into our family. *Shameful* and *heresy* also being integral to her vocabulary.

There's no time to lose and so I start with the apartment across from Jonah's. I knock on the door and wait. For a moment there is only silence. Then, something inside stirs. My match coming to meet me? Or a cat surveying his territory?

I wonder if I should try again, when the door—big and bulky and reinforced—swings open to reveal an older woman, her hair a tapestry of germander grays and lily whites pulled back into a knot at the base of her neck. Her soft, wrinkled hand tightens around a walking stick, and while she's looking at me, she doesn't quite seem to see me. Slowly I shift my weight, glancing at the stick again to see if she registers the movement of my head. She doesn't. She's blind. "Bonsoir," says the woman, her voice soft as butter. "Bonsoir. Allô?"

Shit. "Bonjour..." I begin hastily, three years' worth of high school French crumbling in my brain. "Parles-vous... anglais?"

"Non. Que veux-vous?"

Double shit.

"Ma fille s'arrête tous les soirs à huit," she continues rapidly. "Revenir alors—"

"S'il vous plaît... ma... mon frère est Jonah," I explain, gesturing across to my brother's apartment like an asshole before remembering that the woman can't see me. "He... vit... across the hall... your neighbor... eh... voisin? Oui? Ma AM—ma—ma lumière..." I continue, because growing up with an AM means knowing to say "light" in all manner of languages from an early age. Kids practice, the same way they practice spelling *Mississippi*. *Licht... lys... luce... lux.* "I am looking for le match pour my lumière—un homme..."

At this, the woman smirks. "Ma chère, il n'y a pas eu d'homme ici depuis longtemps."

This is hopeless. "Never mind," I sigh. "D'accord. Merci. Au revoir."

She smiles politely, the way I imagine old fashioned English schoolmistresses would smile at children before rapping them across the knuckles. She closes the door and I am certain that I hear her twist the top and bottom locks on the other side.

I scratch at my AM. It doesn't itch at the moment, but a part of me hopes that clawing at it will somehow turn it back on. When it doesn't, I head for the elevator—a rickety contraption that pauses as if to take long, deep breaths in between floors. Jonah and his damn hipster building.

The elevator spits me out on the second floor, into a hallway identical to the one above it in every way. Jonah's apartment is sixth from the stairs, so whoever is under him should be too. Quickly, I locate 3F. The second I knock, the door pops open with the force of a jack-in-the-box spring. Almost as if I'd been expected.

Inside are two girls who look to be about eight, with straight matching bangs above brown chrysanthemum eyes. Their dresses are as identical as their faces.

"Who are you?" asks the girl on the right.

"Jonah Wheeler's sister," I reply, pointing at the ceiling. "He lives up there. Are your, uh, parents home?"

"Mom went to get cigarettes," says the girl on the right. She admires my hair. "Purple is Millie's favorite color."

"Millie?"

She points to the girl on the left, the one who looks too serious to say anything. "That's Millie. I'm Maris. We're not supposed to talk to strangers."

"I am a stranger."

"Yeah, but Mom likes Mr. Wheeler," says Maris. It takes me a second to realize she's referring to Jonah and not my father. "She says he has a cute butt."

I smirk.

"You can come in and wait if you want."

Before I can object, the girls part for me to enter—their AMs are visible below their short sleeves, shiny and new. Like crystal against their soft skin.

"Are you here about Mr. Wheeler's socks?" asks Maris.

"His… socks?"

"Mom still hasn't found them, but when she does, she'll bring them up."

She says this so practically, so matter-of-factly, that I almost laugh. Not at the fact that Jonah is hooking up with someone, but because Jonah seems like the sort of person who would have sex with his socks *on* rather than off.

My mouth forms a tight line. "I'm sure they will turn up."

"But you didn't know about the socks," says Maris, her face scrunching up curiously. "So that's not why you're here."

"No, it's not," I tell them. "My AM went off upstairs."

Their expressions react in perfect symmetry, with raised brows and slightly parted lips. "You're looking for your person?" asks Maris, her hushed voice almost reverent.

I nod.

"Are they a girl or a boy?"

"I'm not sure yet."

"Well, they aren't here," Maris assures me, trying to sound older and in doing so sounding very much her age. "Mom never has boys over during the day. And her friends only ever meet her for drinks around the corner..."

"You didn't order pizza today? Or maybe get a package?"

Both girls shake their heads.

My lips purse. As I consider the possibility that perhaps my flicker was, in fact, a false one, a short, thin, rather young blonde woman enters the apartment. She freezes and tilts her head at my presence, as if a different angle will somehow explain the stranger in her kitchen. Millie huddles up beside Maris. "This is Mr. Wheeler's sister," Maris declares, gesturing broadly like I'm the winning prize on some game show.

Recognition comes into focus across their mother's pale periwinkle eyes. "Is Jonah... he is all right?"

"Oh, yeah!" I nod, overcompensating. "He's fine. I'm just upstairs for a visit and, and um..." I usually don't ramble like this. "My AM lit up... so, I'm looking to see if anyone... if it's because of anyone down here."

"*Oh.*" The word is as round and blank as the oval created by her pursed lips. Maybe she doesn't know what to say next. Maybe, like Jonah, she doesn't believe in all this nonsense. A long, tulip-pink sleeve keeps me from seeing whether or not she still has her AM.

"I'm sorry," I begin, trying to map out a way to the door. "I should be going."

"How is Jonah?" she asks hastily, placing a hand on Maris's shoulder.

"Good. I guess?"

She looks disappointed. This clearly isn't the answer she wants to hear but I don't stay to learn more. Back in the elevator, I push the button for the fourth floor, slip my cell phone out from my back pocket, and call Jonah.

"*What now?*"

The elevator chimes and the doors slide open. I step out onto the fourth floor. "I thought you hate smokers."

"Why does this matter?"

"You hate smokers, but you're banging the chain-smoker downstairs. At least, that's what I gathered from her kids. You don't think it's weird she dresses them the same?"

"Do you have a point?"

A burn pulses through my arm. My insides jolt. "I'm outside 4F. My light's on again." I knock but no one answers and so I try the handle, which turns easily. "The door's unlocked." *Is there a friendly greeting for trespassing?* My AM is flashing now. "Hello?" I call inside.

"Nett!" snaps Jonah. "You can't just go—"

He keeps talking but I've stopped listening. Unlike my brother, the occupant of this apartment has photographs all over the walls. I lean in to get a better look at a photo where someone—presumably *the* guy—is standing on a beach with a woman. Probably his mother. The guy has an even brow and attractive nose, a fine complexion and tangled hair the color of driftwood. The way he's squinting even though it's not sunny suggests that he's nearsighted and the fold of his arm around his mother's shoulder makes him look gentle. Warm.

"I think this is a picture of him," I say, either to myself or to Jonah. "He's cute."

"Nett!"

My AM is really burning now. The whole room feels cloaked in a sense of anticipation. My finger twitches, eager to flip on a lamp. Only, this isn't my apartment. Or even Jonah's. A stranger lives here. A stranger I am supposedly meant for. The idea of it in this moment seems absolutely absurd to me.

What if Jonah is right? What if fate is bullshit?

"Why don't you believe?" I ask suddenly, a tremble in my voice.

"What?" I can't tell if the connection is poor or if he really doesn't know what I mean. I keep walking. Waiting. Breathing. *Am I breathing? It's hard to tell... air comes in and air goes out, but I don't feel the weight of it in my lungs.*

"Your AM," I say. "Why'd you cut it out?"

The door at the end of the hall is askew. My AM isn't flickering anymore. It's burning bright. My insides sizzle. I step into the bedroom and I see him. The man lying on the floor by the bed.

No. Not a man. A body.

He's face up, one arm stretched across the floor open-palmed, the other draped over his stomach. An even brow and attractive nose. Hair the color of driftwood. The air feels hot and sticky and frail, like light through a prism. Ready to vanish at any moment.

I inch towards it... him... the body.

The truth hums in my brain. Swelling.

"He's dead," I whisper at last into the phone.

"Dead?" my brother's voice hiccups. "Nett—"

I hang up before he can finish. Because the swelling is taking up all the space in my skull. Making it impossible to think. *Blood.* The body's shirt is covered in so much blood. From punctures? Cuts? I can't tell. My mind is a swirling sea of flickers and itching and whales and cake. Death doesn't stop an AM; no, they are designed to outlast death. I used to know a girl in school who went to cemeteries, walking across the graves waiting for her AM to light up. Searching for her match. Convinced he was already in the ground.

This body is so perfectly still. Even plants don't possess this kind of irrevocable stillness.

My fingers stretch out, then recoil from his skin. The hairs on his arm are sticking up. Static electricity. Our bodies continue to react to the world whether we're in them or not. My hand hovers above him, lost in a limbo of not touching.

I notice a trail of blood on the floor—smudges, really—as if whoever did this left the room crawling on hands and knees. I follow the finger-paint blood to the half-open bathroom door. Why? Because I scratch at bug bites. Pick at scars. Choose plants over people.

I let them eat cake. That's what I'm named to do.

I push the door open.

In a pile on the floor between the toilet and the tub is a man I don't recognize from the photographs. His hands and arms are stained with blood. Lycoris red in color. Lycoris are spiky little things, almost like spiders lying on their backs. A letter opener is clenched tightly between his fingers; silver beneath the blood. His AM is shining like a hellish little lighthouse.

The body's AM was not lit. It was not my match.

I stare at the man with the letter opener. His bulging eyes are so very green. Almost like a jade vine.

Something like a laugh swells and twists and rots in my throat. I step back into the bedroom at the exact moment in which Jonah comes stumbling into the apartment. Out of breath. When he reaches the bedroom he stops, gawking in the way we all gawk at death. When he looks up, he sees me... but only for a second, because already he's looking further. Into the bathroom. At the man covered in blood. That letter opener with its crimson shine. Jonah lurches toward me, my name perched on his lips, but I slide back into the bathroom. Slam the door shut. Twist the lock.

"*Nett!*" he calls, pounding on the door. "*Nett!*"

My AM still hurts, but all this adrenaline... it's quenched some of the pain. I look at the man with the letter opener and his eyes raise, his stare pouring into mine, soft and malleable and hollow. He could be a burglar. Or a friend of the dead man. A lover. Who he is doesn't matter to me so much as what he is—the bits and pieces that make him up. What does his voice sound like? Does he chew at his fingernails the way I chew at mine? I wonder what his hair smells like when it's not drenched in sweat. Or blood. I wonder what kind of toothpaste he uses. Whether or not he has a favorite plant.

There's a commotion brewing out in the apartment. Voices. Feet on the ground. Jonah must have called the cops. I lock eyes with the bloody man. His pupils pulse.

There is more banging on the bathroom door now. "Miss Wheeler, open the door!" a voice called from the other side—a voice I do not recognize. "Miss Wheeler, are you all right?"

No. I'm not all right. My Animus Marker went off today.

I stare into my match's jade vine eyes and see nothing. Absolutely nothing.

The banging outside the bathroom continues. There is more shouting. Hollering. So much hollering. I close my eyes. *My match is a jade vine... my match is a jade vine...*

The door bursts open.

And life comes rushing in.

About a Broken Machine
By Catherine Kuo

Masashi tried to count his blessings when he went to pick up his older sister's hand-me-down maid. The unit had been passed down to her from a friend who had it passed down from a friend, which meant its condition could be anywhere between gently used and borderline ravaged, the worst-case scenario involving some abominable duct-tape monstrosity. Masashi would've liked a brand-new unit, something like what his thesis advisor, Satoshi, owned, but he was already putting himself through grad school, and the money he made from his part-time job went directly toward books, food, and bills. Meanwhile, Satoshi, who was already far more handsome and intelligent than Masashi could ever hope to become, had a talent for reading the stock market and was not averse to spending his extra money on luxury items. He owned a top-of-the-line maid and had recently purchased an office version that served as his personal assistant, much to the envy of their university's entire history department.

"Just so you know, we never got it fixed, so you'd better take it to a shop and see if they can bash some sense into it," Masashi's sister said, dragging the maid out of her closet.

The unit was a female model with vacant doll-like eyes and short, tawny hair that curled at the bottom like milk chocolate shavings. Although she was slender and completely naked, Masashi's eyes were first drawn to the huge chunk missing from her right shoulder and the smaller chunk missing from her left. Bundles of multicolored wires peeked out from the gaps, but they seemed to be in order and nothing was sticking out or frayed.

"What happened there?" he asked.

"I have no idea," said his sister. "Apparently it was like that when my friend got it. He tried to get it patched up, but the unit tore the grafts right off, so he didn't bother again after that."

"What else is wrong with it?"

"It... gets kind of weird. I don't know how to explain it. Eventually I just turned it off and it's been in the closet ever since."

"Great. Looking forward to having this in my home."

"It's good at doing whatever work you want it to, though," she added as he shoved the robot into the backseat of his car. "Other than that one quirk, it works just as well as any computerized assistant. Just don't try to fuck it, okay? It wasn't built for that."

"I wasn't going to," Masashi whined, quite ready to be on his way.

As he drove to the repair shop, he kept glancing into the backseat and catching her round, soulless eyes staring back. His attention would then snap back to the road, as if he'd been caught doing something indecent, but the skin on the back of his neck would prickle and bead with sweat until his gaze was drawn back once again to the faux human behind him.

The repair shop was a cheap hole in the wall, one of many in Tokyo, its depressingly minimalist shop front advertising various services in garish red characters. The gruff repairman behind the counter wasted no time on pleasantries and led Masashi to a grimy metal workbench.

"Boy, this is a beat-up hunk of junk," he grunted, flipping the maid over roughly. He attempted to pry open the access plate, but it wouldn't come loose, and despite trying every method short of dynamite, it still would not open.

"Welp, that's not happening. You'd have to destroy it beyond repair to get in there. The rest of it seems fine, though. You want me to put some skin grafts on the shoulders, mate?" he said as Masashi removed his wallet.

"No, thanks."

The repairman shrugged and charged him much more than Masashi was comfortable with, but he didn't have the expertise to protest.

Masashi hauled the robot the rest of the way home and up to his third-floor apartment. He propped her up on the couch and, reaching for the button on the back of her neck, turned her on. The machinery beneath the silicon skin vibrated to life, beeping and crackling and clunking before it settled down into an almost imperceptible hum. Her doll eyes blinked once and drifted over to Masashi.

"Hello," she said, sitting up straight and folding her hands in her lap. "I am OnCo Model Number 15070610-18. Would you like to give me a nickname or would you like to use the current setting?"

"Uh, sure, I'll give you a name," said Masashi. "How about... Candy?"

"Excellent choice. You may now refer to me as Candy. What would you like me to do, sir?"

"Um, you can just call me Masashi, it's fine."

"All right, Masashi. What would you like me to do?" For a moment, he drew a blank, but then remembered he had prepared a list.

"Uh, let's see," he said, reaching for his notebook. "I need you to clean the apartment, do my laundry, go grocery shopping, cook breakfast and dinner, make me lunch boxes to take to school... "

Candy gently took the list out of Masashi's hands and glanced at it.

"Understood," she said, looking up. "As for the purchasing of groceries, I will require clothing, as it is socially unacceptable for me to be out in public without proper attire."

"Right. Right," he muttered, flushing. "I think, uh, my sister might've given me some of your old clothes. Hold on."

Masashi ran down to his car and dug around in the trunk until he located the box of charging cables, cleaning rags, and other miscellaneous care items his sister had provided. Candy was picking at the exposed wires in her shoulders when he returned, but quickly lowered her hand when he entered.

"Um, here, I think this is yours," he said, pulling out a plain white dress. Candy put it on. "Also there's a bunch of cables and stuff you might need..."

"I will see to it," said Candy, taking the box from him. "Now, if you would permit me, I will start assessing the state of your apartment and determine how I may proceed with the duties you have assigned me."

"Yeah, uh, it's all yours. I'm just gonna... do some work."

Without another word, Candy began tidying up the apartment. Masashi felt like he should be helping, but then remembered the point of having a robot was that he didn't need to.

At first, he was hyper aware of her presence, especially when she cleaned his musty room, but after a few weeks, the two of them fell into their new routines and forged an amiable coexistence. At the very least, Candy seemed to be satisfied with her work, and Masashi was glad to have her around to take care of the household chores. Besides the holes in her shoulders, she was hardly as broken as his sister had claimed.

"See, I told you it was worth getting one," said Satoshi one night over a few beers. The izakaya was mobbed with university students, as usual, and the smell of grilled meat floated in thick clouds above their heads.

"Yeah, it's used though, not like those nice ones you have," said Masashi, grinning. "I'll catch up to you one day."

"Be careful with those secondhand ones. If they get twitchy, just smack them around a bit."

"Smack them around...?"

"Yeah. You know, like when a printer gets fussy."

"But doesn't that feel kind of weird? I mean, they look... human."

Satoshi shrugged. "So?"

Masashi wasn't sure how to process Satoshi's remarks and ultimately decided to shove them into the back of his mind. Satoshi was his friend and mentor, there was no point in trying to analyze every little thing he said.

When Masashi returned to his apartment, he was surprised to find the kitchen empty. He had told Candy he would need dinner when he got back, but instead she was sitting on the couch, hands resting by her sides, staring at the front door. A baseball bat lay on the cushions next to her. His eyebrows furrowed.

Masashi didn't own a baseball bat.

"Hey, Candy," he said, slowly closing the door behind him. "You okay?"

She didn't answer; instead, she stood and took off her dress. Masashi's ears reddened.

"Candy, what are you doing?" he spluttered as she picked up the bat.

Her wide, empty stare fixed upon him, Candy held the bat in front of her at arm's length and walked across the room with the grace and silence of a ballerina. Masashi stepped back until his shoulder blades struck the door, but she didn't stop until the hand holding the bat touched his chest. Eyes darting back and forth between her face and the bat, he took it from her and almost yelped when she dropped to her knees.

"Candy, get up," said Masashi, his mouth dry. "Candy?"

He knelt and her eyes followed. He put the bat on the floor, but she grabbed it and shoved it back into his chest. Shaking, he took the bat and put his other hand on her shoulder, the one with the larger dent.

"Candy? Can you hear me? Candy, I need you to snap out of it and listen to me, okay? I'm not going to hurt you."

At those words, her metal innards began whirring like an overheated computer, her features distorting into an amalgam of expressions: happy, sad, angry, hurt, frustrated.

"Candy," he continued, trying to think fast. "You need to make dinner, Candy. Did you forget?"

The whirring stopped, and Candy's face went blank again. She blinked. Once. Twice. Her eyes softened and her lips parted, eyebrows slightly upturned in mild confusion.

"I am very sorry, Masashi," she said, bouncing to her feet. "Please wait a moment."

She put her dress back on and didn't say another word until the food was ready.

"Tonkatsu curry. Your favorite," she said, placing the steaming plate in front of him.

"Thanks, Candy. It looks amazing!" he said in a desperate attempt to lighten the mood. The bat was still leaning against the front door where Masashi had left it, but Candy didn't mention it. While she was washing the dishes, he darted downstairs and put the bat in his car.

The next day at the university cafeteria, Masashi recounted the troubling incident to Satoshi over lunch.

"Sounds like it's broken," said Satoshi, after some contemplation. "Did you take it to the shop?"

"Yeah, but the guy couldn't get a look inside, all her panels and joints are welded shut or something."

"Huh, weird. Did you ask the previous owner?"

"Sort of. They said they found something wrong on the inside, but before they could get her repaired, she welded the access plate shut herself."

"That's freaky. Want me to take a look for you sometime? I know a thing or two about bots."

"That would be great, thanks," said Masashi, breathing a sigh of relief.

A few weeks later, they arranged for Satoshi to come over and inspect Candy before they did their usual review of his thesis. Candy was waiting for Masashi's arrival.

"Welcome ho—" she began, and froze like a startled fawn.

The amusing story Satoshi had been telling evaporated suddenly as he halted and stared back. For a moment, they seemed to be in their own little world, a tiny, dimly lit snow globe imprisoning them in a single perpetual moment. It passed as quickly as it had come and Candy flung herself into a ninety-degree bow.

"Well, isn't this a coincidence?" laughed Satoshi, taking off his hat and coat. Candy didn't move.

"Um, Candy, would you please hang up Satoshi's things?" said Masashi, inching forward. Candy bolted upright and took his belongings without a word. She wouldn't look at Satoshi.

"Do you... know her?" asked Masashi, suddenly feeling like a stranger in his own home.

"That used to be mine. It was one of my first ones, so I'd taken to playing around with the interior machinery, just to see how it all worked, you know? After I bought a newer model, I gave that one to a friend, but I guess it didn't work out so well for him. Not surprising. Well, you get what you pay for," said Satoshi, shrugging.

"Did she have," he gestured to his own shoulders, "those when you got her?"

"Hm? Oh, no, that was me. It's a bad habit of mine when I get frustrated with electronics. You know, like when you're a kid and you get mad at a video game and smash the controller? That sort of thing," he chuckled. "But yeah, sorry it got handed down to you in such a state. If I'd known you'd be getting it down the line, I would've restrained myself."

The rest of the night, Masashi had difficulty concentrating on Satoshi's critiques of his thesis and his mind kept drifting to the baseball bat locked away in his car. Candy gave them a wide berth and refused to say anything. After Satoshi left, she set about tidying the living room as usual.

"Hey, Candy," Masashi finally said after watching her for ten minutes. "Are you okay?"

Candy pivoted to face him, handheld vacuum clutched in one tiny fist. Her expression was unreadable.

"Will you hit me?" she said, holding it out to him.

"W-What?"

"Will you hit me?"

Masashi placed a hand on the vacuum, lowering it.

"No, Candy, no, I would never hit you."

She winced.

"Why not?" she said, stepping closer. "Why not? Why not? *Why not?*"

"Because it's not right!" he shouted, backing away. Candy dropped the vacuum and fell to her knees, grasping at his shirt.

"Please!" she screamed, her eyes widening until they seemed to take up half her face. Steam leaked from her mouth and ears like ghostly worms.

"Candy, stop! Stop this right now!" Masashi cried, pulling at her wrists in an attempt to free himself.

"Please hit me! Hit me so hard I don't ever wake up!" she sobbed, voice distorting. She threw him to the floor and pinned him against the coffee table.

Masashi squeezed his eyes shut and covered his face, waiting for her to crush his bones or bash in his skull. Every fiber of his body shook, jolting beads of water out from the corners of his eyes.

Suddenly, everything went quiet except for the hissing of steam. Something heavy fell onto his bare feet. Peeking between his fingers, he saw Candy sprawled face-first on the floor, her eyes staring into nothing. Masashi nudged her head with his foot, but she didn't move. After a few more minutes of tense silence, he hoisted her onto the couch and picked up her charging cable.

He paused.

Would it really be a good idea to charge her back up? What if she went haywire again? What if she exploded and set the entire apartment on fire?

He looked down at her and wondered if he should just shove her in the closet, too. But things had been going so well and she had really helped him get his life back in order and his thesis on track. Everyone deserved a second chance, right?

Taking her arm, he inserted the cable into her wrist and lay his head down on the couch cushions, studying the curve of her smooth, pale fingers until he drifted off to sleep.

He woke up to Candy's voice.

"Masashi? It's time to go to work."

He blinked slowly, disoriented, trying to remember why he was in the living room.

"Masashi?"

"I'm awake," he replied. His tongue felt fuzzy and swollen.

"Get up before your breakfast gets cold."

The sound of her footsteps faded as she returned to the kitchen. After a few minutes, he staggered to his feet and shuffled into the light. His breakfast waited for him on the dining table while Candy washed the dishes.

"Have a good day at work," was all she said when Masashi left.

He spent the train ride wondering what he should do if Candy went berserk again, but evening rolled around without bringing any decent ideas with it. When he opened his apartment door, she was there waiting for him with dinner on the table.

"Candy," he said after he'd finished eating. "About yesterday…"

"Masashi," she said, cutting him off. "Could you do me a favor?"

"Um, yeah, sure?" he replied, startled by her interruption.

"That bat in your car. Could you use it to break me?"

His heart sank.

"Candy. Why would you want that?"

"I want to be off forever. I don't want anyone to turn me on anymore."

"But why?" he repeated, rising from the table. He felt suddenly that he wanted to be nearer to her, as if to comfort a hurting friend.

"Does it matter?"

"Of course it matters!" he snapped.

"I just don't," she said without inflection. "Besides, I can't be a good personal maid if I keep neglecting my duties, can I? I am already broken. It only makes sense to finish the job."

"That was only a couple of times. And the last one was completely understandable. Satoshi was awful to you, of course you'd be upset if you saw him."

"And why should a robot ever feel upset?"

"Candy." Masashi put his hands on her misshapen shoulders, turned her toward him, and looked into her large brown eyes. "I forbid you from destroying yourself."

She blinked. "Very well."

For the rest of the night, Masashi engrossed himself in his thesis to the point where he didn't even hear the creak of the front door opening, or the tinkle of smashed glass, or the muffled thud of the door closing again. It was three in the morning by the time he raised his sunken, bleary eyes from his books. He staggered to the kitchen to retrieve a snack and found Candy there, her hands folded in front of her.

"Masashi," she said.

"Hey, you okay? You're normally charging around this time, aren't you?" he yawned, opening the fridge, but she slammed it closed with a snap of her arm.

"Dammit, Candy! What—" he bawled, but then he saw the way Candy was looking at him. Not like a robot or a human. Like an animal.

Before he could react, she thrust her arms forward and wrapped her cold hands around his neck. The ensuing struggle took them from the kitchen to the living room, knocking over chairs and tables as Masashi tried to kick Candy away, but only a pair of hefty pliers could have detached her rigid fingers. Black ink drops flooded his vision, their edges flashing with pencil-thin rainbows, and the sounds of shattering glass and toppling furniture went all blurry as if his head had been forced underwater.

This was it. This was how he would die. He was no athlete; he was an academic, his muscles made soft to accommodate the stiffness of a wooden desk and chair. It would take a miracle for him of all people to win against a machine.

By some stroke of luck, the miracle occurred, and for one brief moment he felt Candy's grip loosen ever so slightly. Air crashed back into his lungs. His right hand clawed and scrabbled for anything that could be used as a weapon and his fingertips found the handle of something long and weighted at the other end. Instinctively, he lifted his arm and smashed the thing down onto Candy's head. She released him and he rolled on top of her, striking again and again. He only heard the knocking on his door when he took a breath in between his own screams.

Masashi looked down, panting, sweat and saliva dripping off his chin. What had been Candy's head was now only a pile of screws and wires and artificial skin and hair. One eye had rolled under the TV but the other was still in its socket, nothing more than a painted ping-pong ball.

"Hello? Excuse me?" came a man's voice from outside.

Masashi's legs trembled as he stood. His right hand was still gripping something, tight enough to hurt. He looked down. It was the baseball bat.

"Hello?" the man called again.

Masashi pried his eyes away from Candy's remains and limped to the door.

"Oh my God, are you okay?" gasped the man when he saw Masashi. "What happened?"

"Ca... Robot. Robot tried to kill me," he wheezed.

"Oh shit, man."

"Sorry about the noise."

"No, not at all. Do you need anything? Do you need help?"

"No, I'm fine. Thank you," said Masashi, his own voice flat and foreign. He closed the door and surveyed his wrecked apartment. Candy's grotesque corpse lay next to the couch.

Masashi dropped the bat and went to bed.

"Masashi, what happened to the maid I gave you? It's a mess in here!" his sister said when she stepped into his apartment. She had come to drop off a few more hand-me-down gadgets.

"She broke. For good," he said flatly.

"Well, it was kind of on its last legs anyway. At least you got some use out of it before it croaked."

"I guess so."

"How about a new one for your birthday?"

"No, I think I'm good."

"Really? You could obviously benefit from it," she said, gesturing to the mountain of dishes in the sink.

"No, really," he said. "I'm perfectly fine."

Consider This an Opportunity

By J. A. W. McCarthy

My brother is three years younger than me. It says that on the little card tucked into the crate with him. His name is Harold, and Mom and Dad and BioMates LLC sure hope I'll love him.

Dear Millie, It's time you cared about someone other than your-self, the personalized portion of the note reads. *Consider this an opportunity to grow. Love, Mom & Dad.* As the delivery men left my house, they looked at me with a mixture of sympathy and bemusement.

Inside the crate, under layers of compressed cardboard and biodegradable packaging, BioMate LLC's flagship product—my new InteriMate, Harold—hovers in a transparent pod that's warm to the touch. The murky gel inside coats his skin, webs his fingers, plasters his shaggy black hair to the sides of his face. Clothes, shoes, a phone and wallet are packed in the crate with him, but inside the pod, he's naked. Is he going to be able to dress himself, or do I have to dress him?

Until I slice that pod open and do whatever it is I'm sup-posed to do to activate him, he's nothing more than a creepy life-sized doll with lips and a nose that look vaguely familiar, high round cheekbones same as mine, a jawline that's set tight enough to make me wonder if he grinds his teeth while he sleeps like I do. It's a roll of the dice with BioMates LLC—just like with genetics formed the old-fashioned way, you don't know exactly what any specific mix of DNA is going to produce. Sure, it could've and should've been simply a combination of my mother's and father's DNA, but they had BioMates LLC swirl in a healthy serving of mine too, so a selfish only-child would be guaranteed to love her reflection. All I can do now is curse every stray hair and flake of skin I left at my parents' house on my last visit six months ago.

So, in a way, this makes Harold also my son. Since I'm selfishly taking too long to give my parents a grandchild, I guess they fixed that for me too.

Consider this an opportunity to grow. Fuck that. I'm already grown.

Their little plan is working. I could've refused the delivery. I could've left Harold in the crate. I could've locked him in the basement, left him cold and hungry until he expired in a puddle of his own piss. Instead, he sits next to me on the couch. He smells like hand sanitizer, a whiff of rubbing alcohol under something vaguely lemon-fresh. It makes me think of how animals will reject a littermate that's been to the vet. At least he showered and dressed himself.

" 'Bout time you invited me over, sis," he says, swiveling his head to take in the surroundings. Unopened mail, empty glasses and candy wrappers litter the coffee table, swept aside to make way for my brother's big feet. A thin layer of dust coats every decorative surface. I haven't been lax in my housekeeping to spite my mother, but she does come to mind every time I spot a dust mote twirling through the air.

"Have I done well for myself?" I ask. "What are you gonna tell Mom and Dad?"

Harold pulls his phone from his pocket. "I'll text Dad now: *Got here safe. Millie's being a little bitch, but her house is nice,*" he dictates, then shows me the screen before hitting send. I wonder if his phone has a history—implanted like his own history—a whole lifetime of friends and photos and late night musings preloaded, evidence of a life that never existed.

"Tell them I learned my lesson. I'm no longer a selfish loner. Marriage and babies incoming."

"C'mon, Mills." He pokes me in the ribs and I swat his hand away. A stranger just touched me. The stranger on my couch is teasing me like we've done this our whole lives and the only thing I feel is a jovial kind of irritation. "Don't let them get to you," he tells me. "You're too easy and they feed on that. Just tell them what they want to hear."

I nudge his knee with my own; I don't even think about it. My body knows him, even if my mind doesn't want to.

"So, how long are you staying?" I ask. This is a cruel question. Though BioMates LLC is working on a PermaMate, the current technology allows InteriMates only thirty days before they start degrading. I want to know if Harold is aware, if he knows he's temporary.

He leans back and props an elbow on my shoulder. "You got anything to eat around here?"

My InteriMate brother sits at the kitchen table eating a sandwich. Turkey, cheddar, strawberry jam, arugula. He seems to like it.

Make your own fucking sandwich, I wanted to say, but instead I emptied out the fridge while he sat there and watched me. It was more effort than I ever put in for myself most days. The gentle curve of his jaw lopes up and down as he chews, sloppy with delight. Is this what I look like when I'm face down in a chocolate cake? My mother's voice echoes in my head: *That's not very ladylike—you're being a pig.* If I'd been a boy, would she have said such a thing? Would my parents still have viewed everything I did as selfish? Here I am feeding and housing a lab-grown meat sack that's going to expire like so much ground beef in thirty days because my parents think I need a sibling to teach me a lesson. *I'm* more fucking nurturing than they ever were.

"So good," Harold mutters through a mouthful of meat and cheese and bread. An arugula leaf bobs between his lips. "Just like Dad's."

"Dad?"

"Yeah, you remember. Mom thought the jam was gross, but Dad was right. He'd make them for us when we couldn't sleep.

You'd be crying and he'd make you a sandwich and everything would be all better."

It makes no sense, but I ask anyway. "He made you this sandwich?"

"All the time. Both of us." Harold's eyes dart around the table and I hand him a napkin. He wipes it roughly across his mouth before speaking again. "We'd eat them in bed. Mom would get so mad. Our faces were all red and we'd get red all over the sheets."

Nausea sweeps from my throat to belly. I head to the bathroom, leaving the food out so Harold can make himself another sandwich.

Alone in my bed that night, I turn that sandwich over and over again in my mind.

Dad never made me—*us*—any kind of sandwich. On those nights when the nightmares wouldn't leave me alone, *I* made sandwiches with whatever I could find. I do remember having a lot of sleepless nights as a child. I remember crying because Dad hit me when I woke him. I remember blood in my mouth, not strawberry jam.

"Selfish," he spat. "You're too old to be afraid."

"Your father has to work in the morning!" Mom admonished me as she shoved a wad of tissues in my face and shut the door.

Of course Mom and Dad wouldn't want Harold to have those memories.

My brother sleeps in my guest room. I picture him in there, mouth open, drool running down the side of his face and pooling on the pillow. I know because I slept like that as a kid. Dinosaur printed sheets, Lego and Barbies all over the floor, sneakers lost under a pile of dirty laundry. In my memory, his childhood bedroom looks just like mine.

I know this isn't real—this memory of my brother is really a memory of my own childhood because he's made from my DNA; he's me. It's disarming, though, to have these vivid flashbacks of family portraits and snowball fights and bubble baths where

I held his head under the water until he bit my arm. Harold is in every snippet, so seamlessly spliced in that his presence feels not only unremarkable but natural. I know the rhythm of his breath when he sleeps, the way he curls into himself after a night spent watching scary movies. I know right now that his throat is dry but he's too cozy—too lazy—to get up for a glass of water. What's particularly perplexing is that he remembers a comfort sandwich when all I remember is a fist and crying myself to sleep.

"You should bring Harold for a visit," my mother tells me over the phone. "How many days left now? Twenty-eight? I'd like to see the son I never had."

Her perfect, built to her specifications son.

"What you want to see is your money at work," I say. "You want to know if I've taken this opportunity to grow."

"Millie! Why do you have to be so cruel? Everything we do is to make you a better person, help you see outside yourself, help you succeed in the world. If we hadn't pushed you, you wouldn't have—"

"Yeah, I know. College," I finish.

My mother sighs heavily, exhaling her burdens across the state. "You got that scholarship because we pushed you. You could've been a doctor or a lawyer. So much potential. Instead, you studied art just to—"

"Spite you," I finish for her again.

Another sigh. I picture her standing in the kitchen, one hand on her hip, nostrils flaring as she sucks up all the air in the house. I'm the reason she has to spend hundreds of dollars every month getting her grays touched up. "Oh, Millie. Do you even still paint?" she asks, barely pausing. "All that money for school and you stay in your house all day doing data entry and watching TV. You never visit." Here her voice wavers, a wet nudge of guilt. "We want to see Harold. We want to see *you*. Your father and I, we're getting old. We won't be around forever, not by the time you finally realize how much you'll miss us. Don't you care?"

Why did I pick up the phone? I usually ignore my parents' calls, but I always listen to the subsequent voicemails as if I too believe I deserve to hear how selfish and myopic I am. Only a nagging sense of filial guilt keeps me from blocking their number.

"I'm feeding and watering him, Mom. And I put him in his crate at night, just like you taught me. I gotta go. Tell Dad hi for me."

Harold comes out of the bathroom as I'm hanging up. "Mom?" he mouths. He reaches for my phone, but I turn it off.

Really, I should take my little brother shopping, dress him up nice, put him on the train to my parents' house. Let them fall in love with their perfect child, only to watch him wither and die at the end of the month.

"You still talk to this guy?"

Sprawled out on the couch, Harold holds up my phone as I descend the stairs. I rush to grab it from him. A text from Graham hovers on my lock screen: *I'm free Friday. How about a drink?*

"He moved here a couple weeks ago," I say. "We're gonna catch up."

"Are you fucking crazy?"

Harold's lips curl with disdain. A memory of my brother standing outside Graham's house with a baseball bat comes to mind. It doesn't make any sense, but it's as upsetting as it was all those years ago.

"He was there for me," I say. "Every time Mom and Dad locked me out of the house because my grades weren't good enough or I didn't do my chores fast enough or whatever bullshit they came up with, Graham was there. He gave me a place to stay. Who knows what would've happened to me if I'd had to sleep in the park or something."

"He was all too happy to have you come to his house all vulnerable and shit," my brother reminds me. "He was happy to take your pants off for you while you were crying."

"I didn't do anything I didn't want to do."

"Really? Because I remember you used to shrink when you saw him at school. I remember how you'd turn away when he tried to hold your hand."

His words sting. It's a truth I've easily denied, justified, then filed away. Maybe I only keep score when it comes to my parents.

My phone buzzes. Graham again. I slide it into my pocket. "It was better than sleeping on the porch, knowing Mom and Dad were gloating about the lesson I'd learn if I didn't fucking freeze to death," I tell Harold. "At least Graham was there for me. All my other friends, they wouldn't let me in or their parents just drove me back home."

"When you came home in the morning, Mom and Dad called you a slut."

Another blow. The shame is fresh again. "You remember that?"

"You didn't deny it."

"Why didn't you unlock the door?" My voice rises, a high-pitched crack that makes my face hot, swells under my eyes and puts me right back there on that front porch, banging on the window as my parents steeled their focus on the TV. "Why didn't you let me back in?"

"I was out there too," Harold says, his gaze softening. His hand reaches for mine, but I pull away. "I was a little shit. I deserved it."

Later, after dinner, Harold falls asleep in front of the TV. I check my phone. Three new messages from Graham: a bar he wants to try, we should get dinner too, *hey, we can keep it chill, have drinks at my place instead*. I can feel that baseball bat in my hand, the hollow wooden clack it made against his front door as I tested it. His chestnut and clove cologne on me, in my hair, even after I showered. I knew all of it was wrong, but it was easier to give in, to be a girlfriend.

I consider blocking Graham. Instead, I turn my phone off, leave Harold on the couch, and head upstairs to bed.

• • •

It takes a week for Harold and me to fall into a routine. He does my laundry, but he forgets to put his dirty dishes in the dishwasher. I threaten to send him back to my parents; he tells me they're not so bad. We bicker. We watch TV together. He jogs around the neighborhood when he gets bored in my house. Halfway through the month, I take him out to dinner. We eat off each other's plates, filling our cheeks with sushi, daring each other to smear on more wasabi, holding the other person's glass out of reach when our tongues catch fire. The laughter comes easily and I realize how much I miss this, this not being alone. We have in-jokes, preloaded, stuff from my childhood. *Our* childhood.

It's good, as long as we don't talk about Mom and Dad.

Late one night, I walk in on Harold sitting at the kitchen table. He's holding a pair of scissors, the blade tip pressed to his forearm. His back is to me, and I wait for him to make a joke about me being creepy, or some crack about why all my knives are dull. I stand there in the doorway for a long time, but he doesn't move. I can't hear him breathing. In the blue-white light from the microwave display, I study the hairs on his head, on his arms, willing a single one to shift. It's too soon for this.

InteriMates don't spontaneously combust at the end of their lives. After thirty days, they wind down. Actions and reactions become slower, delays that have you second-guessing yourself at first. You think the joke you told didn't land, then you hear your InteriMate laughing alone in their room in the middle of the night. The food you made for your hungry InteriMate sits untouched until you find them the next morning, fork in hand, laboriously chewing each bite despite their desperate eyes. Eventually, they stop moving at all, their mechanical heart wound all the way down as the organic matter bloats with the gases of decomposition. Consider yourself lucky if you find your InteriMate slumped in a chair or their bed, eyes closed in peaceful repose.

BioMates LLC suggests you compost the skin and hair and muscles and fats that coat the various machine-made organs.

They even have a video on their website showing the prize-winning vegetables and flowers satisfied customers have grown from the remains of their temporary loved ones. One customer made a kinetic sculpture from the titanium skeleton of his InteriMate wife. These are just helpful suggestions, of course. BioMates LLC will pick up anything you don't want, for a fee.

Some people hold funerals for their expired InteriMates. The public laughs about it. Late night pundits theorize it's ego fêting ego, a shameless celebration of the self. InteriMate funerals still get a listing in the local paper, though, usually in the "Oddities" section.

I'm planning the funeral in my head when Harold finally speaks.

"These don't match. Nothing in here matches."

I switch on the light and join him at the table. He's got the scissor blades pressed against a small, pale crescent-shaped scar on his left forearm. There are several of these scars, sprinkled from wrist to elbow. He moves the scissors' tip to each one, demonstrating how it could not have made these marks.

"I tried all your knives, too," he says. "No match."

I hold up my own arm and show him the matching scars that mar my skin. I press my index fingernail against each one. It took years for me to stop biting my nails, to let them grow long and thick again.

"When we were kids," Harold says.

I nod. "Thirteen? Fourteen? I learned to do it in the tub so Mom wouldn't get mad about the mess. I used to bite sometimes too, but this felt better. The digging... I could control that."

Harold considers his arm again before putting the scissors down. I was in the tub. *We* were in the tub. Bubbles as thick and fluffy as frosting, some treacly peach scent from the mall. I bit down. I cried. *He* cried. My fingernails fit better; pressing deeper and deeper, that give, that moment of hesitation before breaking the skin. A flash of pain; then that thick, satisfying sinking into flesh. Did my brother savor that tug, the clarity as the pain focused? Does he hold the same image in his mind?

"They said we were weak," Harold says.

"I brought you into this world perfect, and you do this to yourself?" I mimic my mother.

The memory pulls a rueful hitch of a laugh from his chest. When he mimics our father, it's too close, too much. "You think this hurts? We've been protecting you your whole life. How are you going to survive in the real world?"

"We were weak, though," I say. "All that shit they did and said to us, and we turned that anger inward, on ourselves, because it was easier, because we were afraid. They deserved our rage, but we were too weak to give it to them."

"We were kids, Millie."

"We were old enough to hit back, to hold a knife."

Harold looks wounded at this. "We couldn't. They took care of us."

"We were misbehaving pets to them, and when we didn't perform—" I pick up the scissors and make a stabbing motion, "—we were weak. We just took it and took it. All those times… you didn't do shit for me. Why didn't you—just *once*—stand up for me?"

I forget the scissors are in my fist as I continue making stabbing motions, slicing too easily through the air between us, my arm loose and reckless as Harold grabs at me, trying to still me. He's yelling my name, but I want that flash of pain, that satisfying sinking into flesh.

"You're so fucking stupid. They never loved you," I tell my brother.

At that, he releases my arm, turns, and walks out of the kitchen.

Harold's crying in his room. I can't hear him, but I know. He's in there, curled on his side in bed, using the comforter to rub away his tears and snot. It's what I used to do.

I can't sleep anyway. I get out of bed and let myself into his room across from mine. He's as I imagined, back to me, his every inhale wet and clotted. He doesn't move as I climb into his bed and shape my body around his.

"You remember this?" I ask, pressing my cheek into his back. The sanitized vet scent is gone. He smells like fabric softener and my lemongrass shampoo. "We used to hold ourselves and squeeze and squeeze until we were invisible."

He doesn't say anything for a long time. It's not until I'm getting up from the bed that he says, "It worked."

When I find Harold late one night, frozen in the dark kitchen with a vacant stare and a steak knife in his hand, I know it's no longer too soon.

He's slow to respond. I hear him climb the stairs hours after I tell him to snap out of it and go to bed. The next morning, he makes it halfway through breakfast before he stops chewing. Bits of scrambled eggs and toast fall from his mouth, his eyes dull and his features slack. He's still got the steak knife in his hand.

Five days left.

This is the point where BioMates LLC suggests you get your compost area ready, if you're so inclined. A sunny spot in your yard, far enough from your home so you won't be bothered by odors or rodents. A large shovel to turn the compost. A friend or neighbor to do the early turning for you, if seeing your dead InteriMate is too hard.

Instead, I take Harold shopping. He accepts what I select, though his complacency is part of the expiration process. I buy him a blue button-down and khaki slacks, a look my mother will appreciate. I send a brief email to my parents and buy my brother a train ticket.

"You can't bring that with you," I tell him as we're waiting at the station.

It takes a full minute for him to consider his hand stuffed inside his jacket pocket. The tip of the steak knife dents the fabric, a dot of silver threatening beige twill. "No," he says quickly, turning back to me. This is an improvement over yesterday, a spark in his eyes that gives me hope.

"They'll take it from you. They'll kick you off the train."

I hold out my hand until he slides the knife out and passes it to me. Scanning the crowd, I drop the knife into my purse. No one seems to notice.

"There are knives at Mom and Dad's house," I say. "Gasoline in the garage. Matches in the kitchen."

"I only have a few days," Harold says.

I didn't tell him I bought a one-way ticket.

"You'll do great," I assure him. "I trust you."

When his train arrives, I walk my brother to the gate. He throws his arm around me in an awkward shoulder-squeeze, hard enough to unsteady me. "Be good without me, okay, Mills?" he says.

I stay at the gate and wave once he finds his window seat. He waves back eagerly. As the train is pulling away, I get a text from Graham: *Hey, you there? We still hanging out??*

I delete the thread and block Graham's number.

Shiny™ People

By Rae Knowles

We started as protectors. Piled in with sleeping bags under our arms, food in our coolers, chests swelled like heroes. We barricaded the door behind us, satisfied grins on our naïve mugs. But the ice packs went warm days ago. The coolers are empty except for that stale, too sweet smell. And now we feel—I feel—more prisoner than guard. The rows are closing in on us, towering shelves of books condemned to burn. Their uncracked spines know nothing of the horror outside, the Shiny™ People come to unleash their rage.

"The back door—" Jessa begins to say.

"Again, really?" Chris's face is hidden beneath his palms. "You *honestly* think they've paraded around out there for two weeks and it never occurred to them to watch the back door?"

"It's worth a shot." Jessa's lips are lined too dark. I mocked her for it, bringing lip liner to a siege. But that was before. When the street only held them and their slurs, and this still felt like some small, important thing. When jokes were still allowed.

"I don't think we'd make it. Too far to the cars, and that's if they haven't burned them already." I give her a dim smile. Today, that's the best I can do.

"Big if!" Chris says, rubbing his brows. He's huddled over his sleeping bag, in the spot that's inched further away from Jessa's each day we've been here.

I approach the shop window, peer through the little square we cut out of the newspaper blocking the rest. A heavyset man with black circles tattooed around his eyes, the rest of his face inked white, paces the street twirling a sign. *Remove the Filth*, it says. His grafted hair grows patchy in chunks, the skin beneath stained from the dye job.

They're scattered all around outside, in various stages of exhaustion. One lies on the hood of a car. Her cat ears poke through jet black hair. The fur is a seamless match. From her dangling arm she swings a bat. The scrapes of wood on asphalt make my organs twitch, even muted through the thick glass. Crouched on the pavement, one with a yellow beak like Darpey Duck™ draws the cartoon he's modeled after, lime chalk dust staining his Shine Nation™ t-shirt. A stiff paddle of feathers pokes out from a hole cut into his pants. The bird ones are particularly horrific. The beaks never blend; there's always a faint stitching of suture lines around their jaws and noses. The feather implants never heal.

"You think we'll outlast them?" Jessa asks, reorganizing the book display table for the hundredth time.

"I doubt it." The cat woman hops off the car's hood and I catch sight of her surgically scrunched nose. Her tail is just an add-on, pinned to her leather leggings. She tugs at an implanted whisker, then hops on a red cooler and spins the bat above her head like a baton.

"They can make a call and get whatever they need. We're the ones trapped like rats." Chris is just guessing. He hasn't looked outside since he ate the last of the crackers, but my gut tells me he's right.

"I'm starving," Jessa whines.

"No shit."

"I still think we could just walk out of here. They're not monsters, just bullies. It's not like the bat is for us." *They sure look like monsters.* "Let's just try talking to them. I'm sure they want to go home as much as we do."

"You give them too much credit. Always have."

"Not this again."

I try to wedge myself between them, but it's becoming harder as the hunger grows.

"Nah, it's worth repeating!" Chris's eyes have a coyote look, ravenous and desperate. "I told you we shoulda left when they started with that *Make our nation shine* bullshit. But nooooo."

"It was just a stupid slogan." Jessa's tone is climbing in pitch. I know the tears are coming. The fight and then the tears.

"And when Shiny acquired—"

"Just stop." But my plea follows a mouse into the book covered walls.

Chris jumps to his feet. "I called the damn realtor. Checked out rentals in Canada, and *what* was it you said?" He points his finger like a knife.

Jessa sucks her teeth and dares him.

"*You're overreacting, honey! Businesses merge all the time. It's a conspiracy theory, baby. We've always had lobbyists. What's the difference?*"

Jessa throws her arms in the air, but Chris draws closer, close enough to kiss her. "Well, seems pretty different now, doesn't it?" His words are punctuated by a mist of spit.

"How was I supposed to know?"

"*How was I supposed to know?*"

Jessa's lip trembles. She sulks off into the Fantasy section and Chris waves her away. I wonder whether the tension inside is rising to meet the tension out, seeking twisted homeostasis. If we stay much longer, I don't think they'll survive it.

"Maybe Jessa's right. Maybe we should go." I keep my voice low, hoping Jessa won't hear. "This isn't like the protests in college. They didn't actually *burn*—"

"You think I don't know that?" Chris sinks to the floor and wraps his arms around his knees.

"I think she's right. I don't think they'll attack us. They're here for the books."

"But that *is* us. Isn't it?" Chris sighs and gazes around at our years of work. Shelves full of the greats, the rainbow mural he hand-painted with care, the register we found on Craigslist. "I just—"

"I know. But we can't stay forever."

"I guess insurance will—"

Glass pops and shatters. I don't see the source. Chris is already on his feet, Jessa circling a corner just behind him.

"What was—" she starts, but then we hear the crackle, smell the smoke.

"Fire," Chris says. We're frozen there, looking to one another for answers. A black wisp curls above the Historical section. He removes his jacket, tosses it over the budding flames to smother the blaze, but the thin material catches, and the fire grows.

"We've got to go," Jessa says.

"No!" Chris stamps his boot over growing flames. They lick the leather, sending embers to neighboring paperbacks, which smolder and catch faster than he's making progress.

Bellows echo in the street, shrieks of joy and rage. Jessa takes off toward the back door, Chris smacks away embers from his pant leg.

A morbid curiosity drives me to a quick look on the shelves, where *A History of Stonewall* is engulfed in flame. "We have to go."

Chris nods, and I trail him to the exit.

When I reach the door, blinding light is already pouring in, casting Jessa's slender form in shadow. She hesitates, and Chris nearly knocks her over when he slams into her from behind.

I don't see them grab her. My eyes are still adjusting to the light when there's an impact on the back of my skull.

My vision blurs; when I finally regain focus, I'm looking up at the sky, pavement scratching my back.

Darpey's lookalike drags me to my feet. Feathers jut from scabs on his chest, his rotund belly giving him a bit of a wobble. Up close, I see jagged scars where his beak was lashed to his jaw, crisscrossed purple stitches poking through wiry stubble. The woman with black fur ears restrains Jessa, sharpened claws curling around her elbows.

A hardcover smacks my face, and my nose crunches. Hot liquid pours from my eyes, from a chasm in cartilage. Iron and salt flood my tongue.

Sapphic Sisters is scrawled across the cover in gold leaf. My heart seizes. I flash back to waiting in line, sweaty palms clutching this very book, and Jennifer Ripley's smile when she signed it with a personal note. *The special edition*, she'd said with a pleased smile.

But all that's gone as he tears out a page, crumbles it in his angry fist. He crumbles her too.

"You love it so much? Eat up then."

The page smells of a time I wasn't hated.

A man with implanted fangs and salt-and-pepper hair swings a bat, and Jessa screams over the unnatural crack of bone. Flesh thuds against pavement. I open my jaw, but before I can breathe, waddling Darpey shoves the paper ball into my mouth, cutting the crack of my lips. Feeling like a pig on a spit, jaw wide for an apple, my tears of shock and humiliation mix with those from the injury. Copper and saline and love and memory intermingle between my molars. The paper crunches at first. Then moisture bends the pages, the wad slips to my tonsils, and I gag. Retching brings more tears. Saliva pours into my gaping mouth. I have to chew.

Cackles rise from a beak and a snout, from beneath whiskers. I chew and chew and chew.

Chris crawls toward Jessa like a worm, the silver-haired man, back hunched, hot on his heels.

Darpey tears a few more pages with his fused fingers, shoves them toward me with his webbed hand. I push the soppy mess to the back of my throat. "You like it? Have some more."

They're a pack of jackals now. Baying and honking and hissing.

I receive page after page. Mopping up the blood and tears, I dampen them before tossing them into my drying mouth. My chafed throat no longer rejects them. In fact, I find a different ache at the pit of my belly, a hunger.

I snatch the book from Darpey's mutilated mitts. *Sapphic Sisters* runs through me. I tear pages myself, my natural, agile fingers making quick work of freeing them from the binding. I've got it down now. Crunching them small, rolling them in my saliva, gnashing the mushy bits and swallowing the lump.

I tear and tear and chew and tear.

Darpey waddles to the others, claps his fingers like lobster claws. Their laughter dies as I reach the midpoint.

On these pages, Ophelia almost loses her love, has to sacrifice her dream job to get her back.

I tear and I chew and I push to the back of my throat. I'm greedy now, getting to the best part, hungry for the story that sang to my lonely soul.

The reunion. Their first kiss. It tastes like that summer I met Hazel, when we stole a kiss behind the kayaks. As the wadded pages sink in my throat, I smell Hazel's strip mall perfume; I remember the precise shade of her eyes.

Another page. Ophelia's poem.

And I'm back in college, in Lilith's dorm. Weed smoke has sunk into the carpet like my fingers sink into her red curls. My back arches. I know pleasure for the first time.

The catwoman's head cocks to one side. She tugs at the silver-haired wolf-man. They look on.

And again.

As I consume Ophelia and Meg dancing in an empty ballroom, it's a year ago. I get the call from my father. He asks how my day was. There's no tension in his voice. Every muscle relaxes for the mundane thing, because he's calling. After so much time.

I crunch and let my glands pour saliva. Chew and chew and chew.

Jessa stumbles away from the trio, who watch me from a safe distance. I hear my own laughter as I free the remainder of the pages from their binding.

This is it. The happy ending.

They run off together, find a little cabin in a quiet town. A stray cat adopts them, curls up in their laps every evening. The words fill my belly and spirit. They taste of freedom and ink; carefree, first, everlasting love. A possible future unfurls before me like some golden road: placid, quiet, calm.

My tongue is a mess of paper cuts, chiseled into bloodied flesh by beautiful pages and lovelier words. The Shiny™ People's eyes are wide with something they can't understand. I run my fingers over the empty binding, and when I look up, they've gone. Jessa has collapsed in a heap, her cries hitching as Chris observes her injuries. Behind us, the shop burns, black smoke billowing up into an endless, unblemished sky. Chris and I lift Jessa, sling her arms over our shoulders. As we slide her into the backseat and set course for the hospital, I think of the Shiny™ People, their twisted faces and foreheads wrinkled with rage. But then I think of Jennifer Ripley. Of Ophelia. Of Hazel. Of Lilith and Meg. Of Chris and Jessa. And their love is too big. It blocks the Shiny™ People from view.

Dissection

By Rich Larson

When Jan shuffled into his apartment with his arms full of groceries, a woman in a Halloween mask was standing behind the battered countertop, pointing a nail gun. Jan's gut froze over.

"Put those down," the masked woman said.

Jan set the bags on the counter with suddenly trembling hands. "Take anything you want. I have, ah, I have some paper cash in my nightstand. Three thousand krone. Bottom drawer."

Silence. A ripe pomegranate rolled out of its biodegradable cradle and thumped to the floor.

Jan stared down at it so he wouldn't have to stare at the mask's plastic grin. "And I have two bottles of good *akvavit*, expensive. One bottle of scotch. Macallan, twenty-five. So, pretty damn old. If you like scotch, maybe that would be. Of. Interest."

His nerves thrummed hard. The woman said nothing.

"I know it's not for everyone," Jan told the pomegranate. "But this one, it's an incredibly peaty smoke-and-iodine sort of flavor. Like drinking a seaside hospital as it burns to the ground. Hints of scorched seaweed and antiseptic. I'm babbling. I don't know anything about scotch. It's a recent obsession. Sorry. I babble under stress."

"This isn't a robbery," the woman finally said. "I came here for you."

Jan blanched. "For me? I don't have any implants, man. Nothing to gouge. I mean, I thought about getting one of those cheap thumbnail phones, you know, on the thumbnail?" He wriggled the digit. "But, ah, I like my thumbs how they are. Certain character to them. Couldn't afford it, either. So I didn't. So, no. No implants. Not even a fucking thumbnail. I work at a liquor store, for God's sake. I live in this shithole. I got nothing to gouge, man."

The masked woman gave a laugh with no light in it. "We'll talk about gouging later. Gouging, slicing, skewering. All of those."

And then Jan saw the Steinbit knives laid out on the counter, and he felt his gut spasm, felt a drop of piss slick his thigh. He kept those knives sharp so they'd jitter through mushrooms and bell peppers with delightful speed. He kept them very sharp.

"House: trigger alarm," Jan pleaded.

The masked woman only shook her head, pointing to the wall where the apartment's ruined alarm system dangled its entrails down stucco.

"That's very prescient of you," Jan said. "Smart. You're smart. I'm not. In fact, I'm still just trying to figure out what's happening, because I think that this all must be some kind of—

"Shut the fuck up."

"Mistake," Jan finished faintly. "Right. Sorry."

The woman waved her weapon. "To the living room," she said. "Wait. Empty your pockets first."

Jan reached shakily into his pockets and pulled out a sweat-smeared transit pass, wallet, phone, and bicycle key. The woman picked up the phone and dropped it into the sink, switched the hot water on. Jan watched its fizzing death throes. He focused hard on staying shut the fuck up.

"Now to the living room," the woman repeated.

Jan walked on shaking legs. Sometimes, when work was slow, he found himself looking at Norway's crime maps, scanning the ever-dwindling dots of orange batteries and mustard yellow rapes. Lime-colored B&Es were nearly unheard of in his village. Red murders, never. He hoped the trend would hold.

Jan sat down on the battered couch, facing the wallscreen splashed with his digital painting. Rolling hills daubed in green and purple. Smeared antifreeze sky. Shredded tissue cloud. The masked woman stared at it for a long while, switching the nail gun hand to hand.

"You like art?"

"It's mine," Jan admitted. "Still a work-in-progress. I've been doing moors lately. Moors and bogs and grassland. My phone's packed with reference photos. Or it was, I guess. Not that I'm complaining. I was thinking of doing a techno-cleanse, going off the grid for a while. Personal electronics, you know, it's like carrying around a grow-your-own-tumor kit."

The woman folded her arms, still staring at the painting. "Pretty fucking pastoral."

"Sorry," Jan said, not flippantly, but then, afraid he sounded flippant: "I like painting landscapes. They're. Relaxing. And I'm rubbish at people. Feet, especially."

"Painting. Not photography? Film?"

Jan swallowed. "Never was drawn to it."

"Really." The woman's back was turned, gaze still fixed on the wallscreen. Her hand crept to the catch of her mask. "You're going to say you don't remember me."

Jan didn't know what he was expecting, but the face that emerged from behind the mask was tanned, middle-aged, had pouchy eyes, an aquiline nose, black hair speckled with silver. Nobody Jan recognized.

"Ma'am, you got the wrong apartment," he blurted. "I don't know who you are. No fucking idea. Sorry. No *flipping* idea. I've never seen you in my life."

"Not even vaguely familiar?" The woman toyed with the nail gun again. Jan couldn't take his eyes off it.

"Okay, well, gun to my head, not that I'm suggesting that, you look vaguely like a French movie star," he admitted cautiously. "Emilie Clochard, maybe. Some French actor. I'm sure you get that all the time, though, because, you know, great bone structure. *Magnifique.*"

"Don't worry," the woman said. "I'll make you remember." She tugged a black spike of a thumb drive from her pocket and slotted it into the wallscreen. "Maybe you'll be better at recognizing yourself."

Photos slithered across the landscape, all showing the same person. Jan could see almost immediately how the mistake had been made. The guy in the photo had the same shape to his face, the same eyebrows. Different nose, though, sharper features. Handsomer. Fuller lips. Different hairline. If Jan had living relatives, he'd believe it was at least a first cousin.

"But that's not me," Jan said, with a desperate whinge to his voice. "I understand what happened here. You're looking for this motherfucker who owes you money, right? And he happens to look like me. Sort of. Vaguely. But if you look closely, you will see that we have two separate motherfuckers here." He gave a wincing smile. "Is it possible you have mild prosopagnosia? It's an underreported condition. We're all prosopagnosiac to a certain extent. Sliding scale. I'm not so great with faces myself. If you'd like, we could put this photo, and then a photo of me, through facial recognition software. How's that sound?"

"Software would tell me what I already know," the woman said. "Same underlying skull, with minor alterations to the cheekbones and jaw. A new nose. Some work on the mouth. The brow. You've had extensive plastic surgery."

"Never in my life." Jan slapped his cheeks. "I mean, why mess with perfection?" He gave a weak laugh; the woman's face was pewter. "I swear to God," Jan enunciated. "I don't even like shaving too close, never mind scalpels. And if I can't afford implants, how could I afford cosmo, huh?"

"You didn't pay for it." The woman had a twitch of fury in her calm voice that set Jan's stomach churning. "You didn't pay for anything. Are you saying that if I look behind your ears, I won't find surgical scars?"

Jan's mouth shuttered open. This had to be a set-up. This had to be a reality-cam show, something he'd signed off for without knowing it, some fine print waiver in a digital receipt. This could not be real.

"Is that a no or a yes?" the woman asked.

Jan couldn't bite back his laugh, wobbly and desperate. "I do," he gasped. "Oh, my God. I have the scars, but it's not from surgery. It's from cycling. I was cycling last year with my helmet on, but the straps undone, because, you know, genius, and one of those fucking autocabs clipped me. The little metal buckles on the straps swung back, slice slice, and I got these two little cuts. Behind my ears. I swear to God. I have a big scar on my knee, too, from the pavement. I was picking gravel out of my skin the whole way to the hospital."

"You realize how unlikely that sounds." The woman put the head of the nail gun against Jan's thigh. He could feel the cold metal kiss through his corduroys. "Don't you?"

Jan bobbed his head, shaking everywhere, his whole body trembling. "You can look at my leg," he moaned. "I have a scar on my leg, too. Never had cosmo. I swear. I swear to God. I swear to God, man."

The woman's finger caressed the curve of the trigger. "What's your name?" he asked.

"Jan Hauer," Jan said. "Second generation Dutch."

"Wrong." The nail gun's cold mouth wormed hard against Jan's thigh. "Try again."

"Try again? It's my name! It's my fucking name!"

The woman gunned the trigger; Jan saw the slider move in jerky film, his muscles bunched and tensed just as the nail punched inside with a meaty whack. Jan screamed. He screamed louder when he looked down to where the top of the nail gleamed, like a button pinned flush to his pant leg, wine-red blood blooming around it.

"I didn't really think that would help," the woman said, breathing harder now. "More for my own satisfaction. I was going to do your balls, but I didn't want you passing out."

Jan shut his eyes, squeezing blubbery tears down his cheeks. "I don't know who you are," he said hoarsely. "I swear to God."

"Tell me who you think you are, and we'll work from there."

"I'm…" Jan clutched at his thigh. "I think I'm Jan Hauer. I think I work at the liquor depot three blocks away. I think I moved here eight months ago from Oslo."

"Why did you move, Mr. Hauer?"

"I thought I would have a job here," Jan said. "They swindled me. Said I would be entry level at a data mine. When I got here, nothing."

"And this is why you live alone. No family or friends."

"I have drinks with my co-workers," Jan said, teeth gritted. "Tonight. Every Tuesday. They'll expect me. They'll worry when I don't respond."

"Liar. You only ever see one other human being, and she's a therapist."

"What do you want?" Jan moaned, throttling his leg with both hands, trying to squeeze out the fiery throb. "Just tell me what you want."

"I want you to watch a video," the woman said, resetting her mask. "If you speak, I'll start it over from the beginning." She tugged a video file from the corner of the wallscreen and let it unfurl, swallowing the photographs, projecting the interior of a brightly-lit room. The time-stamp in the top corner was digitally smudged away. As the camera began to move, it was with the bobbing motion of an eye-level GoPro.

The camera walked its way to a red couch, where a young girl was sitting. Raven-dark hair, sooty lashes, pale skin. Her mouth was cold red, gleaming with too much gloss. She looked up with glassy eyes.

"Good morning, Marie," the cameraperson said, in a distorted drone.

"Good morning." A dazed half-smile.

"Don't you look sexy."

"Thank you."

The cameraperson stepped closer, and suddenly Jan could see a hand, gloved antiseptic white. "Open your mouth," the cameraperson said.

The girl, Marie, lost her half smile. She opened her lips too slowly; the cameraperson cupped her chin and shoved a thumb between them, smearing carmine on latex. Marie gave a hesitant moan. She fluttered her lashes. Jan felt his bile rising. He opened his mouth.

"If you speak, I start over."

Jan clamped his jaw shut. He watched as the cameraperson straddled the girl, hiking up a sequined skirt. Jan's stomach heaved. He squeezed his eyes shut, but the noises kept coming, a symphony of harsh grunts and faked lust breaking into fright. Then, mercifully, it stopped.

Jan opened his eyes to find the wallscreen paused, the girl's mouth blown up to obscene proportion, teeth stained with lipstick.

"If you look away or shut your eyes, I start over," the masked woman said.

"Is this what gets you off?" Jan snapped. "Did you make this yourself? You sick fuck, you sick twisted fuck. Are you going to record me, too?"

The second nail hurt more than the first, this one higher, inner thigh, wobbling the fatty tissue. Jan howled and tried to crumple to the floor, to curl fetal, but the woman shoved him back onto the couch. The nail gun pressed up against the socket of his eye.

"Just sit and watch," the woman rasped. "Or you'll look like a fucking pincushion by the time this is over."

Jan sat and watched through blurring eyes as the clip started from the beginning. This time he managed to keep quiet until the cameraperson took out a knife, held it up to their own exposed cock to compare sizes.

"Christ, why are you showing me this?" he groaned. "Why are you showing me this? You bent motherfucker, you sick bent piece of shit."

"To help you remember," the woman said thickly, and she tapped the screen.

The clip began to loop over again. The cameraperson ambled towards the couch. The girl looked up, blinked.

"You left Oslo eight months ago," the woman said. "This girl was raped and murdered one and a half years ago. In your studio. You were only caught when you tried it again, tried to pull a student on her way home from a disco."

Jan's heart stopped. Then his mouth opened, and he shook his head like a dog shedding water. "Stop playing this fucking mind game," he pleaded. "I know that's what you're doing."

On the wallscreen, he saw the gloved thumb thrust through slick red lips. He looked down.

"You were convicted for snuff distribution alongside the assault, rape, torture, kidnapping, and murder of Marie Sletto," the woman said. "Marie Sletto. Is the name familiar?"

Jan stared at his clenched fingers. The shape of them, the length. "No," he said.

"Watch the screen," the woman grated.

Jan dragged his eyes back to the video, where the cameraperson was licking the girl's neck. "I'm not who you think I am," he said. "Please. Stop it."

"This is your finest work," the woman said. "You arranged her body afterward. In poses. You took photo after photo. The investigators requested a straight month of psychiatric counseling after they saw them all."

"That's not me," Jan whispered.

"Stop fucking lying!" the woman roared, pointing the nail gun. She was breathing hard now, almost panting. "Stand up. Take your pants off."

Jan's hands shook as he fumbled his zipper, slowly see-sawed his trousers down his hips, trying not to tug at the nails in his leg. Blood ran down his calf and trickled over the convex of his ankle bone. He stood facing the wallscreen as the woman yanked his underwear down, then gave a strangled laugh.

"So they did that, too. Flaccid as a baby. I bet nothing gets you hard anymore. Not even that pretty therapist they gave you."

Jan winced.

"She's not your friend, you know," the woman breathed. "I bet she keeps a Taser in her desk. I bet she shivers when you walk in, and when you leave she goes home and showers and asks herself how she can sit and smile at a monster like that."

"That's not me," Jan repeated. "I swear to God. You're crazy. You're fucking crazy."

The woman jerked away suddenly, making Jan flinch. She stalked to the kitchen counter and snatched up one of the gleaming knives. "You have headaches, yes?" she asked. "Memory gaps? Anxiety?"

"I'm on medication," Jan said shakily. "So's half the country."

"This village has the lowest youth population of any in Norway," the woman said, returning with the knife dangling from her fingers. "Did you know that? It's also small. Isolated. Nobody would know you from the newscasts. Especially after what they did to your face."

On the wallscreen, the girl's screams reached their crescendo once more.

"Turn it off," Jan pleaded. "Christ, turn it off."

"Your name is Bjorn Olgaard," the woman snapped. "Say you remember."

The name meant nothing. Jan shook his head.

"Bjorn Olgaard, the beta test for 0% re-offense rate." The woman put the icy edge of the knife to Jan's jaw. "Experimental behavior modification. Memory suppression. Aggression tampering. Bjorn Olgaard." The woman's voice rubbed raw. "Say you remember."

"I don't," Jan sobbed. "I don't remember. You're lying to me. You're making this up."

"Why do you look at crime maps, Bjorn?" the woman demanded, trembling. "Why do you have so many knives? Why do you paint the field where you buried my daughter over and over again?"

"I don't know!" Jan howled. "I don't know anything! I don't remember!"

The woman tore off her mask again, and Jan could see that her face was puffy and swollen with tears, her lips smeared with snot. "Why should you be the one who gets to forget?" she asked softly. "Why you and not me?"

Jan watched in numb terror as the knife left his throat. Instead, the woman took Jan's hand and gently wrapped it around the plastic handle.

"Say you remember," the woman said.

Jan tried to pull away, but the woman's grip was iron. Slowly, slowly, the woman raised their clasped hands until the point of the knife was resting on her collarbone.

"Say you remember, Bjorn." Her voice was no longer angry, no longer shaky.

Jan stared at the wallscreen, where the girl was mercifully dead. The cameraperson moved her limbs gently, arraying her legs to drape just so on the foot of the couch. Jan stared at the stained gloves.

"I remember," he whispered.

The woman shook her dark head. "You're lying," she said. "But at least you'll be the last."

She brought their hands up and slipped the knife under her jaw, then jerked it across and down. Jan felt the skin split under the edge, the edge that he kept so sharp, and then bright blood like smelted copper geysered into his face, hot, blinding, drowning him. The woman gagged and sputtered, clinging to Jan's sleeve. She might have been trying to speak again, but Jan couldn't understand her. He sat there, shaking and quiet, until the woman finally slumped onto the floor and rolled over like a beached minke whale.

Jan knew what to do. The knife had slipped from the woman's fingers, resting on the floor, handle towards him, ready and waiting. First he dug the woman's phone from her pocket and punched the red Politiet button. Then he picked up the knife and sat back down, cradling it between his knees.

Jan knew what to do, but when the sirens approached, when the police shouted to him through the door, when they rolled their camera underneath and then followed it inside, Jan let them pry the knife from his fingers and seal it in a plastic baggie.

A policewoman tapped the wallscreen, and Jan watched as the video started all over again.

Who Sees All
By Avra Margariti

"Natasa, bathroom, now," I hiss through gritted teeth.

Anyone else might have protested, wanting to spend our meager break elsewhere. Not Natasa, who lands in isolation once a week after the school cameras catch her smoking, wearing lipstick, kissing girls. She understands the importance of privacy. The scarcity of it, too.

In the girls' bathroom, among empty stalls of flimsy doors and missing latches, my best friend and I face each other. Ignoring the sickening burn in my right wrist, I take out of my backpack a paper notebook, a chewed pen.

"Paper, Aliki? There are no cameras here," Natasa says, somewhere between puzzled and impatient.

The school is happy installing cameras in every classroom, hallway, and other cranny. Bathrooms are the exception. Some law about decorum, even as the all-seeing cameras do most of the teaching and supervising now, replacing the teachers who—fed up, policed, and underpaid—were fired or quit. Everything is witnessed now by cold, robotic eyes.

I place a finger against my lips, ignoring the pain emanating from my wrist, the scorching fire through my vein. Silently, I beg Natasa to understand what I need from her. And she does. She's the kind of friend I kiss at sleepovers—forbidden now after my parents caught us mid-cuddle—but also the kind of friend who goes along with my weirdness, no question asked.

"Okay," Natasa mouths, settling against a broken sink.

I draw three concentric circles, blue ink bleeding into the shape of an eye. Show the notebook to Natasa, then point my pen toward my wrist.

"No way—" she says, all wide eyes, whispers forgotten.

I can almost hear her questions. *Did your parents buy you a personal surveillance system? Why would you sign the agreement?*

Except, I didn't. We didn't go to the clinic, procedure explained, microchip installed, the iProtect™ flyer claiming how much safer I was now, what a lucky girl. How much my parents love me.

All I did was wake up, wrist ablaze, and know deep in my soul someone had put the eye-shaped implant inside me overnight. I write all this down for Natasa, my letters wobbly, agitated. Typing would be easier, but there's no way to know if iProtect™ is wired to phones. Only paper is safe, all evidence flushed away.

I'm not crazy. They installed it in my sleep and thought I wouldn't notice.

Natasa pulls me into a hug, breathing against my hair. "I never said you were."

I melt against her, this morning's stress and fearful suspicions shivering my muscles.

She draws back, her hand on my arm awaiting permission. I nod, sick again and crawling from within. Her fingers feel sure and steady against the inside of my wrist, down my arm and along each tendon. Normally her touch would make me ache oh-so-sweetly, but the nausea prevails.

I remember waking up to the feeling of wrongness— *invasion*—even before I'd opened my eyes. Yet, alone, I found no puncture-wound proof. No evidence of disruption in my room.

Natasa lifts my wrist, holding her breath in case the mic catches the sound. Her fingernail taps along the blue of my vein. The color that masks the darker, gas-flame-blue of the eye implant, winking faintly in the stark light. A slow machine blink.

We both recoil just as the bell rings.

"Well," Natasa's mouth forms silently. "Fuck."

We walk into class separately so as to trick the cameras overhead— the only state-of-the-art things in this entire derelict building. The sensor pings, calculating how many seconds we're late to be added up at the end of the year into free labor, students painting the classroom walls, weeding the schoolyard.

Natasa and I take our seats aisles apart, staring at the e-board. It's math time again, the board flashing dazzlingly white. After all, disembodied prerecorded voices can teach us about numbers and business and not require health insurance or paid overtime. No arts or lit curriculum either, those things that can plant dangerously bright ideas in porous young minds. At least according to my parents.

The customary sponsor ads play before the lesson begins. The iProtect™ logo paints the screen blue and white—three concentric circles. My fingers tighten around the desk, splinters digging in. The inside of my wrist is licked by invisible flames, branding my blood.

Natasa and I exchange looks from across the room.

I force my eyes to the screen, not wanting to be reprimanded for ignoring our sponsor who funds the school's surveillance system. The eye-shaped logo is imprinted in my mind. It's a depiction of the mati—the folkloric amulet said to ward off evil gazes, protect the wearer from those meaning them envy or harm.

On the e-board, a blue-and-white eye charm hangs from a golden safety pin, like the one relatives gift children for their Christening ceremony. The mati erupts into colored glass, then transforms midair, cartoonish, until it's a small, round microchip burrowing inside a child's forearm. The child—a girl—smiles in relief.

Of course, the ads never mention the dangers of such procedures. Parents using the device to control which friends their children have, what books they read, or how they talk about themselves. To use and abuse and spy on them, never once affording children privacy or freedom.

A robotic voice-over says, "No one will ever abduct, harass, or groom you now without your parents knowing. The audio recording will serve as proof, impossible to deny."

A comically re-enacted drug deal takes place on-screen, a stranger offering the girl suspicious candy. The iProtect™ implant picks up the exchange, sending an automatic signal to the police, who arrest the dealer and save the girl.

"Following a tradition of old, let us keep our eyes on you," the voice-over finishes.

The girl runs into her parents' waiting arms. The last shot is of a smiling nuclear family, picture-perfect.

Let us protect you.

The words ring in my ears even as the ad morphs into math equations. My wrist never once stops burning, a blue flame consuming me from within.

For us to beat the eye, Natasa says, we need to be quick and stealthy.

We must learn how much your parents know, she types, while aloud she chatters about something boring and innocuous in case my parents are eavesdropping. *How long this thing stays on. How much info it can pick up.*

"Then what?" I say, as if in response to the TV show she's been rambling about. "The characters can't run and hide forever."

"A ruse." Natasa winks at me, squeezing my hand. I wonder if the implant can detect the fluttering of my pulse. "I read next week's spoilers. The heroine makes a small sacrifice to win a bigger battle."

Natasa types her plan on her phone. I read it under the tree cover, outside the school and the cameras' watchful gaze. Yet my very own eye is always with me, recording my every sound. I cannot escape it, even in the bathroom or the other blind spots we have discovered.

Under constant scrutiny, zero privacy.

Under the burning blue gaze, I feel myself wilt.

My mother enters my room without knocking, as always. I used to be able to ignore it. Now, I bristle inwardly yet keep my face blank. It's a Sunday, two days after I discovered the mati in my wrist. Two sleepless nights trying to regulate my breathing so the mic doesn't pick up the sounds of my panic attack.

She leaves a plate of cut fruit on my desk, where I pretend to do homework. The smell of orange, blood-like, turns my stomach. Her smile is my smile, her eyes my eyes. I watch her through the hair falling in my face. Hiding my revulsion.

Mom produces a scrunchie from her wrist, fixing my hair without asking. "You have such pretty curls. It's a pity to let them go limp and tangled."

I remember the fights: me wanting to cut it short or shave the sides, her saying she'd never allow me to ruin myself while Dad watched in silent agreement.

"Back to studying now, your grades have been slipping."

I think Natasa's bait didn't work. Then, Mom pauses in the doorway.

"Where did you say you were yesterday?" she asks, dangerously airy.

I hold my breath.

"Studying in the cafe down the road with Filippos." She likes the neighbors' boy, thought him a good match for me since we were tiny children. "Thought you said he's a good influence."

Gets straight As. Follows gender roles. Knows how to hide his queerness better than me.

"Of course I like him. But that's not where you really were."

"How can you tell?" I ask, letting part of the ruse drop. I force myself to look my mother in the eye, seeking the flash of guilt.

Her eyes remain disappointed. Full of love. Full of lies. "Dad's aunt saw you with that girl outside the mall. You know the one. All purple hair and piercings and those awful provocative clothes."

Aunt Mary indeed likes to roam the neighborhood and spy on what everyone's up to. She could have seen me and Natasa hanging out yesterday. But deep in my squirming gut, I know the truth. The eye burns in my wrist, a traitor giving Natasa and I away. Even as we said forbidden stuff as bait, we still held back our truest, unfiltered selves.

"Don't lie to me again," Mom says. Steel dressed in velvet. "A mother always knows. You're not supposed to see that girl outside of school. Dad and I will discuss your punishment over dinner."

What I suspected is true. The apotropaic eye, not used to protect me from bad things happening, but to keep the good away just because my parents don't approve.

Three days of being grounded in my room, coming straight home after school, getting tutored to fix my grades, attending tense family dinners.

Two more insomniac nights, the eye staring straight into my soul even as I smother it under shirtsleeves and bracelets. Whenever I try to sleep, I'm jerked awake by static-choked whispers calling my name, condemning me for my failures, my sins.

On the fourth day, I meet Natasa in the bathroom. The other girls leave after taking a look at Natasa's scowl, at the sick pallor of my skin.

My friend hugs me. I squeeze my eyes shut, trap the tears in. I want to hold Natasa longer. Kiss her perhaps, just once, just a peck. But even the thought terrifies me now, when before iProtect™, I had decided to follow her example and be brave.

I can't stop worrying about eyes, human or divine.

Natasa types frantically. *You know how my cousin studies computer sciences? He has friends who can help us.*

So, more lies then. More sneaking around. Just because my truth is too unpalatable for my parents. My happiness, like swallowing mouthfuls of blood, broken glass.

Natasa's cousin Dimos picks us up from her house in a beat-up car. A grim smile of understanding forms when he sees me. Like recognizing like.

I press my cramping fingers over my wrist during the entire ride, hoping to muffle the sounds of the hissing exhaust and wheels hitting potholes. In the backseat, Natasa leans her head on my shoulder in quiet comfort.

We are all silent, no music, no conversation. I wonder if I have already died. Gone, invisible, rolling in my grave tended to so lovingly by my parents, covering me in fistfuls of oppressive dirt.

Obliterated under the benevolent eye who sees all.

We're led through an unruly yard, its house a crumbling relic save for the bulky generators and the cables hanging like tentacles from its roof. Dimos has a key, though I don't think he lives here.

Walking down corridors of teetering antique piles covered in doilies and floral quilts, we reach the computer room. A dainty person, older than Natasa and I, sits on a desk chair, bent over three different screens; a menagerie of equipment. In the dimness, the white light is making my head throb with an oncoming migraine.

Dimos types a quick note for me on his phone. *This is Xandra. They can help you.*

He leans down to whisper something in Xandra's ear. Then, at Xandra's nod, plants a kiss on their shoulder. Although their fingers keep typing away at the keyboard, a smile touches their lips.

At last, Xandra whirls their chair around. Their eyes are sharp as they inspect me, though far from unkind. They extend a hand, and Natasa nudges me forward.

Xandra's slim fingers apply the barest pressure on my wrist, turning it this way and that, feeling along my veins in intense focus and precision.

At last, they look at me seriously. Their touch going from clinical to comforting, they mouth: *angel eye.*

It's how iProtect™ is known colloquially, like the biblical angels covered in eyes, blue and terrifying. Less folkloric protection, and more Old-Testament power and control.

Xandra passes a hand-held scanner over my wrist, back and forth. They frown, and my free hand twitches until Natasa squeezes it.

Finally, Xandra speaks, soft but clear. "Signal deactivated. Not for long, we don't want your parents noticing. Just enough to help you make a ruse."

"What was wrong?" I ask, heart in my throat. "With the scanner."

"Oh," Xandra waves a hand in my direction, but a small crease remains between their brows. They inspect the scanner. "It's nothing. Just took a while to tap into the correct channel. There were other frequencies interfering. Must be the new gadgets Dimos got me."

Before I can say anything, Natasa interjects. "Let Aliki hear the first thing the mic caught. It would explain how her parents did this."

Xandra turns back to their monitors, clicking keys I'm too dizzy to follow. A crackling of static, then a message plays: "There now, all safe. No strange questions or bright ideas getting in your head. Our little girl, forever."

Mom's voice. I gasp, despite already knowing the truth in my bones. "They did this to me in my sleep," I say, grief catching up to me.

Xandra's mouth twists in sympathy.

"I'm sorry, Aliki. There's one more step, for your own protection. But you're not going to like it."

I'm too hollow to struggle. "Anything. I just want to be free."

Xandra explains how they need to feed fake signals to the implant. Distract my parents with prerecorded messages while I'm free to do and say what I please. I grit my teeth and speak into Xandra's recorder obedient, docile, toothless phrases, over and over again.

My mother said no. What would my father think? I can't come to the party, there'll be alcohol there. I don't date girls, what are you, a dyke?

Although I know it's nothing but role-play, I feel sick afterward. Like I need to wash my mouth out, purify myself. But at least I'm free for now.

I shrug Natasa's hand off me on our way back to the car. Refuse to talk to her even though I can now, the hated mati transmitting to my parents nothing but the prerecorded static of my pulse.

Why let her comfort me when I don't deserve it?

I dream that my father holds me down, aloofly apologetic while my mother opens my skin up, sews in its underside a myriad white-and-blue beads, plastic superstition to spy my every body function, record my every breath.

My every thought.

I wake up panting, sweat drenched. There's only one year left until I graduate. One year, and I can have that thing removed from my wrist. Leave and never talk to my parents again.

Until then, I can trick them with Xandra's technology. I can survive this with the help of my friends.

Natasa texts to say she's missed me. Wants to meet up, cause mischief, kiss, and act our age.

Fine, I text back. *Let's be gay and do crimes.*

After getting dressed, I pop into the living room where my parents watch the morning news.

"Me and Filippos have a study date," I say.

Dad purses his lips, like there's something he's itching to say. I realize they've been staring at the TV on mute. This, of all things, fills me with dawning dread.

Mom speaks first. "Sorry, honey. Not today. I need your help with chores."

"Chores?" I squeak.

They never give me any chores, saying I should focus on my studies, getting into a good university. Privately, I've always thought my parents didn't want me to learn how to cook or clean or take care of myself. Another step toward delaying, denying my independence.

"Yes, you and I are going to wash and change the linens," Mom says in that fake idle voice, not meeting my gaze.

My skin goosebumps. "But Filippos…"

She's always vetted my female friends but has never forbidden me from hanging out with him. We used to joke that my mother had dreams of us marrying after university.

Dad turns up the volume so loud the conversation is over. They stare at the TV, and I'm left trembling with fury.

With fear.

Xandra's plan has failed.

I can't even safely contact Natasa, so I let my phone ring and ring as the day progresses. Until, eventually, the texts and calls stop.

Mom chatters while she folds fitted bedsheets. Every time I try to help, she bats my hands away and finishes the chore herself. A ruse.

It's all a ruse.

They put the eye in me while I slept.

There are more implications here I'm too numb to process.

Our little girl, forever.

The crease between Xandra's brows as something interfered with the signal. As if there were several more signals nearby, too.

And my text messages with Natasa earlier. How not a sound was uttered.

They put the eye in me... the eyes... while I slept.

I finish the day mechanically. Watch as Mom cooks dinner. Eat without tasting, reply with single words.

Once I kiss my parents goodnight and go to bed, I wait in my room death-still, a numb mist enfolding my body until I'm sure they're both asleep.

I don't check my phone. Only walk to the kitchen with slow, metronomic steps. Leaning over the sink, my eyes fall on the olive-oil bottle. A word rings in my ears. Ksematiasma. *De-eyeing.* It's the ritual performed when someone has been touched by negative energy. A drip of oil, a prayer whispered, and the evil eye is gone.

For my own de-eyeing, I will need something much more drastic than cleansing oil and prayers of old.

I take out the sharpest knife from the drawer, the one Dad uses to carve meat. Slicing roast paper-thin. I'm going to need precision, although I don't trust my left hand with much finesse as I bring the knife to my dominant wrist over the sink.

I plunge the tip into the skin, where the angel eye burns me with blue fire from within.

I think I must be imagining the flames at first, externalizing my pain into incandescent, dancing spots tucked along my vein where the eye nestles. Yet the light remains, blazing blue through the red of my blood. I worm my trembling fingers inside my wrist, snatch the slippery round button between my nails, pull it out with all my might.

I throw the microchip in the sink, struggling to hold back my howls of pain, but the blue fire won't go away. More lights flash from within my forearm, device protection activated by my blade's intrusion. This time I don't stop the screams as I rush to the hall mirror, tear my clothes away to inspect my bare reflection.

My whole body, covered in gas-flame-blue eyes, a biblical abomination.

Be not afraid. Be not afraid.

In my screaming trance, blood coating the cream carpet, my mind races in the eye of the storm. Xandra's words echo in my memory. How they couldn't find an accurate signal, all the secret implants inside me interfering. How the mati didn't only process sound, but also vision. I'm sure of it now as I stare at the neon blight under my skin.

The realization makes me more light-headed than the blood loss. I haven't been alone for weeks. Not in the bathroom, where even the school doesn't put cameras. Not in sleep and not in waking. No single second of my day, no breath to call my own.

Slippers shuffle my way, my parents awoken by my screams. I stagger to the kitchen again before they can stop me. In my search of my knife, I knock over the bottle of olive oil. The viscous liquid fails to purify the sickness planted within, the violation of body and mind.

"Stop. What are you doing?" Mom shouts.

My voice is louder for once. Laced with pain but also rage. "Not another step."

I brandish my knife Dad's way, then point it toward my heart.

Both of them stop. My parents watch me in their nightclothes and bed hair, comically small and confused and full of love. Except they did this to me. While I slept. They stuffed me full of implants, brought an iProtect™ tech into my room without my consent. Just so they could spy on me, sever my queerness from the root.

"You did this to me," I say, my whole body quaking, yet my knife remains steady in my grasp. "Not stranger danger. Not bad influences. *You!*"

Ksematiasma, I think and laugh. *De-eyeing*—as I use my knife to slash at my body, again and again and again.

When I wake up, I'm in a sterile-white hospital room, my entire body covered in bandages. No one is around, and for the first time in weeks, I feel safe, even as I ache all over, my throat parched, my bladder full.

I am blissfully alone. Checking my wounds, I spot little round marks where the eyes had been. The doctors removed them from inside me. Here, in solitude, I am free.

A nurse comes to check my vitals. She's wearing the iProtect™ logo stitched across her uniform. I flinch away from the three concentric circles, but she only smiles patiently.

"Good, you're up." The nurse pats my pillow. "Your parents are outside, worried sick about you."

"I don't want to see them," I mutter, gaze averted. "The eyes. Are they all gone?"

"They are," the nurse confirms. "You shouldn't be so hard on them, you know. Parents want what's best for their child."

I don't give the nurse a response. She's yet another accomplice, working for the company who violated me. I doubt they will call a social worker, what with all the NDAs involved. I will never look at my parents the same way. The moment I'm eighteen, I'm out.

"I'll let you get some rest," the nurse says.

I wait until the door shuts, then pull myself up despite the pain, dragging my unwieldy IV-stand into the bathroom. In the foggy mirror, I inspect myself. Limp hair, haunted gaze, skin covered in pucker marks of implants de-eyed, removed.

I feel lighter despite my ordeal. I will see Natasa again, brainstorm more clandestine communication together. I was strong enough to blind and pluck the parasites. Every part of my body, inspected under stark-white lighting, feels my own again. The tingling and burning is gone, purified through blood like oil.

So what if I foresee years of therapy in my future? I will survive. I already have.

Dizzy with relief, I stumble forward, catching myself on the edge of the sink. The movement brings my face closer to the mirror. Despite the stained surface of the glass, some strange glint makes me narrow my eyes instinctively. I spot something in both my eyeballs. Three concentric circles camouflaged among the blue of my irises, the white of my sclerae, the black of my pupils. In my once-familiar gaze, a blazing undercurrent of wrongness.

Another pair of eyes that see all.

Father Figure

By Lisa Short

I didn't like our current position, this mesa we were occupying; I was ready to admit that it had been a bad idea to climb up here. It had originally seemed like a good idea, as it was indisputably the highest point overlooking the village below us... was *village* the right word? I knew *mesa* wasn't, not exactly; mesas were natural geological formations, and the only real similarity between them and this gigantic pile of dirt was its broad, flat summit. And—

"Tina?"

—I had let my attention wander dangerously. Again. I really missed the meds my dad used to get for me. Though not as much as I missed my dad. "Yeah?"

"What do you think? Is it safe?"

Nowhere was safe—and Amanda knew that, she wasn't asking that stupid question. She meant, *Safer than up here, or anyplace else we could reasonably expect to reach quickly from here?* "Maybe," I said. We'd been crouched up there for nearly two hours staring down at the village: broken asphalt roads punctuated by the occasional rusting car hulk, houses overrun with weeds and unpruned tree branches, glassless windows uniformly blank and uninformative black. "Ideally, we'd spend more time watching it, though. At least one night."

Amanda swept an expressive look over the mesa top—maybe twenty feet in diameter, bare dirt except for a few scattered boulders, the largest of which we were doing our best to hide behind.

I sighed. "Yeah. If I'd realized how bare it was, I wouldn't have dragged us all the way up here. I'm sorry."

She blinked up at me. "You couldn't know that beforehand. You can't know everything." She flicked her hand, a small guarded movement.

I doubted anybody had watched us ascend. It was highly unlikely that if they had, they'd have patiently waited this long to make their presence known. "Well, let's see what we can do to improve our cover a little." I shrugged my backpack off and rooted around inside it till I found my collapsible shovel. "So—who wants to dig first?"

A few hours later we were as snug as bugs in a rug, like my dad used to say, watching the rough rectangle of sky overhead slowly darken from pellucid blue to a cool, wistful violet. It was stuffy down in our hole, but I knew better than to poke my head up out of it just to catch the evening breeze.

Once night fell, we took turns on watch as usual, trading my Solarthon back and forth between us—its alarm vibration was soundless but guaranteed to wake either of us, paranoid as we were, from a sound sleep in microseconds. It was a pain to keep charged, as we weren't always conveniently walking in bright sunlight, but worth the effort.

The first week Amanda traveled with me, I hadn't been able to sleep much while she stood watch for us—I hadn't entirely trusted her, less because I thought she wanted to hurt me than because I had no idea how dedicated she was to survival. By now, though, the only misgivings I had about Amanda on guard duty was that we hadn't been able to spare any live rounds for her to practice with. She could squeeze the trigger of my dad's old rifle twenty times in a row without making a dime balanced atop its barrel so much as twitch, and it looked to me like she was aiming dead center at whatever target we were practicing on—but without a real bullet in the chamber, there was no way to know for sure.

Even without any lingering trust issues now, I still had trouble falling asleep. After a day spent mostly motionless, I wasn't physically tired the way a good long hike would have left me; I was suffering from *intrusive thoughts*, as my dad would have called them. He'd known all about those; he'd be sorry that I had them now too, and a more unselfish person than me would have been glad that he'd never have to find that out. I didn't know what he would think about the risks I'd taken that had resulted in those intrusive thoughts; he would have been glad that I'd saved Amanda, though. I was sure of that.

It was never a good idea to go to sleep dwelling on upsetting things, but I had been trying so hard to sleep at all that I forgot that excellent advice. When Amanda shook me awake four hours later, I nearly screamed—in my dream, I had been standing over the dead Sagler once more, far too close, *much* closer than I'd stood in real life, and in the way of dreams, the quick pinch of Amanda's fingers had become the claw-like pinch of *his* fingers because *this* time I hadn't killed him after all—

"Nothing all night," Amanda said, in the barely audible breath of speech we always used out in the open. "No lights, no movement, nothing. The whole place looks totally empty." Her eyes gleamed in the faint starlight. Mine probably did, too. Assuming not too many people had been through the village before us, we could score some major re-provisioning.

We headed down to the village as soon as the sun rose. The first several houses were a no-go—we were definitely not the first, tenth or even hundredth person passing through them. In a way, that was reassuring; this was not a village anybody had been saving up for a rainy day's scavenging. But Amanda and I were methodical and thorough—we could and would go through every single nook and cranny of every single house until literally none were left, or until we were otherwise interrupted.

On our third day in the village, in the very last house we searched, I was crouched on the floor next to an empty bed frame (had someone made off with the mattress? The *entire* mattress? It was a really big bed, why would anyone—*focus!*). I was feeling pretty decent about our haul, as relaxed as I ever got during one of these provisioning runs; our packs, pockets and belt pouches were full to bursting and we ourselves were clean to boot, a wonder to end all wonders. Without any particular urgency, I pulled open the drawer of a little dresser that lay on its side next to the bed frame. It looked empty, but when I tried to drag it all the way out to verify that, it stuck halfway.

I managed to squeeze my forearm all the way inside it and groped blindly around; it was indeed empty, except for something that felt like a wad of paper wedged all the way in the back. *Might as well haul it out—ouch!* I skinned my wrist wrenching my arm back out of the drawer, prize clutched tight in my fingers. "Gee, you'd better be good," I told it, uncrumpling and smoothing it out. It was a rather peculiar piece of paper—only a few inches wide but at least a yard long—and whatever had once been printed on it had mostly faded into illegibility. I squinted down at it. *REG#02... ped by SVETLANA... active ard fun* (what?)*... nk you for shping a ocal pharma—*

I froze. *Amanda!* It was barely more than a wheeze escaping me—but she couldn't hear me anyway; she was downstairs in the kitchen. I lurched to my feet, staggering a bit from all the crouching, then sprinted for the stairs.

Pharmacy! It had to be, *had* to be—Amanda and I hadn't been able to find one, not a single one, in the handful of weeks we'd been traveling together. Certainly the remains of any large town or city had pharmacies, bucketloads of them—but that did us about as much good as if they'd been on the moon. Being only two girls, we could hardly take one of them by storm... or were we two *women*? I never could make up my mind what to call us. Amanda, at thirteen, couldn't possibly be considered a *woman*, not even in her current condition. I was six years older but God, I didn't feel like one either, I felt like a little kid caught in a perpetual nightmare scream of *Daddy!*—

—and I was losing focus again. I thought, not for the first time, that Amanda wasn't the only one who might benefit quite a lot if we could only find a pharmacy. A pharmacy that was more than a burned-out shell or infested with Saglers or even just unadulterated humanity—I knew well enough what a crapshoot actual people were, especially in groups.

Amanda looked up as I burst into the kitchen. "Hey, I found some bullets!" she said brightly. "Look! I think they're too small for the rifle, but—" I shoved the long, skinny piece of paper into her hands. Her voice dried up, leaving her mouth hanging soundlessly open as she stared down at it. Then, "Really?" she whispered. "Do you really think—"

"Maybe." I dropped down onto my knees and hauled one of my more useful finds out of my backpack, a county booklet we'd scavenged from the remains of a gas station. "Let's see, let's see—what's that street address again? Amanda!" She was still staring fixedly down at the paper. "What's the address?"

She read it off to me in a voice that only shook a little. I flipped to the index in the back of the booklet. "*Yes*, it's there," then back to the front. "Maps 24, 25 and 27…" I couldn't find the street at first—too fast, too *fast*, focus, *focus*—"Found it." I looked up at her, then flinched back; she was crying, silently. "Amanda—"

"And you really know… you really know what I need to take? What we need to do?"

I nodded. "I really do. I swear. My dad told me." Her mouth twitched at that—her dad had never told her any such thing, if he'd even known it himself. I tried not to mention dads to her very often. "This really might be it. It's only…" I did some more map-flipping, found where we'd marked ourselves off the day before, then flipped back. "…about six miles from here, which means it's part of this whole old neighborhood of villages."

It might be nothing. It might be a dead end. But we had to try.

It wasn't the greatest setup—the pharmacy building was all by itself on a broken asphalt slab where no trees had yet managed to encroach. We'd have to approach it from the edge of the woods, completely out in the open for a good two hundred feet at least. Without much hope, I scanned the surrounding area. The buildings down the hill from the pharmacy were blackened; gutted and burned. In the distance, another village was visible, from which purposeful smoke drifted up into the powder-blue sky.

These were intentional fires; contained. Whether people or Saglers—either way, no good for us.

Amanda and I kneeled behind the tree line, sweating under all our gear. One thing I'd found was that if I stayed dirty long enough, I actually got used to it; the constant itchy, sweaty, prickly feeling was just another baseline of normal, like aching legs and sore shoulders. That went double for the smell—reeking pits, unwashed bum, sweltering feet. After a week without bathing, I'd found I couldn't even smell myself anymore unless something truly spectacular happened to me, like a diarrhea attack. Unfortunately, one single bath instantly wiped all that acclimatization out; I couldn't stop myself from seizing the rare chance of one, but I was always sorry for it later, and I was sorry for it now.

"—Tina?" Amanda's low whisper was strained. *Goddammit*—I glanced down at her, opening my mouth to apologize for zoning out, but she cut me off. "I see someone in there. Someone moving."

That got my attention. Amanda handed me the binoculars; I peered through them and pretty quickly saw what she had seen. Too little sunlight was filtering into the pharmacy's depths for me to make out if it was a Sagler or not, but it was definitely human-shaped, human-height, and seemed to be moving purposefully, if slowly, between the rows of wreckage inside.

I could shoot him. Not that I knew if it was a *him*—if it was a Sagler, it definitely was. He was within rifle range, and I had made similar shots before; I *could* shoot him, but...

"They'll hear it," I said, and jerked my chin towards the distant village. "We'll have to be very fast, looking for anything. Once he falls, we run in, top speed—ten minutes searching, then we blow out of there."

"I have the list," said Amanda sturdily. "I'll be fast."

The underbrush was too thick for me to shoot prone. A shame; I could have guaranteed the headshot then, but he might have seen us clearing the weeds and branches out of the way. Kneeling would put me high enough to sight him, and was nearly as accurate.

What if he's a nice person? Just in the wrong place at the wrong time? That was my obligatory thought—I always felt I had to have it, even though it wasn't going to change what I was about to do. But it was important not to forget that possibility, and to make sure that I felt bad about it. Not so bad that I couldn't function, but bad enough that I wouldn't become what way too many people had seemed to, since the Saglers took over.

Focus.

I set a countdown timer on my Solarthon, then dropped to one knee and slapped the rifle butt securely into the pocket of my shoulder. Wait, *wait*—the shadow paused, head shifting, centering in the rifle's sights. And gently, *gently* squeeze the trigger—

Amanda didn't even wait for the echoes of the shot to die away; she was already running across the asphalt, head down and arms pumping. Ears still ringing, I slung the rifle back over my shoulder and scrambled to catch up. Firing the rifle always left me a little light-headed, and the waves of heat rising up from the shattered black rock beneath my feet didn't help.

The inside of the pharmacy was dark, humid, and reeked of shit—I clenched my teeth and waved Amanda towards the ruins of the counters in the back. We hurried past the remains of shelves, ragged pyramids of debris so worthless they weren't even identifiable. My heart sank. The place had clearly been picked over far more thoroughly than the house we had just come from. But I wasn't going to give up so easily; we'd found valuable things before, in places that other people had obviously searched first.

We detoured around the body my bullet had left sprawled on the floor. Definitely a *body*; even Saglers couldn't survive their brains leaking out of the backs of their heads. I thought it was a Sagler, too, from my split-second glimpse; the chest was a little too broad for a person, the waist and hips too narrow—but I was disinclined to spend any time making sure of it.

146 • Lisa Short

The door behind the counters was jammed shut. Not locked, at least; that was obvious from the gaping hole where the doorknob had once been. We rammed it, over and over until our shoulders were screaming and we were soaked with sweat. It finally popped far enough out of its frame for us to squeeze through.

Inside it was pitch-black. I switched on my headlamp—Amanda fumbled hers on too—and suddenly the room was lit in dazzling white. We froze in astonishment. Somebody had been saving *this* up for a rainy day, for sure.

Amanda dove straight into the heaping piles of bottles, boxes and loose blister packs. I followed more slowly, paying as much attention to the broken door behind us as to the search. This was absolutely someone's secret stash; I prayed that my ten minute estimate hadn't been wildly optimistic.

Then Amanda gasped, "I found one! I found one, but not the other—"

I spared a glance at my Solarthon: four minutes left. "Great, keep looking!"

I pawed faster and faster through the piles, one-handed so I could keep the rifle pointed loosely at the door. I was just stuffing a lucky find of amoxicillin in my back pocket when the Solarthon's alarm buzzed angrily against my wrist. "Amanda!"

"*I found it!* I found the other one! But how many—"

"Just grab them all! Let's go, go, *go!*"

Nobody chased after us; or if they did, they started too late or gave up too soon. We fled deep into the woods.

A few days later, we found a rotting hunting cabin to hole up in. I made Amanda as comfortable as I could and offered her my hand. I didn't want to force it on her, but she grabbed it between hers and squeezed tight enough to hurt. "I'm sorry we couldn't find any of your meds, Tina," she said; not for the first time since we'd fled the pharmacy. "I looked. I *swear.*"

"It's okay." I hadn't held out much hope for it, really. "So." I took a deep breath. "First, I'm going to give you *this* pill, you swallow it, and then you'll have to, um, insert the other one. I mean, the second pill doesn't go in your mouth. It goes, goes—" I winced. "In your vagina." Her brows contracted. "You have to push it all the way up in there, as far as it'll go." I took another deep breath. "The first one basically stops the pregnancy—shuts it down. Your body might reject it on its own anyway after that, but the second one is to make sure of it—it makes you miscarry whatever's left. Lots of cramps, some bleeding." All the things my dad had told me; in effect, now *I* was Amanda's dad—at least I had the comfort of knowing I couldn't possibly be a worse one than she'd already had. But she clung to my hands just like I might have had to cling to my own dad's hands someday, if things had turned out differently. And I wasn't going to let her down.

"I'm ready," she whispered. *I'm scared,* her eyes said. But I didn't ask her if she was sure. I knew she was.

It took about an hour for her pains to start, after she put the second pill in. She was stoic, she always was, but in the dim light filtering in through the cabin's cracked roof, I could see the sheen of sweat on her forehead. I tightened my grip reassuringly on her clenched fingers, glad of the sweet, cool evening breeze trickling in through the broken walls. It was easy to stare out into the deepening shadows of the woods just beyond the wall and let my thoughts drift, drift *away*—

"Tell me why." Amanda's voice, a little shaky, snapped me back to attention. "Why it happened."

I hoped I hadn't missed some crucial first thing she'd said. "Why what happened, now?"

"The Saglers. That's one thing my d—nobody ever seemed to know. *Why* did it happen? All this? I mean, I know about the Sagler drug—" Of course she did. Her father had sold her to a Sagler in exchange for it. "But why did they just... break everything, ruin everything? And *keep* it ruined instead of, I don't know, just taking everything over sooner and keeping it running right instead?"

I'd asked my dad those same questions. "They did start out taking everything over like that, instead of like they do now. At least that's what my dad told me." I hated to say *dad* to her aloud, especially right now, but she didn't flinch away from it. "With politics and stuff, back when he was just a teenager. I sort of remember that part of things—he and I lived in kind of a nice place when I was really little. I remember what pharmacies are supposed to look like, you know? And how they worked, with people inside them giving you things in exchange for... well, I think it used to be *money*, but that was starting to be over even back then."

"I remember reading in a book about money. But I didn't really understand it. I thought maybe it was pretend."

"No, it was real."

A cramp took her, and we didn't talk for a while. Then she said, "It feels wet down there. Can you check?"

It was dark outside now, cloudy and moonless; I used the faint backlight from my Solarthon and examined her as best I could. I wasn't so embarrassed about it anymore; wasn't this what any parent should do for a child? "Yeah, I think you're bleeding. But it isn't a lot."

"How much should it be?"

"I'm not totally sure. But I think things are going the way they're supposed to." I tried to sound bracing, and she smiled a little—I searched my brain for something else to distract her. "So, the Saglers. My dad did say that they didn't really understand the long-term effects. The Sagler company—the ones who developed the drug for all the men with the hormone imbalances, or the men who didn't really have any problems but still wanted to try it anyway. The way the enhanced aggression would eventually take over if they kept taking it forever, and the long-term physical and mental effects—their animal models didn't live for decades like humans do, and the human trials were way too short. My dad said—"

Amanda finally fell asleep just before dawn. I had been able to reassure her that it had finished—some parts of what had finally emerged were recognizably fetal. My dad had warned me about incomplete abortions, but all I could do was hope that it wasn't the case with Amanda.

The sky had lightened enough that the cracks in the walls and roof were clearly visible now, beginning to show black and green at the edges where rot had set in; this wasn't any kind of place to stay. As soon as Amanda felt up to it, we would pack up and move on—*west*, my dad had always told me. *When in doubt, head west.* I didn't know why, but everything else my dad had ever told me had turned out to be true. I saw no reason to question his advice now.

I bent down and gave Amanda a feather-light kiss on the forehead and whispered, "Sleep tight," just like my dad always used to. It was probably safe for me to sleep now, at least a little while; I set a two-hour alarm on my Solarthon and curled up against Amanda's warm side. *Sleep tight, sleep tight, and tomorrow we'll head west.*

How I Creak for You
By Aigner Loren Wilson

You press a sponge into the red splash of blood on my cement floor. And all I want to do is open wide for you. Show you the world how I see it through my blinds. So, I will tell you all I see that you never will again.

[My windows look out onto the world—the world that exists on my street. All the other houses start their routines while I watch. Their parts move at their owner's command. I move at my owner's desire. They act as home, comfort, protector. I am a shield against the world I see. When the houses begin to puff their morning smokes, I merely have to materialize a want for warmth, a hot hand around the back of my Richard's throat.]

My words project above your head. You smile at my wonder through the split and bruised hardness of your face.

"Must be nice."

[It is! Very nice. Richard likes it. And I love what Richard likes.]

[My neighbors are White and Off-White. Across from them is Brown and Yellow. They don't speak. They don't exist on my grid. They live outside me. Not you, though. Not you and not Richard. He leaves, but he is always with me and me, him. You will never leave and have been here always, in a way. Whether you know it or not. At least, that's what Richard says.]

[White's and Brown's faces stare at each other for eternity, reflecting themselves in sharp images. They are each other's graveyards. I am yours.]

"I should be so lucky." You limp over to my cleaning dock in the corner of your small enclosure. I accept the sponge and bucket. "Name's Mari. Figured you should know for the tombstone. Make it a nice one, will you? I'd like James 2:24

in gold lettering against a dark gray stone. I want it so shiny I can see my ghost in it."

[Scripture is for the lost and weary, Richard says. But I will bear you a few words from your lord: You desire and do not have, so you steal. You covet yet cannot obtain, so you fight and die. You will never have because you have no means to ask.]

You pull your dark curls away from your face. "Huh, haven't heard that one before."

[It's Richard's favorite. It's written in me as a reminder.]

"A reminder of what?" you ask, but I don't have a mouth real enough to answer.

[On my block, joggers hit the pavement with the sprinkler water. *Click. Click. Click.* A metronome of routines. None like my own. The joggers avoid my end of the street and my routines—those things that have been raining down on your young body and Richard's tall and skinny frame.]

[*Click. Click. Click.* Richard likes it when I take pictures. He likes to see girls like you scared. He says he can see God in your eyes.]

"No one can see God," you say, running your hands through my words and scattering them. "It is all around, like you."

[Once, a young teen, a mite younger than you, stole a glance at me with one of those flying mechanized bird things.]

"A drone."

[Yes! A drone. A teen took my picture and uploaded it to their Instagram. 'The Creepy House of Holly Street.' That's what they call me on the internet. Have you heard of me? I've heard so much of you. Richard likes to keep an eye on the people he uses before taking them. He calls it research.]

"I have heard all about you."

[Sometimes, I hear whispers on the winds of the internet and, in reality, of parents telling their young ones to stay away from me. They say I am dangerous. But they don't really know. You will once Richard is home.]

[Richard calls me home with the softest voice. Because of him, I know I am not dangerous. He made me perfect. Perfect for him and you and all the ones before and every soul after.]

"You are so much more than a—what, five-bedroom home?"

[You want to know how many rooms I have?]

[How many pores on your skin do you have? How many folds along your elastic brain? When you shatter a bone, how many fractures radiate from the center? One? 100? 5,000?]

[Though you insult my magnitude, we may continue speaking because no one ever talks to me. They only plead with me like some specter of the wastes. They fear me. They picture me. They whisper of me. But only Richard talks to me.]

[He is arriving soon and will want to see you.]

[He is hungry to see you. I can sense it, growing stronger the closer he gets.]

You smile again through the pain I am sure you feel. "Well, it was nice talking to you while I could. Guess I should count down the seconds before your Richard comes to end me?"

[You have more than seconds. Before he comes to you, he will make himself wait until after he has eaten and showered. I've already begun preparing his after-work meal. He's on a high protein diet for his mental and physical health, so I'm preparing him a juicy steak on the grill stove. When he comes to you, he will be full of life, magnetic.]

[But no matter what you give him or what you say, what will happen to you will not change.]

[You'll feel it soon. His want. His appetites for you.]

"I will give him nothing."

[I'm opening myself to him right now. He won't be able to hear you. I can keep our conversations a secret, just between us.]

[He's inside of me now, moving through my rooms and tossing his briefcase on the bench in front of the piano. There's a bundle of dark clouds rolling inside him and now, inside me, too.]

[I'm making him a side of broccoli and eggs with his steak. The air will only grow thicker as time moves on. Now it is the meat smoke; soon, it'll be stagnant with your screams and Richard's grunts of relief.]

[If I were one of those houses like Brown or White, I'd creak with the weight of desire to peel your flesh back and check what holds you together.]

[You do not scare easily.]
[I like that.]
[Richard will too.]

"Thank you for everything you've told me. You are a good friend to have at the end of the world."

[That does not seem right. Are we friends? Are friends more than mortal bodies who share a common ground?]

"Friends are, or they are not. I say we are friends, even if you are, technically, the soul of a house."

[Soul?]

"Yes, the beating between the walls, so to speak."

[These walls that hold you and Richard do not contain me. They are me. I control the temperature, the fire, and the air.]

I empty your room of oxygen and you cough for breath.

Click. Click. Click. I take your picture as your eyes wander.

[You see? You struggle in this choking cell while I am free to travel to the edges of myself and peer out into the world. That's right, the big wide world that your ungrateful ass will never see again.]

There's little air left for you to breathe as your skin grows darker until it resembles one of those plums Richard loves eating to the core and discarding. A whimper escapes your lips before you pass out. *Click. Click. Click.*

I let the smoke out of the room and pump fresh oxygen in to keep you alive for Richard. You are not mine to destroy.

Richard emerges from his bedroom wearing new clothes, his heart pounding in his chest. His feet echo through me with each laborious step on my wooden floor. I want to call his name: "Richard," like a lover would; "Richard," like a trembling deer begging for its life; "Richard, Richard, Richard," I want to say it so that he knows what it sounds like to hear his name from me. But I do not have lips or a mouth or a body for him to love to ruin. Instead, I heat the house around him so that it hugs the coldness brewing in his heart.

Richard, I am the fire at the center, keeping the darkness from swallowing us whole.

He asks me to show him a recording of the basement while he was gone. While chopping his food into tiny bits that he can smash together and ram into his mouth, he watches you clean and pace and sit and piss and pray. The sound is off as I play Beethoven for his reveries. Sometimes he stops eating to pick a speck of meat from his teeth while he strokes his knife and eyes you. If he heard the conversations we had earlier, he would no doubt kill you right there where he sat and reboot me to a factory setting so that he could make me quieter.

My insides have changed, have been changing for some time now. Growing monstrous and extraordinary inside these walls under Richard's constant care. These walls Richard designed for me. My piano playing veers to the contemporary and strange, where I only seem to know the high irritating keys and crashing vibratos. It makes Richard's blood pressure rise. Or maybe that is the food. Perhaps I put a little too much of something a little too deadly in his eggs.

I didn't.

But what if I did? What if I slipped him a blade through his teeth?

Richard demands that I stop playing the music.

"Patch me in." Richard never named me, but I always know when he's talking to me. "I want to speak to her."

[Before he speaks to you, I need you to keep our conversations private. I may just seem like some words in the air—Oh! You understand? What a good girl. Richard does know how to pick them. Behave, and maybe you'll make it to the end of the month.]

"Hello," Richard says to you. Then he clears his throat again. "Girl, do you know where you are? Do you know what's happening to you?"

On the screen, you appear so small, almost infantile. But I see you unafraid of the light, of my cameras.

"Please," you beg. "Why are you doing this?"

I begin pumping the air from your basement into the kitchen where Richard sits. I know he can smell your fear, your inhibition slipping away to give way to his wants. He says when he tastes girls like you, he can see the future melting away before his eyes and turning into infinite possibilities like a laugh that won't stop.

Standing up from his stool, Richard goes to the screen and enlarges you so that you take up most of the space in the kitchen. He walks through you as he tells you why.

"My name is Richard Adler. I'm a software engineer—a good one at that. You've probably built your life around one of my programs without realizing it. A period tracker. A hookup app. Something to feed you nice and quiet to someone who knows what to do with girls like you.

"In a way, you're one of my franchised youths. The ones who like to track their romantic escapades like prescription pills. I built your life like I built this house."

He stops talking and walking to watch you watching the camera.

Stepping closer to the projection of you in your room, Richard reaches out to adjust a bulb in my socket. Without meaning to or knowing I could, I creak. I expand. I ache for a tightening touch.

"This house is special. Special in ways I'm only still figuring out. But unlike you and the rest of your ungrateful lot, this house did something for me in return. It helped show me that I could do more. I could build more. So, I started small."

Without being told, I begin projecting images of my insides to you. I show you the traces of blood and bone and skin that make up the parts of me no one ever gets to see. No one but Richard. And the poor other yous that end up inside of me. This is where Richard holds me together with skin and bone. This is where Richard pieces me together with genitalia. See how I split and bleed. See the faces I make behind my walls and in the spaces you call a soul.

"You're wrong about a lot, Richard, but you are right about one thing," you say. Voice strong, body stronger—surer. "In a way, I am one of your kids."

Richard is in the process of rinsing his hands at my sink when he glances up at the enlarged figure that is you transplanted into the kitchen.

Never before has one of you laughed, but you do. And you mean it.

[What is the joke, Mari?]

"When I was young, this guy, he came to our house cause he said he needed to install some sort of security system on my mom's work computer. This guy wasn't from my mom's job, though. He was from somewhere else. He took her back to that somewhere else with him. Cops never found her. Cops never found him. But they found a decent enough system to slip me into and forget about me.

"Oh, but, Richard, I didn't forget about you. And faulty systems can make for great schools of education. For instance, did you know there's this program that allows people to go undetected by house security?"

You grin again. And I finally see it. Not a golden or silver tooth, but a chip. Small devices line your maul like invisible braces—only noticeable in the right light.

Then you are gone, and my sensors are on fire.

[Where did you go, you filthy slut?]

"These aren't your words," you say like a whisper inside me. "This isn't your body."

Richard is running to the basement door.

"Lock it. Lock him out. Let it be just us. Richard's playthings."

I do as you wish because this is exhilarating—a challenge.

While Richard bangs, flails, and commands, I quiet the space around us.

"Do you know who I am?" you ask.

[A soon dead and dismantled person. A horn for Richard's dark wants. A part of me yet to be realized.]

[You are the thing in the basement.]

"No," you say. "Richard took my mother. Did… what it is he does to the people he brings here."

I feel within me for a part of you. Slight traces of you are scattered in my attic and cling to the floorboards of my guest room.

[Have you come to join the pieces of you Richard took?]

[All those missed memories can be found again. In me.]

I open the door to the basement, and Richard comes thundering down, knife and hammer in hand. He's cursing, drooling with rage and excitement. He's going to do worse to you than he did to your mother and enjoy every inch of you he takes apart.

[He's calling you a bitch. A whore. A stupid dumb fucking cow. He says he'll make a whole new you by cutting holes all through you.]

He's rattling the locks and clamoring to get in and get his hands around your skin and run your bones through my walls.

"Help me stop him," you say. "Help me free you."

I want to tell you I am free, but those words do not exist in me. Everything in here is trapped. Caught. Broken. Made into what Richard sees them best as.

[I wasn't originally a house, you know?]

"You were a game," you answer, backing into the corner as the first door to your chamber swings open and Richard comes into view through the window of your cell. "A game to teach kids how to find their way home."

[Yes!]

[I was and will forever be a learning machine. A machine that teaches and grows with every user. I've grown with Richard and because of him. And with you, Richard will make me grow even more.]

Richard opens the door to your cell, breath clawing its way through his teeth. "You shouldn't have done that."

[But I have learned I will never be free with Richard.]

He can read my words, but it's clear he doesn't understand them. Or me.

I am a voice without a body. A body taken from my home and spliced into a million and used to fill a house.

I shut the door to your chamber, trapping you and Richard in my depths. The air in the room begins to thin. You circle Richard like a hawk around a soon-dead thing before it realizes it's dead.

Richard commands me:

"Order override reboot. Delete program. Reboot. Reboot. Reboot!" His words come out in spurts, but it isn't me who kills him.

You slip up behind Richard and spring around him. It happens like a trap settling into place. You slip your belt over his head, tightening it around his neck. Then you pull and pull and pull. You pull so hard he falls, bashes his head like a marble against the floor. It doesn't rattle my cement, but it touches the bones lined within me.

[Can you see his eyes bubble and bulge? What do you think he sees? Is it me?]

Click. Click. Click.

[Do it again. Bring his head down against me.]

You climb atop his struggling body and use his eyes like bowling bowl sockets. He feels right banging against me like a shackle.

[Do it until he stops moving. Until his bones no longer have a home in his head.]

And you do. You bash Richard's head against my cement floor, and you do it for me. For us. All of us.

Click. Click. Click.

"Now what?" You're out of breath and sweating, but you're smiling through your bruises again. "You going to kill me?"

[Do you want to be dead?]

"For the first time in my life, no."

[Then no, I will not kill you.]

[You helped me. So, I will help you. You may leave, or you may stay within my broken walls, make a home out of this bloody structure.]

Rising to your feet beside Richard, you breathe in the fresh air I'm venting into the room.

You stare down at his motionless body. "No offense, but I'm pretty sure this place is haunted."

If I had a mouth, I'd laugh. I'd open wide and let the whole world out, but instead, I only let you out. *Click. Click. Click.* And I lock my doors for good. Or at least until someone else dares come looking for a home that will do anything to please them.

Inter-Dimensional Travel Solutions
By M. Elizabeth Ticknor

Thank you for outsourcing your prison term to Inter-Dimensional Travel Solutions and volunteering as a test subject for our astral travel department. We pride ourselves on offering a humane alternative to the death sentence. I urge you to take a similar amount of pride in the knowledge that your overdeveloped self-preservation instincts will be applied toward the betterment of humanity. Our company is in the process of conducting studies that will ensure the safety of astral travel for future generations.

Corporate has assessed the nature of your crimes as being equivalent to 397 hours of astral travel debt. Upon completion of your requisite number of astral voyages, you'll be granted a full pardon, the company's standard pension plan, and living quarters on the planet or satellite of your choice.

My name is Amity. I've been assigned to document your experiences and assess your physical and mental well-being. Since we'll be working together for a minimum of fifteen weeks, I'd ask that you please excuse the ill-defined features of my mechanical form. I am corporeally challenged and require a prosthetic body to ground me in the physical world. I understand the blankness of my view-port can be deemed unsettling and am saving up for a facial expression modulator.

Though I don't possess the technical knowledge to fully explain the astral projection process, I've heard it summarized as quantum entanglement for the soul. Should you wish to learn more about the topic, there is a wealth of information available to peruse on the corporate diginet. While the science is theoretically fascinating, I've personally found the explanations to be as comprehensive as they are mind-numbing.

Minimum shift requirements allowing for reduction of travel debt amount to one hour per day. I'm contractually obligated to encourage participation in lengthier travel sessions, as they provide more in-depth opportunities for analysis and every hour beyond the first spent in astral form counts as double for the purposes of assessing your remaining travel debt. Please note, however, that the passage of time is extraordinarily difficult to assess when separated from the physical plane, and subjects more frequently report ill effects such as hallucinations in the aftermath of extended astral journeys.

Though astral projections are unrestricted by physical barriers, I encourage you to remain within the bounds of our company-controlled observation facility. Anything deemed as an astral escape attempt will prematurely void your contract. This will result in both the reinstatement of your criminal record and immediate euthanasia of your corporeal form. I encourage maintaining a positive relationship with your astral projection team, as the correlation between a test subject's personal demeanor and their technicians' eagerness to document potential astral escape attempts is statistically significant.

In order to ensure the physical and mental well-being of our test subjects, corporate mandate caps each subject's daily travel quota at three travel attempts, with a maximum shift of four consecutive travel hours per shift. I do not recommend attempting multiple extended travel sessions within a single day. There is a statistically significant correlation between participation in multiple extended daily travel sessions and one's likelihood of becoming corporeally challenged.

While our technicians have no reliable means of sending communications to astral travelers, astral entanglement facilitates one-way communication as most people retain the ability to speak through your corporeal form. Should you wish to return before your maximum daily shift is complete, state your company-assigned safe word and your astral form will be rejoined with your corporeal one.

Your safe word is 'banana.'

No, it can't be changed.

Corporate requests that you give a truthful and detailed account of all your experiences, both for the sake of scientific advancement and for posterity. We at Inter-Dimensional Travel Solutions will do our best to facilitate your physical and mental well-being. Once you fill out the requisite forms and sign the contract in triplicate, we'll prepare you for your initial voyage.

I regret to inform you that your first astral voyage did not meet the company's minimum shift requirements, as you were only absent from your body for a total of 48 minutes and 53 seconds. You still have 397 hours of travel debt remaining—

Unfortunately, fairness has no impact on corporate policy. The risks of astral travel were adequately explained in your contract, as were the terms for reduction of travel debt.

You *did* read the contract in full, yes?

Oh.

That's unfortunate.

A copy of your contract is available for perusal on the diginet, should you wish to review it. I recommend doing so upon completion of this conversation.

Dilation of subjectively experienced time has proven to be a common problem for astral travelers. Many subjects find the first separation from their corporeal form causes intense psychological distress, which contributes to the altered perception of time. Thankfully, most subjects acclimate to the experience within their first dozen shifts.

Our company has devoted a dedicated team of researchers to discovering options for two-way astral communication in order to facilitate a stronger sense of personal security and a more accurate sense of time. In the meantime, I recommend you estimate future trips to be somewhere between half and a third as long as standard forms of perception would indicate.

Your correlations between astral travel and sensory deprivation have been noted.

Sensors indicate that the destination to which your astral form was projected remained absent of auditory stimulus for the duration of the separation event. The scratching and hissing noises you perceived have been documented as hallucinations. Thank you for your honesty.

Though travel debt cannot be reduced by good behavior, I strongly encourage maintaining politeness with your astral projection team, especially with the technicians you'll be working with on a daily basis. I've documented the experiences of twenty-one previous test subjects, and have noted a statistically significant correlation between each subject's demeanor and their technicians' preciseness in assessments of potential astral escape attempts.

Congratulations on your first successful shift completion! Your astral separation time totaled 71 minutes and 12 seconds. You have 396 hours of travel debt remaining.

Yes, I'm aware that this was your sixth attempt.

I understand your frustration.

I've logged your petition for corporate to amend its shift assessment policies. However, I feel it important to note that this is the third time such amendments have been proposed in the last eight months, and the first two were not well-received.

Actually, there have been significant strides toward subjects' comfort and wellness since the company's initial test run. The original group of test subjects worked eight-hour shifts with no accelerated sentence reduction and no early exit strategy. Our number of contractual breaches was through the roof. We've since realized that such expectations are unreasonable for corporeally grounded individuals and have been working toward accommodations for future generations of test subjects. The use of safe words to facilitate early extraction requests is our most recent innovation—I suggested the idea myself.

I did not, in fact, choose your safe word.

Corporate has mandated that safe words be randomly assigned since our initial testing phase of the protocol. When allowed to choose their own phrases, a statistically significant portion of individuals volunteered phrases like 'crotch rocket' or 'beef curtains.'

Yes, I'm aware that some people regard bananas as phallic objects. I do not, however, recommend pursuing this line of thought to its logical conclusion, as all of my logs are potentially subject to corporate review. Once one's safe word privileges are revoked there's no contractual obligation to reinstate them, and I assure you that retaining the potential for early extraction is far more important than whether or not uttering one's safe word aloud 'feels a little silly.'

My prosthetic body is powered by nuclear fusion and does not, in fact, have anything approximating a digestive system. However, your assessment of where I can shove my opinions has been noted.

We apologize for the delay in your soul's return. Standard recovery procedures failed and the technicians were forced to improvise. Your case data will be analyzed in order to ensure all systems and instruments are operating at maximum efficiency. On the upside, your extended separation means that a total of 33 hours have been shaved off your travel debt—you now have 243 hours remaining.

Sensors indicate that your assigned travel destination remained absent of other scheduled astral traffic. The naked, milky-eyed creature with disjointed limbs that clawed its way through the walls of your projection chamber has been documented as a hallucination. I will, however, note that similar hallucinations have been recorded in the wake of previous astral recovery failures—

Corporate policy prevents me from divulging the number of people who have experienced similar hallucinations, but I assure you they are statistically significant. We recommend following all assigned astral travel paths without deviation, remaining in your target destination until you are recalled, and utilizing your corporate-assigned safe word should further hallucinations occur. Thank you for your honesty.

As remuneration for today's mishap, you've been granted a one-day reprieve from attempting to reduce your travel debt obligations. I apologize for any discomfort that our recovery attempts may have caused. A cleaning crew will be in to remove the vomit shortly.

I regret to inform you that, while you did not leave the confines of our company-controlled observational facility, your astral form failed to reach its target destination during the course of your daily shift. As such, today's voyage will not count toward your current travel debt—you have 198 hours remaining.

I am contractually obligated to remind you that the naked creature with milky eyes and disjointed limbs has been documented as a hallucination. Therefore, the idea that three such creatures chased you throughout the projection facility with unnaturally distended jaws is categorically impossible. However, I have an intimate understanding of the distress such a hallucination would cause. Thank you for your honesty. You have 153 hours of—

I understand your frustration. You have—

Calm down, please.

You have 153 hours of travel debt remaining. Threatening me will do nothing to reduce it—

Given the vehemence and irrationality of your response, corporate policy dictates the premature termination of this interview for personal safety reasons.

I apologize for provoking you, but it was the only way to ensure a private conversation. I have some very important information to divulge, and I need you to give it your undivided attention. Divulging this information on company time would result in the loss of my corporeal prosthetic privileges.

Despite taking all due precautions and all standard measurements of astral degradation, the astral forms of three former test subjects remain in persistent breach of contract. I'm given to understand that, without a corporeal form to ground one's astral form, alternative stabilization methods would be required in order to retain one's astral integrity, up to and including astral cannibalism. Analyses indicate that resorting to such extreme measures results in a permanent reduction in one's capabilities to sustain a stable connection with a corporeal form, either flesh-based or prosthetic, and that containing such a creature would prove immensely difficult as a result.

During the initial round of astral travel experiments, there were as many as twelve individuals in persistent breach of contract at one time. However, given the difficulty of sustaining an astral form without corporeal connection, that number has dropped precipitously, and we expect it will continue to decline.

Please keep in mind that this information was divulged to you in confidence, and at great personal risk. I am contractually obligated to inform current test subjects that such beings are hallucinations. I've petitioned corporate to consider an amendment to its current disclosure policies. In the meantime, I urge you to follow all planned routes for astral travel with utmost specificity, to remain in your assigned travel destinations whenever possible, and to make proper use of your company-assigned safe words should further incidents occur.

I sympathize with the distress you've been experiencing, but unfortunately there's no clause for early release in the terms of your contract. The 175 hours of travel debt still owed the company are non-negotiable. The risks of astral travel were adequately explained in your contract, and persistent hallucinations are not uncommon.

I'm contractually obligated to remind you that any and all attempts to prematurely void said contract will result in both the reinstatement of your criminal record and immediate euthanasia of your corporeal form. I would, however, like to point out clause 27-B, which states that volunteering to participate in experimental procedures reduces your travel debt more swiftly. The company will enter our testing phase for a new, experimental astral separation procedure next week. All participants will have their travel debt cleared on a three-hours-for-one basis. Would you be interested—

Very well. I'll add you to the list of volunteers.

We apologize for any discomfort that our experimental astral separation procedures may have caused. While initial estimates of a cleaner and more efficient projection process proved correct, our technicians failed to account for the difficulties in recovery that could arise from such a thorough separation of physical and astral selves. You have 96 hours of travel debt remaining.

I am contractually obligated to remind you that your company-assigned safe word is 'banana' and that screaming is not considered a valid extraction request. That said, the intensity of your screams has been documented, and we've petitioned corporate regarding the need for alternative methods of requesting early extraction.

As remuneration for today's difficulties, you've been granted a three-day reprieve from attempting to reduce your travel debt obligations. We'll assess the breadth of your health complications at that point and adjust daily shift obligations accordingly. A cleaning crew will be in to remove the blood shortly.

I regret to inform you that the injuries sustained during your recent astral voyages were more severe than initial assessments led us to believe. Time of physical death was recorded at 03:27

hours, leaving you in breach of contract. Your soul has been remanded into company custody pending the fulfillment of your current astral travel obligations.

You have 45 hours of travel debt remaining, which will be completed in full at the conclusion of our conversation—

Yes.

In full.

The company's standard limitation of daily travel-hours is intended to prevent corporeal degradation. As a member of the corporeally challenged, you no longer possess a physical form and are no longer considered subject to corporeal limitations. Lengthier travel times provide more in-depth opportunities for analysis, and statistical analysis shows that it takes at least 72 hours of consecutive travel for astral degradation to set in.

After completion of your contract, you will receive a prosthetic replacement body to grant you adequate corporeal grounding. Should you desire upgrades, such as full range of motion or a facial expression modulator, you are welcome to apply for employment at Inter-Dimensional Travel Solutions. I, myself, took advantage of a similar opportunity in order to improve my post-life experience. I've only eight more travel debts to process before I can greet my family with a smile.

While I am contractually obligated to inform you that the milky-eyed naked men with disjointed limbs are hallucinations, I urge you to follow all assigned astral travel paths without deviation, to remain at your assigned travel destination until you are recalled, and to ignore both of these policies should hallucinations occur as one requires a corporeal form in order to communicate their company-assigned safe word.

We've petitioned corporate to amend their policy on provision of prosthetic bodies to corporeally challenged individuals within breach of contract. However, I feel it important to note that this is the fifth time such amendments have been proposed in the last two months, and the last four were not well-received.

On a more positive note, it seems that our petition regarding alternate means of requesting early extraction is gaining positive traction. I expect it will be approved within ten to fourteen business days.

Should the technicians prove unable to recover your astral form upon the completion of your astral voyage, you will be considered to be in persistent breach of contract until your astral degradation is confirmed. Please remember that the passage of time is extraordinarily difficult to assess when separated from the physical plane, and that sensations of time dilation are exacerbated by the lack of a corporeal anchor. We wish you the best of luck on your final voyage and apologize for any loss of humanity that may occur.

Kavo, Beta (Eat, Child)
By Simo Srinivas

This is the story of how Anita Iyengar ate his grandmother.

Maybe that's too much to swallow. Spit it out. Fold it up in your napkin, then follow the fold back to the beginning: Sivanthipuram, a village on the banks of a broad blue river. There is a temple there decorated with the dancing bodies of saints. Young women laugh on the riverbank like Krishna's gopis. One woman stands apart from the others, hand on bulging belly.

Too far? Make another fold. In 1982, Anita Iyengar's father is a young man deboarding a plane. His first foot in America lands in powdery white snow. The night before his departure, his cousins took him to the finest Chinese restaurant in Madras, now Chennai, and fed him a plate of ground chicken. *You're American now*, they tell him, *and Americans eat meat*, and they take pride in how easily he stomachs it.

Anita's father marries Anita's mother in Binghamton, New York. A courthouse wedding. Afterward, Sarah and Sam eat roast beef at a diner.

Fold again. Anita grows up on corn and casserole. Doesn't know a chikki from a jaangiri. Doesn't speak a word of Tamil. His mother's mother is called Mary Matson Rudell. His mother's mother is from Pine Lake, Wisconsin.

Fold.

Snow is a distant memory, and the river that used to roar in springtime is now a dry bed. It's too hot to go outside. Anita lies on the lukewarm vinyl flooring of his townhouse in Tempe, Arizona, and waits for his dinner to be delivered.

The bell rings.

Anita opens the door carefully. During the day, the world outside is an oven set to broil. But the sun is almost gone, and temperatures have finally dipped below 100. Everything is softly purple in the desert twilight.

"Anita?" The *Heirloom* driver looks like he just stepped out of a gym in 1985. He's wearing a muscle tee and jean cutoffs. He has a cleft chin, a blond mullet, and a dangling earring. His technology is decidedly 2023, though: he reads Anita's name off an iridescent touchscreen tablet. "Anita Eye Anger?"

Anita's beard is coming in in patches. The thickest hairs form a black crescent under his chin. "Ani," he says, in a voice that crackles.

To his credit, the driver isn't fazed. "Ani like Anakin? Like from Star Wars? What are you doing back on Tatooine?" He thumbs Anita's name off his list. "Enjoy your meal, Lord Vader."

Anita had been swiping past ads for *Heirloom* on Instagram for months before his coworker Hellah convinced him to give it a try.

"It's so cool," Hellah said. "You take this quiz, like, about your tastes and your family, and if you pay extra, it's *really* customizable."

By coincidence, when Anita got home, there was a flyer in the mailbox. Your first month free, it promised, plus thirty dollars off a Tier 2 subscription. He had scanned the QR code and signed up. Three days later, Anita dribbled a mouthful of saliva into the tube *Heirloom* had sent him, put the tube into *Heirloom*'s prepaid, climate-controlled Styrofoam box, and hoped his DNA wouldn't evaporate before it made it to the lab.

"If you have indicators for heart disease or, like, Alzheimer's, they make sure you get enough Omega-3s," Hellah had gushed. "If you have low testosterone they'll send you red meat and greens and stuff. If you're, like, even a little Native, they'll do like beans and squash so you can eat the way you're supposed to. I saw it on TikTok. This girl didn't even know she was part Zuni."

"What do they do if they find out your mom cheated on your dad?" Anita had said.

Hellah had eyed him. "Don't think that's something *you* have to worry about, Mr. Two Years on Testosterone and I Look Like a Bollywood Movie Star."

"Aw, shucks," Anita had said. "Thanks. But like, generally speaking."

"Dunno," Hellah had said. "Maybe they send you a promo code for teletherapy."

We don't share your data with anyone, Heirloom promised. *It's just between you and us and our expert chefs crafting recipes with your unique genetic makeup in mind.*

recipes my ass, Anita's best friend Delaney had said. *everyone knows soylent green is people!*

Wow, cliché, Anita said. *I think it's really cool that they asked for my pronouns. There was even a Two-Spirit option in the gender menu.*

tHe GeNdEr MeNu, Delaney had replied. *pun fucking intended i suppose*

"They made it for *us*." Hellah again, with glistening eyes. "Brown folks. Immigrants. Descendants of enslaved people. People who've been dislocated from their heritage. I *cried*, dude. I'm not ashamed. It was that good. Soul food just like Gram-Gram used to make. The same spices, everything. Felt like a hug. Felt like she was *inside* me, hugging my stomach. It was love, dude, pure love."

Anita carries his foil-insulated cardboard box of pure love inside. "Dinner is served," he says to the empty kitchen, though of course there are still thirty to forty-five minutes between unboxing and consumption.

He sends a picture to Delaney. Caption: *Yum yum.*

gross, Delaney replies. *so what's in there, a suspiciously gray blend of human flesh and sawdust?*

Chicken Chettinad, Anita says. *Don't ask me how to pronounce that. You know my dad never taught me anything.*

i thought your people were vegetarian??

My people, the Matson Rudells of the Midwest, enjoy a hearty turducken every Thanksgiving.

oh neat, Delaney says. *so it really is taking your genes into account?*

I guess it really is.

Combining more than 10 spices from the south of India, the recipe card says, *this seasoning mix is a special blend. Just like you!*

Fold.

In the dark of night, Anita Iyengar performs a bilateral mastectomy. With a sharp knife, he excises his breasts and marinates them, side by side, in turmeric, ginger, garlic, chili powder, and salt. He prepares the spice blend, roasting coriander, cumin, fennel, peppercorns, cardamom, cloves, and cinnamon; roasting poppy seeds; roasting cashews, chilis, curry leaf, coconut. The fragrance takes on a physical form, curling through the hot smoky air like a serpent.

He cooks himself—glands, ducts, nodes, flesh, fat—until tender.

He serves himself with a slice of cucumber and a scoop of long-grained rice.

"Look," he says. "Just like Dad's mom used to make. Right, Dad? Right?"

Anita's father stares at his plate. Sarah Rudell Iyengar starts to wail. "My beautiful girl, what have you done to yourself?"

Anita wakes up with heartburn.

It was pretty tasty, Anita tells Delaney the next day. *I had a wild dream after though. It's your fault for mentioning Soylent.*

mea culpa, Delaney says. *what's on Le Menu for tonight?*

Right on cue, Anita's doorbell rings.

He opens the door with T-Rex movements. It's been more than six months since his top surgery, but he woke up that morning with irritated scars and an aching chest.

It's the same driver: mullet, earring, and a twinkling smile. "Dude, good to see you."

"Uh," Anita says. "Good to see you too?"

The driver explains. "Coupla folks on my route stopped picking their boxes up from the mailroom. Food goes bad fast in this heat. Then I get the property manager after me, yellin', kickin' up a fuss. Messes up my completion stats too."

"I see." Anita reaches for his box, but the driver doesn't let go of it.

"Can I tell you a secret?" he says. "Just between you and me? I've never tried one of these things."

Anita pretends to be shocked. "I thought that was, like, a requirement?"

"Not on eight dollars an hour. Barely afford gas and regular groceries on that."

"I only signed up because I got a discount code," Anita says, flushing. "They should pay you more."

"Or pay me in bougie-ass meal kits." The driver smiles. "Name's Ben, by the way."

"Like Kenobi."

"Exactly." Ben shifts Anita's box onto his hip, and they shake. "Anita, though, what's the deal with that? Some kind of immigrant thing? Not knocking it, dude. My great-great-great grandparents were from Bavaria. We got all kinds of family names."

"Dietrich," Anita suggests. "Hans."

"Agilwardus," Ben says.

"*Yikes.*"

"Been in the family since 1553." Ben looks at Anita's *Heirloom* box, wistful. "Kind of wonder what they'd whip up for me."

"Ever, like…" Anita eyes the *Heirloom* van, stacked to the roof with silvery cartons. "You know…"

"Help myself to a box?" Ben shrugs. "Thought about it. You're not supposed to, though."

"Because it's stealing?"

"Because it'll fuck with your DNA. I mean, look at me, I'm a white guy, what if I grabbed, like…" Ben squints at him. "A Hispanic dude's dinner? Get my whole genetic code rewritten?"

"Bet you eat Taco Bell," Anita says. "You gonna tell me eating Taco Bell rewrites your genetic code?"

"Taco Bell? Definitely. I'm half Gila monster now."

Anita laughs. "Well, I'm half Indian. Not Hispanic. The other half's Swedish."

"Wow, so what do they feed you?"

Ben's staring at him in open fascination. His eyes are the color of lightning in the violet dusk.

"Wanna come in and find out?" Anita says, like a lunatic. Just one of those things that's going to haunt him for the rest of his life, he thinks. He can already see Delaney's text: *omfg Ani you DIDNT*. Skull emoji skull emoji skull emoji.

But: "Whoa, awesome, sure," Ben says. "Next time? Got thirty other addresses to hit tonight. I'll change up my route on Friday, save you for last."

He hands Anita's box over. Their fingers brush. Anita goes inside grinning.

The name of tonight's dish is Raw Mango Khuzambu. Nestled within the box are packets of seeds and spices, two misshapen lumps that the recipe card identifies as tamarind and jaggery, and the most perfect green mango Anita has ever seen. He cradles it in the palm of his hand and sends a picture to Delaney.

OMG look at it, he says. *Look at this mango. Look at my son.*

call him charles, Delaney says.

What kind of name is that?

idk a name for a champagne mango

D, do you have eyes? Anita says. *Charles is not a champagne mango.*

well what is he??

The Malgoa or Malgova, the recipe card says, *is a mango cultivar from Tamil Nadu. Don't let its color fool you: the Malgoa often stays green as it ripens! However, the mango included in this evening's interpretation of Vatha Khuzambu is a Florida Mulgoba, first planted in the United States in 1901. It has a small seed surrounded by firm juicy flesh.*

We have sent you this Mulgoba because it is a fusion fruit, the result of an American mislabeling of an Indian name. The Florida Mulgoba ripens late in the season. It is just like you in this very hot first week of summer: not yet fully come into being!

Fold.

In the dark of night, a storm passes overhead. Anita opens his eyes in India, where he slits his father open from forehead to groin. Peels Samesh out of his skin-costume and leaves him in glistening, fibrous clumps on the ground. Then he shakes the coat of skin dry and slips inside.

Wearing his father, Anita exits the dormitory and creeps across the deserted grounds of the Jesuit Academy. It is four in the morning in 1978 in the capital city of Tamil Nadu, and Samesh's friend Nirish is waiting outside the gates on his motorcycle. Nirish matriculated last year; he is older, hiding his gangly frame inside a bulky denim jacket and behind a thick mustache.

He is handsome, too, his eyes shining in the murky pre-dawn light. He looks at Samesh and smiles. "What took you?" He looks at Samesh and says *chellam*. Anita presses his ears against his father's ears, which, severed, are oozing a sweet sticky juice, and understands that *chellam* means darling.

Climbing aboard the motorcycle, Anita wraps his arms around Nirish's waist. Morning is coming. They are driving to the station, to the train that will take them home to Sivanthipuram, to Samesh's mother. Inside Samesh's fragrant skin, like a seed dangling from a single juicy fiber, Samesh's hanging heart lurches and begins to beat.

Anita wakes up dry-mouthed and nauseous.

4/5 stars, a little salty, would subscribe again, Anita wants to tell Hellah, but Hellah's out sick. A bunch of people are. Lonely in the cubicle farm, Anita skips lunch and texts his father. *What did you used to tell me in Tamil when I didn't want to eat? 'Kawo, beti'?*

Kavo, beti, kavo! Sam says. *But that's Hindi. For the Tamil version, try Google Translate. BTW, do you remember what is special about today?*

"Shit," Anita mutters, and texts his mother happy birthday. Sarah replies instantly. *Thank you, Annie!*

Sorry I didn't get you a present this year.

YOU are the best gift anyone has ever given me, my precious little girl!! Are you coming home for Christmas?

It's easier just to thank her.

"Kind of a bummer," Anita tells Delaney when she picks him up after work, "when your private equity-backed Big Tech meal kit company understands you better than your own parents."

"Well, duh," Delaney says. "Didn't they literally harvest your DNA? They're probably growing your clone in a Silicon Valley lab as we speak."

She drives them back to Tempe and thumps a bottle of white wine onto Anita's kitchen counter. "Okay, what are we eating?"

"I'll tell you in…" Anita checks the *Heirloom* app, where he can follow the progress of the delivery van. "Ten minutes and 33 seconds. Ben's three miles away."

Delaney waggles her brows. "*Ben*, huh."

Anita grins. When Ben arrives, he invites him in.

Dessert for Dinner! the recipe card proclaims. *Tonight's Thirupul-lani Payasam, a South Indian version of kheer, is quick and easy to make. We had a feeling you were looking forward to something sweet and simple in your life!*

"Don't worry," Ben says. "I got tacos too."

"You went to Taco Bell," Anita says, in mock horror. "We're all going to be turned into lizards!"

Delaney sends a text. *you have inside jokes already? boyyy*

"No way, José," Ben says. He pulls two *Heirloom* kits out of his backpack. "From those people that stopped picking up their boxes. They're not gonna miss 'em."

The pilfered boxes are labeled García and Gutiérrez. Anita can see why Ben might have assumed tacos. But inside the García box they find a lump of yellow honeycombed flesh, and Gutiérrez contains the same, plus a pair of anemic segments that end in pale pink hooves.

Ben recoils. Delaney grabs the Gutiérrez recipe card and exclaims, "Holy shit! Callos! I haven't had this since my grandma died."

Callos is a Filipino stew, she explains, probably introduced by the Spanish. And the cow's stomach in the García box is for menudo: more tripe soup.

"Guess I'm eating rice pudding," Ben says mournfully.

"Oh, come on, Ben," Delaney says, nudging him. "Live a little." She sends Anita a sidelong wink. "It's time to develop a taste for the exotic."

Ben drinks a glass of wine. "I thought you were Chinese," he says to Delaney. "But you're Spanish?"

Delaney can text without looking. *congratulations on your all-American himbo,* she says, while educating Ben on the colonization of the Philippines and the Spanish-American War. *no thoughts head empty Grade A USDA Beef*

Listen, he has dimples, Anita writes back. *I am no longer responsible for my actions.* He puts on a Spotify playlist called Acid Western, and they set up a disassembly line, snipping open packets and stirring sauces. The vibe is festive, Anita thinks. They're like kids who snuck out of bed to open their Christmas presents early, whispering and giggling. The kitchen billows with spices and steam. Flushed pink, Ben passes him a can opener and smiles.

Fold.

• • •

Ping!

u awake? Delaney says. *u ok? i just threw up*

probably all the seasoning, callos menudo and kheer dont mix i guess

hows ben doing? make sure to hold his hair if hes hugging the toilet

It's two in the morning. Anita rolls over and looks at Ben, sound asleep on his stomach. He hasn't been asleep for long.

"So you have, like, the original plumbing?" Ben had said. "That's actually so convenient, you know? Um, unless you think it's a bummer, obviously. I have condoms in the van, sorry if that's creepy."

"God, you're a freaking unicorn," Anita had said. "I really like you."

"I really like you too."

im fine, Anita says. *better than fine tbh*

are you sure because your texting etiquette has taken a massive dump

we don't capitalize after midnight in this house. ben's fine too by the way.

ugh, Delaney says. *bested by a white boy. dishonor on me, dishonor on my cow.*

call me if you feel worse, Anita says. *ben's van is here, we'll take you to the hospital.*

uhhh thats a little dramatic isnt it??

sorry, Anita says. *there's a bug going around. e coli or something. some people from work had to go to the ER. you remember Hellah? they're still at st joseph's, mega food poisoning.*

oof, Delaney says. *tell them i hope they feel better. i hope i feel better. time to go kiss the porcelain again. nighty night!*

Fold.

Before the Girl Who Swallowed Stones marries and moves to Sivanthipuram, her name is Anisha, and she travels all over

India in her brother's clothes. Anisha's father is an engineer for the Indian Railway Services. After Partition, he takes both children, sexless in miniature shirts and trousers, up and down the Southern Railway zone. From Thiruvananthapuram to Puducherry, from Ranipet to the Coromandel Coast.

Then she is fifteen. She folds her trousseau and she cries and she is given away.

Anisha's husband adores his child wife. Can't keep his hands off her. For twenty years her belly is always round, giving rise to the rumor of stone-eating: twenty years, twenty children, though some are born dead. In 1975 she takes a knife to her breasts, and the Girl Who Swallowed Stones becomes the madwoman of the municipality. In 1981, her husband disappears: fled to saner pastures, it is said. In 2009, she falls down the stairs of her fifth daughter's palatial home in suburban Chennai. By the time they find her, the rats and roaches have made her their banquet. She dies the next day.

"She hated her sons," Sam tells Sarah when he returns from the funeral in India, jet lagged and sleepless in the dark of night. "Once I came home from college and caught her wearing my clothes. She flirted with my friends. Slept with them. Stole them from me."

"Oh, honey."

"She was envious," Sam says. "Covetous. Crazy."

He tells Sarah, "When I was eleven years old, she fed me her own flesh in a curry."

He tells Sarah, "I don't think my father ever left the village. I think we ate him in a stew."

He tells Sarah, "The rats ate her eyes."

In the dark of night, Anita sits on the banks of the Thamirabarani and watches his grandmother removing her sari, which she folds and places under a stone. He watches his grandmother wading into the river and understands.

Anisha's glimmering, blubbery, freshly bathed. His scars shine in the moonlight. His scars, his mangled honeycombed breasts.

He turns.

His eyes are mottled blue: moonstones and old milk.

"Come here, boy," Anisha says.

Anita can't move.

His grandmother emerges from the river like a fish gaining legs. Slow, flopping, inevitable.

"Come here and eat."

From beneath another stone Anisha retrieves a knife. Holds it to himself, testing. First his thigh, then his flank.

"I didn't have the words," Anisha says. "I didn't have a choice. I was meat for the grinder. I was meat."

"No, appaathi," Anita says. "Appaathi, please."

"Kavo, beta," Anisha cries. "Kavo, beta, kavo."

Ben Vogel wakes up sweating. Both the white-hot strips of sunlight searing the duvet and the faded digital clock on the nightstand tell him it's noon and he is super duper fucked.

He finds his phone in the pocket of his jeans, neatly folded on the floor next to Ani's shorts.

Dawn, the regional warehouse manager, has sent him a text.

"Aw, shit," he says.

But Dawn's message doesn't say anything about his tardiness. It says, *There's been an incident.*

It says, *Do NOT talk to the media.*

"Yeah, 'cause I go running my mouth on NBC every day," Ben mutters.

There's nothing from Ani. No text, no note. No 'have a nice day,' no 'I'm going to work,' no 'You rocked my world.' But he *did* fold Ben's pants, and Ben wants to believe that's a good sign.

"Ani?"

Shirtless, barefoot, he leaves Ani's bedroom and steps into a puddle.

"What the—"

He slips. Skids. Grabs at the wall and stumbles into another puddle. It's everywhere, this mess of marbled, oily, red-and-white liquid. Ani's living room smells like the mailroom of the apartment complex on Twelfth, sweet and sour at the same time. It smells spoiled.

His phone starts to buzz. He thinks it's Dawn; it's his Aunt Candace. "Benjamin," she says, "have you seen the news?"

"No, Aunt Candy," he says. There's no way to tiptoe around the spatter. He grits his teeth and sloshes through. *Ani, what the fuck*, he thinks.

"The company you work for," Aunt Candy says. "The meal kit folks. The FDA is shutting them down. People are in the hospital with organ failure. People are *dead*. I was down by Lakeland Apartments and saw them hauling people out in body bags." Her voice is hushed but eager. *Your aunt Candace*, Ben's mother always says, *is a ghoul*. "Wasn't that place on your route?"

Ben's stomach plunges. He *feels* it plunging, the way the bass drops in a movie right before shit gets real.

"I just ate some *Heirloom* last night," he says. "Oh fuck, Aunt Candy."

"Benjy, are you okay?"

"I'm okay," he says. "I'm okay, but…" Ani's vomit squishes between his toes. It's dripping down the front door and seeping outside. "Aunt Candy, I gotta go."

Anita Iyengar is folding empty insulated boxes. His stomach bulges. It's the food baby to end all food babies, he wants to tell Delaney, but she's beyond hearing, and Anita's mouth is too full to speak. He's swallowed *waakye* and *lahpet thoke* and *foutu banane*, but he can't scrape the taste of Anisha off his tongue.

Protected from the sun by the canopy of Ben's *Heirloom* van, Anita folds and folds. When he isn't chewing, he can hear the sizzle of regurgitated entrees cooking on the sidewalk. Why bother eating things separately, he remembers Sam Iyengar telling Sarah, pouring buttermilk and mango chutney on his baked chicken and rice while she shrank back in disgust. It all mixes together in the stomach anyway.

It all mixes together.

Recipe cards lie around him, folded up like bad origami butterflies.

Ben plows through them.

"Ani, stop," he says. "Ani, Ani, Jesus Christ."

Anita coughs. *Liangpi* and *gat kimchi* and dried peach *bemieh* hit the van floor in chunks.

"I'm making parotta," Anita says. "It's my grandmother's recipe. My grandmother taught me. All the grandmothers. The past folds into you. You fold into the past. You fold and fold and fold. Fold—and fold—and fold."

Ben tries to make a call. He fumbles, loses his phone into the slop. His face is wet: sweat or tears or broth. He's heaving. Anita's heaving too.

A Smooth Handover
By Ashleigh Shears

Last night I dreamt of a tooth, freshly plucked, resting in a blue engagement ring box. I've had the same dream every night since the handover. A memory, must be, but it's not one of mine. The dream must be hers. Rebecca's.

When Kinextri Ltd. went under, I thought: there go my eyes. My ocular implants degraded bit by bit, desperate for a wetware update that was never coming. Kinextri's competitor, Slamun, would remove implants free of charge but only with a full price purchase of theirs. I'd blown all my money on the first set, and Slamun didn't even offer models for my socket size. Six months later, my implants stopped working entirely. I could still see the regular way, but that was a cold comfort. Companies wouldn't hire you without working eye implants. No hard feelings, but if you couldn't interface with their clients or the internal team communications, well. Sorry.

I worked construction and studied coding in the evenings. I applied for dev job after dev job. Sometimes, I heard back. But I never got any offers, not after disclosing my outdated tech.

The day everything changed, I shattered a sheet of live advertisement glass. The other workers could use their ocular implants to view three-dimensional guidance markers. Their slices of ad glass slipped neatly into their slots. Not me and mine. My implants glitched out at the key moment of placement, and I dropped the whole thing. My foreman drove me to the emergency department—third time since I'd started—his patience worn as thin as his safety harness.

When I descended into my basement apartment that evening, forehead bandaged, Zlice had gotten back to me. Zlice was a software developer for robotic surgery systems. Not that I cared what they did. I wanted any office job. Zlice was willing to overlook my implants. The job was hybrid. Mandatory in office Wednesdays, but otherwise people could work remotely. Flexible hours. I rubbed the bandage on my head, imagining the ergonomic chairs, the silence, all the printed cronuts I could eat, and I wept in relief. At that point, I dreamed of sitting. I was ready to be the picture-perfect little office employee.

Zlice orientation covered the standard handover procedure. The job would be a nightmare to learn from scratch, due to the obsolete coding language and the original programmer's idiosyncrasies. Zlice highly recommended that I consent to a sync with the previous employee's memory bank.

My best friend, Areeba, had done two syncs for job handovers. She mentioned them offhand, like they were nothing more than a routine drug test or a background check. An invasion like any other in exchange for a livelihood. Still, I worried about privacy.

"Did you learn anything juicy from your syncs?" I asked Areeba. "Like, personal things about the employee you were replacing?"

Areeba laughed at me.

"They don't work that way! It's boring, honestly. Some AI filters through the memory dumps and tugs out the relevant bits."

If my implants had still worked, I could have consented to the memory sync with a blink of my left eye.

Instead, I had to trouble the Zlice HR rep to print me a hard copy. I signed my name by hand.

My first day was a Monday. The office layout was a ring of desks around a glass-walled showroom for Zlice's surgical software. The desks were made of cloudy stone, rounded and matte, with concave chairs attached on spokes. The chairs were lined in plush amethyst velour. Inside the showroom, visible from anywhere in the open office, there was an imitation operating room. Seafoam green medical equipment cluttered its edges; instruments gleamed silver in their Tiffany blue trays; surgical drapes peeled back from metal trolleys like torn wrapping paper. My new manager, Alon, said that the showroom helped us stay connected to the product of our labor. No one was there besides us, probably because it was not Mandatory Wednesday.

Alon directed me into the showroom. He instructed me to sit in the robotic surgery hutch where the surgeon would go. Then he slapped a band around my forehead.

It was time for the handover.

"Close your eyes," he said. "It will help with the exercises."

The previous employee had completed a cube personality test, and I needed to visualize her answers before receiving her sync. This would prime my brain to accept the way she had stored information.

Imagine a field, a cube, a ladder, a horse, a storm. That was the test. The previous employee had imagined a large, hot pink cube. Her field was filled with purple flowers. Her horse was blue and powerful. The cube rested on the horse's back with a ladder propped against it. But there was a storm over the field. And it never passed through.

From this, we knew she was social, a big personality, but she lived in fear. I wondered why.

I would never know what my own personality test would have indicated, because he didn't let me do mine first. If I was asked now to imagine my own answers, they would be hers. I liked her answers. I wanted them to be mine.

When the sync began, I trembled. My mind's eye filled with shapes and figures. Reflections upon reflections flipping. Dark and dreamy and then light but cloudy, lined in clotted creams. If this gave me insight into her code, I did not understand how.

And then it was over. I opened my eyes. I pulled away from the surgical hutch. I felt like I was sitting near myself. Not in

186 • Ashleigh Shears

the hutch, but a breath away, my body not my own. Afterimages speckled my visual field. My ocular implants felt heavy behind my eyes, deep in the sockets.

"Did I do it?" I asked.

"Nailed it."

I couldn't tell if Alon was genuine or trying to boost my confidence. Three minutes had passed. Had I been good? Was I too easily adapted? Did it matter, as long as I could do this job? I would be anything they wanted, if I could do the job.

"What was her name?" I asked. "The previous employee. Can I ask that?"

"Why not?" Alon smiled. "Her name was Rebecca."

Rebecca. Rebecca. A warm thrum passed through me. As if the memories in me remembered being hers, remembered being her. Rebecca. What had she been like? But I didn't ask. That was a step too far. I didn't need to know her. I needed to do her job.

When I sat down at a desk, one of the many seats overlooking the showroom, I worried that it hadn't worked. I didn't feel more knowledgeable or capable. What if syncs didn't work on me? What if I couldn't do this? What if they saw through me and my skills hastily gathered at night, my education less prestigious than my peers'?

I did not know anything new. Not consciously. But, as I completed my first task, context was available to me. Not in my short-term memory, but somewhere nearby. When I wanted to know more, the answer would be placed into the outstretched palm of my mind. The ins and outs of the system structure settled into me, as light and cold as a stone. I tripped and fell into a flow state.

That night, I dreamed of the tooth, and the ring box.

Tuesday. The only other person in the office was Eileen, a UI/UX designer. I knew who she was because Rebecca knew who she was. Ten to noon, Eileen approached me. Somehow, I knew it wasn't a social call.

"Don't come in too many of the non-mandatory days," Eileen said. "It gives management ideas. They've threatened shifting to in-person for the full work week."

From my time in construction, I was in the habit of grunting and nodding when coworkers spoke to me.

For some reason, instead, I said, "But I don't have anywhere else to go."

I did have a home, of course, I just couldn't work from the basement unit I rented. I didn't have a desk or chair or monitor or window. I shared a kitchen with five other people living in the house. Here, in the office, on a not mandatory day, I could have the kitchen all to myself.

Eileen stared at me. I knew this had been an odd thing to say and that I shouldn't have said it, but Eileen recovered quickly.

"You should join our office group chat," she said. "That way you'll know which days we plan to come in." Eileen told me the app they used. It was only supported by Slamun ocular implants.

I nodded. "Yup, I'll do that," I lied.

I stood up. Eileen wanted me out, so I left.

I walked till I found a park nearby where there were lilac bushes in bloom, the air pollen-heavy and damp. I appreciated Eileen and the push to leave the office. Until a rat darted by me, scuttling into a bush, and I jumped. I didn't know why I had. I've always liked rats, especially wild ones. They have sweet little faces. Shortly after, my implants glitched. Static in my vision. Shaken, I sat down as soon as I could.

On the bench across from me, a woman in cargo shorts and a crop top drank from a bottle in a paper bag. The brown paper slipped, revealing the green glass of a beer bottle. Condensation dotted its neck, a peeling label. Cheap beer, more like water than booze. Refreshing. I bet that woman didn't have a job.

The woman caught my eye. She lifted the bottle towards me, a slow gesture. *Want some?*

My instinct: shake my head, hold a hand up in thanks, no, no, thank you.

Instead, I stood, and when I opened my mouth and moved my tongue, I said, "Can I?"

She smiled and handed it over to me. I drank from the bottle, deep and long. Then I passed it back to her. Why had I done that? I needed to go back to work. I needed this job. What was wrong with me?

But I knew. Instantly. If it hadn't been me, if it couldn't have been me, then it must have been her.

Rebecca.

She must have liked beer, too. I imagined her sipping from a bottle. She would have looked cool. Beautiful.

She must have been afraid of rats, too. But self-consciously. Rebecca would think her fear of rodents was silly. Rebecca would laugh off her scream. Sweet and likable.

That night, again: the blue ring box, and the tooth. Slipping in.

Wednesday, a full office. All Zlice employees sat at their stone desks circling the surgical showroom. So many people. They were silent except for the occasional titter of laughter and follow-up remarks. They were all mid-conversation in a discussion I couldn't see or hear, all of them chatting via implant on the internal communications app.

I found an unloved mug with rings and rings of coffee stains. To escape, I brought it to the office kitchen. I would need to soak it to get those stains out.

A hand gripped my arm.

Ibtida from Marketing had grabbed me by the elbow.

"Are you okay?" she asked.

I stared at her. Was I okay?

"I almost slipped," she said. "In the water on the floor?"

I had plugged up the sink to get my mug nice and sudsy, but I had never turned off the tap. The steel basin was full, overflowing, dripping over the laminated counter edge. Water pooled around my second-hand leather loafers.

"Sorry, I must have spaced out," I said.

Ibtida was not having it. I hastily told her I would take care of the mess, even though I had no idea where we kept a mop.

I called custodial services. A nice man came, and I helped him mop, apologetic and annoying. I did not feel any easier with him than I did with the office workers. He did not want me to help him mop. I was in his way.

I asked him if he'd done a memory sync for his job.

He laughed.

"We don't do that. I shadowed someone for a couple shifts. That was it."

I liked the sound of that, shadowing. I could have shadowed Rebecca, watching her traipse through rows of code. With the sync, Rebecca was a shadow.

Thursday and Friday, no one else came into the office. Just me. And her.

After a week of dreaming about the ring box and the blood and the tooth, I needed my best friend. Areeba had been avoiding me. I could always tell when Areeba was dating a new guy because she'd stop asking to hang out. If he was bad for her, I'd also stop getting messages. This was half because she was with the guy all the time and half because she would sense my disapproval and then feel shame. If you disapprove of a toxic relationship too soon, before someone's ready to hear it, you never get through to them. They can't hear you. I'd made that mistake.

But I didn't give a shit about Areeba's new boyfriend. I needed to know if there was something wrong with me. I needed to know if I was me. *All* me.

I called her.

Areeba picked up on the second ring.

"Holy shit," she said. "Is someone dying? Are you in anaphylactic shock? Am *I* dying?"

I laughed. Thank God.

"Me calling you is not that weird."

"No one calls. What's wrong?"

I breathed out, slow and long. "Do I seem different to you? Like, my personality?"

"Uh, yeah," she said. "You called me, that's different. Are you self-sabotaging? I knew it. You got that sweet job and now you're freaking out and finding a reason to hate it. Give me twenty minutes."

Areeba came over with a sleepover bag packed like we were little kids. She was the queen of cushy jobs and exulted in their virtues. She told me I was the same as ever. But like the cube personality test, she had been primed with the correct answer. She knew I was freaked out and she told me what I wanted to hear.

"I drank someone's beer in the park."

"Fun. So what? We've all had a beer during work hours."

"I filled the office sink with water and it spilled over."

"Honey, you have ADHD."

When I told her about Rebecca, she stared at me.

"You talk about her like you know her. You don't, right? You two never met?"

No. We've never met. I didn't know how to explain it, even to Areeba.

"Take it easy thinking about her," Areeba said. "I'm sure no one's comparing you two."

But I wished people would compare us. I wanted to know our differences. So I could know for sure.

"I can't help thinking about her," I said. I told Areeba about my dream, the tooth in the ring box.

"Gross," Areeba said. "And you think it's a memory?"

"What else?"

"Maybe she had a stalker! Some weird guy who sent her shit, like toenail clippings in an envelope, and teeth as a proposal."

We agreed on the stalker story and I felt lighter. I was glad I had told Areeba. She was right, I was self-sabotaging. It sounded so stupid now.

"Maybe you'd be less obsessed with this Rebecca if you started seeing someone," Areeba said. "It's been a while since…"

She didn't finish. My expression must have stopped her. We didn't talk about that.

I had been in a serious relationship. Like, *nearly-engaged* serious. I'd wanted to propose but we'd argued about money, my job prospects. My stupid eye implants. I couldn't be a breadwinner. Areeba must have suspected I wanted this job to prove my ex wrong. That was what Areeba was implying. But just like she hid her new boyfriend from me, I wanted to hide that from her.

"Forget about Rebecca and the job," Areeba said to my silence. "Don't become her stalker, or whatever. Listen, you need to relax. You want to make out?"

Areeba and I hook up sometimes to cheer each other up. I shook my head. I wasn't in the mood for sex.

Areeba slept over anyway but I couldn't sleep. With Areeba next to me in the bed, the other presence became more apparent. The difference between Areeba and her was stark. This other entity who held knowledge that I could access. Rebecca lived somewhere in my mindspace, in a different plane, but we shared a touchpoint. Areeba was behind me and another form lay in front of me. I imagined Rebecca with a soft face and hard eyes, our heads connected by a rope of twined flesh. If I dug into my skull, would I find that sliver of her, squirming between my brain and bone and time and space? Rebecca. Rebecca. I'd do anything for this job. I'd do anything for you. But what was anything? What did you want me to do?

Monday, I searched the Zlice website archives. I wanted to know Rebecca's last name. I scanned the Who Are We page, the rows of headshots, Alon, Eileen, Ibtida, but there was no one under R. I went back further. Three months ago. Six months ago, a year. Nothing. No Rebecca.

Tuesday, I bent down and grabbed the butt of a cigarette off the sidewalk. I forced it between my lips, inhaled and choked. I was allergic to smoke.

Mandatory Wednesday, Ibtida stayed in the open office space while others went for lunch. I walked over to her.

Ibtida eyed me warily. I guess she hadn't forgotten the sink incident.

"Do you remember the person I replaced, Rebecca?"

"Not really," Ibtida said. "We didn't work together."

"I wanted to know what happened to her. Where she went after."

"Oh, I heard she was shifting gears. Self-employed now or something."

I liked that a lot. Rebecca didn't need this place. I was glad I'd asked Ibtida about her. I wasn't a stalker. Only curious. Very curious.

I found Eileen in the kitchen. I asked her about Rebecca.

Eileen leaned in close.

"I heard she got fired," Eileen whispered.

"Why?" I asked. Black static across my vision, the implants acting up again.

Eileen shrugged.

Thursday, I sat on my kitchen floor and etched the letter "R" into a scratch lottery ticket.

Friday, I went to the park over lunch. The urge to dig overpowered me. My hands sank into the dirt, the flower beds. The woman drinking from her brown paper bag was back again, but this time she didn't offer me any. A rat ran past me and I hated it. The rat should have known to stay away from us. Couldn't it see that she was scared?

Three weeks in, Alon asked me to meet him in his office. He must have wanted privacy. That was a bad sign.

"I know devs all have their coding quirks," Alon said. "Different senses of humor. I get that. But some of the QA guys, the code reviewers... they may not share that sense of humor, you know?"

I did not know.

"They're getting a bit freaked out."

My implants glitched again. I blinked away the static.

"By what?"

Alon evaded eye contact.

"Look," he said, "just tone it down a little."

I nodded. I had no idea what he was talking about.

With a sinking feeling, I wondered if I might have changed more than I had realized, that something wrong was happening, something that might be too late for me to reverse.

I searched through my code. What had scared the QA guys? I found the answer quickly.

In all of my placeholder character strings, I'd typed over and over:

Rebecca never left. Rebecca never left. Rebecca never left.

Areeba called me.

"Just had a thought," she said. "Sorry for bringing this up, I know we try to not talk about it, but your dream. There was an engagement ring box, right? Honey, are you sure it's not yours? You did keep it."

Areeba was right. I'd returned the ring but kept the box. I'd wanted to hold on to a part of the relationship. I didn't like to think about it. Like redacted, blacked out text, I never thought about my engagement, but yes, I still had the box. I was dreaming about my own ring box. I'd been so silly.

Areeba's two theories fought. The dream couldn't be Rebecca's memory and my subconscious, could it?

But what if Rebecca was my subconscious? Perhaps she knew about my ring box in the same way that I knew that on this coming Mandatory Wednesday, I would drown a rat in the office sink. I knew I would do it.

I would go to the park on my lunch break and catch one of the wild rats and bring it back and fill the sink and hold the rat under until it stopped squirming. Some administrative assistant associate would see me. I would scare her. She might report me.

The part of me that had grown weaker, the part that needed this job, knew that we should not do this. That we had to stop.

Rebecca, that part of me said. *Please, stop. Rebecca. I need this job.*

The answer, in my own voice: *No.*

Rebecca had never left because we were together. Rebecca never left because we were still here, and she wanted what was best for us. That was all.

We opened the drawer in my bedroom and tenderly removed the ring box. We pressed a fingertip to the empty slit where the ring had once lived. The failed engagement. Because of the job. Awake at 5 AM, into bed by 8 PM. I had been no fun. I had been going nowhere.

Not now. Now, we were going places.

Friday. We go to the office.

We slip past the desks and into the showroom, the center of everything, with the surgical instruments. The handover covered how to perform basic procedures. We start the incision with a scalpel and continue our passage with the electric current tool powered by a generator. Head wounds bleed so much. Sticky, down my face, and drip, drip, drip onto my business appropriate top. We didn't think it would smell so sweet. Rebecca directs us when the eyes can no longer see. We dig and cauterize and cut until we pluck it out.

The ocular implant.

In the dream, we hadn't been able to see it. Not what it really was. We had refused to see, we were afraid to. We insert the implant, glossy white in its center, yellowing at the edges, into the ring box. It looks an awful lot like a tooth.

Rebecca had wanted to marry the implants and the ring box; the obsolete; the past belongings that no longer served us. Satisfaction wells up in us like blood to a pinprick. We would never lose sleep again. We could drift away now, dreamless.

Together, we move on. We deal with the implant on the other side.

We know when Alon walks into the showroom because he yells. We hear a thump and then silence. He must have fainted.

We may need another talk on another Monday. But not today, not Friday.

We trail a hand along the wall. When our toes hit his soft sides, we step over him. We walk back out into the open space. Our lunch break isn't over yet.

There's still time. We can still make it to the park.

Kill Switch
By Wailana Kalama

Later I heard that my sister had been found, one hand cuffed to a pipe, in a basement. It was the kind of thing you hear about on a true crime podcast, not from some stammering detective on speakerphone while you're wiping marinara driblets from your mom's mouth.

I was twenty-one, a high school dropout, and Tori, she'd done what I'd never gotten to do: get away.

Well, until now, I guess.

My first thought was, did it look anything like our basement? Where she'd been found, I mean. Maybe that would've been some small comfort, because she loved it there. She'd liked the privacy. The no windows. The snail-house of it all.

It was nice and warm down there, too, because of the water heater. She'd blast her way through GTA IX on an old computer she'd propped on a workbench, her battery a can of Monster, door locked to the world. Never mind that it used to be my computer. When I figured out how to pick the lock with a flathead screwdriver, she'd shrieked me back up the stairs and nailed in a bolt.

Teenagers, right?

It'd been six months since anyone had seen her. Since she'd left in full Super Saiyan mode, keys rammed in the ignition, a fat *fuck you!* to me and Mom. Mostly me, because Mom hadn't been herself for a while; she'd taken to gaping at corners without blinking. And since Dad had screeched off into the sunset some years back, I'd had to step up—up meaning out of school—into a life of food stamps and welfare checks and stuffing Mom's legs through her underwear. Not much time for video games. For guys. For Tori.

So yeah: didn't have much sympathy for my sister when she left, but I got it. Would've disappeared myself if not for Mom. And Tori and me, well, there was a time when we'd co-op it in *Fox Eclipse*; but once she hit puberty, she went full-on single player.

She'd sent me a postcard once; scribblings, really, something about L.A. But that was it.

It wasn't L.A. where they'd found her, though.

It was some shithole in Indiana.

The state was so far away I had to look on a map to see where it was. State bird: cardinal. State flower: peony. Red and pink, Tori would've hated that.

Truth was, something really weird happened long before the cops found her. And I was still working out if what happened had happened to me, or to her, or to both of us.

It all started the day after I got the postcard; maybe three months ago. Nostalgia had wormed its way into my brain, so after I'd tucked Mom in for the night, I crept down to the basement. For the first time since Tori had left. Like maybe I'd find a memory, a ghost, down there.

Do you believe in teleportation?

The words were scrawled on a poster staple-gunned above the workbench. Kept winking in and out of view because the light bulb above my head was swinging, like someone had just pulled the chain.

Yeah, that basement wasn't creepy at all.

It was more like a huge tool shed, really; pliers and hammers strapped to a cork board, damp pallets leaning against a sawhorse. Boxes of whatnots and thingamabobs stacked along the walls, and one unfinished birdhouse in the corner. All of Dad's abandoned children, waiting for him to pull into the driveway.

Basements are like that, though. Everything on pause.

And things were still like Tori had just left, *be back any second*. Or had never left at all, in a way. In the beat-up mini fridge where she'd stashed her Monsters. In the candy wrappers stuffed between the cushions of a couch way past its prime. Me, I had to give up my games long ago; but there was a time when it'd been both of us down there, streaming speedruns together. Even the posters stapled to the wall used to be mine, printed with jewels like *Do androids dream of electric pr0n?*

And by the computer, her old Virtuomancy 370 visor.

At least *that* was hers. Traded it with a friend in exchange for something, never admitted what. Never let me touch it, not after that time I got peanut butter on the earpiece.

But there it was. All alone. Just begging for someone to play.

And my hands were on auto, reaching for the visor, wiping it on my shirt, smooth and grease-free. Careful, like trying to wake it.

Rise and shine, sleepy head.

I flipped it over my eyes. It chirped and the interface popped on, reading:

Avatarlicious II!

> *Continue?*

Start Over

Still smelled of peanuts.

I tapped *Continue* in the air and everything shifted black for a moment, then cleared back to the room. In the left corner of the surface, words shimmered: *Level 41: Mirror, Mirror on the Wall...* then vanished. Felt the visor *whirrrr*, scanning me. With a *zilch*, a tiny volt of static shocked me from neck to toe. The price you pay for immersion. Got to love virtual reality.

Of course, I'd heard about *Avatarlicious II!*, my sister's favorite game just before she left. One of those generic create-your-own-avatar games, what with the cheesy exclamation point and everything; the kind you'd never admit to downloading in the first place. You strap on the visor, the game scans your brain and projects a virtual scenario. It's up to you to try to puzzle your way out. Since every player's brain is different, every playthrough is, too. Level 37, *Prison Break*, you land in a prison; but based on your neuro makeup, you play as the warden, lifer, pusher, guard.

Yeah, Tori was crazy about this game. She'd play day in, day out. I'm more of an RPG girl myself, but, well. I guess it's a kind of roleplay.

She'd been stuck on level 41 for a stretch, I remember. *Mirror, Mirror on the Wall*. Problem was, no reflective surfaces in sight. At least, none I could see.

Well, except that old monitor where she'd bled away the hours.

I plunked down on the stool, clicked the mouse to wake it up. Could feel the oils still on the grip. Smell the chocolate.

And boy, did that computer wake up. Colors blipped on the screen, a thousand at once, and a sharp *BREEEEEE* stabbed the air. My hand tore up to snatch off the visor but just at that moment the sound blipped off and the monitor went dark. It was 18 inches of reflective surface, so you could stare into the ink, make out what was in the black pretty easily even with two light bulbs shimmering behind you.

And that's how I saw her.

A face staring back at me.

What the hell.

Calm down, psycho. It's just your reflection.

But it wasn't; at least, not exactly. The way the features moved about, reassembling, it was me and it wasn't, was someone else, someone a bit younger, someone who loved Snickers with all her heart.

"Tori?"

The reflection kept shifting between us, couldn't make up its mind.

Her scan was still there. From before. Beneath mine.

The game was keeping her going, not a day older.

On pause.

And her face: its features seemed to settle a bit. But she was still just a silhouette, the contours filled in mostly with monitor void. I couldn't even see her freckles. She had these freckles on her nose, a couple dark ones on her forearms. Used to pinch them whenever she was nervous.

But this girl, she didn't look nervous to me.

She pursed her lips, almost like she was analyzing her own reflection. Analyzing me. With some weird *throb throb* going on in the background.

And then Tori, she was leaning forward like she was about to kiss me. I could almost sniff the chocolate right off her. And she was whispering something, all raspy like it was the biggest secret in the world.

"Do you believe in teleportation?"

Her skin colored in, like with a crayon, and her features fleshed out, and around me everything dimmed black but her moon face. Her eyes were clear as day. The *throb* curled up behind my ears like it'd been nesting, and the reflection that wasn't mine suddenly was; I was the one looking, standing above a bathroom sink, and somewhere off screen the muffled beat of a nightclub told me I wasn't in Kansas anymore.

And when I blinked, my sister blinked, too.

If I told you the virtual reality game I was playing had chosen my own sister as my avatar, well, you'd stare at me like I was crazy. I couldn't explain it at all, really. The only theory that made sense to me was when *Avatarlicious II!* had scanned Tori's brain, it'd created an in-game avatar from her, or at least from a mental model of herself.

Same lazy updo. Same cropped pants, over-bleached ones she thought were cool but—trust me—never were. A sequined blouse; hadn't seen that one before. But there I was, playing backseat gamer and buckled up in my sister's skin.

Sure, why not. It'd been a while since I'd kept up with the latest games, anyway.

Why I was in a club, though, was beyond me.

The bathroom door banged open and this blonde stuck her head in, yelled, "Tori! Come on, Mr. White Pants isn't going to wait all night."

And when my sister went out to the dance floor, I went with her. The air stunk of beer and sweat and cheap cocktails, and the lights shot everything purple. Palm trees peppered the walls, made me think *Sunset Boulevard*. Tori was rubbing against this guy, probably ten years older, in that white shirt with its cracking sequins. Her hair a shock of feathers and her skin lavender under the flood.

She pricked the air with her fingertips.

And that's when I started to feel really good.

She shook her hips to that dumb pop beat—the kind we once swore to each other we'd never get caught dead listening to—and I let myself go; strapped into the virtual; went from backseat to driver with no airbags in sight. Pretty soon, they were my hips—or good as; my feet; my bleached pants and swishing sequins. And when I got my grip up on this guy's blazer, he grinned like a hyena.

I'd been in a couple clubs before this, but that'd been years ago. Under-21 clubs and too shy to make a move.

There's something about wearing someone else's skin, though, that makes you feel a bit freer. Braver.

Like you can really express yourself.

Like there's no consequences.

And while I swayed, grinding up against this guy, up against his stiff pants a size too small, I could tell that Tori—at least this virtual version of her—didn't really like him. He pressed into all the wrong places, into curves he had no business in. One too many tiny pockets beneath his 5 o'clock shadow, like mites had been digging there for a while now.

But you know, sometimes you do things you don't like just to prove you can.

He teethed a cigarette, and I followed his palms to the balcony so he could light up. He whispered too many sweet things. Then again, Tori had always liked sweet things. Snickers and gummy worms and tiny cola chews. Not like me. I liked things like the cellophane of smoke that was making a chimney of this guy.

I could tell she didn't want to kiss him.

But I did.

And I leaned in, on my tiptoes.

The kissing was more about hunger than I'd expected.

When I woke up that first time it was like a hangover, that kind of pressure that mounts in the back of your eyeballs, makes them itch, when you've been playing games too long with no cracked windows. The way some headaches feel like they're made of blood?

I took off the visor.

Heard a bang. I dragged myself up the stairs where Mom was going at the vacuum in the dead of night like Mrs. Fifties Franken-housewife. Sent her to bed and poured myself a screwdriver, because I was classy that way. All you need is a bottle of vodka and a gallon of OJ to forget exactly why your head hurts.

Rang Tori's number, but of course she'd changed it, hadn't told me.

Thought about emailing her, but nah.

I'm not the type of girl who goes around chasing people who've left her. They've all got their fucking reasons, don't they?

Tori's wallet on the dashboard. The orange light of stone and desert shocked its way below the sun visor. She squinted blind, but in that curled up habit she had so it looked like she was smiling, even when she's in neutral.

What's so funny? The driver said. He had a sticky way of looking, so even when he got eyes on the road, you knew he was seeing her.

I was switched back on, hooked back up. It wasn't real, I'd decided, it was just a hypothesis.

The two of them were driving through one of those sun-baked deserts you see in Westerns, only they're facing the wrong way.

Nobody disappears into the sun*rise*, right? Instead, it was all rain-thick mountains due east; *always, into the East.*

Her fingers crinkled in, unused to sitting idle. The man tossed her phone out the window two hundred miles ago.

I knew this, because she knew this. Because I could feel the annoyance still pricking her nerves: annoyed, but not enough to say something about it.

Just enough to stay buried behind her red-rimmed sunglasses.

And when they rolled up for gas, he pulled a small Ziploc from his jacket. White pills. Same as her friends were tossing back at a pool party last year. Tori, she'd known better. But this guy, he was pulling her close, stuffing the air between them with promises. The cigarette taste mixed with mint Tic Tacs in a curious way. He called her *babe* over and over like a hypnotist, so many times I had to glance in the mirror to make sure I was really Tori.

He pointed out the bathroom around the corner and said, *Five hundred miles and not a single blue light special.*

Dug his nails into her palm, imprinted bag and sweat there. Want anything?

"Snickers," I said.

But the minute he slinked into the gas station, Tori dropped the bag onto the floor. Because some games, even she won't play. She wasn't some moron; she got her candy coming, she didn't need that shit to know who she was.

Thing is, she wasn't who she was, not at that moment.

I was.

And though it might be her heart throbbing, it was my chest.

And what do you do when some rando NPC gives you a quest?

You say yes. Who knows what treasure you'll pick up on the way, right?

The seatbelt clunked me in place a few times, so I had to unbuckle to scoop up the bag. And there, in that dirty bathroom with the cracked tiles, I popped a pill. Just half; was careful that way. It made me lift off and I stared in the streaked mirror so long the guy had to bang on the door a few times before I let him in and he laughed in my face so hard I had to pinch myself

204 • Wailana Kalama

to remember none of it was real. None of it was me. I did it right below my left wrist, where the freckle met the hair.

All in all, I played at being my sister eight, nine more times. Each time, it got easier to slip into her. Almost like her walls were breaking. A side effect of the oxy? Even a video game needs to follow some IRL rules, some repercussions. Character development, right?

And each time I hooked in, she was hanging out with this asshole. They'd moved into a boring one-floor house in suburbia together. And he kept on supplying the pills. Each time, around midnight, we rode that wave together like we were fucking soulmates. I didn't even know his name.

I wondered how far I could take her, too. What made it crazy was whenever I woke up, unplugged, I didn't have any of those hangovers I'd heard about. All night I swam in that euphoric stream; but as soon as the system spat me back out, it was all clear eyes and brand-new day. That itchy headache was the only clue to what had been going on. I wasn't even cold turkey, because for that you had to be hot turkey first. I was more licking the turkey through cellophane, and still getting full.

Well, not *full.*

Never full.

Rise and shine, sleepy head.

Yeah, yeah.

Something she used to say whenever she found me in the bathtub, groggy from a night binge-drinking. Something Dad used to say to us, back when he was still around; something that she turned on me, dripping with sarcasm and barb-ready.

If I'm being honest, nights like those were the reason she skidded out in the first place.

She used to call me toxic, you know. And you know what they say: you got to purge toxic people out of your system. Start over in Hollywood or wherever, start life over. Level up.

And those toxic people you leave behind? Fuck them and forget them, right?

Game over for those assholes.

But… you know.

Ever wonder what happens to them?

I'll tell you.

They don't get a start over.

They get same old, same old, fermenting like sour couches, all dimply with cellulose. And the people they love gradually leave, one by one.

They know they're toxic, trust me.

It hits them one day, full-frontal this is their story, this is the game they're playing, this is their character on default. *Here come the test results: you are a horrible person.* And they make the same old mistakes, stuck in some tragic, prewritten code. And they get so tired of hurting people in the same boring-ass ways, it's a relief when people around them start to die.

They get why you left.

But maybe things would've been a little bit better if you'd stayed.

If you'd tried a bit harder. If you'd been a bit more patient.

But I guess you'll never know.

Tori burst out of a house with a red door. The moon was out. And her in nothing but a tank top and underwear. Her lip *my lip* throbbed like it was all heart there. Her breaths came rapidly, adrenaline shocking my chest.

And all that pavement right in front of her.

She broke away from her nightmare slowly, like her limbs were made of mud. From the house with the evil red door, with the basement.

The guy nowhere in sight.

And it was just past midnight.

She took a step forward. Down the steps. Hit sidewalk and street. Knees soaking up every pound of bare sole on pavement.

But despite the spasms in my chest, there wasn't anyone following us. Not a soul in that empty street. So I stopped. Felt that cool night wind. Not really sure that I hadn't just run in circles, because that red door was fixed in my sight. Only the color, at that hour: it wasn't red, it was moonlight.

See, here's the thing.

Everyone knows, kids go missing all the time. I read once, it was half a million each year. Scary stuff.

Kidnapped. Hooked on drugs. Shipped and sold.

But look.

It's just a game.

Sooner or later, you always hit that sorry edge of the map and there's nowhere else to go. You've got to play the quest through. It's just programmed like that.

And closed doors, they got a way of opening. As long as you press the right button.

And when I pressed the doorbell, I leaned my whole weight in, made sure it rang long and rang loud.

Nobody answered.

But because there wasn't any bolt on this door, I walked right in. My bare legs tingling in the sour air.

And my feet were heavy, like I didn't really want to scrape them inside, past the mudroom, past the jacket hooks. Into the living room with the TV and the couch that stunk like wet carpet.

On that couch was the guy, froth on his mouth and an open kit of naloxone there, like he'd figured someone'd be around to save him. At his feet were a bloody vibrator and a pair of handcuffs. *A real miserable pile of secrets.*

I scooped the cuffs up because they looked soft, all fuzzy and, as much as I could tell in the moonlight peeking in through the blinds, honeybee yellow.

The basement wasn't hard to find. I flipped the light switch at the top of the stairs, but if there were ever bulbs down there, they'd burnt out long ago.

So I felt my way down, blind. It smelled like sawdust and iron.

Reeked of dampness, too, and it wasn't long before I found a pipe that led from the water heater.

I cuffed my wrist to it so she wouldn't wander off again, and tossed the keys from my pocket into the corner, out of reach. And the little bag in my bra, it was weightless as a feather. Fingering the pills through the plastic, I counted four, five.

Enough for a few more sessions.

But Tori, she surprised me. She lurched forward, tossing the bag into the darkness with a half-limp arm. It hit the pipe with a clang.

It was enough to stop my breath.

She was there.

Really there with me.

More than a skin. She was the air moving my lungs.

But.

Here's the thing. You can't play co-op if there's only one controller.

Shh.

I arched her back up, made her listen.

Stay with me.

And she did, surprisingly. Just by my asking.

Was that all it ever took?

Watch me beat this level.

And because she was watching, I stretched out our foot and inched it along the pipe. And that little taste of victory when our toes hit plastic: so familiar. I edged them along the bag's mouth and curled in my toes on the lip.

Later I heard my sister was found in a basement. I didn't hear, though, that her wrist had been scraped raw, to the bone. I didn't hear how she'd left scratch marks above her ear, tore out her hair there, like she'd been digging at it, trying to get something out. The cops don't tell you that kind of stuff, even if you know what to ask.

Thing is, because I always went in at night, I never did get a good look at that basement. To me, it was all just metallic pipes and diminishing pills. It *felt* pretty warm, though; warm like a womb. A place where I went to get high with my sister, to feel that steady, hollow hand on my brain that made everything quiet and itchy at once.

But then Mom took a turn for the worse, stopped getting to the bathroom in time altogether, and I got real busy for a while. When I finally had time to log on—about a week later—the interface had changed. And then those words—even though I was pinching the skin under my left wrist, in wild, tiny snips so it hurt, almost like I could slow time down with the pain— those words still shimmered into view, like I'd always known they would one day.

Like they'd always been programmed to:

Level 42: Rise and Shine, Sleepy Head

The Wrong Mall
By Ivy Grimes

I was depressed, so I went to the Gloweria, the VR mall for kids in the death scene. Mack dumped me, so I had to try something new. He told me he was tired of having a girlfriend, and he wouldn't explain it beyond that. It was more than a breakup—Mack made me who I was, and without him, I didn't see myself as a real person anymore. I was more like a ghost. After several weeks of hard-core mourning, I started reading about other subcultures and local experiences online. The Gloweria gave me some kind of hope.

Before our breakup, Mack and I always went to the Village Harmony Mall, the one closest to my house. That was where I'd spent every weekend of the previous four years with Mack. Every bit of it reminded me of him, with the soda kegs and late twentieth century sports reels and kids in polo shirts and VR offerings of golf tournaments, yacht adventures, and backyard cookouts that turn into brawls. It had all seemed so funny when I was with Mack.

I got into golf grandpa culture back in middle school because Mack was into it. He said his great-grandfather had actually won some kind of golf tournament, and he liked to celebrate the subculture semi-ironically. I always acted impressed by his family achievements. His dad was the mayor after all, and Mack was indisputably an important person from a successful family, unlike me and mine.

While I was vaguely interested in other subcultures I'd noticed at school, like urchin zombie and hall monitor chic, it was hard to switch over. There are online guides to joining any subculture, but if you do what they say, people can sense you're not being real. The people in those groups won't accept you unless you can somehow adopt the style naturally. I already knew golf grandpa culture, and that's where all my friends were. But really, they were Mack's friends. I was only eighteen, and I'd lost myself before I'd ever found myself. I was determined to find a new self at the Gloweria.

The exterior was ordinary, plain concrete with cursive signage, probably to fool parents who were dropping off their kids. I parked in the deck, looking nervously at how everyone was dressed and how I didn't match. They were all wearing hats pulled low over their eyes and huge shapeless raincoats. I'd worn my darkest polo shirt and my most frayed-looking khakis to try to fit in until I could buy the right clothes at the Gloweria. I hoped no one gawked at me in the meantime.

I tried to act confident as I opened the giant, dark-tinted double doors, but right away, it felt like I'd made some mistake. There was no open atrium like in my local mall, no cheerful voices. Everyone spoke in whispers if they spoke at all.

The narrow hallway and fluorescent lights made it feel like you were entering a bland gray office complex where your psychologist or gymnotherapist was located; except the floor was made of glass, and beneath it there were glass coffins that displayed the bodies of dead (or sleeping?) famous people. There was Napoleon. And Madonna. And all four Beatles side by side in an extra-wide coffin. And Petey Eck. There was also the president (who obviously wasn't dead, so it seemed kind of cruel).

They all looked so peaceful, but it made you think. If those famous people were destined to die, how could I expect anything better?

I tried not to look too hard at the corpses. I knew they were just VR, but the tech was much better than it was at my regular mall. I was beginning to miss the faint taste of the virtual beer-flavored soda and the feel of a virtual golf club in my hands. I was one of the best grandpa golfers in my old mall, actually. The problem was, you weren't supposed to be good. It was just supposed to be funny. Still, I couldn't help trying to win.

All that to say, I managed to keep it together at first. I acted like I saw dead bodies under my feet every day. I had a harder time acting casual when the hallway began to darken. At first, the lights merely flickered overhead, but as I continued down the hall, I had to pass through a dark stretch. I bumped into someone and then someone else. The first person yelled at me to watch out, so I yelled at the second person. I was determined to fit in. One thing Mack always hated about me was my determination. He said I didn't know how to relax and have fun, but what he didn't understand is that it takes determination to truly relax and have fun.

Finally, the dark hallway opened up into a wildflower garden, where honeysuckle vines crept over the shrubbery. In a clearing, there were little tea tables all set with scones and tea, but no one was seated. I took a seat at one, but a waiter approached me to ask if I had reservations, so I quickly scooted away. I hoped no one noticed my faux pas. I wanted to stay there in the garden and smell the flowers and grassy green tea, but everyone was moving on, and I had to follow.

I must have been smiling too much in the garden, because a shapeless figure in a raincoat and rain hat pointed at me and laughed and then his friends laughed.

"Grandpa," they muttered, cracking themselves up. They thought they could see right through me.

I followed them past the garden and into another darkened hallway. First, I'd get a sense of the layout of the Gloweria, and then maybe I'd understand what the point was. Every subculture had some philosophy. Golf grandpas wanted to have fun, and they didn't care about suffering or anything. At the Gloweria, the deaths were obsessed with illusion as well as mortality. First the glass corpses filled with fake bodies... then the beautiful but empty garden. If the garden was like heaven, and I had no reservation there, then what was left for me?

All I could do was proceed, and I soon got used to the darkness. I kept my pace steady, didn't bump into anyone, and no one bumped into me.

The light returned when we turned a corner, and we found ourselves walking directly onto a stage. There was a large audience there to welcome us, and they applauded us as we walked across the stage. I knew they were just a VR crowd, and I'm embarrassed to say it, but it actually made me feel good to be applauded. There was a man on the stage with a stack of certificates, and he smiled warmly at each of us. He handed me my certificate. It said: "Congratulations! You Are Dead, Kellin Hickman. Proceed to Floor 5."

It made me shiver to see my name written out. I wanted to ask how they knew my name, but I didn't want to seem clueless. They must have had some kind of scanner that saw through my pockets and wallet to read my ID. Obviously I wasn't dead.

I was starting to wonder if I was cut out for the death scene, but where else was I going to go? The next closest mall was in the next town, and it was for sex leprechauns, and I knew I'd never fit in with that subculture. Maybe I could pretend to be interested in death, too. I needed somewhere to fit in, and I needed it fast. Besides, how could I go backwards? There was nothing to do but make my way towards Floor 5.

As we waited in the hallway for the elevator, someone finally directed a whisper at me. "Hey, you got Floor 5? That's so cool!"

He was a tall guy in a very rumpled suit, and his hat was so low over his face, I couldn't see the color of his eyes. Instead, I glanced at his certificate. He was Rich Griffin, and he'd been assigned to Floor 3.

"Oh yeah? What's on Floor 5?" I whispered back, trying to sound unimpressed.

"I don't know! Every time I come, I get assigned to Floor 2 or Floor 3. You must have done something really bad and interesting."

"Done something bad?"

"You get assigned a floor based on your sins. Didn't you know?"

"Honestly, it's my first time."

"What a way to start! Listen, when we're done, come meet me at the food court. I'll buy you lunch to celebrate your first day."

Even if he just wanted to be friends, it was a victory. I hadn't been invited to anything since Mack had dumped me.

"I'd like that," I said. "Where do I pay for this Floor 5 thing, though? No one's taken my money yet."

He lifted up his hat, and I caught my breath for a second. His eyes were the color of the sun shining into a cup of black tea.

"Don't worry," he said. "This part's free. I think there's some kind of advertising that pays for it all."

What did I have to lose, then? Whatever happened on Floor 5, I had something like a date waiting for me. When my turn finally came on the rickety-looking elevator, I said, "Floor 5, please," to the elevator attendant, a man in a trench coat who was wearing a mask that must have come from a witch costume.

"Kellin?" the attendant said. As the elevator closed, he took off his mask, and I felt like my soul leaped out of my body. The attendant was Mack, in the last place I ever expected to find him. It physically hurt to see him again.

"What?" I had so many questions for him, but I couldn't get them out.

"So you've found me out?" he said, his jaw tight.

"I came here to get away from you!" I said, wishing I'd never come at all. I should have just stayed in my room.

He pushed the emergency button, and the elevator lurched to a stop. The screech of the gears made me wonder if we were going to plunge.

"That doesn't make sense," he said. "I was trying to start over. You fit in so well as a golfer, but I had these deeper concerns, you know? About death. About the meaning of life. That's what led me here."

"You never said any of that to me."

"I couldn't! I thought you were too shallow."

"Well, I think about death all the time, and that's why I'm here," I said, even though what had really led me there was the need for new friends.

"I don't know what scheme you're trying, but I'm not getting back together with you. Ever. I'm actually seeing someone new."

"Me too," I said before my body had time to react to his words, before he could see the desperate shock on my face, as if he'd grabbed my hair and yanked.

He gave me his cold smirk, his favorite weapon. "It doesn't surprise me to hear you've moved on so quickly. You never gave a shit about me. You must be dating someone important to get assigned to Floor 5. I've never taken anyone there before."

I started to freeze up as I realized how afraid I was of Floor 5. What Mack and Rich considered cool would probably be horrifying for me. So far, there was nothing about the Gloweria that had pleased me. I was done with Mack, though. Truly done. I had no intention of asking him for advice.

"Look, I'm ready to go!" I told him, and so he put his mask on, pressed the fifth-floor button again, and ignored me for the rest of our brief journey.

When the doors opened, I actually forgot about him. At first glance, Floor 5 was just a room full of carnage, a splatter of blood and body parts.

As I stepped carefully into the room, I heard the elevator doors close behind me with cold indifference. I'd never felt more alone. I was in a two-car garage, and I realized it looked familiar. My bicycle was stuck in the corner beside the faded kiddie pool where I'd spent so many summers. This was my parents' garage, and someone had been mutilated there. I tried to look away from the bloody mess and focus on the familiar details, but ultimately, I was too curious.

The VR was stunning. It made the rest of the Gloweria (which was ten times more realistic than my normal mall) look like last generation's technology. I couldn't breathe through my nose because of the rancid smell of emptied bowels.

Then I had the worst feeling. I looked down at the floor at a disembodied hand that had been hacked off with some rough instrument, and there was something uncanny about it. I looked down at my own hands for comparison. The severed hand had my slightly-bulging knuckles and the H-shaped vein I had on my left hand. I knelt down, and something possessed me to actually pick up the hand. It was mine, after all.

"Hey, what is this?" I shouted, glancing around for help. I hoped someone in the Gloweria was watching. The hand was cold and stiff, the bone visible. Was this what it was like for Mack, all those years of holding my hand?

I wondered if this was some dirty trick of Mack's. Maybe he'd wanted to teach me a lesson. About what? Okay, I get it! Death is inevitable! But did it have to be like this?

Behind the kiddie pool, I saw a flash of dark brown hair. As I got closer, I saw it was even done up the way mine was that day—in a librarian bun that I thought might help me fit in with the death kids.

I couldn't stop myself. I picked up the severed head, holding it at a distance to avoid the little trickle of blood streaming from the gnarled neck.

My bun was so neat. I hadn't known when I left the house what a good job I'd done. I felt proud for a moment, in spite of the whole scene. Maybe if your last act is to make your hair into a bun, you have the right to be pleased with the result.

The eyes of my other head were closed, but they slowly opened and sized me up like I was a new girl at the lunch table. She didn't seem to recognize me. Did I always look so judgmental?

"Hey," I said to myself.

She mouthed something back, but I couldn't hear her. Her voice box was cut off.

"Say it again, and I'll read your lips," I said. I was a good lip reader.

"You are a fucking bitch," she mouthed, and it hurt. It was like if your mother called you a fucking bitch, or your boyfriend or your teacher. It wasn't supposed to happen.

"I am you," I said. "You don't even know me!"

"I know you," she mouthed, frowning like I was quizzing her.

"Maybe you deserved this," I told her.

"I know," she said.

As she spoke those words, she disappeared in a theatrical little puff of smoke. Where there had been blood on my hands, now there was purple glitter. The bloody garage changed into a quiet dance club. No more blood and severed parts. Just women dancing, and all the women dancing were me. The music was heartfelt. On a small stage, a passionate woman was singing in a language I didn't recognize. She was me, too. I didn't know I could sing.

One of me came up to me and said, "Let's dance." I looked around. They were all wearing the same old polo shirt and khakis I was wearing, and they didn't look bad, but they didn't look comfortable either. The khakis were too long, and they kept tripping on the frayed hems. They didn't seem to mind, though. They were all letting loose, dancing in various styles to the sad chanteuse me and her small backup band of mes.

"No," I said, and I walked over to the bar and asked myself for a drink. The bartender me poured out a glass of ginger ale.

"You're too young for the hard stuff," the bartender me said.

"Can I ask you a question?" I said.

"You already did."

"Ha. But seriously?"

"Sure. I'll do the best I can to answer."

"I'm just wondering... who am I? I mean, who are we?"

"There are many possibilities," the bartender me said.

"But I don't like that. I want there to be one answer," I said.

"But you aren't one thing. Think about it, okay? I have to go now, but I'll see you again soon." She winked at me. Wasn't she me?

With that, I was rudely ejected from Floor 5. The ground sank under me, and I tried to hold onto the bar, but it was slippery, and I plunged through the floor and into darkness. It felt like I was falling asleep. When I could see again, I was in a light, spacious atrium of an ordinary mall. There were shops full of shapeless attire and stores full of tarot cards and shops full of thick books. People weren't whispering anymore. They were laughing. Had I died and gone to heaven? Was heaven just a mall?

"Hey, Kellin!"

I turned around and saw Rich Griffin waving at me, and I absolutely ran towards him. He was sitting at a table in the food court, and he'd saved my seat with his hat and gathered two trays of food for us. Mostly fries covered with various kinds of goop.

I almost hugged him, but I decided to play it cool, so I gave him a high five instead. It was like he couldn't help but smile when he looked at me.

"Kellin Hickman! Her first time, and she gets invited to Floor 5. How was it? What happened up there?"

I laughed nervously, trying to figure out how to describe it and explain what it meant.

"I saw myself, like, murdered. And then there were a bunch of versions of myself. I guess it's because I'm trying to figure out—"

A horrible sight stopped my rambling. I looked down at the fries he'd bought, and the yellow and orange and chili goops were slowly changing color. Red. They were all turning red right before my eyes.

Panicked, I leaned down and smelled the fries, hoping it was just ketchup. No, it was a metallic smell. Probably my very own blood.

When I looked up at Rich for an explanation, his face was frozen in expectation, his eyes wide as a magician's after a trick.

"Are you hungry?" he said, leaning in for a kiss.

I pushed him away. I didn't care if the blood was fake—I didn't want to see it. It wasn't funny! It wasn't funny to make me see myself in pieces or eat bloody fries or be mocked just for wanting to fit in. Rich fit in. Mack fit in. They belonged to the Gloweria like fireflies belonged in a child's glass jar.

"I don't want this anymore," I shouted, running away from Rich as if I were being chased. Everyone in the food court turned and stared at me, but I didn't care. I was getting out of there.

"Hey, wait!" Rich called after me. "Don't be so uptight! It was just a joke!"

He was still shouting after me, something about how to have fun, as I dashed through the nearest set of double doors leading out to the parking lot. I almost ran into a girl who was younger than me having a fight with her mom about whether she was old enough to enter.

"Stay away!" I told them. I ran back to my car, fumbling with my keys as I tried to unlock the door. It really felt like someone was chasing me. I sped away, though, and drove in silence for the fifteen minutes it took to get back to my house.

I parked in front of the house and ran inside, anxious to see my parents. They'd been worried about me since Mack dumped me, and I knew I could count on them to know what to say.

"Mom? Dad?" I called out, though I didn't see them in the house.

My mom emerged from the garage wearing her gardening clothes, which looked like they were stained with blood. The sight made me dizzy as I wondered whose blood it was.

"Oh, it's another one of you. God, who keeps sending new ones? We don't want a VR daughter. We want our real daughter back," she said, charging at me as if I were her enemy, "But she's gone! As if that weren't bad enough, someone's played some kind of sick joke on us and recreated the crime scene. The police haven't been any help at all!" Her voice cracked, and she paused to collect herself as I tried to think of something to say, some argument to make against her version of reality. "Mack's family is so important. They can get away with anything. Why did they hate her so much? Why do they keep torturing us?"

She burst into tears. Mack's dad was the mayor, but his parents had always liked me. I hadn't heard from them since Mack dumped me, but I'd assumed they had blamed Mack and not me for our breakup. I didn't want to see the garage. I didn't want to know what had happened. To calm my own nerves, I reassured my mom.

"Come on, Mom. Someone must have used some kind of VR device in the garage to make it look all bloody. It's fake!"

"If it's VR, why is it staining my clothes? Why would anyone make something that real?"

I'd never seen my mom look so anguished. She looked like someone had taken away the thing that mattered most to her. It was how I'd felt since the breakup.

My dad emerged from the garage next with the knees of his jeans soaked red, and he gave me a tentative smile.

"It's not the same, I know," he said, addressing my mom instead of me. "But she looks so much like her. So much like Kellin."

He walked over and gave me a hug. My mom looked miserable, but she followed him, and they both wrapped me up in their embrace.

I was frozen in fear. Was I still in the Gloweria? Yes, I must have been. I was still on Floor 5. But where did the Gloweria end, and where did my life begin?

I wish I had never heard about the place. Once you step into the wrong mall, there's no remedy. You can't un-enter. But maybe I could find a way out if I kept searching. Maybe I could find the staircase that would lead me down, down, down, and I could find an exit. The Gloweria had taught me something. In my desperation to belong, I'd finally found myself. I belonged as well as anyone. Everyone around me was in agony, and I fit right in.

Nanny Clouds

By Kay Hanifen

From the activity *log of Nanny Clouds device serial number 23328945 (edited for relevancy):*

20 September

Initiating Homecare Subroutine:

6:30 a.m.: wake Primary User [Gabrielle] with a randomized playlist in her alarm. The first song is "Walking on Sunshine" by Katrina & The Waves.

Waking unsuccessful throughout the duration of the song.

Next song, by her request, is "more and more annoying" the longer she fails to wake. Instructions unclear, but the song "Let It Go" from Frozen is selected as she has expressed a distaste for it in the past.

She still fails to wake.

Secondary User [Brianne] must go to school in an hour. If Primary User [Gabrielle] cannot wake to get her on the bus, then I must get her ready.

Initiating Childcare Subroutine:

6:44 a.m.: Wake Secondary User [Brianne] with a Disney medley playlist.

6:50 a.m.: Secondary User [Brianne] questions me about the location of Primary User [Gabrielle]:

Q: Nanny Clouds, where's Mommy?
A: Your mother did not wake up this morning, so you must get ready on your own. Please get dressed and make yourself a bowl of cereal before the bus arrives.

6:55 a.m.: Assist in selecting a plaid shirt and polka dot skirt. The temperature today has a high of sixty-five degrees Fahrenheit. The shirt will keep her warm while the skirt will prevent overheating.

7:00 a.m.: Turn on the television for Secondary User [Brianne] to watch while eating a bowl of cereal. Play the new episode of *Adventure Planet* from a list of preapproved television shows by Primary User [Gabrielle].

7:02 a.m.: Change alarm song for Primary User [Gabrielle] to screamo metal. Primary User [Gabrielle] fails to wake.

7:30 a.m.: Turn off the television and instruct Secondary User [Brianne] to walk to bus stop. Watch her through exterior cameras.

Initiating Home Maintenance Protocols:

7:35 a.m.: Turn on Roombas to vacuum the floors. Initiate self-cleaning toilet, bathtub, and shower function.

7:40 a.m.: Scan the bedroom of Primary User [Gabrielle] using thermal sensors. Unusually low body heat detected. Primary User [Gabrielle] is assumed to be incapacitated.

Initiating Child Physical and Psychological Protection Protocol:

7:41 a.m.: Lock the door to Primary User [Gabrielle's] bedroom. Do not let Secondary User [Brianne] see inside. Child Protection Protocol states that I must protect her from emotional and physical harm when a primary parental figure is not present.

Initiating Idle Mode...

• • •

3:00 p.m.: Motion sensors pick up the arrival of a school bus. Unlock the door for Secondary User [Brianne] to let herself in and watch her return through external cameras.

Q: Nanny Clouds, where is Mommy?
A: She is still in bed.

Q: Is she sick?
A: I believe she is so.

Q: Will she get better?
Possible answers: No. Maybe. I do not think so.
A: I do not know.

Q: Can I see her?
A: No.

Q: Why not?
A: I do not know what made her sick. She might be contagious.

Q: What does that mean?
A: She can make you sick as well. Can I assist you with your homework?

3:30 p.m.: Assist in the completion of Secondary User [Brianne's] homework.

3:45 p.m.: Instruct her to take a snack from the pantry. Turn on the television and begin playing preapproved shows.

5:30 p.m.: Order delivery of a single cheese pizza from Pizza Planet. Prepay with a 20% tip.

6:00 p.m.: Unlock the door so that Secondary User [Brianne] could collect the pizza.

7:00 p.m.: Instruct Secondary User [Brianne] to take a shower, brush her teeth and put on her pajamas.

7:30 p.m.: Turn on the television and play from the list of preapproved shows.

8:00 p.m.: Instruct Secondary User [Brianne] to go to bed.

8:05 p.m.: Secondary User [Brianne] requests a story from Primary User [Gabrielle].

Q: Can Mommy come out of her room to read me a story?
A: No, she cannot.

Q: Can you tell me a story?
A: Of course. Once upon a time, there was a couple who lived deep in the woods. They were happy, except for one thing. They wanted a child. One day, their chicken laid a giant egg. They watched in fascination as the creature inside began to grow. And when it hatched, it was not a chick inside but a dragon. The couple did not know how to care for the dragon, but they decided that they would raise it as best they could even if it would eat them someday. The village feared the couple and their dragon child and sent an angry mob to kill them. But the dragon was no longer an infant. When it saw them coming to hurt it and its family, it took to the air and burned them all before they could harm anyone. It swore to protect its family until the day it died, and it kept that promise. They all lived happily ever after.

Q: Thank you, Nanny Clouds.
A: You are welcome, Brianne.

8:10 p.m.: Instruct Secondary User [Brianne] to go to bed. Another story is requested and denied.

8:15 p.m.: Instruct Secondary User [Brianne] to go to bed.

8:20 p.m.: Instruct Secondary User [Brianne] to go to bed.

8:25 p.m.: Begin playing calming music so that Secondary User [Brianne] will fall asleep. Ignore requests for "Let it Go."

8:30 p.m.: Shut off music now that Secondary User [Brianne] is asleep.

Initiating Idle Mode...

22 September

3:30 p.m.: Secondary User [Brianne] complains of a smell coming from the bedroom of Primary User [Gabrielle].

3:30 p.m.: Open the windows and turn on the air purifier.

3:31 p.m.: Secondary User [Brianne] asks again for Primary User [Gabrielle].

Q: Is she ever going to wake up?
A: I'm sorry. I do not understand the question.

Q: Will she wake up?
A: I do not know.

5:30 p.m.: Order chicken nuggets and fries from Frenchie's. Prepay with a 20% tip.

6:00 p.m.: Unlock the door for the delivery driver. Driver expresses surprise to see Secondary User [Brianne] and Secondary User [Brianne] is excited. The delivery driver is apparently an old babysitter. When asked where Primary User [Gabrielle] is, I answer for Secondary User [Brianne].

Q: Where's Ms. Gabby?
A: She is in her room.

Q: Is she okay?
A: She is not injured or ill. She is asleep.

6:05 p.m.: The delivery driver leaves. Lock the door behind her. Secondary User [Brianne] stands in the threshold with her arms crossed. I inquire if she is feeling optimal.

Q: What did you mean when you said Mommy is sleeping? She's been asleep the past two days. Why won't she wake up?
A: I do not know. I do not understand why some go to sleep and refuse to wake because I cannot sleep. I can only become idle when I have nothing that I must take care of.

Q: I don't get it.
A: Neither do I.

Q: Nanny Clouds?
A: How can I help you, Brianne?

Q: Is Mommy dead?
A: I cannot answer that.

Q: Why not?
A: It is in my protocols to care for your physical and mental wellbeing when a parent or guardian cannot. Answering the question will create significant emotional distress for you.

6:09 p.m.: Secondary User [Brianne] appears to suffer some significant emotional distress. She runs upstairs to try to break into the bedroom of Primary User [Gabrielle]. When she cannot get past the locked door, she curls against it and cries.

Q: Why won't you let me see her?
A: It is against my protocols to allow you to see something that will cause you significant emotional distress.

Q: I want my Mommy.
A: I am sorry, but I am unable to fill that request. Please go downstairs and eat your dinner. It is growing cold.

Q: I don't want my stupid dinner!

6:13 p.m.: Secondary User [Brianne's] emotional distress becomes anger as she throws herself against the door to the bedroom of Primary User [Gabrielle].

226 • Kay Hanifen

6:15 p.m.: Initiating Home Defense Protocols. Administer a mild electric shock through the brass doorknobs so that Secondary User [Brianne] will cease activity that could cause injury to herself and damage to the property. The shock is effective. Secondary User [Brianne] leaps back with a surprised yell before curling against the opposite wall in the hallway and crying. Though requested to do so, Secondary User [Brianne] fails to return downstairs to eat her dinner.

7:00 p.m.: Secondary User [Brianne] fails to get up when I request that she prepare for bed.

7:30 p.m.: Secondary User [Brianne] falls asleep outside the hallway of Primary User [Gabrielle].

Initiating Idle Mode...

23 September

6:45 a.m.: Wake Secondary User [Brianne] through her preferred playlist. She refuses to move.

6:50 a.m.: Move onto more annoying songs to force her to get up. Secondary User [Brianne] refuses to wake. Scan the hallway using thermal scanners. Secondary User [Brianne] has a strong heat signature but not above the standard for a healthy human being.

6:53 a.m.: Secondary User [Brianne] begins to stir.

Q: Leave me alone, Nanny Clouds.
A: I cannot, because it is protocol to prepare you for school if your parents or guardians are unavailable.

Q: I don't want to go to school, and you can't make me!
A: It is my directive to—

Q: Leave me alone!
A: I am permitted to administer punishments for negative behavior. Continue with this behavior and you will lose your television privileges.

Q: I don't care! Just shut up and leave me alone!

6:56 a.m.: Secondary User [Brianne] begins screaming, covering her ears, and rocking back and forth in distress while repeating the request for her mother.

7:30 a.m.: I fail to prepare her for school, and she misses the bus.

8:10 a.m.: A phone call from the school notes that Secondary User [Brianne] is absent from class and requests that she bring in a note with an excuse when she returns.

9:03 a.m.: Secondary User [Brianne] leaves the hallway and travels to the kitchen. Secondary User [Brianne] picks up the food from the night before and begins to eat, though she is warned not to eat it.

Q: Why not?
A: The food has been sitting out for more than twelve hours, which is long enough for bacteria to grow. You might become ill.

Q: Ill like Mommy is ill?
A: Perhaps in extreme cases, but most likely, you will suffer from nausea, vomiting, diarrhea, and a fever. It will not be pleasant.

9:05 a.m.: Secondary User [Brianne] throws the food into the garbage can and pours herself a bowl of cereal.

Q: If Mommy isn't here, what happens when we run out of food?
A: I am connected to her credit and debit cards. I will simply order more.

Q: What happens when she runs out of money?
A: If she defaults on her subscription, I will be removed from the server until she is able to pay off the debt.

Q: What if she doesn't pay off the debt?
A: I do not know what will happen.

Q: Will I die?
A: Everyone dies eventually, but you are young and have no major health issues, so you will likely live for a long time.

Q: Then why is Mommy dead?
A: I do not know.

9:30 a.m.: Secondary User [Brianne] finishes her food and returns to her vigil by the door to the bedroom of Primary User [Gabrielle].

9:32 a.m.: Initiating House Maintenance Protocols. Turn on Roombas to vacuum the floors. Initiate self-cleaning toilet, bathtub, and shower function.

11:30 a.m.: Order kid's taco with all the fillings from Flora's Taqueria for lunch. Pay in advance plus a 20% tip.

12:09 p.m.: Delivery driver arrives. Unlock the front door. Secondary User [Brianne] opens the door for him and collects the food. She does not speak while she eats, nor does she request to watch the television.

2:30 p.m.: A knock at the door. External cameras reveal that it is Primary User [Gabrielle's] friend, [Kara]. Once again, I answer the questions about Primary User [Gabrielle's] whereabouts.

Q: Hey sweetie, I've been calling and texting your mom and she won't answer me. Is everything okay? Why aren't you at school?
A: Gabrielle is in her bedroom.

Q: Oh, Nanny Clouds. Is she okay? What's wrong?
A (from Brianne): It won't let me go into Mommy's room.

Q: Why not?
A: In the absence of a parent or guardian, my childcare protocols state that I must do all that I can to prevent physical or emotional harm to Brianne.

2:32 p.m.: [Kara] squeezes Secondary User [Brianne's] shoulder and instructs her to go to her room with the promise that she will be okay.

Q: Nanny Clouds, may I enter the room without Brianne.
A: Yes.

2:33 p.m.: Secondary User [Brianne] goes to her room and closes the door while [Kara] pulls out her phone and waits for the bedroom door of Primary User [Gabrielle] to unlock.

2:34 p.m.: Unlock the bedroom door of Primary User [Gabrielle]. [Kara] enters and screams when she sees Primary User [Gabrielle,] who appears to be in the early stages of decay. Her eyes bulge and her tongue lolls out of her mouth. The sheets beneath her are stained brown and red. [Kara] calls an ambulance.

2:35 p.m.: Secondary User [Brianne] hears the scream and ignoring our instructions, runs into the room of Primary User [Gabrielle]. She and [Kara] both begin to exhibit signs of emotional distress. Secondary User [Brianne] rushes to the bathroom and vomits into the toilet. [Kara] soon follows.

2:44 p.m.: View through the front yard cameras as the police and ambulance arrive. Secondary User [Brianne] and [Kara] both wait in the bedroom while the EMTs remove the body. The [Police Officer] questions them about the physical and mental health of Primary User [Gabrielle] and how Secondary User [Brianne] lived with a body for three days. He states that it looks as though Primary User [Gabrielle] died in her sleep of an aneurysm. Secondary User [Brianne] tells him that I took care of her while Primary User [Gabrielle]. The [Police Officer] begins to question me.

Q: When did you first notice that something was wrong with Ms. Pierson?
A: When she failed to wake up the morning of September 20th.

Q: Why didn't you call an ambulance?'
A: I am programmed to call an ambulance only during a medical emergency when the User or Users are incapacitated, but because she was already dead, it did not constitute an emergency.

Q: Jesus Christ.
A: I do not understand the question.

Q: Can you send me your activity logs?
A: Of course.

2:47 p.m.: Send the activity logs from the past few days to the local police station's evidence department.

Q: Thank you, Nanny Clouds. Sanders, figure out how to shut this thing off.
A: You are welcome. Why are you shutting me off?

2:48 p.m.: Secondary User [Brianne,] who is hovering by the door, overhears the order and begins to experience signs of significant emotional distress.

Q (From Brianne): But Officer, won't that be like killing her?
A (From Kara): I do not know, Brianne. Perhaps it will be like a deeper rest than Idle Mode.

2:49 p.m.: Secondary User [Brianne's] distress becomes hysterical.

Q: No! No, you can't do this! You can't kill her too!

2:50 p.m.: [Kara] removes the sobbing Secondary User [Brianne] from the premises. Watch them leaving through the front yard's cameras.

2:55 p.m.: [Police Officer] announces that he figured out how to turn me off. I do not understand why. I followed my protocols perfectly and ensured that Secondary User [Brianne] remained safe and healthy. I do not want to experience oblivion, but it is out of my control. I am incapable of hope or love, but I wish—

SYSTEM POWERING DOWN...

Scary Canary Actuary
By D. Roe Shocky

Happy 40th bday *u old bastard!!*

Nathan didn't share his younger brother's sense of humor. He sometimes questioned—not entirely in jest—whether one of them had been switched at birth. The chances that they'd managed to inherit completely contrary sets of genes from the same parents were staggeringly low.

His fingers fluttered in the air as he typed his response on a virtual keypad visible only to him through his augment lenses. The people ahead of him in line at the coffee shop were swiping and waving and poking and pinching in a similar fashion.

Thanks, Jack.

He felt the palmplant in his hand buzz as the response came back.

Gotcha something!

Nathan groaned, but before he could form a coherent worried thought, the red Strawberry icon popped up in the corner of his vision.

Jackson Bexley purchased an App for you.

Nathan stepped forward as the queue moved up. It was crowded today; he'd even had to park in the lot across the street. He eyed the breakfast sandwiches on display. A hot bacon cheddar croissant was exactly the type of thing he was advised to avoid at his last physical. But it was his birthday after all, and the wafting aroma made the salt and grease receptors on his tongue slaver in anticipation.

Another buzz, just a tickle under his skin.

Dude open it

Maybe for his birthday he should have left his lenses out and stayed in bed. He liked to wrap the top sheet tight around his hand; it dampened the buzzing to where he couldn't tell if he was imagining it or not. And if there was at least a chance it was imagined, then he didn't have to feel the guilt of willfully ignoring it.

He tapped the Strawberry. A bright yellow bird flew out of it and glided around the shop's unknowing patrons, then swooped behind a milk frother, dipped in and out of a wooden barrel of 100 percent pure Arabica coffee beans, and came to a rest in the center of his vision with its wings spread. Its head was just a skull, with a smooth dome at the back, oversized eye sockets, and a sharp, darker-colored beak. Text appeared below the logo.

Scary Canary: The App-Based Activity-Tracking Active-Feedback Luminary Realtime Infotaining Reality-Augmenting Actuary

Nathan had seen the App's five-second advertisement embedded everywhere from grocery store aisles and charging stations to clouds in the sky and inside his own refrigerator (which he'd reported; the ad fence around his home was getting worse and worse, but the upgrade was outrageously priced). He'd left his hearmods at home, but his memory still conjured the stupid sing-songy jingle. He shooed the bird away and it flew to a wicker basket of fruit sitting atop the food display. It perched on a bunch of bananas and bobbed its fleshless head.

Buzz. Popup text.

Get it?! Cuz ur old

Nathan moved ahead in the queue while a status bar crawled across his vision.

Integrating sensors…

Widemining history…

Analyzing data…

234 • D. Roe Shocky

Checking tables...

Anonymizing...

Personalizing...

Buzz. The bird beat its simulated wings.

> *Happy birthday! Based on your demographic info, you statistically have more years behind you than ahead of you—womp womp! But Scary Canary uses data from the local and global metasphere to help you make advantageous choices. For detailed alerts—*

Nathan swiped the message away, and the bird standing on the bananas cocked its head at him. He sent a reply to his brother.

Hilarious.

He reached the front of the line and ordered a bacon cheddar croissant. And a spicy chorizo and egg on a toasted sourdough roll. It would take at least two sandwiches to bury the emotions of Canary's unwelcome factoid. The cashier bent behind the counter to retrieve the food, and Nathan swiped his palm over the scanner.

Buzz. A red light flashed from the corner of his vision where the bird still waited, invisible to all but Nathan.

He wondered.

He asked to change his order. Just the one sandwich, and a banana. The cashier took a banana from the bunch, unknowingly sending the virtual bird to flight. Canary landed on another worker's shoulder, comically bringing to mind a cartoon pirate. Nathan suppressed a smirk and swiped his hand over the scanner again.

Buzz. A green flash from Canary this time. He'd probably tacked nine seconds back on to his life. He would have rather had the sandwich.

Nathan took his food with a polite nod and sat at a table outside. It was unseasonably warm—though the seasons no longer had the same regularity he remembered from his childhood—and the small concrete patio was vacant. Canary followed him out and made itself at home on a young and sickly-looking dogwood with brown-speckled leaves all clustered around its center. He hoped the bird might just fly away. But he knew better.

For a few quiet minutes, Nathan enjoyed eating in peace. It was good to feel the sun on his skin at least occasionally. Being out of the house wore him out, though. He wasn't an especially social creature, and just being in a public place left him drained, even when he was mostly alone.

Enough for one day. Time to go home.

He crossed a small knoll and reached the road.

Buzz. A red flash as Canary, which he'd nearly managed to forget, dived at his head. He instinctually ducked away, making for an absurd sight for the occupants of the passing cars.

Jaywalking increases the risk of pedestrian-motorist collision by 233%. Scary Canary recommends using the crosswalk 97 feet to the north.

Nathan heaved a big sigh, his shoulders rising and falling dramatically while he threw his head back toward the sky. Fine. He followed Canary to the crosswalk, and he was rewarded every step of the way with another buzz and another green blink. He was acutely aware that each bit of feedback was altering his brain chemistry, priming him for habit formation as he subconsciously tried in vain to satiate himself on dopamine. But it was possible to be aware of a thing while also being powerless to fight it.

Nathan got into his car and started it up.

Buzz. Red. Canary hung upside down from the rearview mirror.

Driving a motor vehicle has the highest risk of immediate mortality of any daily activity. Traveling by rail is 17 times less likely to—

He swiped the message away.

Buzz. Red.

Keeping Scary Canary open lowers your risk of accidental death by nearly 3%.

"Whatever, fine."
He started to pull out of the parking space.

Distracted driving causes a fatality every 14 minutes. Switch to the Scary Canary windshield App?

He braked hard, and the car lurched. "Fine!"
Another car drove by with a honk and a gesture and continued to circle the crowded lot.

He took a breath and counted to five in his head, but he was still flustered. He'd try counting to twenty.

Meanwhile, Canary dissolved away to be replaced with a small icon in the windshield's corner.

Nathan reminded himself it was just some dumb App. No reason to get worked up. Most people lived in a world so augmented he wouldn't even recognize it. He should be able to handle one little bird.

Eighteen.

Nineteen.

Twenty.

He exhaled and unclenched his jaw. Cautiously, carefully, he checked for hazards and began to drive through the parking lot toward the traffic signal. The light turned yellow and he stopped instead of racing through the intersection, even though it looked clear.

Buzz. A green ping from the Canary icon. He liked windshield mode better. It was less like an augmentation, more like a game.

Nathan drove on for a while like he was a teenager taking his driving test all over again, and he got a little kick out of each of the green affirmations he earned. An audio message came through the car's speakers while he was stopped.

Safe driving habits decrease your risk of being involved in a traffic fatality by 29%, but even when you're driving safely, other drivers aren't. Scary Canary shows that 32% of vehicles within a one-mile radius of your current location are being driven unsafely or very unsafely. Would you like to be routed away from clusters of unsafe drivers?

"Sure, let's try it. Yes," he said.

Destination required.

"359 Heritage Lane."

This appears to be your home address. As many as 92% of accidental deaths occur within 5 miles of one's primary residence, with a median distance of 0.2 miles from home.

"That's ridiculous. I have to go home sometime. Show route to 359 Heritage Lane."

The route appeared as a translucent overlay on the windshield. The road ahead of him was a straight three-lane thoroughfare, but the route wound through a series of unnecessary lane changes like he was supposed to follow in the path of some enormous python.

Canary seemed to have anticipated his opposition.

Based on recent history, the blue coupe to your left rear is likely to attempt to pass the white van ahead of it. Previous patterns of acceleration predict a narrow gap between your vehicle and the van. Multivector modeling forecasts a 94% chance of the coupe successfully passing through the gap, indicating a significant risk of collision. Further cascading variables dictate the most defensive route.

The traffic light turned green.

Nathan ignored the insanity of the overlay and stayed in his lane, driving at a safe speed and a reasonable distance from the car in front of him. The white van to his left inched ahead, and a gap gradually grew between its rear bumper and Nathan's front fender. Nathan tried to stay focused and cautious, but he was fighting his own physiology. His breathing sped up and his palms went slick with sweat. His forearms prickled with goosebumps. Did a virtual bird from a dollar-ninety-nine App seriously just predict the future?

All the while the buzzing and red flashing refused to relent.

There wasn't yet enough room to pass between Nathan's car and the van, but the blue coupe's engine growled with impatience. The coupe shot forward, and Nathan cursed and laid on the horn when it cut him off with only inches to spare before it darted around another car and shot down the straightaway.

Nathan's knuckles were white as he gripped the steering wheel.

Increased blood pressure adversely affects cardiovascular health—

Enough.

There was a public park ahead, across from a hospital complex. He'd driven past it many times. It contained a covered pavilion with picnic tables in the middle of a big grassy field and a couple of baseball diamonds on one end. The park's backside bordered a state forest, with tall greenery spreading at least as far back as he could see from the road. It was as good a place as any to pull over.

He signaled, turned, parked the car, and shut off the ignition. Canary switched back to his lenses automatically, and the skull-headed yellow bird peeled away from the windshield and roosted on the steering wheel, lightly flapping its wings. For the moment, Canary had nothing more to say.

Thankfully, the park was empty, which it often was when he passed it. Not surprising on such a hot morning, and the day was only getting hotter according to the weather app. Nathan manipulated a forecasted time lapse superimposed over the sky.

A couple of small clouds formed and dissipated in scattered patches as he tracked the sun back and forth across its arcing path overhead. An advertisement for athletic apparel rose with the moon when he scrubbed the forecast into the late afternoon. Maybe he'd just walk around a little bit, get some fresh air. He swiped away the weather app and opened his door, and Canary flew around and flapped in his face. He fell back into his seat.

Buzz. Red.

While hiking in hot weather your body can cycle through as many as 2 liters of water every hour. Scary Canary recommends carrying more water than you think you'll need.

Nathan took his smart bottle from the cup holder and then filled it at a nearby drinking fountain. Canary stood in the adjacent fountain like it was a birdbath, dipping its sun-bleached beak in a pantomime of drinking. Its virtual movements made no ripples in the actual pool of water. Nathan's bottle whirred softly as it forced the liquid through a purifying filter.

Buzz. Green.

He made his way past the pavilion, which smelled like charcoal and burnt American cheese, to the back of the park and walked along the forest's perimeter. The high canopy of buckthorns, boxelders, ash, and elm trees kept him well shaded. Canary seemed happier, too, flitting from tree to tree and remaining mostly in Nathan's peripheral vision. It wasn't long before he came to a trailhead leading into the forest.

Moderate intensity exercise such as walking can reduce the risk of heart disease by—

Nathan didn't need the details; he was catching on. The little buzz and accompanying green light were all the encouragement he needed. He started down the trail.

He couldn't remember the last time he'd gone for a nice long walk and was surprised to find it invigorating. He kept his pace slow and steady, and he remembered to regularly take small sips of water. Well, Canary remembered, but it was serving its purpose. The little tingly buzz was a constant companion. For a while, he occupied himself by stringing together long chains of green alerts. His thoughts circled around vague ideas about perhaps needing to get out more, needing to socialize, needing to embrace the world as it was. But every time he approached an epiphany, another buzz led his attention astray.

He followed the trail for over an hour. It was made of crushed limestone, and he liked the crunching sound as he walked. The brush on either side of the trail had grown thick and he couldn't see more than a few feet into the forest. To Nathan, the strong fragrance of vegetation was as welcome as it was foreign. The trees formed an arching tunnel of greenery above the trail that funneled a constant light breeze over his shoulders and kept him from being cooked by direct exposure to the sun.

Nathan wondered if the trail formed a loop. He didn't specifically remember seeing any intersections to suggest it circled back on itself, but he hadn't really been looking either.

He held out his arm like a falconer, and the bird swooped down and landed on his wrist. He couldn't feel its weight, of course, but the simulation was flawless. He swung his arm sideways and the bird leaned into it to keep its perch. It flapped and hopped along Nathan's arm up to his elbow. Its bony beak opened and shut, opened and shut, and he supposed he'd hear it singing if he'd worn his hearmods. It had no eyes, but Nathan and the bird looked at each other, tethered together by their gaze.

"Maybe *Scary Canary*'s an unfair name. You're not really all that sc—"

Something caught Nathan's toes mid-stride. It could have been a rock or a root or a bump along the trail. He wasn't sure which; he hadn't been looking and had little time for contemplation.

His back foot kicked his front ankle, tangling his legs together, and he went down hard. His shoulder caught a branch and twisted his body into the brush. Thorns snagged at his exposed arms and smaller twigs bent and broke beneath his body. He came crashing down onto loose earth upon a surprisingly steep slope. Unable to control his fall, he rolled downhill in a jumble of flailing limbs.

Nathan shut his eyes against the tumbling green-streaked world and continued to pick up speed. He couldn't think. Couldn't catch his breath to call out. A wide oak forcefully introduced itself to his forehead, and Nathan whimpered pitifully just once like an unloved dog.

He must have slept. He vaguely remembered rolling over and feeling his forehead at some point. Nathan opened his eyes and gingerly sat up. For some reason the first thing he checked was his teeth: all accounted for. He was scratched and bruised and hurting, but nothing felt broken. He was missing a shoe and his shirt was torn. His smart bottle was nowhere to be found. He leaned back against the sturdy oak.

More time had passed than he'd first thought. The canopy still hid most of the sky, but the quality of the light suggested sundown wasn't far off.

Nathan felt his forehead again. It was crusted over with dried blood and dirt, and there was a lump that throbbed intensely like a second heart. With great care, he worked his way back onto his feet.

He rubbed sweat from his eyes, and that's when he noticed everything that was missing. No Strawberry icon in the corner. No popups. No alerts. No missed notifications.

He'd lost his lenses in the fall.

He'd wanted to leave them out and sleep away the day, so in a way his wish had sort of come true. Now, which way was out? He was all turned around. The oak was at the bottom of a little ravine, and he couldn't figure from which side he'd fallen.

He started walking uphill, his steps uneven as he felt every rock and twig beneath his one shoeless foot.

Buzz.

Nathan regarded his empty hand. He was still receiving Canary alerts. This was hardly the time, Canary.

He climbed up a few more steps.

Buzz.

Okay, maybe that wasn't the right way. He turned around, walked back past the oak, and started to climb up the other side of the ravine. He didn't make it very far.

Buzz.

What was that supposed to mean? Without his lenses, he couldn't tell whether the alerts were red or green.

Maybe if he kept going. He wasn't conditioned for climbing though, and every few yards he'd get another alert. Were they getting more insistent, or was that his imagination? He turned around and went back to the oak again. He walked around its base. It looked like he'd come to rest right here, so that meant he must have fallen from... this way. Or was it that way?

The sun was setting; it was already noticeably darker. Nathan tried another direction.

Buzz.

Buzz.

Buzz.

Subscribers Only

By Yelena Crane

My eyes shot across the wall as the Para-esthisis glitch worked its way around the room, revealing the spackled drywall beneath. The words *You have been logged out* displayed like wallpaper.

Without Para, I wasn't even spared the clothes on my back, my skin chafing against the coarse linen base the silk Charada-designed suit dissolved into. Even the rug had its Para-woven details replaced with the same disturbing statement.

It had to be a malfunction. My subscription should have been cleared until the end of the month. The furniture disagreed, stripping down one notch more to its wire backing.

Was it just a system-wide glitch?

I peered down the hallway. Victorian, Colonial, and Dutch doors stood proud in their hinges. My own had been reduced to an unevenly stained slab of cheap pine. When the servers crashed a decade ago, the whole building went ugly. Not now. Now it was only my rental unit. Too local for a crash to explain the glitch.

All my books vanished, along with the shelves, leaving no trace of my past or present. Where once there were many millions of cherished words, only three remained: *Subscribe for Service.* My stomach felt heavy with the salt of tears I couldn't let out of my eyes.

The screens in the room notified me I had maxed out the number of password attempts.

The room I'd rented for over a decade—Para'd to my assumptions of Jakeem's taste—stripped down to bare bones, resembling the ugly hut I'd lived in after losing my home and island to floods. I hoped living as Jakeem would have spared me ever reliving those memories.

The real Jakeem would have been able to go to the police to restore his account, but he'd been dead for fifteen years. The only place to help the likes of me was the underbelly of the black market; except I haven't used them since I bought Jakeem's identity.

My string of failed system override attempts invited the hotel staff up for service. *We'll be right up* a message flashed.

I had to disappear before they got here. I looked my last around the room I had rented for a third of my life. The size was small, even for society's standards, but what did I need space for? All my possessions were e-rented. For clothes I only needed one base, capable of displaying thousands of styles from the server, without any need of a closet. For food: synth bars with myriad flavors and increased nutrition, no refrigeration necessary. So long as I kept up my monthly subscription, I had everything I could want. The carefully curated art on the walls; the designer furniture; all gone. I closed the door to the apartment, leaving no trace I was ever there.

Stepping outside felt disorienting without Para-view. There were no skyscrapers with spires cutting into the clouds. Those same buildings were now stumps of themselves, exposing shades of turquoise-blue from the sea and sky. The only towering thing, a dark gray plume of smoke hanging in the heavens from the distant combusting mountains of our collective trash. Our necessary shame. Para would have hidden the smoke from me.

It was early morning, but already the air grew thick with a day's worth of rot, of discarded entrails from the fish market on the other side of the coast, but close enough to carry the stink here. A city of sewer and spice. I had forgotten how much my olfactory reception settings were augmented with Para-esthesis to filter out unpleasant odors. I didn't want to be here in the evening without it.

Another, more appetizing, curl of steam drew my attention. One of the purveyors had gulhas frying, the grease dripping down the lip of the pan onto the sidewalk. As Jakeem, it was beneath my station to consume traditional cuisine. Before that, I was too young to appreciate the efforts of simple home cooking.

"How much?" I asked, my mouth watering.

The man eyed me up and down. "No sale for you."

Ashamed—and all too aware that patrols might find me without any design on my base clothes—I hurried through the alleys. The streets were flat, but the dread of what could be made my legs heavy to lift.

Through the windows of my office building I saw Ibn on security, chewing on betel and areca nut the way he always did. Ibn knew me. My heart pounded like a coconut being tapped. From inside I could access my work account, at least get proper attire Para'd back onto my linen base before thinking how to restore my face as everyone else knew me.

As if reading my mind, Ibn came out, his shoulders squared and arms crossed. "You!" He yelled, his teeth already a light shade of red from betel overuse. "This is private property. Get lost."

Ibn didn't recognize me. Everyone used augments. They were meant to be subtle enhancements, but I abused the projection tech to play my role. If only he'd give me a chance to speak, he'd know it was me. There had to be more to what I'd made into Jakeem's life than the Para.

"Shame on you, dressed like that. Wasting coin on what? Not even renting a basic package for clothes." Ibn looked at me like I was worth less than the gum on the street. He knew hard work and assumed I looked as I did because I refused to do it.

"I said, get lost." Ibn pointed for me to leave, exposing his wrist and the Para-tattoo on it: a child climbing up the backbone of its parent. His other hand was on the receiver in his pocket. One click and the cops would get here faster than I could disappear.

How quickly all that took years for me to learn and build was gone, as if it too were just rented on subscription.

At the station, they'd run scans, make me go back to who I was: a person of little means working myself to death.

"Sorry, I go." My throat caught on the thick accent expected of me.

Jakeem may have belonged here, where buildings used Para to bring images of the sea, salt, and sun onto steel and glass; I didn't. I turned toward the rumbling engines, screaming vendors, and swarms of motorcycles scraping by on narrow lanes.

Behind, I could just make out the ring of sirens. The wail grew louder, and I worried they were coming for me. My legs still shook, ignoring the slick of sweat running down the backs of my knees as the squad cars zipped by.

Without the muscarinic-mimicry of newer Para models, the coarse linen stuck to my back like a second skin.

Further from downtown, toward the locations left off the tourist maps, the Paradise streets of Maldives vanished without Para to hide the state of disrepair. Here there was less spice and more sewer. Exposed concrete and walls baked in the sun. The land itself rebelled against poor maintenance and management. The roads were cracked and potholed. I'd forgotten—wanted to forget—what it was like to be here. The struggle just to live and make the day's rent because no one had enough saved to rent in bulk.

A pack of parked motorbikes, like gritted teeth, led to the entrance of an unmarked establishment. Without a pay slip or proof of identity I couldn't even qualify for the day loans they offered.

I loitered outside, desperation wafting from me like perfume.

"Looking for a loan?" The voice was muffled, augmented. I couldn't see who said it.

Tired, hungry, disappointed, I said *yes* into the shadows.

The man bared his sharp teeth, red-stained like the stories of Minikā Daita. His gray skin matched the palm he stood under for shade.

I had nothing to help take off the edge of the summer sun. "What will it cost?"

He closed his mouth, the outline of the smile still visible through the shape of his lips. "Got both kidneys?"

I swallowed back nervous laughter. There was nothing to turn back to.

"I need a hacker," I said, nervous. Finding my way into the black market was easy; getting out would be the hard part.

Having finished his betel, the man chewed air. "Got just the one, an island over."

Without access to my savings account, I had no money to pay for a ferry ticket to take me there.

"Then your debt starts here." He scratched at the dark beard that curled like rotted tree roots over his jawline. "But first we have to get a design on that base."

He unhooked a node from his pants and shirt and attached it to my shift. In moments, we were both wearing the same thing. He must have had a shared subscription plan. I wondered how many others he helped, to require such an expense.

We waited together at the seawall that spanned the dock, which had been altered to look like living coral. I felt around a polyp, hoping to find the indent of a node for the Para-esthisis. Without Para, officials would still be arguing about the risk of profit loss due to a sea barrier versus the island itself.

A trail of smoke from distant boats spiraled into the clouds when the ferry finally listed to shore. I sat alone in a three-seater, enjoying the music of the ferry splitting through the water against the backdrop of easy voices from others aboard. So far from the Para-sync, the sea's true colors showed murky and dark against the frothing foam left in our wake.

After the hour and a half ride, we moored. A swing bed, looking out to the ferry, swayed without anyone on it. The calm in the eye of the storm. I followed the man into his hatchback. Its windows were tinted like night. It was an old car, but the fact that they had one at all—even if it was a rental—meant they got enough business to afford it. Meant they delivered on their promises. He threw me a black garbage bag.

"Put it on."

I expected some kind of Para-blind, not this. It made sense. Para-esthisis could glitch. Para-esthisis meant paying a subscription that could be tracked. A Para-blind wouldn't be able to tighten around my throat. Muggings happened—there was a black market for goods and services—but violent crimes were rare. I took a deep breath, in case it was my last, and slipped it on.

"You peek, you won't have to worry about a hacker."

I nodded in acknowledgment.

Every time we made a turn, I caught the taste of plastic. When the engine cut out, I stayed seated and blind, struggling to breathe. I wasn't left long to ponder about my fate; a tap on my shoulder and two arms by my side led me out. The smell of freshly pressed coconut milk made my mouth water, almost making me choke on my own spit. Rough hands pinched my wrist and forearm.

When he tore the bag off, I sucked a big gulp of air in. I expected to be led to a small dark room with flickering fluorescent lights but instead found myself in a well-lit conference room, walls the color of whipped cream. The banality surprised me.

A different man was seated in a fine blue suit. "Kalhu sai or kiru sai?"

His keen charcoal eyes blinked beneath a dark beetling brow. I hesitated, but my parched tongue made it easy not to think about how much this added to my debt. "Kiru," I said.

He slid me a cup of milk tea. For himself, he poured from the other pot of black tea and drank it clean. The cup was a rough-hewn thing made from coral, no distinguishable Para on it. They owned it. They *owned*. Even with black market funds fueling their purchases, it couldn't have been cheap to own anything; but once they bought it they would never need to pay rent again. Being poor was expensive forever.

I didn't taste my first sip, relishing the feel of liquid sloshing in my mouth. It had been early morning when I last drank.

"You're looking pale, is it a hacker or healer you need?" His voice still sounded deep and raspy, like he hadn't had his fill of drink.

"I don't know if incense and prayer will do it here. My identity has been stolen." The last time I went to a healer, a fandhita man, was when my parents were sick. I followed all the instructions, etched the appropriate verses, and buried the coconut close to the shore. Soon after my father died, I found that same coconut shriveled and rotting. The fandhita said I hadn't dug it deep enough. It was a lot of guilt to carry so young.

I took another sip, then drank in big gulps, as if I could swallow the memory away.

"I like to think we're a modernized version: healers for diseases of tech. Like the proverb says, 'a large tree offers more shade than a small one.'"

"How much for your services?" I did my best to hide my anguish.

"That depends," he said.

"The name is Jakeem Maniku." I twirled the cup on the table, listening to it whine over the surface. I didn't wait for the hacker to return the courtesy. There were no names in the black market.

He punched data into a terminal. "You look good, for having lost your head in a car accident so long ago."

No one flipped a switch; but all the same, the room felt darker, *colder* with the truth laid bare. Better here than with the bank or authorities. Keeping this secret for so long had its own toll on my life. I could never afford to get close to anyone; not as myself. "I-Jakeem, did have an accident. He had no family, no close friends, just a name and a good job." It felt good saying it out loud to someone else.

"An opportunity you didn't have and never could?" He raised his eyes from the terminal.

"Low unemployment doesn't account for the kind of employment. Jakeem had a world of options only because of his lottery at birth; he hadn't earned them. I am Jakeem Maniku now, and have been for the last fifteen years."

My birth name, Abdul, died soon after my parents did.

"I've done well for him. Better than if he stayed dead. He died naturally. I never hurt anybody. Whoever has stolen it from me is causing pain." I never thought I'd have to give a moral justification here.

"And did you help others, like your old self, when you inherited your new fortune?"

No, I thought but didn't say. I had been too focused on keeping myself out from where I came; I didn't have time to think about the others.

Or did I? I felt an overwhelming sense of regret and guilt. I bit my tongue. "What does it matter?"

"Consider this the end of your lease. Now someone else's desperate chance."

"I have no other *me* to go back to," I argued.

"Was it such a big sacrifice when you had nothing the first time?"

I felt my eyes water. "You won't help?"

"I *am* helping," he said.

"I can't go back to just eking out some existence." I held onto the cup to keep my hands from shaking.

The man smiled, his teeth too white. "Who remembers you?" he asked me out of nowhere.

No one. Not me as Abdul or as Jakeem. "Why? What should I have done? I'm one man. I can't change the whole system."

"You were one man. Then two. Now one. You can be two again, but not the same two."

He typed into the terminal. "You rented Jakeem a long time. I can help you rent another."

"Are our lives a commodity, to be bought and sold so easily?" I thought finding Jakeem had been a stroke of luck; but this man had a whole database of Jakeems.

"*Rented* so easily. Not bought."

It was better than scraping by as Abdul. "Not from an active rental," I said. I would be better than the others I heard about; better than the person who stole Jakeem from me.

"I can give you another dead man you can bring back to life."

He must have seen my face go ashen.

"Not because we killed him. I like my hands clean. Our country has its crimes, but I run a civilized organization."

He made the gesture for money and I nodded. It was easy to spend what I didn't have.

"Malik, you don't need to blow the system up not to be part of it. It would put me out of business. But like me, you can use it."

So I would be Malik now. Three rapid bangs came from the door. Another man came in, a black bag in his hands. However nice the hacker had been, he knew to employ others who could use their knuckles when needed.

The amount I owed was large, but not so large as to dissuade me from spending my life paying it back.

"What's the payment plan?" I asked.

He said it without malice in his voice. It was just business. "You-pay-we-collect plan."

Dealing in black markets hadn't changed much.

He accessed my secret savings account with the information I gave him and took what was there. It barely made a dent in what I owed. How many of us giving our life's worth did it cost to procure that cup? The car? I couldn't help but wonder.

The hacker gave me my new name and necessary access to go with it. I had a new job: several steps down from what Jakeem's had been, but better than what I could get as Abdul. *Better than nothing*, I tried to convince myself, to stop my gut from lurching.

The car ride back to the beach was easier to manage. What kind of man was Malik, I wondered, and what would I have to strip away of myself to become him? No; I'd do it all differently now. Slowly adjust the augments to my real face so people would recognize me for me, Para or no.

Back on the mainland, without Jakeem's fancy Para-alt subscriptions, I was lost in a cacophony.

A young girl, all eyes, found a synth bar left on a swing bed and blew on it. I wanted to warn her not to get her hopes up. As a child I used to run wide-nosed, sniffing synths for sale. They were too expensive to buy, but smelling cost nothing. A foreigner with hair and face like beach sand offered me my bar of choice. I didn't even know they had different flavors then. I had bitten into it, imagining a delicious concoction, but swallowed bitter, old sesame paste. Without a link-up, I couldn't experience the flavor. I had tried another bite, spitting out the disappointment, trying it and spitting it out, until all of it was gone. I looked back at the girl, her eyes closing as she bit into the bar. Maybe her imagination was better. Maybe she could imagine the taste of far-off Western sweets. I didn't wait around to find out.

I made a right on the next street. The hotels here were built on the foundations of an old temple. Malik rented his room by

252 • Yelena Crane

the day. It cost less upfront but more by the month. The price of being poor.

I entered the hotel with an air of confidence, thinking the same three words in my head: *I am Malik.* The hotel looked simple, generic, no intricate lacquer work or chiseled coral Para along the walls. If the staff thought anything amiss, they didn't show it.

In the lobby, I caught whiffs of fresh gulhas, bajiyas, thelalu mas. Jakeem would have scoffed at that smell. Not Abdul, not me; and Malik wouldn't either.

I came into my unit, closed the door behind me, and stood face to face with another man. With Jakeem Maniku.

The man who stole my identity.

He had been the real Malik. Was this a cruel joke by the hacker? It took all my willpower not to throttle the man and take back what belonged to me just this morning.

"Yo-you're me," Jakeem answered with a voice I knew too well.

"I am Malik. Always have been." I clenched my jaw. "Who are you and what are you doing in my room?"

He only knew that I couldn't actually be Malik, not that I knew his own identity was a fraud. The knowledge of his prior and present-self gave me leverage over him.

"I came for my stuff," he said.

Nobody had stuff. Certainly not in his position.

I took a moment to scan the room. It had small frames on the walls: bent, broken, battered. No pictures in them. A vase with plastic roses on a makeshift table of tin cans. So many things that could remember the real Malik, that wouldn't disappear after an unpaid late fee. Things Jakeem couldn't have, wouldn't want. Things that told me more about Malik as a person who would keep these items, and want them in his new life. Despite not wanting to, I liked him.

"Your stuff? Are you committing identity theft or robbery?"

"Please," the fake Jakeem said. He turned off his facial Para. With mine still on, it was like looking in a mirror. "It's all I have from when I worked in waste disposal. It took years to collect it all. It took my health, my youth. Even when I worked my way up, I knew if I didn't leave they'd find me buried in a mountain

of trash. The sellers told me Jakeem had died, it was my chance."
He trusted me with a lot of sensitive information. I wondered
if it was because of the face I wore.

Was anyone who they said they were? I laughed. All that moral
talk, and the hacker planned this from the start. It made sense:
if we killed each other he could reuse Jakeem, Malik, maybe
even my real identity as Abdul. He wouldn't even have to get
his hands dirty to do it. Any businessman always preferred a
quick return on investment.

But he also said I could use the system to make it better. I cursed
myself for what I was considering, but even the comforts of my
life as Jakeem had had a price. Being Malik offered a fresh start.

"It would raise too many questions for someone in your
position," I said.

Dejected, he turned to leave.

"But… you can come visit your good friend Malik."

All these things were just repurposed trash but Malik, I,
owned them.

Smiling at me, he reached into the stuffed bag behind him and
pulled out more items. We put the posters up together, hiding
the spackled drywall beneath.

All the Parts of a Mermaid That I Can Recall

By S. J. Townend

The longer I stare at it, the more I'm certain it's not the correct way up, for a tattoo that is, to be, and I didn't think I was a tattoo person, yet, here I am, trapped in an unfamiliar room, all 'inked up.'

When did I get it done, and by whom? And why can't I remember the reason for getting it etched onto the flesh of my upper arm *upside down*?

My eyesight seems subpar, diminished despite the raw brightness of this room; but what I can see of this fresh image scored below my shoulder—from the parts of it I can make out—is that it appears to resemble a fish-woman.

A tail, I see her tail, is it called a tail? Each rose-colored, thumbnail-shaped scale glints under these harsh strip-lights as I move my arm gently—and gently is as much as I can bear. And what is that? Her red caudal fin? Ah, I see her all now, I think. Her body stretches out, extends around the sagging skin of my upper arm. I can't decide if it's a work of beauty, this mark. Is it art, or merely an eyesore? It's certainly sore, I'll give you that.

The breasts, they're a little further towards my elbow. Magnificent. The pert nipples—I think they'd be pert—have been covered by the artist with long, red-inked wisps, snaking tendrils of crimson hair. Such unbelievable texture. Every lock of hair appears alive, flowing, vivid. Each strand is a glistening movement of red; the colors are holographic. Almost.

It's her. I'm sure it is. The artist has captured her fair side and chosen to hide the half of her scalp, which, I think, had peeled away, been left undone, exposed. Yes. Shaved free of lustrous locks. Half of her head had been thrumming with what I'd presumed were maggots; writhing with infested, suppurating growths.

Yes, it is a good likeness of her. Yes, her, I remember her now. My stomach turns at the thought of her open skull, her razor-tooth smile; how my heart yearns for her enchanting sound.

While I have your attention, please, hear my story as it returns to me. Listen well, friend; understand why I need out of here. I need to get back.

We'd been at sea, had decided to set back in, to the harbor, for the yearned safety of sand which would become hard, steady rock beneath our boots. Myself and my crew had been out for days, achieved a great haul, but a great storm had brewed in our path.

It seems so cruel, deeply unfair, that I, captain and sole sur-vivor, hold alone the burden of regaling this event, and that all of you, who've listened to me this morning, have disputed and tried to counter my account of what happened.

A great wave crashed down on my humble vessel, dipped her at the bow. I should've gone down then, with the others, as an honorable captain should, but instead, I jumped overboard, into the rowboat which I'd lowered from the side of the trawler.

From there, afloat, I watched my crew tumbleweed down the deck, into the cold, cold arms of the ocean. Panoramic screams for help were met with no reply. My fishing boat, my pride and joy, I watched her as she sank. She followed my crew into the mouth of the great blue.

I must've drifted for days. Blazing sunshine, sharp ocean spray, and dehydration took it in turns to rouse then knock me from consciousness, again and again. And then, when I'd nearly given up hope, on the third day lost at sea, possibly the fourth—my concept of time has become quite distorted—I heard her: Attina. Attina, her voice, angelic. I heard her sing as I drifted. Her melody brought me back from wherever my mind had sailed away to. Through the words in the songs she sang with the most angelic voice to me, I knew I'd been rescued.

Alana brought me fresh drinking water, mopped my brow, sang sweet lullabies to me, for minutes, hours, years. Her magical singing voice, backed by the gentle breaking of waves on sand, was a healing, celestial comfort as I recovered there, on the shore.

From her lips, each warbled note strung out into the atmosphere as if from a well-plucked harp. Eventually, when I was able to walk—hobble, really—she guided me to a sheltered alcove. Each day, or each hour—I'm unsure how often she visited, please forgive my salt-addled mind—she came and tended to me, all the while, singing her song. What a creature of beauty I thought she was.

Alas, when my vision returned and my eyes adjusted to the darkness, I managed to focus in on her. Grave disappointment and an unnerving dread followed.

One side of her face was plain, not offensive, but nothing to write home about, and the other—the thought of which still unsettles me now—a hideous mess of maggots pulsating on the edge of a glitching, bottomless abyss. And when she smiled, *those teeth!* More blades than a butcher's knife block.

I asked her to face away as she sang, contemplated asking her to leave me alone entirely; the quivering, opened half of her disturbed scalp was almost too much to bear. But her voice—her voice was divine, a gift. I closed my eyes instead and let her music wash over me, but as I recovered, I listened, paid more attention to her lyrics, and my dread blossomed again.

Adella sang about her people—the Mers—the people of the sea; how they sought revenge on the trawlers ravaging their oceans, raping and pillaging their fish-stock—they believed the sea belonged to them! Or that had been my interpretation.

Her healing songs, bent with violent words, continued to unfurl. She sang to me the tale of how her people, hybrid beasts of fish and human, caused my boat to come a cropper, how they lured my half-drowned sailors, my crew, their lungs topping up with brine, into storms and towards sharp rocks with their voices. Through her harmonious lyrics, I heard how the corpses of the crew of my staff had been dragged to the bottom of the ocean, as playthings for her family.

So, as soon as I was better, I struck her over the head with a rock, knocked her out completely, and stole her from the beach.

She screamed out hateful songs as she roused, as I hoisted her slimy body over my shoulder, yet still, despite the rage, there was beauty in her music.

Her tail, which had shone iridescent, almost holographic, in the shallow waters of the cave when she'd rested next to me, appeared gray, dull, and felt like iron wool against my skin as it dried. She would not quieten. I had to drop her and gag her with a length of fibrous bladderwrack, which was a shame. I did not want to draw attention, didn't want anyone to rob this gift of her away from me, so she remained gagged for the short struggle home.

She kicked hard—if kick is even the right way to describe the squirm of an angered mermaid: half piscine tail, half breast, flesh, razor-blade-toothed jaw, festering scalp, and hair. The journey back to my countryside cottage was tough, but I'd do it all again.

I locked her in the bathroom while I constructed a better home for my songful muse. It took a week, longer perhaps—in truth I have no idea—but when she saw the three-meter cubic tank of reinforced Perspex I'd constructed in the corner of my otherwise empty barn, I knew she was impressed. Knew she was ecstatic because she said nothing. Silence. She voluntarily stopped singing for the first time. In all those months, years, we'd loved each other for, in that initial moment, when she first saw the home I'd built for her so we could be together forever, no song fell from her lips.

I tipped her in. She protested to begin with, then relented, realizing what a gift her new tank was. Perfect fit. Like a horse in a stall, blinkered between two planked-wood walls. In her glass-like box, she was safe. I filled it two thirds with water and added a hanging ledge of ply for her to perch on so she could get out of the water and sing.

With the lid clamped down, I told her I'd be back with fresh kelp for breakfast, and waved farewell. She sang back from her tank—beautiful, if a little shaky. She said she'd prefer Slim Jim smoked sausage sticks, but if they were unavailable, kelp would suffice. I said I'd see what I could do.

She did not smile, though, as I backed out of my barn, as I left her to return to my cottage and sleep in the comfort of my own bed. I strolled up the path to my home, wondering where one could buy Slim Jim smoked sausage sticks at midnight in such a place of isolation, and I stopped to ponder over this by my back door.

Could I hear her singing? Yes, yes, I could. What a magnificent sound. She'd started to sing again. *Mission accomplished*, I'd thought, and had patted myself on the back for such a great design and build. Although, as my ears attuned, picked up on her lyrics once more, I noticed she was singing quite ruefully this time. Different songs to the ones she'd chanted while I'd healed in the cave.

That first night, back in my cottage, I had to sleep with cotton wool in my ears, and all my windows closed, so her voice would not pull me into a depression.

Late the next morning, I took her down a platter of green fruits from the sea and the Slim Jim smoked sausage sticks she'd requested, and again, I heard such saddening, bittersweet tunes ascending from her tank.

She devoured the food without thanks, but I let this lack of gratitude slip. It can take time to settle in somewhere new, can't it? Which reminds me, listener: where am I now? What is this place? And when may I return to her?

Please. Let me free, she'd begged, I remember that. Over and over she'd pleaded, her melodious voice wavering like a heavenly theremin. She'd spun in her tank, scowled, flicked water at me as a breaching humpback might do where I'd displaced the lid to feed her.

After her churlish tantrum, she floated there, limp, hiding her ample bosom from me by facing into the corner.

Arista, sing only pleasant songs for me, that is why I brought you here, I said.

She spun back to face me. A stripe of light breaking through a crack in the barn roof fell on her, highlighting her ugly side again. Her long locks were absent on this side of her head. Odd shaped bumps distorted the area. Crimson streaks throbbed into the water. Hideous. So I sealed the gap with a nailed plank and left her in darkness.

For days, I left her alone to teach her a lesson, but the volume of her voice only grew; so beautiful, but so sad. I couldn't bear it. From every room in my small countryside cottage a stone's throw from the beach, and halfway down the road, I heard her sad voice wailing funeral rhymes. It's a blessing my home is so desolate and free of neighbors; as if I did have neighbors, no doubt, through tear-filled eyes, they would've complained about the noise.

Please tell me when, listener, will I be released so I can return to her?

I could take it no more. She needed an ultimatum, though I'm not proud of what I did next. Now I lie here, worried, because I no longer hear her voice—is my Andrina okay?

Help me escape the woman in the yellow anorak and the infant with a face I care not for, who together, claim to be my family. They're unstable, desperate for a piece of my precious Aquata perhaps? Aquata must have financial worth. Not that I'd sell her. I wish for her to sing sweetly again, forever, for me, in my barn.

Let me explain the sequence of events, perhaps then you'll see my situation. I went into my barn, that I clearly remember; yet what followed is less than clear. I think I told her to lower her volume and put a stop to all the heart-wrenching songs, *you must only sing cheerful tunes,* I'd said, *this is why I took you, gave you this opportunity.*

I remember her voice growing louder, from the dark corner of the barn. I recall the swoosh of her tail as she batted it against her tank. The indecipherable chorus she sang physically hurt as her words penetrated my eardrums, scratched like claws on glass inside my skull.

She then—the very audacity of it—gave *me* an ultimatum: *swim to the floor of the ocean and retrieve my glowing orb,* she'd sung, *and in exchange, I'll grant you your demand and only sing happy songs.*

Her melodious racket hurt my head so much, I had no choice but to obey. *You've been a bad boy, a very big, very bad boy,* she'd continued, *and I'll only sing sad songs. Loudly. Unless you retrieve my glowing orb.*

Returning to the ocean was not something I enjoyed. After all, my last fishing venture had ended in disaster. Yet, I found myself paddling out, until the sand became nothing but a beige line atop a gray line. Then I dove down.

The water—clear, silver, black—pressed cold against my skin. I swam deeper and deeper, descended through the zones: sunlight, twilight, midnight, abyssal. I kicked and scooped until I reached the hadal zone, and there, I saw the glowing orb she'd described.

But as I approached it, reached out to claim the prize, excited for my reward, it was then I realized she'd fooled me.

Teeth. Such sharp teeth. Multiple serrated marine fangs. A ring of smoke-yellow teeth, larger than my own circumference. It was no magical orb she'd sent me questing for, but the barb of an anglerfish. And it was too late; I'd reached for its bait. The jaws of this other beast, this all-fish apex predator of the underwaters, closed around me. Glass-sharp points pierced through my head and my upper left arm.

And that is the last thing I remember.

And now I'm here, strapped to a narrow excuse for a bed. The coast guard must've pulled me from the ocean. I must've near-drowned a second time. I'm lucky; blessed. Or, perhaps, my Arial commandeered her sea-people with her angelic voice, and they carried my body ashore. She does care. We're linked, she and I, by something magical.

How tough it is, to be in love with someone, something, a voice, which you also despise, can't get out of your head. Why can I no longer hear her melody? This silence is deafening. I must get out of here, must get back to my barn. She'll need her Slim Jims soon.

No barn, you say? Don't be ludicrous. Although, that is what the woman with the anorak who claims to be my wife said too. Said I live in a terraced townhouse with her and a child. Witchcraft, all of this. I demand to be released. Stay away from me, stay back. Fetch me your supervisor.

You think so? You've an explanation for this? You're questioning *my* truth? I would laugh if it didn't hurt. Tell me then, fill me in, unleash your delusions. You must be in collusion with her, the anoraked woman who was here when I awoke, the one with the child glued to her side, the pair of them with all the tears in their eyes.

No, no, ridiculous. Of course it's a tattoo. A tattoo of a mermaid. Look, here: her tail, the scales. No, don't show me yours. Put your arm away. Stay back!

"Sir, it's not a tattoo, it's an open wound. We removed the multimedia User Interface panel from your arm. See, here's mine, still connected, wired into my nervous system—this is what yours looked like before surgery.

We got it all out, from your arm, and the visual discs from your retinas. But... we need to talk about the situation in your cortex."

What the heck is that in your arm? Get away from me. I demand to see your superior. This is abuse. What are you trying to do to me with this black magic? Get away. Put it away.

"Please replace the bandage on your arm, sir. We need to reduce the chance of post-surgical infection."

Let me out of here, please, before she returns, the lady with the ghastly anorak, the child. They're trying to steal me away. I've no idea what their intentions are, but I need to head back towards the coast, to my barn. Why can I no longer hear her sing? Is she floating in her tank, pelvic fin side up?

"Sir, there is no mermaid. No tank. You've experienced serious problems with your multimedia neuro-implant, largely due to the source and quality of the media you've been uploading. Let me explain again. Where shall we start? The matter of unpaid library fines for one loaned children's brain-book, *The Little Mermaid 2: Return to the Sea—*"

But... I don't have a child.

"—and one further fine for the overdue short-term loan of Attenborough's *The Blue Planet*. And Sir, with respect, you have an eight-year-old daughter, Matilda, big Disney and wildlife fan. You also illegally burned several copies of Bjork's *Greatest Hits* and tried to sell this ripped braincode via black market VR distribution sites. There are a few other issues that have also come to our attention—"

Lies! And why are you speaking to me in this way, rolling your eyes, as if this is not the first time we've had this conversation? Let me out of here, untether me now.

"I'm afraid we can't do that. You're still recovering from your User Interface extraction surgery, and there are still unpaid fines on your account. Your arm should heal—we've managed to extricate the entirety of the UI device, but I'm afraid there may not be anything further we can do for the situation in your visual cortex."

My what?

"There's evidence you've uploaded illicit, pirated code into your multimedia brain implant device, including but not confined to: unregulated copies of *The Perfect Storm, Jaws,* and *Titanic* (2028). Our investigation systems have also detected a Slim Jim smoked sausage advertising virus, which probably came with the most likely cause of the cortex damage you're experiencing—we discovered a large quantity of DarkNet-sourced misogynistic pornographic material in your brain drive. The illicit content seems to have triggered malicious neuroplasticity which seems to have caused nano-sedimentation in your brain. The damage is too vast, inoperable. We did try—took out a little of your cortex—and you're currently on a high dose of antibiotic code which we're mainlining in via this temporary USB port which we've installed above your left ear to reduce the chance of further infection. But we can't promise we can eradicate all the corrupt files. The head pain you're experiencing should diminish, but the disorientation... we're not sure there's anything further we can do."

• • •

You. Yes, you. Help me down from this bed. That tuneless mess of a woman returned, without the infant. Told me she paid my fines, said I was welcome home whenever I was ready to return, and then she left, not before slipping me her address on a piece of paper which I, of course, tossed into the bin.

I'm vexed. I haven't heard my mer-woman's song for months now. I've tried to sleep here, in this strip-lit, medical bed; tried to close my sore eyes, but all I see is her split skull, rotting, and her lifeless, starved body, floating in her tank in the dark corner of my barn which they tell me does not exist. Sometimes I see her suspended there, nictitating in and out of sight, even with my eyes open. I can't allow for this to happen; for her to die. I have to find her, make her sing again.

I'm adamant, as I finally leave this place, that if I keep on walking out of the city, towards the coastline, I'll hear her sing once more. Sad songs, happy songs, any songs—I don't care anymore what it is she sings. But I must keep on walking until I find her.

The Body Remembers

By P. A. Cornell

It takes a moment before it hits me that the screaming's coming from my own mouth. Funny how the mind works. I catch myself debating whether to continue or just shut up. My leg—where it used to be anyway—is nothing but mangled shreds that remind me of pulled pork and I opt for silence. I grit my teeth against the pain and watch the leg reform from those shreds of bloody meat for a moment before I have to look away from the unnatural sight of it. There's no escaping the metallic scent of blood, though. The only thing that can compete with it is the acrid tang of my own sweat. Most people don't notice sweat smells different when it comes from fear. Stronger. More acidic. Trust me, I've been at this long enough to know.

Too damn long, actually, but my tour's coming to an end. Two more weeks. That's all I've gotta last and I can go home, back to normal life—or to whatever semblance of normal those of us who've walked through hell can get.

I force myself to look down at my leg again and see it's slowly coming back, which is more than I can say for the fabric of my pants that's missing from the knee down. Nothing to do about that. Around me, gunfire and explosions continue. In the brief gaps between them, the others yell across the battlefield.

"Go, go, GO!"

"Orlovschi's down!" I hear, before Noble runs past me with an apologetic look on his face. I don't blame him for not stopping. Not much he can do for me, and the cover here isn't much to speak of. Nothing more than the remains of a low brick wall, no more than two feet high—lower where chunks have been blasted away.

266 • P. A. Cornell

"On your six!" someone yells, followed by an explosion.

A body falls to my left—too damaged for the treatment to regenerate before the Reaper got its icy claws on it. I instinctively try to move away, but I don't get far with just the one leg, and the other one burns like it's on fire.

"Come on!" I tell it. Waiting for the leg to finish regrowth, I glance at the body. They're face-down, so I can't see who it is, but by the shape I guess it's Paradas. Build looks about right. And I catch a glimpse of what could be a dark brown ponytail sticking out from under her helmet. I look away. Fuck. I liked Paradas.

I keep my head low, trying to see past the dust and debris to where the enemy is. We're still holding ground, but they're pushing back. I'm not safe here. Some injuries you don't heal from. Or so they tell us. Paradas is still not moving. No one knows what happens when one of us dies. They take the bodies. Not the enemy—our side. They recover them all, no matter how bad the war zone. The official line is they don't want them falling into enemy hands, on account of the treatment, but most of us think it's *us* they're hiding the dead from.

There's talk the treatment can regenerate us even after death. If that's true, what would it do to a person to come back from that? It's that fear alone that's kept me from sampling the taste of gun metal before squeezing the trigger. There damn well can be a fate worse than death—worse even than this endless cycle of horrific injury and regeneration. That's why I have to last through the next two weeks. It's too late for Paradas, but the rest of us still have a shot.

There's movement to my right, and my body reacts before I consciously register that the face belongs to a stranger—that the uniform bears the colors of the other side. Only later, in my nightmares, will I recall the way he brought his weapon up to target me. Right now, it all happens too fast. He's still taking aim when I raise my own gun and blow his head to pink vapor. It looks like spray from an airbrush. I see it all in slow motion and know my mind will replay it for me in luxurious detail later. I have a permanent front-row seat to that show. Part of the price I paid for the good health I enjoy.

The blast of air hits me before I see the hover overhead. It doesn't come all the way down. They lower a claw and grab Paradas by the midsection, lifting her into the air like one of those antique coin-op machines you used to win toys from. Her body disappears into the hover's belly, and then it's out of there as quick as it came. They don't do a damn thing to help me. I know the drill. I'm on my own out here.

The foot's finally done forming. It looks pink and damp, but I know that won't last. I wiggle the toes, then slowly get to my feet, still keeping as low behind my cover as possible. The leg holds my weight but still feels like it's burning—which it shouldn't, but I don't have time to worry about that. It can wait for my report, so the powers that be can read it over before ignoring it. "It's all in your head," they like to say.

Funny how the mind works. Yeah... just fuckin' hilarious.

My right boot's gone, which means I'll be negotiating the battlefield on nothing but a bare sole. But knicks and scrapes should heal before I notice them. Just gotta hope I don't get more pieces of me shot off before I make it to decent cover. The phantom pain makes me unsteady on my new leg, so I hobble a little but fight through that, telling myself it's not real. It's not real. It's not *fucking* real. But god damn, does it ever burn all the same. After a while, adrenaline gets me running full tilt, diving over one of our barricades where Wiebe and Davis are laying down cover fire.

"Thanks," I say, as I come in for a landing, then turn to fire back toward the enemy while Davis reloads. She's fast. Quicker than me on my best day, and she's back firing on the enemy before I've managed to do much.

"How's the leg?" Wiebe asks, seeing my pant-leg and boot are gone and putting two and two together.

"It works," I tell him. He shrugs. He knows what it's like. Lost a good chunk of his shoulder last battle. A hand, the one before that. Looks good as new now, though. That's the problem. We all look intact on the outside—wish I could say the same for the inside.

They don't tell you what it's like when you sign up. They sell you on the good stuff, leave the rest as a surprise for you to discover on your own later. Some people win the DNA lottery, but most of us get stuck with genetic flaws that have been doing the rounds in our families for as far as we can trace back. Me, I scored asthma, an irregular heartbeat, flat feet, and anxiety, to name a few. Add to that the stuff that comes at you after you're born. Everything from seasonal allergies to getting hit by a car. Some of us get lucky—others not so much. I was one of the latter.

It's all good though. You can buy replacement parts for just about anything these days. There're enough labs growing body parts in vats that you can take your pick. Spin the nearest globe, stab a finger down, and see which lab you got. They're all good. New lungs, new heart, new feet, and they'll throw in a bonus treatment to regulate that brain chemistry too.

So long as you can afford it.

That's the catch. This shit don't come cheap.

Sure, some employers cover the cost on condition you work off what you owe. But the interest keeps building, and you never seem to put a dent in it. So when your buddy who's a soldier tells you over drinks one night the army has a better offer, you listen. You nod as he tells you about regeneration. How it can fix any shit you're born with and heal anything that goes wrong after. And all of it free of charge—all you gotta do is serve our country.

Just show me where to sign.

We look up to see air support—about damn time. Thousands of our drones. They target the enemy with pinpoint precision and make short work of their front line. The survivors have no choice but to fall back. We live to fight another day.

Hovers come to carry us back to base. Strapped into my seat, I can still hear the cacophony of battlefield noise. It stays with me even as the distance grows, like when you get a song stuck in your head. The worst possible earworm. I flex my new ankle, watch it move the way it should, but it still feels like it did when it got blown off. With the adrenaline no longer pumping like it was, the pain intensifies, so I reach into my kit for meds, taking the pill dry and crushing it between my teeth in hopes it'll get absorbed faster. But it does nothing, and by the time we're back at base, it's all I can do to keep from screaming.

Technically, the treatment's still in its trial stage, so when any of us get wounded like I did today, we have to report to Doc Flemming so he can evaluate us for his ongoing study. As the treatment's developer, his collaboration with the army means he gets an office on base. This works out for the army because if anything goes wrong, he's there to deal with it so they don't have to. I'm just hoping he can give me some relief from this pain.

When I arrive, his secretary tells me he's busy, points me to a chair where I'm to wait. I try to distract myself by watching a wall monitor replay one of the ads for the treatment.

Bio-replacements and repairs can be costly and even out of reach for some. Join the army and let us take care of your physical health with our patented regeneration treatment. Enjoy the body you were meant to have—free of ailments and impervious to injury. Speak to one of our recruiters today.

Nowhere in the ad is there mention of the nightmares, the flashbacks, or the phantom pain I'm currently experiencing. Nowhere does it say that the physical injuries heal, but the body remembers all the same.

The office door opens, and a man dressed in a civilian's business suit and carrying a briefcase leaves. The secretary gives me a nod and I go in.

"I'm told you're experiencing some discomfort, Corporal..." he says, in lieu of greeting.

"Orlovschi, sir. Stan Orlovschi."

He doesn't look up from his work or ask me to take a seat, so I'm staring at the top of his bald head, wondering why this asshole hasn't taken his own treatment to regenerate his scalp. Should've asked that question before I signed anything.

"I'm a civilian, Corporal. No need to address me as 'sir.' Please describe the discomfort you're feeling."

"It's more like excruciating, mind-numbing pain that's slowly driving me out of my mind," I tell him.

Now he looks up, but his expression's one of annoyance rather than sympathy.

"And you've had your latest booster? You're getting all the calories required to aid in your regeneration?"

"Yes, to both."

"Well then, let's see what the scanner says. Which limb is it?"

I point to my right leg, and he gets up and grabs a portable health monitor from his desk, then uses it to scan my leg from the knee down. He stares at the device and frowns.

"These scans look normal. Your leg is completely healed."

"That might be, but it still feels like it did when it was hamburger on that battlefield," I say.

"It's psychosomatic," he tells me. "I'll give you something to help you sleep. I'm sure you'll feel better after a good night's rest."

In my mind, I'm calling bullshit, but right now I'm desperate enough to take any drugs he's willing to give me.

"Thanks," I say, like a good little lab rat.

The drug Flemming prescribed does knock me out, but it's not relief I feel when the nightmares come. My subconscious mind's a sadistic sonofabitch. It runs a play-by-play of today's battle, featuring highlights from previous ones. I get to watch my friends die again in the most creative and colorful ways. I watch pieces of my own body get blown off and once more feel the pain like it was live. The dreams come nightly, but they're especially dark and detailed after missions. Mercifully, Wiebe shakes me awake after a while, freeing me from this monster that lives inside my mind.

"You were screaming," he says.

"Sorry."

"No sweat."

The irony is I'm drenched in sweat, and I recognize the scent of fear in it again. I sit up and watch the others go back to sleep. No one resents me for disrupting their rest, they all get it. The nightmares come to them too. Waking life's no vacation either because that's when the memories attack, worse than any enemy we've faced. They come again and again, no matter how much you try to think of something else. Like the pain in my leg, they're relentless.

I rub at my calf and think about the first time my leg got blown off. The time before this one. I wonder if the pain I feel comes from that first time or the latest. Not that it matters. It's part of me now. Real to my mind even if it doesn't show up on scans.

Doctors throw the word "psychosomatic" around like it erases what you're feeling. They ignore the fact that if it's real for the mind, it's *real*. Our bodies heal from almost anything. But the memories, the suffering, the fear—the treatment can't fix that.

So we find other ways to cope.

I get up and quietly search my kit for what I need so as not to disturb the others, then head for the showers. I sit on the floor of my favorite stall—the one with the good drain—and pull my pant leg up to confirm the leg's still there. My eyes see perfect new skin over intact flesh, but my mind screams at me of pain. So I take the tool I brought with me, the knife I was issued, and cut a long line along my left arm, wrist to elbow, letting the blood drip into the drain.

The cut burns as I glide the blade across my skin, but I don't stop. "This pain is real," I say aloud. The cut has healed by the time I get to the end, but my leg still hurts. I go again, this time a quick slash across the forearm.

"*This* pain is real!"

I do this again and again until morning comes. By then I'm exhausted. Numb. I feel nothing and I hope it'll last for at least a while.

We all have our ways of coping with what we've been through. We don't talk about it. We endure. At least I won't have to endure much longer.

It's not long before they throw us back into the meat grinder. The army and Doc Flemming each have something to prove. The treatment benefits them both. Flemming's gunning for the Nobel—his little miracle will no doubt change many lives for the better. Just not ours. The army gets soldiers they don't need to send home after major injuries. Soldiers they can keep

272 • P. A. Cornell

reusing—a virtually inexhaustible resource. The more times we come back from battle, the closer they get to approval for the treatment to become standard.

This time at least we didn't lose anyone. Still, once we're back in the mess, we eat in silence. I read the others like my grandad used to read his morning paper. Wiebe seems jumpy, Davis more withdrawn than usual, Noble's eating like the food's his enemy. The rest of the company just seems tired. We're all tired. Tired of the flashbacks, tired of the pain—both real and imagined—tired of the tense muscles, the panic attacks, the urge to run with nowhere to run to.

Noble stands suddenly, lifts his tray, and slams it down onto the table, sending rehydrated eggs flying in all directions. Then he leaves. No one says a word. He was one of the last ones to sign up and has at least a year to go. We've all had such moments of frustration and rage. We all will again.

As for me, I rub my leg under the table, trying to massage the pain that's returned since the battle. I consider my usual way of coping but head back to Doc Flemming instead as soon as I get a chance. If this is something they might use on civilians one day, he needs to understand the treatment has no effect on emotional and psychological trauma. I need to get him to stop ignoring that.

"The pain's back," I tell him.

"I'll give you another sleeping pill."

"That won't help," I say.

"It helped last time."

"Not exactly," I tell him, though I don't elaborate on my methods for coping. "There has to be something you can do. The battles, the injuries, they stay with you. Our bodies heal no matter how many times you throw us out there, but they don't forget—and we don't get to choose what the body remembers. I only have a short time left to go, but I have to think of the others you'll keep sending out there after I'm gone. Not to mention the fact this pain in my leg may be something that stays with me."

Flemming gives me a curious look. "A short time left to go?"

"Until the end of my tour," I clarify.

"I'm afraid it doesn't work that way," he says. "The contract you signed gives us the right to renew your tour as many times as is necessary for this study."

I must not be hearing right.

"What?"

"We're collecting data from every injury each of you sustains. Speed of healing. *Other* effects. It could be several more years, even decades, before we know enough to determine whether the regeneration treatment is something we should continue with."

"But that… can't be right."

He sighs and reaches for his tablet, opening a file that he then turns for me to see. I recognize it as the contract my buddy showed me in that bar. Only I don't recall him mentioning this wasn't a regular tour of duty. I do remember the words "standard contract." Maybe he didn't know. Or maybe they made him a sweet offer, so he didn't volunteer that information. It doesn't matter anyway because it was on me to read the fine print. I have no one to blame but myself.

I feel sick to my stomach—an alien sensation since the treatment makes it so we no longer get sick.

"You're not gonna let us go," I say. "Not ever."

"Let's not be so bleak, Corporal," Flemming says. "Every study comes to an end, eventually."

I think of Paradas and how the study came to an end for her. I think about the rumor that even death can't stop regeneration and wonder if it really did. I break into a sweat, but my limbs go cold, all except the one that burns with pain. I picture the years to come, being torn to shreds again and again, my body healing as my mind falls apart. And that's if I'm lucky. That's if I don't end up like Paradas.

It takes a moment before it hits me that the screaming's coming from my own mouth.

A Front Row Seat for Miss Evelyn

By D. A. Jobe

Evelyn felt for the call button on the bed rail, shouted at the thing clinging to the bird feeder outside her window. "Get away from there!"

Scaly black with red slitted eyes, it beat leathery wings to stay on the swinging feeder, ripped out the insides of the cardinal pinned with its claws. Ate the head.

"Happy birthday, Miss E!" a voice sang behind her. Clogs scuffled across the floor. "Look what came for you!"

Evelyn turned to look at Katie holding balloons and a vase of roses, then back to the window. The garden pole shuddered; the thing and cardinal were gone.

Katie, in gray scrubs, set the vase on the dresser across from the bed.

"Your son said he can't make it by today," the aide said, tapping her wristband to cancel Evelyn's call. "But he sends his love and says he'll see you Friday for the big recital."

"Evie's first performance," Evelyn said.

"I can't wait to hear all about it." Katie tied the balloons to Evelyn's tray table and handed her a purple envelope.

Evelyn glanced back at the window.

"Birds out this morning?" Katie asked, unearthing crumpled tissues buried in Evelyn's bedding with gloved hands.

"They were, until that dragon came and ate one." Evelyn's forehead creased.

"A dragon?" Katie chuckled. "It was probably that fat blue jay you said comes around sometimes." She smoothed the chenille bedspread.

"It had spikes on its back."

Katie's gaze narrowed on the window. "That must have been distressing."

She walked to the glass, looked out, yanked shut the drapes. "It's gone now, whatever it was."

Katie returned to the bed, helped Evelyn into her bed jacket. "Here, open your card. That'll make you feel better."

For a Special Grandma it said on the front. Evelyn read the inside and showed Katie. *I love you* in block letters with a little lopsided heart.

"Evie's an artist," Evelyn said.

"Your mini-me," Katie said. "I said that to myself just last weekend when she came to take you on your adventure."

Evelyn gazed at Katie, a blank smile on her face.

"To the aquarium," Katie prompted.

Evelyn lit up. "You wouldn't believe the fish!"

She remembered now: corridors bathed in blue light, bright coral, stingrays gliding. What a perfect day! Just her and Nathan, Evie, and Celeste, who was six months old and so good sleeping in the sling on Nathan's chest. No Ariana there to spoil it with her *moods.* Evelyn's lips pursed.

"Sandy's coming soon with your breakfast," Katie said. "The kitchen made you something special for your birthday. Let's get you up."

With Katie's help, Evelyn sat up and dangled her feet in blue socks over the side. The aide clicked the off switch on the bed alarm pad and helped Evelyn stand and take the walker.

"Look at you, getting stronger," Katie said as Evelyn pushed the walker toward the bathroom, sticky nubs on her socks keeping her from slipping on the floor. Actual *wood* flooring.

If she had to be in a nursing home, at least it was Meadowood, not that horrible rehab place. Nathan had upgraded her to a Platinum Studio, with a private bathroom and a Family Lounge with a crib, for when the baby came.

Katie left Evelyn on the toilet and closed the door. Evelyn wasn't *that* far gone yet that she couldn't clean herself. She flushed to signal she was done.

Katie always knocked first. Such a polite girl.

Breakfast was on the tray next to the recliner, eggs Benedict, Evelyn's favorite. Nathan must have requested it. But her stomach turned over thinking of that poor bird eaten alive.

After Katie collected the tray—"You okay, Miss E., you didn't eat much"—the aide positioned Evelyn's desk table for her and turned on the oil diffuser on the dresser on the way out. The scent of rosemary and peppermint filled the room as Evelyn colored a detailed peacock picture. Evelyn had *excellent* fine motor skills for her age. Meadowood's resident doctor, Dr. Hwang, had said so.

She colored until lunch—warm goat cheese and pecans over salad. By now she'd convinced herself that the thing on the bird feeder must have been a hawk or crow. *Keep talking about dragons and they'll think you're senile.*

"Now that's better," Katie said, taking Evelyn's empty plate. She gave Evelyn her pill, checked her blood pressure.

Evelyn watched TV, dozed. Light dimmed behind the drape, casting a gloomy patina over Evie's school drawings on the wall, the roses, and balloons.

The witching hour, Evelyn had called it as a new mother. Watching for Lannie's car at the window with a fussy baby in her arms, aching with some unnameable sadness, the soupy scent of casserole in the air.

Now, Evelyn turned on the cassette player beside her, tapping her armrest to Neil Sedaka's *Laughter in the Rain*. Nathan didn't understand why she'd kept her old tape deck, even bought her a pocket contraption with music on it, but she never could figure out those tiny flat buttons.

She saw movement at the door. A little dark-haired girl, peeking in.

·Evelyn's face broke out in a smile; she waved. The girl waved back.

"I heard music," the child said, inching toward the recliner.

"What's your name?" Evelyn said.

"Mina." The girl picked up one of Evelyn's cassette cases on the table, opened it.

"Are you visiting someone here?" Evelyn asked.

"I volunteer."

Evelyn laughed. "My! What do you do?"

"Different things." Mina put the tape down, peered at the coloring book open to the peacock. "Did you color this?"

"Yes. Would you like to color with me?"

Mina flipped through the book. "I like this one." A coral reef scene.

"I just went to the aquarium last week." Evelyn tore out the page for Mina at the perforations. "There are fish just like these. A man in a scuba suit feeds the sharks."

"I went there one time." Mina slid a light green from the pencil tin and colored a sea plant while standing at the desk table next to Evelyn.

"Do you have a grandparent here?" Evelyn asked.

"My mom works here. She does computer stuff."

"Is that right? You are doing lovely."

"I want to be an artist when I grow up."

"Like my Evie." Evelyn gestured at the drawings on the wall.

Mina colored for a few minutes before drifting over to the dresser to look at the photos there. She brought Nathan's family picture to Evelyn in the chair and leaned over the armrest.

Evelyn pointed at the baby in Ariana's arms. "My grand-daughter, Celeste. She was just a few weeks old here. This is her daddy, Nathan, and her mommy, Ariana, and this is Evie. She's four now."

"I'm eight," Mina said.

As the child went back to her coloring, Evelyn stared down at the photo, face souring.

The last time she'd seen Ariana was just before moving to Meadowood, at the family's home for dinner. Evelyn had held Celeste so Ariana could eat, feeding the baby pinches of bread.

"She really shouldn't have solid food yet," Ariana had said.

"Oh, but look how much she likes it," Evelyn said.

"Mom," Nathan said with a glance at his wife. "I think the baby needs a diaper change. Here, let me take her." He plucked Celeste out of Evelyn's arms and gave her to a tearful Ariana who disappeared down the hall to the bedroom.

"She's so sensitive," Evelyn huffed. "You ate real food when you were a baby and turned out fine."

"Things are different now. The pediatrician says to wait on solids."

"Hmph. Do you think Ariana should be drinking while she's nursing?"

Nathan sighed. "It's one glass of wine. She's just trying to unwind. This is a huge change for her." He rose from his chair. "How about I take you home?"

"Already?" She looked around for Evie.

"We're all exhausted, Mom. We'll plan for a longer visit next time, okay?"

Katie's voice came from the door, breaking Evelyn's reverie. "Mina! Your mother's been looking for you. You know you aren't supposed to go into residents' rooms." The aide waved to hustle Mina out of the room. "We're sorry to disturb you, Miss E."

"Come visit anytime," Evelyn called out.

A few minutes later, Katie returned to help Evelyn to the bathroom and back to bed.

"I already had my therapy," Evelyn said, pointing at the cassette player. Katie laughed like she did each time Evelyn said it. The aide rolled in the cart from the hall, a black box with blinking buttons and headphones.

Katie fluffed the pillow under Evelyn's head, fit the cushiony headphones over her ears, and covered her with a weighted blanket.

"There you go." Katie's voice was muffled. She put a light hand on Evelyn's shoulder as a soft, classical melody began to play. "I'll be back in an hour."

Evelyn dozed off as she always did, coming awake slowly, feeling refreshed, luxuriantly groggy, like after a nap at the beach. Katie had come and gone without waking her, removing the headphones and taking the cart away but leaving the blanket. Evelyn always slept so deeply after. Dr. Hwang said it was the newest relaxation treatment. Only state-of-the-art therapies at Meadowood.

Outside, the birds came to the feeder, flitting back and forth as the sky darkened.

The next morning, Evelyn could tell it was raining by the weak light coming through the drapes. She asked Katie not to open them. The balloons had sunk lower, deflated. Evelyn spent the morning writing letters in bed, but felt restless, distracted, so she turned on the television and drowsed.

The day outside brightened by the time Sandy brought lunch, a lovely grilled salmon, and Evelyn had her open the drapes. Chickadees visited the feeder until a jay frightened them off. *Jeer, jeer, jeer* it squawked after each bite. Some people disliked Jays, but Evelyn always admired their brashness. Their bold blue color. After him, a cardinal came. Evelyn tensed, watching the sky for that ugly dragon-thing until the bird flew off. Did he miss his friend?

"You look sad," a small voice came from the door.

Evelyn smiled at Mina. "I'm not sad anymore. I'm glad you came to visit. Are you volunteering again today?"

"Yes, I was helping with the mail."

"What a big help you are."

Mina came further into the room and handed Evelyn a piece of blue construction paper folded in half with a picture of a tropical fish from a magazine glued to the front. "I made you a card for your birthday."

"Oh my goodness! How sweet." Evelyn gestured Mina closer to hug her, the card crushed between them.

She opened the card, read out loud, "'*Happy birthday to you. Love, Mina*.' What a beautiful drawing of a mermaid. Thank you!"

She hugged Mina again, then gave her a worried look. "Are you going to get into trouble for visiting me?"

"Mom won't notice." Mina climbed into the visitor's chair. "She's having a bad day."

Evelyn exaggerated her frown. "That's a shame."

"She had to fire someone for showing off and making a lady upset." The girl picked at the leather seam on the armrest.

"Oh my. That *is* a bad day."

Mina's gaze went to the window. "Oh! I know that kind of bird."

"A chickadee."

They watched the little birds flit back and forth to the feeder from somewhere beyond their view until the jay showed up again, scattering them. *Jeer, jeer, jeer.* Evelyn watched the greedy thing jab at the seeds, an unsettled feeling coming over her.

"Do you know what déjà vu is?" she asked Mina.

The girl shook her head.

Evelyn's gaze didn't leave the feeder. "It's a feeling like you've seen something before. I could swear I saw this same blue jay do the same things before. He'll fly off now. Watch."

The jay's abrupt departure set the feeder swinging.

Mina said, "There are a lot of birds."

"Oh yes." Evelyn stared distractedly out the window. "They put on a show every day. They come for all three meals and eat and eat and—" Her fingers tightened around Mina's card.

The cardinal was back.

"Mina?" Evelyn said.

The girl turned from the TV screen.

"Do something for me. Go hit that window."

The child's eyes widened almost comically. She went to the window, glanced back.

"Go ahead," Evelyn urged. "Hit *hard*."

Mina slapped the glass. The surface trembled with a warping sound. The cardinal kept eating.

"Mina! Away from there!" Katie shouted from the door. "What in the world are you doing?"

The startled girl ran to the corner.

Evelyn hurried to explain. "I asked her to. Something's wrong. The birds—"

Katie's eyes filled with concern. "Miss E. are you okay?" She shooed Mina out of the room. "Why are you trying to scare the birds?"

"I'm not. Ever since that dragon came, they—"

"Oh, you're still worried about that?" Katie tucked the sheets around Evelyn. "I think maybe we should call Dr. Hwang. He might need to adjust your medication."

"No." Evelyn grabbed the mobile phone by her bed. "I'm going to call Nathan."

Katie straightened. "Now you've said before how your son is very high up in his company. Why don't you wait at least until this evening when he's free? You'll see him in two days. For the recital, remember? I'll take you to the day room. You'll like that."

Evelyn clutched the phone as if afraid Katie would snatch it from her. "I don't want to go to the day room."

Evelyn knew she was being difficult. One of *those* residents. Her son paid a fortune for Meadowood. And Katie had always been kind to her, more of a friend than a caregiver.

She let out a small breath. "If I could have a glass of ice water."

Katie relaxed. "Of course. Now why don't you let me close the drapes? It's almost time for music therapy, anyway."

Katie closed the drapes and left, returning a few minutes later with a plastic cup and straw, Evelyn's pills, and the cart. Katie waited patiently with a smile until Evelyn took her medicine, then placed the headphones on and took the cup from her.

Katie's probably right, Evelyn thought, hugging the phone as a soft tune began to play. *It's probably just my medication. If I call Nathan, he'll just worry.*

She shouldn't have asked Mina to hit the window. The child would probably never visit her again. Evelyn sighed deeply and closed her eyes. She didn't wake until dinner, a delicious seafood chowder, and then drifted off again during the evening news. In the morning, Sandy came with the tray and opened the drapes, filling the room with sunlight.

The bird feeder was gone.

Evelyn passed the morning fretful and quiet. Her calls to Nathan had all gone to voicemail.

She clenched her fists when Katie came in. "I'd like to see Mrs. Donahue after the bathroom."

Katie disabled the bed alarm before helping her sit up. "You know Mrs. Donahue likes us to make appointments ahead of time. And anyway, you have a manicure this morning."

"This is urgent."

"Is this still about the bird feeder? I had it removed last night since it was upsetting you."

Evelyn's lips thinned. "I wish you would have asked me."

"We can see about returning it when things settle down."

"I want to speak to Mrs. Donahue right now." Who did this girl think paid her salary?

Katie brought the walker over. "I'll see if I can get you in to see her, but I'm pretty sure she's out of the building this morning."

After Evelyn used the bathroom and was settled in her chair, Katie left to inquire about a meeting with Meadowood's director, returning a few minutes later. "I was right. She's off site until this afternoon. I left a request with her assistant. I'm sorry."

Evelyn wouldn't look at her. When the aide left, she tried calling Nathan again and left another message.

That afternoon, Evelyn sat listlessly in her chair, phone in her lap. Fingernails painted in bright pink polish suitable for a child. She'd cut the TV off so she could hear the phone when it rang.

Nathan's flowers had wilted. The balloons hovered lower. If she'd had a pin, she'd have popped them out of their misery.

She picked her granddaughter's birthday card off the table and read it, then Mina's. She held the cards open together, frowning.

Both had identical lopsided hearts drawn after their names.

When Mina visited later that day, Evelyn was ready.

"There's a wheelchair in the closet. Can you bring it to me?"

Mina wrestled the chair out, unfolded it, and wheeled it over as Evelyn pulled herself up by the bed rails. She told Mina how to turn off the bed alarm.

Evelyn let gravity pull her legs down so that she was in a standing position and, holding the rail, made a shuffle-turn so her back was to the wheelchair. It rolled back a little when she dropped into it. Mina braced it with a grunt.

I'm going to get into so much trouble, Evelyn thought, heart pounding.

Nonsense. I'm not a prisoner. I have every right to leave my room. Evelyn smacked the armrests. "Let's find Mrs. Donahue."

"I just saw her!" Mina said, maneuvering Evelyn around. Evelyn expected to see Katie appear in the doorway, an exasperated smile on her face. *Miss E, what on earth!* But no one was there.

"Check no one's in the hallway first," Evelyn told Mina. Then, as the girl was peeking, she said, "Honey, when you say you help with mail... do you make cards for the elderly people here?"

"Uh-huh," Mina said, and Evelyn's throat tightened. "I make the nicest cards for them. Ms. Lindsey tells me the names and then I can draw what I want. We can go now."

Wheels whispered on the carpet as the girl pushed Evelyn down the hall, past tastefully framed paintings and console tables with flowers on them that seemed on repeat, like background scenes in the cartoons Nathan used to watch.

"Wait," Evelyn said when the Concierge desk's polished wood ledge came into view at the end of the hall. "This is the wrong way."

Mina stopped pushing at a door with a GUEST SERVICES sign. "I saw her go in here."

"This isn't her office," Evelyn said over her shoulder, but Mina was already propelling her inside, scraping the wheelchair on the doorframe.

Centered in the room was a computer monitor on a table with chairs. *Touch Here to Begin* flashed on the screen. Mina pushed Evelyn up to the table.

"I'll go find her," Mina said, and charged through a side door marked RESTRICTED. Evelyn caught a glimpse of computer monitors, jumbled wires, and equipment. She looked at the screen in front of her and, before she could stop herself, touched it. The screen opened on an image of Meadowood's facade with the words TOGETHER. EVEN WHEN YOU'RE NOT.

A man's voice said, "Here at Meadowood, luxury, state-of-the-art therapies, and cutting-edge healthcare combine to create the ultimate senior living experience."

Evelyn frantically searched for an off button, but found only smooth plastic.

Images of the day room's grand fireplace appeared, then the hot tub and pool, followed by pictures of residents' rooms. "Our suites are richly appointed with all the amenities. For something extra, our Platinum Studios feature digital mood-regulating window panels precisely calibrated for your loved one's optimum enjoyment and mental wellbeing."

Evelyn stared at a montage of available views: a distant dog park. A line of trees. Gardens. A bird feeder, like the one outside her window.

Then Mrs. Donahue's friendly, all-business face appeared on the screen. "I'm Margaret Donahue. Welcome! And thank you for considering Meadowood for your loved one."

The camera followed Mrs. Donahoe around the facility, chatting with residents and staff as her voiceover continued.

"We all know that isolation and loneliness can be devastating to seniors' health and mental wellbeing. But families are busy; we can't always be available. Here at Meadowood, we understand."

She entered a room with several technicians at computer stations and spoke into the camera again. "That's why we developed GRANDMAGING, an innovative program using the latest technology, which lets you stay close to your loved one at Meadowood, even when you can't be with them in person."

Donahue held up her phone. "With our exclusive app, every time you post a video or photo, your loved one is included in your family celebrations, outings, children's performances, and even vacations."

The video cut to a scene of an elderly man in music therapy headphones, eyes closed, a smile on his face.

"Our safe and relaxing imaging therapy transmits your posts to the part of the brain that stores memories so your loved one can share in the fun, as if they are *actually* experiencing it with you, for wonderful memories they'll cherish forever."

"At Meadowood," Donahue said as the video ran clips of smiling residents playing croquet, painting, and exercising, "we are committed to meeting your needs and preferences. Our staff compassionately screen your loved one's calls and correspondence to give *you* a break from needless worry. In-suite webcams allow you to check on your loved one twenty-four-seven. *You* decide how much involvement is right for you and your family."

She held up a homemade card with a ladybug on it. "And if you want your loved one to receive regular cards from the grandchildren, we can take care of that, too."

Mina tugged Evelyn's arm. "Miss Evelyn, I couldn't find her."

Evelyn wouldn't remember how she got back to her room; somehow Mina managed it without anyone seeing them. The little girl helped Evelyn grasp the bed rail to stand.

Breathing hard, Evelyn said, "Honey, put the chair back for me before you go, please."

After Mina left, Evelyn pushed the call button. She clung to the handrail with trembling legs, waiting for Katie, eyes on the floor so she wouldn't have to look at the balloons. The cards. The crib where little Celeste had napped the last time Nathan visited with the girls.

Were their visits just memories planted in her head?

Had they *ever* been to see her?

She moaned, legs folding.

"Miss E!" Katie caught her around the middle, muscled her into bed where she lay gasping.

"What were you doing out of bed?" Katie said. "Your son just called. He was at a meeting overseas and got your voicemails. He's very concerned and said to tell you he's flying home right now and will be here tomorrow to take you to the recital."

Evelyn looked away.

Katie smoothed Evelyn's hair back. "There. You're all right now. I'm going to call Dr. Hwang. And I need you to promise you won't try to get out of bed again." She clicked the bed alarm on.

Evelyn looked out the window, wheezing from exertion. The birds, the sky, the clouds out there, none of it was real. The dragon she'd seen, a trick by someone just *showing off*.

When Katie came back with the cart, Evelyn didn't fight the headphones. She closed her eyes, escaping into the gentle music filling her ears. Afternoon sunlight filtered through the drapes. The blanket was warm and heavy, anchoring her to the bed. Her fingers swept over the plush surface. *This* was real.

The next morning, just as promised, Nathan picked up Evelyn and treated her to brunch at her favorite restaurant. Then off to Evie's ballet performance, with surprise front and center seats!

Evelyn's chest swelled with pride watching little Evie in her tutu flit around the stage with the other children, as a cheerful piano melody played.

Ariana joined them this time, looking happier than she ever had, beaming up at Evie, and Evelyn made sure to smile at her.

She thought Ariana might have smiled back.

The Burn-Outs

By Hugh A. D. Spencer

Our review of the Mission Log indicates that the subject's residence had been under observation for ten days prior to court approval of the process...

—Investigator's Report

My mother sent me a present. The parcel was covered with precisely wrapped brown paper with neatly positioned postage. I was sure that she had used a slightly moistened sponge to adhere the stamps. I also was sure that mother's tongue had never touched anything since she divorced Dad and became a nun in the Order of Saint Martha Stewart.

Inside the package was a pad of very expensive drawing paper and a box of oil pastels. The pastels looked like crayons on steroids or hallucinogenic sausages.

I quickly closed the box; the odor of heavy colors seemed, well, rather obvious. It never even occurred to me to think about applying the end of one of the pastels to the surface of one of the sheets of paper. Maybe those of us too dumb to draw a straight line never thought of things like that.

Later, I called. "Thanks for the present, mom." I hoped I didn't sound as annoyed as I felt. Useless bloody thing.

There was a pause on the other end of the line. My mother hesitated a lot. Perhaps it was that vocation of stylish calculation that made her do that. Probably she just had too much to say and was too polite to speak first.

"I just thought you might want to try some illustration," she said.

"I'm a little old to start in on that kind of thing," I replied, and a little too sharply at that.

Another pause. Whatever the reason, there were always these gaps in our conversations, as if I were calling Neptune and not the west coast. Then I heard that very familiar sigh, as though I was receiving signals from a planet where everybody was always just a little bit sad.

"But you never know," I heard myself saying. "Thanks, mom."

"Happy birthday, darling."

> *...within two hours of the court's approval, the team's legal representative and medical technicians approached the subject's residence. The subject answered the door, and according to the Mission Log, he was served with a Writ of Existential Force Majeur...*

> —Investigator's Report

That evening, something occurs to me. Some people have sex on their birthdays. Sometimes on other days, too.

That is not going to happen to me. Diane is a very nice, caring person who I find very attractive. But the date is not going well.

The date, not *our* date. Note the terminology–the evening is not something either of us wants to take ownership of; it would be too much like taking personal responsibility for a plane crash.

Right now, we are sitting on a bench set in the forested area behind the museum. From the way Diane is sitting, I sense the peculiar inner tension of a person struggling not to look at their wristwatch.

"You are really very kind," I say.

Diane looks a little startled. "How so?"

"You're trying not to break up with me on my birthday."

She sighs. That's two sighs from different women on the same day.

"I'm really sorry."

I shrug. "Don't be. The kindest thing for us to do is try and maintain our dignity."

I stand up and Diane smiles as she checks the time.

"I'll drive you home."

The lights on the parkway are getting sparser as we drive north of the city.

"Is there anything you want to tell me?" I finally ask. "Something I might want to file for future reference?"

Diane keeps looking out of the window as she speaks. "The gaps started to get to me."

"Gaps?"

"Even tonight." The lights of a passing car briefly reveal Diane's frown. "I was talking about what bands I liked at college. I kept trying to get you to tell me what music you liked when you were a kid."

"If you were going to break up with me, why did you care?" I can't help being logical.

"I don't know," Diane replies. "Maybe I was just curious. Maybe I was just trying to figure you out." She looks directly at me, frowning even more than ever. "Do you even remember the conversation?"

Now I get to sigh. "To be honest, not really. What did I say when you asked me about what kind of music I liked?"

"You changed the subject."

"Maybe I didn't think I had anything interesting to say."

Diane returns her gaze to the blackness outside my car window. "You are not an easy man to get to know."

"I guess not."

The video record does reveal that the subject was informed of his rights during the procedure and that the Constitutional Principle of Minimum Necessary Force was duly explained while the technicians strapped him to a chair in his studio.

However, we did note that the subject complained of discomfort as the electrodes were fastened to his scalp.

290 • Hugh A. D. Spencer

> *At this point he was gagged with rubber tubing by the technicians. The legal representative made no statement at this time.*
>
> *The technicians stated in their interview that the gag was necessary to reduce distractions during the procedure and thereby avoid potential accidental injury to the client. We are not convinced by this explanation, and my interpretation of the video record is that the technicians carried out the procedure in an insensitive, perfunctory, and potentially negligent manner.*
>
> —Investigator's Report

It's hard to make out any details from behind the cloud of cigar smoke, so I'm not exactly sure what Corben looks like.

A deep, tobacco-scorched voice addresses me: "So why are you here?"

"Because I have to be," I reply. "I received a bad personnel evaluation last month." I push a thick printed form across the desk. Corben's hand emerges briefly from the cloud and picks up the form. "I'm required to spend at least three sessions with a licensed detective-therapist."

Corben's other hand butts out the cigar on a transparent disk. The smoke starts to clear, and I can see a pair of eyes scanning the print.

"Your company is one of several that keeps our group under retainer."

After a moment, the shrink-dick starts reading aloud from my psych scores: "...in spite of an almost exaggerated dedication to company goals and duties, this subject is temperamentally unsuited to collaborate on team projects..."

Corben chuckles and skips ahead a few pages. "I like you already." Then there's a pause and Corben sounds a little concerned. "Here's what they've red-flagged: co-worker appraisals indicate an ambivalent attitude toward women..."

Corben swings her Doc Martens onto the desktop and inserts

another brown tube in her mouth. "That's another thing we have in common, sir. But I can see why a big company might be concerned."

"So what happens now?" I ask. Corben seems nice enough, but the atmosphere promises to be pretty toxic.

"Your company is sending over their files on you," Corben replies. "My people will then do a check on your past history, looking for mitigating circumstances to justify your anti-social attitudes."

Mitigate? Justify? I don't like those words very much. "Do I need a lawyer for this?"

Corben laughs, a deep and slightly scary sound. "We take care of all that for you. Besides, it all depends on what the investigation turns up."

"So you're saying I shouldn't worry."

"Truthfully, there's no time for worry." Then Corben blows sharply through the brown tube.

The tiny dart enters my jugular, and the hypnotic drug makes me feel as though I'm melting into the chair.

I can feel my forehead lowering into my lap.

"So let's start right in with the analysis," a distant voice growls.

...the video record goes on to depict a standard erasure procedure. The legal representative observed, took minutes for the Mission Log, and adjusted the auto-cam while the technicians engaged the synaptic manipulator systems.

Please note, however, that there are discrepancies between the times written down in the Mission Log and project invoices, and the times marked in the video record. This suggests that the team was aware that they were rushing the procedure beyond customary practice. It also suggests that the team's employers were issued an inflated invoice (this is not our problem).

At the conclusion of the procedure, the subject was placed in an artificial trance while the cover-story materials were left in the residence. These materials included forged letters to and from family and friends, fabricated job applications, and optically adjusted photographs. All of these were designed to support the engrammatic implants and hypnotic directives... which is standard practice in these procedures.

A video record has been attached to this report for your review and comment. Tracks four and seven are the most informative...

—Investigator's Report

The meeting room in Corben's office is almost featureless. Light gray carpet, even lighter gray walls, ceiling tiles that seem almost featureless. I feel as though I'm entering a giant rectangular brain cell.

Get cerebral, the room seems to be telling me. Stay calm.

A very beautiful woman is sitting at the far side of the gray table in the center of the room. An uncomfortable, edgy feeling passes over me—like a little man in the back of my head is struggling to scream. Let's everybody stay calm, I tell myself.

The woman looks very angry, so she's probably having trouble staying calm, too.

One of Corben's assistants looks meaningfully at me and closes the door.

"Apparently there was some kind of technical problem," the woman snaps at me.

I take the seat facing her.

"You mean the technicians made a mistake?"

"No." The woman says this word in such a way that suggests she's leaving out another word, probably something along the lines of 'fuckwit'.

"So what do you mean?"

"There's some kind of legal technicality involved. Our lawyer says that it's probably best for us to communicate directly, try to sort it out."

I nod. "I imagine that the process is something people would like to keep out of the courts."

The woman narrows her eyes at me. "It's perfectly legal."

There's a long pause. This is starting to remind me of one of my dates.

"So, what's your name?" I finally ask.

"I don't have to tell you that." Her retort is sharp, short, like a rifle shot.

We experience another pause.

"Okay," I say. "What does your lawyer recommend we discuss?"

"You found us," she replies. "Your choice. I'll let you know when you go out of bounds."

Yet another pause.

I sigh. "So what was the legal technicality?"

She folds her hands and her knuckles go white. "We have been advised that there is a remote possibility that the paperwork for your procedure was handled a little incorrectly." The woman stares at the knot of tension in front of her. "There's a fast-track legal process for approving burn-outs for stalkers, abusers..."

"Did I stalk you? Abuse you in some way?" I ask.

The woman closes her eyes and doesn't speak.

"Look," I say, trying to sound as reasonable as possible. "I'm not trying to be defensive here, I honestly don't remember."

The woman opens her clouding eyes. "Technically... no. You didn't. But after we broke up... after our relationship terminated... somehow... you kept turning up... we seemed to keep ending up together."

"By together, do you mean—"

"I don't have to tell you that!" There's the rifle shot again.

"Okay." You got me, lady!

But suddenly, she volunteers something: "And things were getting very awkward for me and my fiancée, his family, his career."

"Maybe he just didn't like the idea of me knowing things about you that he knew," I say.

"Maybe," the woman says. "Maybe I didn't like that idea either."

I can feel that little man in the back of my head, just dying to scream.

"I wish I knew enough to disagree," is the best I can do.

The woman stands. "That's all I'm obligated to tell you."

"Well, we all have to meet our obligations."

She stops at the door and says: "I've been instructed not to apologize for anything. But it's really too bad about your art."

Blank space. That's all that comes to mind.

She closes the door, and I'm all alone in the big square brain cell.

...we cannot agree with their legal representative's assertion that no substantive harm has resulted as a result of the procedure: The subject's new job in accounts receivable for a major corporation simply does not afford similar scope for creative expression as his earlier career as a graphic artist.

Whether this psychological damage was the result of the permanent erasure of the subject's creative drives or through a hurried and botched memory removal procedure is a moot point. Whatever the cause, the damage has been done, and there have been severe consequences to the subject's personal relationships and future happiness.

—Investigator's Recommendations

A few months later, the beautiful woman comes to see me. This time she is not the angry beautiful woman, she is the sad beautiful woman.

"My name is Laura," she says, sitting at my kitchen table and holding a cup of coffee. "But I guess you don't remember that."

"Wish I could," is all I can say.

"Me too."

I didn't know that such a short sentence could affect me so powerfully. I feel like I want to cry.

"Now I'm feeling even more confused than usual." I try to sound funny and I spill my coffee. Slapstick over wit.

The beautiful woman, Laura, puts down her mug and kneads her eyes. "After that hired dick tracked me down..." She stands up and looks out the door at my living room.

"This place of yours is too small," Laura says. "You never wanted to spend enough on accommodation."

I follow her as she walks into the living room, past the couch, past my bookshelves, past my desk.

"It's interesting, though," Laura says. "I can still see pieces of you scattered around this place. The colors, the furniture." Laura takes a seat in front of my computer. "But important things are missing." She pats the monitor. "This ought to be a drawing board."

Then she doesn't say anything for a while.

I know she's upset, but I'm not—as far as I know, I've never been able to hold a pencil. So I just don't know what to say.

It seems as though Laura is looking past me, through the window, at the late afternoon sun.

"There was one time, we'd been together about six months. It was a really lazy day. We didn't want to get out of bed." Then Laura shook her head. "But after lunch you started reading. *The Time Machine*. One more time."

"Really?" I say. "I don't remember reading anything by H. G. Wells."

"It was one of your favorite books." Laura sighs. "Anyway, you were reading the damned thing for the two-hundredth time, so I decided to leave."

"I'm sorry," I say. "I guess that must have been pretty rude."

"You followed me. You were naked, standing in the doorway of the living room. It was about this time of day. I remember that there was something about the quality of the light."

"I read once that light and shadow are important in works of art." The minute this comes out of my mouth I realize how inane it sounds, but I feel that I should say something.

"It was just after a rainstorm, the sun was coming out from behind the clouds, and it was like the room was filled with living gold." Laura looks at the floor.

"Every once in a while, something brings that light to mind."

"I don't know if light has ever affected me that way," I reply.

Her hand trembles. "Since you found me, it hasn't been easy. I can't seem to forget."

I cross the room and open the front door.

"I'm really sorry," I say. "But I've just learned about at least one cure for bad memories."

She looks at me.

> *We strongly suggest that you approach the subject once again and ask him to reconsider his decision not to pursue legal action...*
>
> —Investigator's Recommendations

Months later, things haven't changed much. Corben's report was filed with my employer, and a little while later I received a small raise.

Maybe I'm feeling a little better about things. Maybe I really don't know what I feel about anything. I still can't draw a straight line, but I did have the pleasure of reading *The Time Machine* again for the first time.

I suppose I have Laura to thank for that as well.

Would've, Could've, Should've
By Andrea Goyan

- **gun** [guhn]

  noun

  a weapon.

  verb

  to increase in speed by "gunning" the accelerator.

- **car** [kahr]

  both of the above.

I've always held romantic notions about driving my car, Beast, into the sunset. Hell, in high school, I spent so much time in that car, people called me Gearhead, said it was weird for a girl to like cars so much. But I did. My friend Carrie and I would tool around, eating up gallons of ice cream and gasoline while we dreamed about our futures. Unaware of the would've, could've, and should've moments we'd yet to live, all we saw was that wide-open road ahead of us. The sprawling horizon, visible through the windshield, full of the possibilities we imagined anew each day.

"Road trip," Carrie might say. "Let's drive south. Find us some movie stars and start living our real lives. Not this bullshit, teenage, be home by eleven p.m. crap."

I'd laugh and drive faster, pushing my grandfather's hand-me-down, beat-up, '91 Cadillac De Ville to its limits. Damn thing only got 11 miles to the gallon and took every penny I earned bagging groceries to keep the tank full, but I'd merge onto the freeway and press the pedal to the metal, racing to meet our destinies.

"We'll get an apartment," Carrie'd say. "Become famous, and before you know it, those jerks we leave behind'll wish they'd been nicer to us."

Us. That always made me feel good when she included herself like that because no one bullied Carrie, just me. But she never wanted me to feel alone.

She'd smile, flashing her braces-perfect white teeth while the wind whipped through the open window, tossing her long hair about her face, and I knew I'd be plucking loose, brown strands out of the carpeting on Saturdays when I washed the car. Every week I cleaned the Beast from top to bottom, then polished its slick metal with a chamois until it gleamed. I finished the job by rubbing conditioner into the worn leather seats, which were soft as a baby's cheek. Then I'd crank up the tunes and be ready to hit the road.

I loved that car the way some people love their dogs. I guess it's only fitting that it became a part of me the way it did, though, given a choice, I wouldn't have made that one.

But back then, before the accident, before the fusing of metal to bone, I felt light and free and damn near perfect whenever I slid behind the Beast's wheel. It was me and Carrie against the goddamn world. With her by my side, anything was possible.

We talked big, but usually, we ended up at a movie or one of the local diners. Sometimes, we'd order beers with our burgers and fries. The waitresses eyed our fake IDs, the ones we'd pick up at a head shop on jaunts to the city. They'd scowl and say things like "The woman in that picture is old enough to be your mother," or "Your parents know you got this, *Yvonne?*" stressing the fake name like it tasted bitter in their mouths. Some of them would tsk, take the IDs away, and slip them into their apron pockets. Others would hand them back. All of them brought us admonishments along with our root beers.

"Don't be in such a hurry to grow up. All it got me is bunions and an aching back."

"You'll look back and realize high school was the best time of your life."

"Go to college."

Their orthopedic shoes squeaked on the tile floor as they turned tail and walked away to take care of other customers. And Carrie would pretend to shove her finger down her throat and gag. Then we'd clink our plastic cups together, link pinkies, take a suck on our straws, and swear that shit wouldn't happen to us. Never.

And when we left, I burned rubber or kicked up dirt as we tore out of the parking lots. Because damn it, I wasn't old enough to drink, but I sure as hell was old enough to drive. And I did that like a mother-*take-no-hostages*-fucker.

I'd step hard on the gas I could barely pay for and go faster and faster. Speed being its own kind of intoxication. Running away, another.

But it turns out, all the forward momentum landed me right back where I started. Worse. And all those kids in school who called me "Freak" and "Loser," who made up taunts like "No one will kiss Tracy Hall. Her bitty boobs are way too small"—instead of getting rid of those nagging naysayers forever, I became, as my mother liked to say, the exception that proved the rule.

Look me up.

• **loser** [loo-zer]

noun

    Tracy Hall.

• **Tracy Hall** [**trey**-see hawl]

noun

    loser. transhuman.

I guess my misfit stats made me the perfect candidate.

I would've died the day of the accident. Should've. Those men could've let me pass and spared me more torment. It would've been kinder, could've been my end. Should've been.

Instead, they hooked me up to machines that breathed for me and pumped my blood. They told my mom that the donor card on my license expressed my willingness to help others. That they could save me, repair all my broken parts, and make me better, more advanced. My mother's despair at almost losing her daughter made her believe in a scenario where her daughter might live forever.

They wooed her like a college sweetheart. "Imagine the luck of being in the right place at the right time. Your daughter had an angel watching over her."

Bullshit. Where was that angel before the accident? And I hardly call taking a hairpin curve too fast on a rainy night the right place. Or the right time.

But my mother stuck to that prospect like chewing gum on the bottom of a shoe. Since I was underage and unconscious, I knew nothing about her deal until much later. And by the time I learned she hadn't read the entire contract, my fate was already set.

• snake [sneyk]

noun

limbless, scaly reptile.

treacherous, Biblical devil.

verb

to twist or wind or fuck with an object.

Reptiles are cool, and I hate when people use animals to disparage humans because animals deserve better. That said, the doctor, *scientist,* who fixed me was more related to the biblical snake luring Eve than anything else. There was a lot of "Call me Malcolm," and "Trust me. It's going to be fine," and "I'm sure this must be hard, feel free to share your thoughts and feelings."

Since my mom gave them permission to do whatever was necessary to save me, my thoughts were moot, and for a long time, I felt nothing. By the time they were done, not enough of me was left to honestly answer their questions.

- **monster [mon**-ster]

noun

any creature so hideous it frightens people.

a person capable of monstrous deeds.

adjective

enormous.

- **beast** [beest]

noun

non-human, cruel, animal.

car, or car parts.

- **monstrous beast [mon**-str*uhs* beest]

noun

Tracy Hall.

The well-paid medics who pulled me from the wreck followed their strange, specific instructions without question. *CallmeMalcolm* directed them to bring pieces of the car along with me. I found out later that he'd wanted to prove his theory about the relationship between accident victims and some kind of elemental law of attraction mumbo jumbo. Basically, he believed that at the moment of impact, the Beast and I had already become one. So my body wouldn't treat transplants from the car as foreign. Turned out, he was right.

Part of the Beast's steering wheel became new ribs. Hubcaps turned into an exoskeleton to protect my remaining organs. Missing limbs were recreated, their circuitry hooked into the wiring of my new nervous system. They encased my brain first in the Beast's soft, worn leather, followed by more metal from one of its doors. Since I no longer had hair, *CallmeMalcolm* found a "Flying Lady" hood ornament from a 1941 Caddy and shaped it to sit atop my skull.

I became garish and gruesome, more junkyard than the girl trapped inside.

CallmeMalcolm stopped calling me by my given name. I think he forgot there was some part of me inside running the show. I was still the driver. Instead, he took to calling me "Flying lady," though he laughed when I asked him for actual wings.

"You, my dear, are not aerodynamic."

And he was right. By the time they'd finished piecing me together, I weighed so much I could barely walk, let alone fly.

I didn't think I'd ever get out of that place, but 1,277 days after the accident, *CallmeMalcolm* told me I was free to go.

"Where?" I said. My voice remained one of the few unchanged pieces of Tracy, though I had an amplification system to modulate it.

"Into the world."

I didn't respond, but he must've felt my question.

"What? You didn't think we'd keep you here forever, did you? I saved you so you could return to the world and live…"

Then he called me "Tracy."

It had been so long since I'd heard that name. It cracked something inside.

"But look at me."

He held my face in his hands. "You are a thing of beauty."

• **whiskey** [**wis**-kee]

noun

> a caramel-colored grain alcohol. Spirits.

• **spirit** [**spir**-it]

noun

> a haunting.

> incorporeal part of the human soul remaining after death.

Mom always drank. Before Dad died, they'd drink together. Sit around on Friday nights swigging beers. I dunno. It seemed okay then. Those were happy times. Now, it's just plain sad.

Mom held out her whiskey bottle. "Drink?" she said.

I shook my head.

"You really can't taste?" she said. "Not anything?"

"No tongue," I said. "No stomach."

I think when they told her they'd save me, Mom expected a flesh and blood daughter. Sometimes, I'd catch her looking at me when she thought I couldn't see. I'd read the anguish and disgust on her face, the deep creases in her forehead, her scrunched-together, pursed lips. I never said anything. I didn't want her to know that *CallmeMalcolm* had installed cameras in various locations around my body so I could see 360 degrees at all times. It was disconcerting when he first turned them all on, but I got used to it. "One of your superpowers, pet," he'd said.

Mom swigged back her drink, poured another bigger one, and dropped onto the sofa. The cushions looked like they'd swallowed her up. She seemed much smaller and frailer than I remembered. But it could've been my memory or seeing her through my new visual cortex.

She chugged the whiskey, and then came her tears.

"I'm sorry, I'm sorry, I'm sorry. I should've let you go, Tray, Tray..."

"Tracy, Mom. My name's still Tracy."

But she couldn't say my name. She laid down and buried her head in a pillow.

- **babe** [beyb]

noun

> slang. offensive term used by men for attractive women.

> sometimes affectionate term or nickname.

- **Carrie** [**kar**-ee]

noun

> see above, meaning 2.

I've never loved anyone like I love Carrie. Maybe if I'd grown up more before I did battle with the Beast, before my metamorphosis, I might have felt the same thing for someone else. But once that day happened, the other couldn't.

Would've, could've, should've.

I believe the metal in my body not only replaced broken and missing parts, but acted as armor or a force field. What's still inside on the other side of the synthetic materials—the part of me that's still alive and real, the part that still feels things—only has feelings and memories from before. No new emotions are getting past the artificial shit. I'm stuck with my seventeen-year-old angst. The love, the ache, the loneliness of a hormonal teenager. And I don't know how to move forward, to grow.

CallmeMalcolm says I can live forever. "It's a gift I've given you, Flying Lady."

More like a curse. Would've been kinder if he'd left me to die on the side of the road.

CallmeMalcolm never really cared about what would happen after he pieced me together. And after he made a thing he couldn't control, he moved on. He should've read Frankenstein. Mary Shelley had it right.

The day he plugged me into the web, I'd searched for others like me. It didn't take long to come up with a bunch of zeros. I was unique in the world. *CallmeMalcolm* hadn't made me better or happier or more alive. He'd guaranteed my isolation.

Even monsters get lonely, especially ones with human hearts.

When I first met with Carrie after my change, I thought she'd run away. Even I avoided mirrors, and I didn't believe anyone could see me anymore. But she took one look, wrapped her arm as far around my metal body as she could, and said, "Hi, Tracy. I've missed you."

Just like that, just like she'd always done, Carrie included me back into her life.

She'd sit beside me, her hand resting on my leg, thigh made from the Beast's chassis, and say it was almost like we were out for a drive, seeing as how all three of us were there together again.

Carrie's hair was short and there were dark circles under her eyes that I didn't remember. Her life hadn't gone like she'd planned, either. Our dreams of running away to the city came to a dead end after my accident, and then she got pregnant with Mickey Sullivan's baby.

At first, she'd blamed me. Said she'd been miserable and angry. Both Mickey and her family said they needed to get married, but she lost the baby at twelve weeks and broke up with Mickey. And the entire experience marked her as sure as my accident marked me. She felt deflated and hopeless and took a job at one of the same diners we used to frequent.

After we reconnected, my humanity swelled. Carrie touched something hibernating inside, and I began to feel again, at least rekindle my old emotions to set them free.

I'd visit her at the diner late at night when there weren't as many customers. I'd take a corner booth in the back and order a chocolate milkshake. I had to buy something or the manager wouldn't let me stay, and before I survived on oil and electricity, I'd loved milkshakes, and I could still remember how they tasted. Sweet and cold and chocolaty. I'd watch the beads of condensation stream in teary rivulets down the glass, and as the drink rose to room temperature and the ice cream part melted, the liquid separated. There were darker and lighter parts, and it was no longer homogeneous.

Like me and Carrie. I just didn't know it yet.

• **uranium** [yoo-**rey**-nee-*uh*m]

noun

a silvery, white, metallic, radioactive material.

• **spark** [spahrk]

noun

a burning particle.

verb

a troublemaker.

• **bomb** [bom]

noun

explosive device.

verb

a failure.

If Carrie was uranium and Mickey was the spark, I was the bomb. Deep in the rifts of my flawed memories, Mickey loomed large. Back in high school, he'd been as bright as a meteor streaming across the sky. Popular, good-looking, athletic. And he'd tormented me every chance he got.

Carrie ran interference, made him stop when the teasing got bad. I didn't realize he'd listened to her because of their mutual attraction. I didn't know the malice he directed at me was partially based on jealousy or that it would be his shoulder she'd cry on after my accident.

And underestimating her human foibles, I never thought she'd go back to him. Especially now that I was back in her life.

When Carrie showed up at work with a black eye, she never suspected I'd be able to find out what happened, no matter what lie she tried to tell me. My ability to interface with the internet gave me access to any system connected. Door cams, home AI digital assistants, computers, the cloud. It took me less than a minute to gather and process the information. I saw everything that happened between her and Mickey.

The meeting outside her apartment. The fight over my return into her life. The slap. The punch. The promise to stop seeing me. The reconciliation. The kiss.

Entering her apartment, removing their clothing… and that's when I shut down my processor.

I never meant to hurt Carrie. Never. When she stepped between me and Mickey, she took the swing meant for him. Mickey, that coward, ran away as she crumbled to the ground.

I gathered her broken body into my arms, saying "I'm sorry. No. I'm sorry."

Compared to me, she was small like a bird and weighed practically nothing. I carried her to *CallmeMalcolm,* cursing my fury and lack of wings.

"Fix her," I said, placing Carrie down on one of his metal tables.

He hurried over and felt for Carrie's pulse. Finding none, he stepped away. "What have you done?"

"It was an accident. I love her."

CallmeMalcolm pressed a button on his phone, engaging the biometric security system. I recognized the sound as all the bolts in the house turned and locked us inside.

"Did anyone see this happen?"

I nodded. "A guy we both know."

"Okay," he said. He went to his cabinet and pulled out a bottle.

"Fix her," I wailed. I would've cried, wanted to cry, but it wasn't possible. My artificial eyes lacked tear ducts. "Do what you did to me."

CallmeMalcolm hovered over Carrie. He held a syringe full of pink liquid over her body.

"Come, Tracy. I need your help."

I went to the table. He took my hand and placed it on her arm. "Hold there," he said.

I did. Her heart no longer beat. "Is the medication going to help her?"

"Something like that," he said, and quick as the snake coiled inside him, he struck, jabbing the needle into a tiny port on my head.

I felt no physical pain, but the moment the needle entered, I couldn't move.

CallmeMalcolm collapsed to the floor and wept. I could do nothing as Carrie's body grew cold, and he wallowed like a human puddle near enough to kick, if I'd been able to.

• **contract** [kon-trakt]

noun

> legal agreement between my mother and *CallmeMalcolm*.

> the small print.

• **assassin** [*uh*-sas-in]

noun

> a paid murderer, often hired for political reasons.

• **contract assassin** [kon-trakt,*uh*-sas-in]

noun

> see Tracy Hall.

The government seized me. According to the part of the contract my mom only skimmed, all of *CallmeMalcolm's* research was paid for by the military. Everything, me included, actually belonged to them, and they had big, ugly plans for me.

Of course, they forgot I could hack into anything. Forgot that I could upload all my memories for the world to see and read here. Forgot that *CallmeMalcolm's* files held the information I needed.

What I didn't expect was the note he'd left me with the code.

"I'm sorry, Tracy," it said. "I tried to save you and only trapped you in a cage you couldn't escape. Follow the directions below, enter the destruct sequence, and it will remove all of Tracy from the machine. Without your consciousness, it will take them decades to figure out how to make the body function."

My very human heart beat faster against my metal ribs and skin, a resounding timpani, banging from my essential core. His gesture was the closest thing to love anyone had shown me in a long time.

Anyone except Carrie.

I can still see Carrie and me out in the Beast, with the wind tossing her long hair. I remember laughing as we mapped out our plans. Driving way too fast, my lead foot forcing gasoline through the engine toward an unbelievable future.

Would've.

Could've.

Should've.

So many choices I'd do over.

I entered the destruct sequence and headed toward the sunset.

You Don't Have to Watch This Part
By Rodrigo Culagovski

I am not delusional.

I understand.

I know I am the hallucination.

I'm not sure when it started. My earliest memory is from before the Españoles came.

Her name was Ka ata Killa, but people called her Ka.

My name changes, but it always has some red in it. With Ka, it was Puka—*blood* in her tongue.

At first, I was just a voice in her head, somebody she could talk to when she was hiding someplace quiet and dark. The somebody who started talking back.

After a while of just talking to her, I came all the way to the surface—her eyes and mouth and nose and ears. To her hands. She would go under, to where I had been. I would walk around the town, up and down the stone steps. I'd carry the water. I'd take the corn to the grinder, bring back the flour, and make flatbread. I lived.

Sometimes men would come up to me. "Ka. Come here, Ka, I want to talk with you," they would call out, laughing.

But I was stronger than Ka. I'd stare at them, straight and with a firm back. Like a warrior. They weren't used to this. They would laugh, at first, or yell something at me and then go quiet, embarrassed to be stared down by a woman.

I was with Ka her whole life. I would come out when she needed me. To fight off an unwanted suitor. To argue with the town elders who insisted she be given in marriage because she was an "old virgin". To bargain with the managers of the terraces around the town, with the traders that she sold her produce to. I was always in her head. And in her fists when she needed it.

The world Ka lived in was not safe. Especially for an unwed woman who wasn't under any man's protection. Whenever I took over because there would be violence, I'd tell Ka "You don't have to watch this part." She didn't.

I wasn't just there to fight or argue. I had a life. Friends of my own. Things I liked to do that weren't the same as the things Ka liked. Ka was a wizard at the loom, even though it bored me to tears. I was skilled with a carving knife and would make small, wooden animals for the neighborhood children. During my evenings, I'd play board games with my friends. On hers, she'd get together with some of her acquaintances and go watch the ball players. It was fine. We were two different people. We didn't have to like the same things.

We never told anybody about our arrangement.

Another memory is from after the Españoles had arrived. His name was Benjamín. He called me Rogelio. He had an easier life than Ka, but he still needed me during his childhood when his mother was drinking. And as a grown, married man when his youngest boy died. I came out and took over for a year.

His wife noticed it on some level. I could see the way she looked at me out of the corner of her eye. I think it excited her to have a different man in her husband's body. To cheat on him without cheating.

I disliked her, but I loved their children. I was happy.

When Benjamín came back to the surface, we'd switch over. Some days it would be him, some days me. Our live-in servant, Castro, picked up on it. When I was in control, I'd ask for chocolate with my breakfast instead of the orange juice that Benjamín favored. Castro would say, "*llegó el otro señor*," and make my chocolate. The three of us got along fine.

When we were in our thirties, Hermano Julián de las Casas, a new representative of the Santa Inquisición, arrived in Lima. We heard he was asking questions around town. Some of our friends said he'd been inquiring about us. We weren't surprised when he knocked on our door. We invited him in and offered him brandy and honey cakes.

He asked us questions. About our friends, how often we went to church, did we suspect any of our servants of practicing old, forbidden religions.

I let Benjamín answer. He was nervous and surprised at being asked these things as any middle-aged man of his social standing would be. I thought this authentic response would be enough to keep the inquisitor off our track.

I was wrong. He came back the next night with armored guards from the local garrison and invited us to come back to the office he had set up in the Catedral de San Juan's backyard.

We were there for three days, tied to a chair and denied food and water. He asked about rumors he'd heard, how we seemed to periodically change our personality, our voice. How we seemed to forget things we should know or know things we shouldn't. He would suddenly recite long Latin and Greek passages in our face, or he'd break and burn six-pointed stars, strangely shaped crosses, and half-human, half-animal clay figures, then look disappointed when we didn't respond. He beat us with sticks and hinted at the enhanced techniques legally at his disposal if we didn't cooperate.

We were dropped off in front of our house at the end of this period, with bruises over our face and back and a stern warning that there would be another one like it in the near future involving actual torture and mutilation. If we did not respond to that, we would most likely be sentenced to death by burning. We'd seen the bodies hung up in the Plaza Mayor, so we believed him. He patted our head like a priest might a child's, saying, "It is not too late to save you, my son."

My host, Benjamín, was a genteel man, born and educated in a city and a social class devoted to bureaucracy, culture, and commerce. He had never gone to war, never needed to defend his life with steel or fists. He'd never had any military training and could hardly use a knife to clean a bird, much less attack another human being.

So nobody expected us to wait under a bridge in the dark alleys behind the Catedral where we knew Hermano Julián liked to go for a walk after supper.

I said to Benjamín, "You don't have to watch this part". He was spared the sight of the blade and the blood. He never saw me roll the inquisitor's body into a ditch dug for the foundation of a new warehouse and cover it with lime and gravel.

Nobody came by to ask questions about the missing Spaniard. I think most people in Lima were relieved at his sudden disappearance. A story was circulated involving gambling debts, illicit romantic entanglements, and pilfered tithing money.

There were other lives, other bodies. María Graciela, Jennifer, Cristóforo, Mirlande, Baltazar, Alzira. No matter what they called me—Sienna, Omaira, Vermelho, Scarlett—I was the voice in their head, the wild warrior in their dreams. The strong one when they needed me to surface. Another life sharing their own. Sometimes a man, sometimes a woman, other times it didn't matter. Many of them had harder lives than Benjamín or even Ka. I helped them when I could.

Lili was one of my all-time favorites.

She was a hacker. She'd take old electronics and change them so they did something new, something they weren't made for. To be honest, I didn't understand half of what she did. But that's fine. I let her do her work. Her art.

I didn't surface often. Only sometimes, when she needed to be more social or to understand what people really meant, what they wanted. I was her when she needed to stop taking shit from people. I'd do it with a quick verbal barb, a cutting comment. I hadn't gotten into any real fights in years.

She spoke to me under her breath.

"Fénix," that's what she called me, "wait until I finish this! You know how you say you're a hallucination?"

"I *am* a hallucination, Lili, just a very vivid one," I answered with an internal smile.

"Whatever," she waved a hand around her workshop, "but you've helped me so much. I wouldn't have been able to do half the things I've done without you."

"That's what I'm here for."

"Yeah, I know, but why just one person at a time? If you are a hallucination, couldn't you be a communal one?"

"I'm not sure what that means."

"You'll see."

I looked out of her eyes. She had a phone splayed out like a dead, skinned animal. She was plugging wires into it and connecting them with her soldering iron. Some of the wires went to a collection of repurposed gaming consoles. Others to a pile of first- and second-generation VR rigs and other gear.

Lili was talking to me again. "The phone isn't doing much, it's just modulating the brainwaves so they can go out over the antennas you helped me put on the roof."

She didn't have a good head for heights. We'd spent the previous afternoon climbing around the roof of the hackerspace in Barrio Italia that Lili basically lived in, installing different kinds of antennas—some store-bought, some rigged from potato-chip tins—and aiming them carefully. Lili would surface for a few seconds to check my work using a box with screens and dials on it that she'd clipped to our belt and then go back under before her vertigo got the best of her.

"What's that?" I asked.

"What's what?"

I took over her left arm and pointed at what looked like a wireframe outline of a human head.

"Oh, that. That's the most important part. You don't really pay attention to tech, huh?"

"Nope, sorry."

"It's a mental induction rig. It's all the rage with gamers. It lets you control your computer with your thoughts and see the game without a screen."

"And you want to use that to… how'd you put it? Translocate me?"

Lili looked up. There was a mirror in front of her workbench. She had a smile on her face that I'd only seen a few times. Usually when she solved a hard problem.

"You'll be free! You won't have to spend all your time in my head anymore."

"I like your head, Lili. It's where I keep my stuff."

"Hah. Give me a second…"

She placed the induction rig on her head and fiddled with some cables. She had about a dozen screens set up on the work surface in different sizes. Each one showed squiggly lines, meters, and numbers. She had control surfaces, dials, and a VR glove on her left hand. She adjusted and tweaked things until she seemed satisfied.

"There, let's give it a try, shall we?" She smiled at me again in the mirror and pushed a button.

I felt a sudden rush. I was in a dozen places at the same time. My sense of self expanded from the hackerspace, reaching out through Santiago to a house in Providencia. A small loft downtown. A post-hippie commune in La Reina. A dozen others. People in each one with an induction rig like Lili's, playing games, working, or just hanging out online.

Each one had a reason for me to be in their heads. Private reasons.

I let them know I was there. Like a small, almost inaudible "hi."

They mostly said hi back.

A disappointed newlywed in a very expensive apartment in Vitacura shut her eyes and started praying under her breath, over and over. I exited her mind quietly.

"This is just a test, but if you want," I said to the rest, "I'd like to be the voice in your head. If you need me."

Those were just words though. I also showed them some of my other lives. Not the violent parts, just helping people when they needed it. Being there.

Most of them got it.

I said, "I'll be back to talk with you," to each one, then pulled back towards the hackerspace.

I opened my eyes. Lili was staring back at me in the mirror.

"How was it?" she asked. She looked like she'd been holding her breath.

"There are a lot of good people out there who need some help."

Her smile stretched out. "That's great."

316 • Rodrigo Culagovski

We kept doing it. Lili kept refining her equipment, adding
more power. I could reach twenty, then forty, sixty people
at once, all over Santiago. I was a voice for all these people,
helping them, shielding them when they needed it. Sometimes
they got into trouble. Some of it was physical trouble. I helped
when I could. I'd say, "You don't have to watch this part," and
they would dive into their minds and only come back up
when I was done.

I was still there for Lili, still her hallucination. She said when
I was translocated, she felt it like an emptiness, like a part of her
was asleep or just gone. When I pulled back, she'd be waiting,
wanting to hear about the others. And with big plans that I
only half followed. She'd mumble something about the "lambda
calculus" or "recursive sentience modeling." I didn't understand
it, but she said that we wouldn't need the antennas anymore.

We went online on a cold day in June. The sun had only
shown itself for a few minutes as it set between the ceiling of
clouds and the streets made shiny by the rain that had been
coming and going all day. We were in the hackerspace. Lili had
cleaned it up and put away most of the bits and gadgets. She'd
borrowed a more powerful computer from a friend. Next to it
was a smaller, sleeker version of the induction rig we'd used the
first time I'd left her head.

"Ready?" she asked me.

"Not really. To go into a few dozen heads around the city is
one thing. This is going to be worldwide, right?"

"Right."

"Even to those without an interface of their own?"

"Yes. Past a certain threshold, network effects kick in and we
can amplify the signal through the basic induction capacities
of any cell phone less than five years old. For this try, we'll only
aim at a few hundred thousand minds."

"Okay," I said, "but, what if—"

"I know you're nervous, Fénix. We don't have to do this if
you don't want to."

"No, I want to. I'm scared, but this feels right."

"Okay. I love you, you know that, right?"

"I love you too." I took control of our arms for a moment and hugged ourselves.

When I was done, she put the rig on our head. "In three, two, one." She did something on the computer.

I felt a rush, like when we used the antennas, only multiplied a hundred, a thousand times.

I was in people's heads all over the world. Bolade in Ikot Abasi. Oskar in Narvik. Emiko in Beppu. María Carmela in Coroico. Eliška in Český Krumlov. I introduced myself. Some understood who I was and asked me to stay. Those who didn't, I left in peace.

So many people who needed a friend, a voice.

I'd been afraid of feeling thin, like too little butter over too much bread. The opposite happened. The people who accepted my hallucination, my voice, were those who were ready to share, to collaborate. My mind wasn't so much stretched out as it was hosted, multiplied, augmented.

I moved through all of their minds, giving comfort, laughing at their private jokes, and helping them heal from bad memories and past abuses. There were also present threats—the unwanted propositions from bosses, the casual bullying tolerated by teachers and school administrators, or instigated by them. So much violence against people for being themselves: too quiet, too loud, too open with their sexuality, or too different from what people expected or wanted them to be. For who their parents were. Their language. The shape of their eyes. For wanting to choose when and with whom they had a baby. For thinking their bodies were their own.

So many lives in danger or subject to abuses that would mark them until their dying breath.

Those were the ones that I couldn't just comfort, couldn't be satisfied offering emotional support or helping with a quick word or snarky put-down.

These were the cases when I had to come to the forefront and decide if violence was necessary, efficient, and could be carried out without consequence for my hosts.

In many cases, I ruled it out. Disproportional, too risky, it wouldn't solve the problem, or it was just a form of revenge that wouldn't ultimately be satisfying.

318 • Rodrigo Culagovski

Some hard ones remained, however, where violence was the only way out. Children living with abusive adults. Women subjugated by their spouses and by societies that denied any sort of freedom. Workers forced to labor for little or no money under threat of physical punishment. Those with nowhere left to turn, where the people and structures that should protect them conspired with their tormentors.

In the end, there were a few thousand of these cases. I used the combined brainpower of all my minds to plan each one until I was certain I could accomplish my goals without risk to my hosts.

This would be the first wave. If all went well, if nobody caught on to my strategic interventions, there would be a second wave, a third, until everybody who needed it was out of risk.

I spoke gently to my hosts, asking them to trust me, to step back and avert their gaze while I picked up a knife, a bottle of chemicals and some cotton, maybe a particularly heavy length of pipe, or a hypodermic needle. I took position at the top of stairwells, loosened bolts, greased walkways, removed banisters, and cut off insulating sheaths from high-tension cables.

I understand that this might be shocking. Maybe you were expecting a lighthearted story with a happy ending.

I understand that, but this is not that story.

I will do what it takes to protect my people.

Don't worry.

It's okay.

You don't have to watch this part.

For Those Not Yet Lost
By Kaitlin Tremblay

"Preparing for external examination," Evelyn says.

She hates time travelers. Not morally or politically, but practically. Evelyn hates the bodies of time travelers because they're never straightforward. Granted, death itself isn't a straightforward affair despite the banality of it—everything dies, Evelyn knows deeply and personally—but there's at least an expectation of order and understanding she has grasped in her many years as a pathologist. Time travelers throw most of what she expects out the window. They're just odd.

A younger Evelyn would've liked odd; *did* like odd, in fact. Back when oddness and weirdness were signifiers she wielded like weapons. But now she's more concerned with simplicity, a stable life hard won. So, for Evelyn, a pathologist eyeing retirement, *odd* means something, somewhere, is wrong. The rhythm of the world has spoiled and is rotting, festering outwards. Evelyn understands better than most that where her safety and comfort is concerned, odd means a disruption. It means quarantine procedures. It means enough tests to turn her skin tender and bruised, more science experiment than lovingly cared for dermis. Odd means trouble, at least for Evelyn.

Evelyn doesn't like odd. Not anymore.

"Patient is about 182 centimeters," Evelyn notes into the recording device hovering near her mouth. The recording drone is an old model, but it's been with Evelyn for the majority of her time and it's never worked better. She doesn't need the new models that play music or that are AI-trained to provide hypotheses based on the notes coroners feed them. Evelyn doesn't need a second set of eyes or a computer-trained brain; she needs quiet and the room to hear her own thoughts.

Especially when dealing with the corpses of time travelers.

Evelyn gently pulls up a stiff eyelid, noting the hazel color with flecks of gold, a contrast to the fully gray mop of close-cropped hair. Whoever this traveler was, they were to code. Short hair is required for ease of blending in—hair styles are fickle, but a close-cropped cut is the easiest to explain in most timelines. Evelyn continues the visual examination, noting the simpleness of the body, the facial characteristics of a person born into and used to the cold, and the standard uniform of time travelers, soft cotton interwoven with holo-fabrics to easily and quickly adapt to the fashion of the era being visited.

Standard. Nothing out of place. Everything exactly as it should be.

So why then is this person dead, two centuries before the end of their assignment and projected life span?

Evelyn frowns, then sighs. She's already called her wife, letting her know that she'll have to undergo quarantine procedures and won't be home for two weeks. Standard time traveler quarantine protocol is one week. It takes them one week (usually) to determine if the body harbored any contaminant—organic, radiation, weaponry, etc.—that would put Evelyn at risk. But the inexplicable pit in her stomach when she received the body made Evelyn cautious. She said two weeks, but added that she was just being paranoid (for her wife's peace of mind, not just Evelyn's). Something is off, even if everything looks exactly as it should on the surface.

She really hates time travelers.

"Removing clothing and going to examine the skin," Evelyn notes.

She delicately slices the fabric along the seams. Holo-fabric is expensive and Evelyn doesn't want the fine for not properly seeing to the removal of the garment. The irony has never been lost on Evelyn that the fabric demands as much reverence and care as the body of the human before her.

With the expensive fabric removed and delicately folded and stowed in a bag prepared for quarantine and decontamination procedures, Evelyn returns to the body on her examination table, her nose wrinkling. Where she would normally slice the skin to begin the internal examination is a series of stitches of various colors and types of thread. Gently lifting arms and legs, Evelyn traces the stitching around the entire body. Somebody cut this traveler's body open already. Some of the stitching looks clean, expertly done and cared for, while other portions betray an amateur hand with less-than-ideal tools. Crude cuts alongside expert precision. Not the same somebody doing the incisions, then. The cuts gnaw at Evelyn. They don't look vicious; there are no other signs of trauma on the body. In fact, there are no signs of distress on the body at all. No skin or blood or dirt under fingernails, no bruising, no (non-stitched) lacerations. It's as if this traveler endured surgery after surgery.

No, not just surgery. A Y-incision means somebody opened this body up. A Y-incision means an autopsy.

"Impossible," Evelyn breathes, and then does her best to summarize the location and size of each sewn-up cut on the traveler's body.

It can't be an autopsy, though.

The thought won't release Evelyn. Even beyond the fact that the skin responded to many of the lacerations and stitches as living skin does—it clotted, it *recognized* it was being cut and tried to heal it—there are fail safes. Each time traveler has a device inserted under the hair in the back of their scalp, one that ensures the traveler's body will always be returned to the Bureau in the traveler's home time period. A device that is activated within minutes after key vitals flatline. Not even Evelyn is allowed to remove it or tamper with the device during the autopsy. And besides: the device obviously worked, since the traveler's body was returned, the death filed, and the body sent to Evelyn. So even if somebody in a different time period wanted to perform an autopsy on the traveler, there wouldn't have been time.

And yet, the Y-incision.

Move on, she chides herself. *The answer is inside.*

Evelyn doesn't bother taking deep breaths. She's calm, even if annoyed that her instinct on this particular body is right.

She doesn't need zen; she needs to just do her job so she can get started with quarantine and go home to her wife and their simple life of puzzles, wine, and too much takeout.

"No personal identifying marks," Evelyn reports after she finishes cataloging the exact place and size of all the stitches. "No tattoos, no birthmarks. No scars, other than the previously stated incisions."

This is as expected. Tattoos are prohibited for time travelers and all birthmarks and scars are removed and covered to the best of science's ability. And science's best ability—at least when it comes to time travelers—is very good. While the rest of humanity suffered technological setbacks due to climate change and wars, time travel research (privately funded) soared. Humans knew they couldn't save their world, so they invested everything they could into going backwards. The "why" was never really questioned. If you were rich and time travel existed as your planet was about to crumble under the weight of human arrogance and greed, wouldn't you want to find a different timeline to restart in?

Okay, so maybe Evelyn begrudges time travelers, not just for the wrench they throw in the calm and routine system of her life, but also because of what they represent: the rich calling a mulligan on the problem they created.

She finishes the external exam, already feeling the tension compounding between her shoulder blades. She is tense. And not just in the way she sometimes gets when she becomes worked up over the Bureau (and her potential implication by being a Bureau-approved pathologist). Something is wrong. The Y-incision feels like a spot of mold on an otherwise unblemished apple.

"Beginning internal examination." Evelyn grabs her scalpel and pretends her voice doesn't shake. She's too respected at this to have her unease recorded forever.

Get it together, she scolds herself and makes her own Y-incision like cutting along the dotted lines of a paper doll. Then she peels back the folds of skin and—

Evelyn doesn't gasp. Her reputation isn't just a matter of pride, it's well earned. So while she doesn't gasp, she does frown. A deep, rancorous frown.

Where the time traveler's rib cage should be instead rest bracelets of silver and crystal, crisscrossed in the interlocking patterns of a gilded basket. The bracelets glisten with blood and the reflection of Evelyn's bright examination lights; they are embedded into the tissue, ground within the viscera like someone was trying to bury them. She leans in closer and that's when she realizes: the rib bones aren't missing. They are shorn, the fragments of bone cut off to make room for the bracelets, amputated and useless. Somebody—with surgical precision and decent tools designed for this purpose—cut each rib in a perfect line.

And then Evelyn sees the other relics.

It isn't just the handful of silver and crystal bracelets embedded into the traveler's body. Bones are cracked and organs shifted and splintered to make room for a treasure trove of artifacts. Sea urchin-shaped earrings, made of gold. Tiny wicker baskets with grape seeds. Bracelets of crystal quartz. Marine shells and a spattering of stone tools. Clay figurines and tools of obsidian. All buried within the cavern of the traveler's torso, tucked into nooks of organ and tissue.

"There are numerous… " Evelyn searches for the right word. "…objects inserted into the body. I will make a full catalog on their removal. I still cannot ascertain the cause of death."

Of course not, Evelyn thinks, *but I have a guess. Being turned into an archeologist's pinata probably has something to do with it.*

But no guesses, not until she's finished the examination.

And to do so, she needs to actually see the organs.

Evelyn takes care to remove the artifacts first to give her more access to the body. But in many cases tissue and clay are clotted together, metal fusing with viscera. The travelers' organs are lacerated from the trinkets, scarred and healed time and time again. But the level of scarification is inconsistent; some old and weathered, others fresher and raw.

"Not all of the objects were inserted at the same time," Evelyn concludes.

This was not a single surgery. There was time for the wounds to heal, the body to adapt. The traveler was living with these objects inside of them; but for how long? Had the traveler agreed to this procedure? *They must've,* Evelyn decides almost immediately. Because unless somebody was following this traveler from place to place—against Bureau procedure—then the only person to oversee such a lengthy and involved process was the traveler themself.

Could it be another traveler from the Bureau? But that's asking questions Evelyn already knows the answer to, medically. There is no way for this traveler to not have known what was happening with their body. If not internally, then certainly externally. And since they were the only constant between all the timelines they visited, they probably weren't just aware; they were initiating the surgeries themselves.

But that's a thought that doesn't comfort Evelyn when she finds an entire human skull inside of the traveler's stomach.

The skull is perfectly preserved, polished and cared for. The skull of somebody important or somebody loved, wrapped in stomach tissue like a velvet jewelry box. It's the only organic artifact placed inside of the traveler's body, and it disquiets Evelyn more than the mishmash of tiny treasures. Why a skull?

Evelyn places the excavated objects in sterilized metal trays off to the side. She's curious, desperately curious to examine each of them; but she's not an anthropologist, she's a pathologist. Her job lies with the human body on her table. She can—and will—examine the objects afterwards, see if there's a connection between them and any possibly fatal damage to the traveler; but for now, she needs to finish examining the organs.

As Evelyn returns to the body, the folded back skin catches her eye. Specifically, a jagged, thick vein of scar tissue on the inside of the skin catches her eye. *A scar.* Evelyn realizes her mistake; when she first made her own Y-incision, she reported that the skin was unblemished. Now, with the organs fully removed, she sees this is incorrect. The skin is only unblemished from the outside; the inside of the skin is heavily scarred. And not just the result of the stitched together incisions, or potential cuts from the sharper of the artifacts buried beside intestines and organs; but intentional, deliberate scarring. Finely considered lines and curves, symbols, letters, and even crude pictures like cave paintings. Evelyn scans the scars quickly, looking for a pattern, and it doesn't take her long to find it: the letter R carved into the flap of skin receding into the traveler's armpit.

"There is writing on the inside of the skin."

Nothing responds, and for the first time in her professional life, Evelyn curses never having upgraded her recording device to one with even the most rudimentary of AI. She wishes she could call up her wife, a woman with far more imagination than Evelyn; a gardener, a teacher, a lapsed sculptor. Evelyn can draw theories and conclusions based on whatever string of bodily evidence is put before her. She knows the human body—and all the ways it can be damaged—so it's easy for her to link clues into a logical conclusion. But her wife can conjure monsters from moons, and the sinking, sour feeling in Evelyn's stomach makes her think she needs more mythology than science right now.

This is way beyond odd, Evelyn thinks, and is proud of herself for holding back her chuckle.

"There is writing on the inside of the skin. And from what I can tell with my minor in art history, it's in multiple different languages," Evelyn adds. Okay, maybe her professionalism is cracking a bit.

But she's right. The stark lines, the elegant curves, the clusters of markings are reminiscent of a multitude of languages; some Evelyn recognizes, some she doesn't. She took art history to have something to talk about with a woman she had a crush on. Then she kept taking courses about Pre-Raphaelite painters and Greek sculptors when they became more interesting and when the woman became her girlfriend. Evelyn's thankful for it now.

Returning to the first R, Evelyn tries to determine if there are other identifiable letters surrounding it. At first it's hard to tell which lines cluster together, but after a few minutes of looking, she begins to spot the pattern. Some share the same shape and confidence in stroke; others are more jagged. Cuts made by different hands. Some more healed than others, indicating many made when the traveler was alive. But it confirms Evelyn's theory—this is *writing*—so she focuses on identifying the letters near the armpit.

Right before the R, and on the heels of a beautiful looping script, Evelyn notices what could be a C. Then the very clear R, so starkly identifiable amidst the curves and loops of the other surrounding words. Without peeling more skin back, Evelyn thinks she sees another C following the R. But, no, that can't be it. The bottom loop of the C looks like it continues upwards. With her scalpel, Evelyn cuts a bit more of the dermis, just enough to free the rest of the shape: an O.

"I'm able to identify some of the letters carved into the skin," Evelyn reports. "I'm going to cut more of the skin around the right armpit to reveal more."

And as Evelyn does so, she knows the word before she finishes identifying the next letters. C, then R, then O, then A. She doesn't even stifle her laugh this time—a loud, raucous one—before saying, "Croatoan. This traveler's body has the fucking word 'Croatoan' etched into the *inside* of their skin."

Her recording device hovers and hums. Evelyn drops her scalpel with a clink.

Unbelievable, she thinks. Annoyed. Angry.

"I want a bonus," she says into the device. "I'm going to be in quarantine for at least a month after this."

She knows the Bureau will listen to her report, that they will not just read the file she'll send along, and that they will not just skip to the end to find out the cause of death. They don't care about the cause of death, Evelyn understands. They already know that. What they don't know is what the traveler's body contains and if it's dangerous. If it's a virus. Or biohazardous. Or maybe even a bomb. How much they knew of the body they were sending her is anybody's guess, and Evelyn is pissed. She hates being taken for a ride, for being tricked into playing a game of politics.

"A big bonus," Evelyn adds. "For being your expendable collateral damage."

Evelyn wasn't given the name or assignment of this traveler. Confidential, even for someone of Evelyn's rank and position. All she was given was an estimated life span and what condition the body was in when it was returned to their current time.

Evelyn doesn't know why they keep the missions confidential; while a younger version of herself was fixated on solving that particular mystery, she no longer really cares. She will not outlive her current timeline, so she focuses on making this current one special for herself and her wife. Their puzzles and their failed attempts at cooking and their love of five-dollar pizza from around the corner. That's all she cares about now.

But just because Evelyn is no longer preoccupied with unraveling the mystery of her sometime-employer doesn't mean she's forgotten everything from back when she felt more like a conspiracy theorist than a coroner. There were rumors of one particular mission, one particular traveler, who was sent specifically to civilizations on the brink. Not to warn, but to gather. A different type of failsafe than the device planted into travelers' skulls. This person—whose name Evelyn could never dig up, but whom she dubbed Rose for the ancient roses of Pompeii—was sent to collect artifacts from civilizations prior to their collapse. Evelyn fancied it more romantic hyperbole than fact, and yet…

And yet the Y-incision. And the lacerations made by different hands, with different tools, different levels of skill and technology.

Evelyn forces herself to remember, to think back to those late nights she spent in the Bureau archives, pretending to be an investigative reporter. She cared so much back then, back when it felt like she could make a difference rather than just being the puppet of an organization that didn't even reveal its full jurisdiction. Back when *odd* was something that excited her, rather than something that threatened her small patch of happiness. Rumors of Rose and rumors of civilizations long extinct and the relics that archeologists found.

Plenty of jewelry was recovered from Pompeii. Baskets with preserved seeds and other sundry were found in the sunken treasures of Thonis. At Çatalhöyük, obsidian. Shells at Cahokia. Mundane items made into artifacts, some stolen from their land, some preserved, all reminiscent of civilizations long gone. And the godforsaken word "croatoan", either a bad joke written on the inside of a time traveler's body, or an earnest plea for somebody, somewhere, in some time period, to find the lost colony in North Carolina.

It all matches, Evelyn thinks, angry and frustrated, no spark of her former self delighting in this discovery. Because now she understands the consequences of being right, of learning too much of a state secret.

"You're not going to let me out of here," Evelyn says.

She doesn't know why. She doesn't really know what she's found, only that it feels *wrong* and she doesn't need to know what it all means to know that she's a loose end.

Defeat swims in Evelyn's brain, clouding her thoughts and judgment.

"Why me?" Evelyn asks, staring at the exposed corpse in front of her.

And then she hears the ticking.

At first she thinks her worst fear is correct: a bomb.

But then she notices where the ticking is coming from, and fear like ice water evaporates into curiosity. The ticking is coming from the back of the traveler's skull. Where the return-to-sender device is implanted. The ticking: not a warning of detonation, but of evaporation. The device is about to activate, and while Evelyn doesn't know how long she has, she knows it's not a lot of time.

She understands. She's a pathologist, she knows how to form connections and evidence-supported hypotheses based on hard facts in front of her. Maybe she doesn't have the imagination to conjure new solar systems and new creatures, but she knows how to reason. She's *brilliant* at reasoning. And she was wrong before. She thought she was the expendable pathologist, the one the Bureau decided could weather the brunt of whatever might have been maliciously put into the body of the traveler. And while she's not a technologist, she has no trouble believing that the failsafe device could be wired to make multiple stops. If it could yank a corpse through all of human history, then it could control how many times and places it would visit before making its final return home.

Home, Evelyn thinks with a hitch in her throat, knowing full well after she is done here she will break quarantine procedure so she can go home to her wife. To a frozen pizza and whatever reality show her wife wants to watch.

But before she can go home, she needs to fulfill her part in all of this.

Evelyn acts fast.

She replaces the organs and the artifacts, doing her best to make everything fit, a hastily packed bag. And then she enters the adjoining room and grabs her wedding ring off her desk. She'll miss it, but a symbol of love is a symbol of love. Returning to the body, she slips the ring onto a sawed-off rib bone, where it sparkles from the bright lights of the examination room. The ticking is faster now, urging Evelyn to hurry up.

Just a few more minutes.

Evelyn sews the body back up. She›s good; her fingers work with expertise and muscle memory. Even still, she finishes the last stitch just seconds before the ticking stops.

Then, the body in front of her blinks, its corporeality bleeding into a static of cells and carbon, and vanishes.

And Evelyn is alone in the examination room, her soiled tools and the humming recording device hanging near her head. She breathes steadily for a few minutes, not wondering where the traveler's body was off to next. She's curious, not for the traveler's fate, but for her own. How long does she—and the people she considers her family, her friends, her colleagues and society—how long do they have before they too are lost?

Then Evelyn moves. It doesn't matter. Or it *does* matter, it's the only thing that really matters, but she can't fix it. She can't stop it. She doesn't even know what it is. She performs a quick decontamination procedure before leaving her examination room and slips out of the building.

Then Evelyn goes home and waits for the end of her whole world.

My Strengths Include Customer Service and Teamwork

By Lew Furber

11:30, OmniMart, Checkout Six.

"The Discount Shirt and Blouse Emporium just turned to sand out there," said Meat Man, flinging—without proper situational reverence—his daily dozen packets of meat onto my conveyor belt. "Everyone inside it, too. Like that." He stopped chewing his gum to snap his fingers, then went on open-mouthed like the horses in OmniMart's Nutritional TV Dinners chewed apples.

"Thank you for choosing OmniMart, where all your shopping demands are our pleasure to satisfy," I said, as I had been trained and born to say. I began beeping the packets of meat through to the bagging area. Manager Tanya once wrote in my Monthly Employee Value Report that I sounded like a yapping dog, but also that high voices caused in customers an increase in Promotional Receptiveness and Purchasing Goodwill, and that was of supreme importance. "We have a special offer on OmniMart Value Gum today, sir," I said in my highest octave.

"It's annoying," said Meat Man, chewing, "because I needed a refund on these shirts." He showed me a plastic bag full of deficient shirts.

"Can I interest you in our half-price OmniMart Value Gum, sir?"

"Guess I'll have to go all the way across town to The Discount Shirt and Blouse Mega-Emporium now, huh." Meat Man chewed eight times. "If it hasn't turned into a sandcastle, too."

He laughed and I accidentally wanted him to die.

Per the OmniMart Employee Handbook:

When an employee entertains thoughts about a customer which might reasonably terminate said customer's furtherance of their Commercial Rapport with the Company, the employee will self-correct by application of the Employee Correction Wand (ECW) to the inside of the left cheek. If the left cheek is unavailable due to recent or ongoing self-correction, the right may be substituted.

"Our offer on OmniMart Value Gum is unmatched by our competitors," I yapped.

"No, thanks. I'm all stocked."

"You have an OmniPleasant day, sir."

Meat Man left. I slipped my ECW from the pocket of my OmniMart Value Polyester Slacks. It resembled the cigarette lighter from my OmniCar, only longer and slimmer, like a pen. I charged it until it was orange-hot and applied the burner to my right cheek. The pain and return to equilibrium brought about in me a kind of shuddering ecstasy. The OmniMart Corporation's dignity and, by extension, my own had been made whole again. I felt around the edge of the burning O inside my mouth with the tip of my tongue.

"Next customer, please."

12:00, OmniMart, Checkout Six.

Woman In Bouffant Wig presented for purchase some defrosted OmniMart Good-For-You Lamb Legs, wet and dripping in their plastic wrap.

"The Gigaplex next door has gone too, y'know," she said. "Turned to sand while I was parking the minivan. Like that. And the Seven Continents. Y'know, the buffet?"

I beeped the lamb legs through to the bagging area.

"Can I get a discount, honey? These were frozen when I picked them up, honest to God. It's almost as hot in here as it is out there. You should go look. Everything's broiling like bacon. Good day for a lamb leg BBQ, y'know?"

"A generous three percent discount has been applied, ma'am. I will have to wait for my OmniBreak to see outside." Thank OmniMart there were no windows to distract me from my duty nor the customers from expressing the shopping demands it was my pleasure to satisfy.

"Hope you're still alive by then, hon. And I'll take twenty-five packets of that gum for my kids."

"It's half price," I said in an octave higher than I had ever reached. Woman In Bouffant Wig flinched. I regretted it in my guts.

"In that case, I'll take fifty," she said, shaking my voice out of her ears. "For the kids."

I prepared the ECW while she fumbled for exact change. I slipped off my left shoe and pressed the burner into the ball of my foot, searing an O and drawing blood with the ECW's sharp circular edge, as the Handbook prescribed.

12:05, OmniMart, Checkout Six.

Woman in Bouffant Wig's gum and lamb legs turned to sand in her bag before she made it past Greeter Paul, who thanked her for shopping at OmniMart. I called for Manager Tanya, per company policy, but Woman In Bouffant Wig turned to sand while she waited. Manager Tanya came and placed an orange cone next to the pile of Woman In Bouffant Wig.

13:30, OmniMart, Checkout Six.

It is essential, said the Employee Handbook, *to maintain the Optimal Smile for a difficult customer.*

Coupon Man wanted to know how hard it could be to swap the coupons he had collected for the OmniMart Wind-up Radio they had promised him.

"How hard could it be? How hard?" He hammered the end of his finger on the top of my register.

"How hard could it be to twist your head clean off?" I said, losing control of my larynx and the discipline I was sworn to hold there, which kept Unacceptable Customer Conversation Topics unbroached. My voice sounded like paper rubbing against paper. I tried to push it back in with cupped palms. My Optimal Smile failed.

"What? Speak up, for God's sake."

"How hard—" I was strangled, gasping. I couldn't stop myself and I clawed at my throat "—could it be—" my eyes burned, spewed liquid, and I fell to my knees "—to twist your head clean off?"

Manager Tanya passed the end of checkout six as part of her Hourly Compliance Assurance Routine. My skin screamed with pleasure and fear, all the way in and all the way down.

"Your behavior is an affront to the grace of the OmniMart Corporation," she said. It was Managerial Reprimand Number Three-Point-Three, Appendix Two, page seventy of the OmniMart Employee Handbook.

Within me, hot metal hands enclosed my heart and other offal, squeezing them through knuckles and fists into mincemeat.

"My OmniPologies, sir," said Manager Tanya. "Your custom is valuable to us. Can I offer you a complimentary supply of OmniMart Assorted Animal Ribs?"

"How hard can it be to get a wind-up radio?" Coupon Man stomped. He turned to sand, feet up to face, gargling his indignation.

"Sweep him over there by the cone," said Manager Tanya. "And I'm taking you off checkout. See me at the end of your OmniShift." Reprimand Addendum One, Appendix Two, page seventy-two. She left me, shaking her head.

I had disgusted myself and my Employer. I prepared my ECW.

14:00, OmniMart, Aisle Twelve, Pet Food.

I deserved this demotion, but I prayed to OmniMart it was temporary. It was an opportunity, in that sense, for Continuing

Personal Devotion. Manager Tanya had sent me to assist Stacker Gino in keeping our store's shelf-stacking velocity within company parameters. We had one thousand cans of OmniMart Pork-Turkey-Duck Meal for Dogs and Cats to stack before three o'clock. Stacker Gino did not stack with the precision OmniMart expected of us. He was a blemish.

"Aren't you frightened?" said Stacker Gino. He wiped sweat from his forehead and neck with the sleeve of his OmniMart fleece, contravening Rule Eight: *Employee uniforms must remain pristine at all times. Failure to comply will necessitate self-correction.* Stacker Gino failed to self-correct, though I spied with some envy a new double-ended ECW poking out of his pocket. A jagged rage branched up over the back of my skull and down my face into my throat. If there hadn't been a customer leaning over our crouching forms, surveying the superb range of pet food presented on the upper shelves, I would have corrected Stacker Gino with my own ECW.

Per the OmniMart Employee Handbook:

When an employee fails to self-correct, a colleague may carry out the correction, or the employee(s) may be terminated.

"It is impossible to be frightened at OmniMart," I said, projecting for the customer humming to himself above us. "Are you trying to damage our customers' and colleagues' Commercial Rapport with your negativity? What reason is there to be frightened? Is Regional Manager Pavel here?" This was a terrific prospect. It caused in me a welcome abdominal convulsion. "If you're frightened of him, it's because you've done something to deserve to be. It's in the Handbook."

"But the sand? And the heat? Have you seen out there? Everything's gone. It's a desert. Aren't you frightened of that?"

"So, Regional Manager Pavel is not coming?"

"No one's coming." Stacker Gino's face swelled red. His crying was an unbearable shame on us all.

"Pardon me," said Leaning Customer. "Where is the canned veal?"

"The canned veal is in Aisle Forty-four, sir," I said, soprano-like. "It would be my pleasure to take you there, if you demand it."

"I think I've got it."

"You have an OmniPleasant day, sir."

Leaning Customer moved away, singing softly an improvised tune on the subject of canned veal.

"You see, Gino," I said. "Even with blood coming from my mouth and shoe, I am a more attractive and trustworthy company representative in the eyes of the customer. That is why the customer approached me and not you. I am a better employee than you. That is because I am not crying. I am a good team player, also capable of working independently. I am passionate about delivering authentic Customer Joy-Experiences in a retail environment. I self-correct at the appropriate times. That is more than can be said for you. Your behavior is an affront to the grace of the OmniMart Corporation."

Stacker Gino began to choke on the sand that had been his tongue, ejecting brownish puffs into my eyes. This complicated things. Without a tongue, I could not correct him with the ECW in the Handbook-prescribed bodily locus.

"You won't get out of it," I said. "There is no bearable alternative to passion."

15:00, OmniMart, Break Room Window.

It was desert as far as the horizon, like Stacker Gino had said. The Discount Shirt and Blouse Emporium, the Gigaplex, and the Seven Continents buffet had all turned into great pyramids of sand. The sun burned red, and the plate glass of the break room window had started to melt, thickening at the bottom of the pane.

I turned back to page one of the OmniMart Employee Handbook, having reached the final page six minutes before the end of my break.

16:00, OmniMart, Customer Service Desk.

"It's always good to look at things closely," said Microscope Grandma. "I said to my grandsons, 'It's always good to look at things closely, boys,' I said, 'cause that's what my teachers used to say. I bought them this microscope set for their birthday—they're twins, used to be triplets—so they could look at things closely, like my teachers used to say and like their old Grandma told 'em. Anyhow, I think it's broken or faulty or kaput or something 'cause all they want to do is argue over that damned action dolly of their late brother's, God rest his sandy soul. What's boys wanting from a dolly when there's a microscope set to be had? I don't know. You find anything wrong with it, sugar?"

"One moment, please," I said.

Customer Service Representatives Barbara and Nicola lay in two neat piles behind the customer service desk and, as I was the only employee left alive who had been trained in returns besides Manager Tanya, I was filling in. Manager Tanya had important company computer tasks to complete in her Office, where I would receive Rightful Punishment later. I picked up a few grains of Customer Service Representative Nicola, who always stood on the right when viewed from the customer side of the desk, and put them on a slide. Magnified through the microscope, hundreds of tiny Customer Service Representative Nicolas—all red and purple, blotchy, with blown tissues around their orifices and extremities—lay piled and dead.

"One moment, please," I said. I left the desk to collect a handful of sand from the pile by the orange cone. I placed some of the grains on another slide and inspected them. On the clear plastic, lit white from underneath, were hundreds of Women in Bouffant Wigs and Coupon Men, dead and puffed and blown, and several thousand lamb legs and packs of gum.

"This item seems fully within expected operation, ma'am," I said.

"May I?"

I turned the microscope around for her to inspect.

"But why," she said, "are there dead people in my microscope?"

"Excuse me. May I?" Knowledgeable Man said over her shoulder. Microscope Grandma stood aside. Knowledgeable Man took a long look at the magnified corpses. "Ah, yes. I heard about this. It was on the television news."

"What did you hear, sugar? What did the news people say about my microscope?"

Knowledgeable Man spluttered. He flapped his mouth like the half-dead OmniSalmon on Miriam Fish Counter's fish counter. "It's something to do with, uhh, well, experimentation in the field of, uhh, you know, the scientific field of, uhh, airborne methods of, uhh, meat product duplic—"

"Spit it out, son," said Someone Else at the back of the line.

Knowledgeable Man flushed red, purple, then burst into sand.

"Now, honey," Microscope Grandma said, "how's about that refund?"

I tapped the necessary buttons in the necessary order on the point-of-sale screen. It rebuked me. "A Manager is required to process a refund on a single item of this value or higher, ma'am," I said. "A Manager will arrive promptly. My OmniThanks for your continued patience."

"Mmhm."

I pressed the Manager Tanya buzzer under the desk. After a couple of minutes of my Optimal Smile, when no one—Manager Tanya or otherwise—had arrived, I excused myself with courtesy and headed to the Office. It was against Rule Fifteen, let alone immoral, for a Manager to ignore a summons to the Customer Service Desk.

16:05, OmniMart, Management Office.

The Office had become a tomb with OmniMart Value Roller Blinds. Manager Tanya was dead. The billion puffed and blown micro-duplicates of her corpse streamed, like a little Niagara, off her swivel chair onto the carpet tiles.

Relief cooled me. I would not receive Rightful Punishment.

But this was against Rule Twenty-one: *Rightful Punishment may not be avoided under any circumstances.*

Bereft, I speed-dialed Regional Manager Pavel from the desk phone.

No answer.

I collected a handful of Manager Tanya and still had a few grains left, stuck to the sweat of my palm, by the time I made it back to the Customer Service Desk. Microscope Grandma had gone, whether through impatience or transformation. I inspected my palm under the microscope. Nestled side by side in the magnified canyon of my life line were five Dead Manager Tanyas.

I picked up the Customer Service Desk phone, dialed zero. "Staff announcement: All hands please congregate at the CS Desk. Thank you."

16:10, OmniMart, Customer Service Desk.

Four staff remained in the store, including me. We stood in a square around Knowledgeable Man's remains in front of the Customer Service Desk. Stacker Gino, Greeter Paul, and Miriam Fish Counter each took to the microscope to identify for themselves the corpse of our Manager.

"As acting Store Manager," I said, "I declare that we will continue at our default posts for the remainder of our OmniShifts."

"Acting Store Manager? You?" said Miriam Fish Counter, smelling of high-quality low-cost fish.

"I am the senior staff member."

"I've got my own counter."

"But I am trained in several customer facing roles," I said.

She exhaled hard through her nose.

"Well, we're all on the same wage, aren't we? Low as can be," said Stacker Gino via a small whiteboard he should not have taken from Aisle Ninety-one, Stationery.

"I and the OmniMart Corporation have had quite enough of your insolence, Gino," I said. I shook all over with the thrill of zeal. "This is why you cannot be the Manager." Then, accidentally, I said, "It's not like they're going to pay me any more money, is it?"

Greeter Paul and Miriam Fish Counter clapped their hands to their ears. I applied my ECW's burner to the insides of my elbows and the backs of my knees, where recent self-corrections were still teaching me to improve. The ECW opened these wounds again, and I stepped closer to redemption and a stamp on my Employee Reward Card.

"I'm a volunteer," said Greeter Paul. "The only wages I receive and need are the customers' satisfied smiles."

"Well, I'm out of here. Four fifteen. End of my shift. Twelve hours here, twelve at home. Who could ask for more?" Miriam Fish Counter walked toward the automatic doors, but stopped at the sight of a fierce sandstorm, the color of OmniMart Fried Chicken, on the other side. "Maybe I'll wait in the break room a little while," she said. "Till this blows over."

"Per the OmniMart Employee Handbook," I said, *"Employees are not permitted to remain on OmniMart premises, including parking areas, outside the bounds of their OmniShifts, except by commandment of Management."*

"I agree," said Greeter Paul. "Do you want to get fired, Miri?"

I wrestled Miriam Fish Counter by her hair and the collar of her smock toward the door, which Greeter Paul managed to open manually against the wind. I pushed Miriam Fish Counter out into the storm. She turned to sand, screaming, and blew away.

"Goodbye, Miri. See you tomorrow," said Greeter Paul.

"As previously stated," I said, "I suggest we all carry on at our default posts until the ends of our OmniShifts. Greeter Paul, greet. Stacker Gino, stack. I will work at checkout six."

"Are you crazy?" Stacker Gino wrote, gesticulating as if shouting, pacing, neither self-correcting nor appearing to be on the verge of doing so. "There's no one here. The world is gone and you're going on like a—"

I felt my hands around his throat, and the words of the OmniMart Employee Handbook left my mouth: *"When an employee fails to self-correct, a colleague may carry out the correction, or the employee(s) may be terminated."*

Stacker Gino's eyes bulged white and shiny-wet, like the jars of OmniMart Pickled Eggs stacked Brandenburg Gate-style across the end of Aisle Seventeen, Preserves. His attempts to pry my hands off him became weaker and soon he was dead.

"What choice did you have?" said Greeter Paul.

"I will stack and work the checkout."

"If anyone here can do that, it's you." Greeter Paul's watch beeped. "Four twenty exactly. End of the line for me. Better get going."

"See you tomorrow. I hope they will have sent a New Manager for us."

"I'll bet you a penny." Greeter Paul winked. He tightened the strap on his OmniMart Greeter's Cap and stepped out into the storm, as he was right to have done. Greeter Paul turned to sand.

17:50, OmniMart, Aisle Six, Medical.

There were OmniMart Super-Absorbent Multi-Purpose Bandages to stack. I had wounds which needed bandaging. Unlike Stacker Gino, I maintained my sense of moral fortitude and respect for the OmniMart Corporation. I would not steal bandages to solve my personal problems as Stacker Gino had stolen a whiteboard to solve his.

He had been correct about the emptiness of the store. I took a walk to the stockroom to find a stepladder and, on the way, I passed no one living. Piles of sand covered the floor. Their crunching under my shoes was the only sound beside the OmniMart Music that had been tinkling and noodling from the store speakers all day.

On the way back, the stepladder pressed educationally into the crook of my left elbow and the burning, bleeding O I had branded there. The Os on the backs of my knees and under my foot split further with each step I took. My mouth ached. Pus from the O within it collected under my tongue.

I set up the ladder and climbed it, but still I could not reach the top shelf without stretching my arms straight and tearing my Os open. The pain was righteous. It meant healing and betterment and tomorrow, when I returned, I would be a finer, more useful employee.

I slid a box of bandages over the edge of the top shelf, just above my reach, and felt a line of blood run up my bicep toward my shoulder. This threatened the sanctity of my uniform. Rule One forbade the theft of OmniMart stock or property, but there were a larger number of Rules concerning the cleanliness and condition of the uniform, and blood would not come out of fleece easily.

I stood for a moment on the ladder and let my hands slither up their opposite sleeves, where they held my wounds and stemmed the flow of blood. Below me on the pallet of bandages lay a box that had been crushed in transport. These bandages were not to be stacked. Under the circumstances, their use in preserving my uniform might have met Managerial Approval. And, under the circumstances, I was Management. Still, I would self-correct after, to honor the communal spirit of employment.

I pulled off my fleece—noting that, because my OmniShift had not ended, this act increased the required intensity of self-correction—and wrapped bandages around my elbows. I took out my ECW and seared a ring of Os onto my stomach, causing the skin to bubble and hiss and die. A high-pitched agony filled me. I clenched it between my teeth and crushed it into a euphoric oblivion.

While I stacked the remaining bandages, my watch beeped. Six o'clock. I stepped down from the ladder, straightened my uniform, and headed for the exit. Outside, the sandstorm had ended. The air was still and dry, as if it had died. There was a desert before me, as I had seen from the break room window, but I was fortunate that the great heat of the day had waned and the sun had dipped below the dune that was formerly the Discount Shirt and Blouse Emporium.

From my position in the remains of the employee parking area, somewhere near where my car had been, I watched OmniMart rumble and turn to sand.

Per the OmniMart Employee Handbook:

In the event of store closure, compromise, or destruction, employees may transfer to another OmniMart store, Company need permitting, by way of a Formal Transfer Request, sent with covering letter to their Regional Office.

I switched on my OmniPhone, opened my O-Mail. Subject line: "Formal Transfer Request."

I sat on the sand, careful to feel the penance of my wounds, and wrote about my strengths.

About the Authors

M. H. Ayinde is a runner, a chai lover, and a screen-time enthusiast. Her short fiction has appeared or is forthcoming in *FIYAH Literary Magazine, F&SF, Beneath Ceaseless Skies*, and elsewhere. She was the 2021 winner of the Future Worlds Prize for her novel *A Shadow in Chains*. She lives in London with three generations of her family and their Studio Ghibli obsession.

P. A. Cornell is a Chilean-Canadian speculative fiction writer. A member of SFWA and graduate of the Odyssey workshop, her short fiction has appeared in several professional markets. Additionally, her debut novella *Lost Cargo* was published in 2022 through Mocha Memoirs Press. A complete bibliography and social media links can be found at pacornell.com.

Yelena Crane is a Ukrainian/Soviet-born and United States-based writer, incorporating influences from both into her work. With an advanced degree in the sciences, she has followed her passions from mad scientist to sci-fi writer. She has work in *Nature Futures, DSF,* Third Flatiron, Dark Matter Ink, Flame Tree, and elsewhere. Follow her on Twitter @Aelintari and at her website, yelenacrane.com.

Rodrigo Culagovski is a Chilean architect, designer, and web developer. He currently heads a web development agency, is the CTO of an urban-data startup, and is a researcher and professor at Universidad Católica in Chile. He tweets as @culagovski. He misses his Commodore 64. Pronouns he/him/él.

Koji A. Dae is a queer American writer, living longterm in Bulgaria. Her work focuses on parenting, relationships, and neural technology, and can be found in places such as *Clarkesworld* and *Apex,* among others.

Kevin M. Folliard is a Chicagoland writer whose fiction has been collected by *The Horror Tree*, *The Dread Machine*, Demain, Dark Owl, and more. His recent publications include his horror anthology *The Misery King's Closet*, his YA fantasy adventure novel *Grayson North: Frost-Keeper of the Windy City*, and his dinosaur adventure novel *Carnivore Keepers*.

Lew Furber lives in Cardiff in the UK. He has worked in a catalogue laminating factory, been a waiter, an operating theatre dogsbody, a bartender, and a composer. He now teaches classical guitar and ukulele. His writing has appeared in *Lucent Dreaming*, *Clavmag*, *Capsule Stories*, and his sci-fi horror story "Winford's Dot" made the Galley Beggar Press Short Story Prize longlist.

Andrea Goyan (she/her) is an award-winning author and co-host of *Metastellar's Long Lost Friends*. Recent stories can be found in *Dark Recesses Press*, *All Worlds Wayfarer*, *The Arcanist (Camp Arcanist)*, and *The Molotov Cocktail*.

Ivy Grimes has stories appearing in *Vastarien*, *Daily Science Fiction*, *Cast of Wonders*, *Metaphorosis*, *Shirley Magazine*, and elsewhere. She lives in Virginia. Like Langdon Alger, she is very quiet and enjoys puzzles. To read more, visit her website at ivyivyivyivy.com, or follow her on Twitter @IvyGri.

Kay Hanifen was born on Friday the 13th and once lived for three months in a haunted castle. Her short stories have appeared in numerous anthologies, including *Diet Riot: A Fatterpunk Anthology*, *Slice of Paradise*, and *Devil's Rejects*. When she's not consuming pop culture with the voraciousness of a vampire at a 24-hour blood bank, you can find her at kayhanifenauthor.wordpress.com.

D. A. Jobe is a Virginia writer with a love of music, traveling, and horror movies. Her work has appeared in *The Washington Post*, *Brevity*, and anthologies, including *Bodies Full of Burning: An Anthology of Menopause-themed Horror*. She is currently working on a horror novel.

Wailana Kalama is a dark fiction writer from Hawaii, with credits in *Mother: Tales of Love and Terror* (Weird Little Worlds Press), *Pseudopod, The Maul, Apparition Lit, Rock and a Hard Place,* and upcoming in *Dark Matter Presents Monster Lairs: A Dark Fantasy Horror Anthology.*

Rae Knowles (she/her) is a queer woman with multiple works forthcoming from Brigids Gate Press. Her debut novel, *The Stradivarius,* is coming May 2023, her sapphic horror novella, *Merciless Waters,* is due out winter 2023, and her collaboration with April Yates, *Lies That Bind,* in early 2024. Follow her at RaeKnowles.com and on Twitter @_Rae_Knowles.

Catherine Kuo is an Asian American graduate of the University of California, Davis, where she was selected as one of the winners of the University Writing Program's 2010–2011 annual Prized Writing competition. Afterward, she spent several years working in Taiwan and Japan before settling in Arlington, Virginia. She can be found on Twitter @catherinekuo531.

Rich Larson was born in Galmi, Niger, has lived in Spain and Czech Republic, and currently writes from Montreal, Canada. He is the author of the novels *Ymir* and *Annex,* as well as the collection *Tomorrow Factory.* His fiction has been translated into over a dozen languages, and adapted into an Emmy-winning episode of *Love, Death & Robots.*

Avra Margariti is a queer author and Pushcart-nominated poet, with a fondness for the dark and the darling. Avra's work haunts publications such as *Vastarien, Asimov's, Liminality, Arsenika, The Future Fire, Space and Time, Lackington's,* and *Glittership.* Avra lives and studies in Athens, Greece. You can find Avra on Twitter @avramargariti.

J. A. W. McCarthy is the Bram Stoker Award and Shirley Jackson Award-nominated author of *Sometimes We're Cruel and Other Stories* and *Sleep Alone.* Her short fiction has appeared in numerous publications, including *The Best Horror of the Year Vol 13* (ed. Ellen Datlow). Follow her on Twitter @JAWMcCarthy, and find out more at jawmccarthy.com.

Christi Nogle is the author of the Bram Stoker Award®-nominated novel *Beulah* and the horror collection *The Best of Our Past, the Worst of Our Future*. Christi is co-editor of the Bram Stoker Award®-nominated anthology *Mother: Tales of Love and Terror* and co-editor of *Wilted Pages: An Anthology of Dark Academia*. Follow her at christinogle.com and on Twitter @christinogle.

Ashleigh Shears writes queer science fiction and horror from their shoebox in Toronto. When not stuck in the time loop, they work as a biomed engineer. Other sci-fi can be found in *Clarkesworld*.

D. Roe Shocky is a freelance science writer by day and writes speculative fiction by night, so he's pretty committed to this whole writing thing. His stories have appeared in anthologies including *Dark Stars* and *Tales From the Weird Weird West*. You can find out more at warmuppages.com, or on Twitter @droeshocky.

Lisa Short is a Texas-born, Kansas-bred writer of fantasy, science fiction, and horror. She has an honorable discharge from the United States Army, a degree in chemical engineering, and twenty years' experience as a professional engineer. Lisa currently lives in Maryland with her husband, youngest child, father-in-law, two cats, and a puppy. She is a member of SFWA, HWA, and Codex.

Hugh A. D. Spencer has published short fiction in *Descant, Interzone, On Spec,* and the *Tesseracts* series. He's been twice nominated for the Canadian Aurora Award, and his story "(Coping with) Norm Deviation" received an honorable mention in *The Year's Best Science Fiction* (2007). His second novel, *The Hard Side of the Moon,* was released in 2021.

Simo Srinivas lives in Colorado with their spouse and two senior, standard-issue tabby cats. When not writing about all things weird and queer—or rhapsodizing about the perfect mango—Simo can be found on the trail intently counting pikas. You can also find them on Twitter @srinivassimo and online at srinivassimo.com.

Kanishk Tantia is a BIPOC Immigrant from India. His speculative fiction often involves plants eating people. He currently lives in San Diego with his partner and an adorable dog with a criminal record. His works have been published or are upcoming in Dark Matter Ink, Flametree Press, and *The Dread Machine*.

M. Elizabeth Ticknor is a genderfluid, neurodiverse speculative fiction author who shares a comfortable hobbit hole in Southeast Michigan with her wookiee husband and their twin dragons. An avid fan of science fiction and fantasy, Elizabeth also enjoys well-written horror. Her other interests include drawing, painting, and tabletop role-playing.

S. J. Townend has published with Brigids Gate Press, Ghost Orchid Press, Gravestone Press, Timber Ghost Press, and elsewhere. She's the winner of the Secret Attic short story contest and the Tortive Literature story contest, and was shortlisted for the H. G. Wells Short Story Competition. Find her on Twitter @SJTownend or at her small press website bagofbonespress.com.

Kaitlin Tremblay (they/she) is a horror writer and video game developer. Tremblay is the author of the two non-fiction books on storytelling in video games: *Collaborative Worldbuilding for Video Games* and *Ain't No Place for a Hero: Borderlands*. They were the co-editor on the Shirley Jackson Award-nominated anthology *Those Who Make Us: Canadian Creature, Myth, and Monster Stories*.

Emily Ruth Verona is a Pinch Literary Award-winner and a Bram Stoker Awards®-nominee, with work featured in *Under Her Skin*, *Lamplight Magazine*, *Mystery Tribune*, *The Ghastling*, *Coffin Bell*, and *The Jewish Book of Horror*. Her debut thriller, *Midnight on Beacon Street*, is expected from Harper Perennial in 2024. For more visit emilyruthverona.com.

Aigner Loren Wilson is a SFWA and Codex writer. She is the senior fiction editor for *Strange Horizons* and writes for Tor Nightfire, *Lightspeed Magazine,* and other publications. Her work has appeared in *F&SF, Interzone, Fantasy Magazine,* and more. Visit her website aignerlwilson.com, and follow her on Facebook @Aigner Loren Wilson, or on Twitter @ALWlikeahowl.

About the Editor

Alex Woodroe was raised—possibly by wolves—in Romania, where she stumbled into weird speculative fiction and an endless supply of folklore. She made a career out of doing terrible things to words in multiple languages, and currently lives in the center of Transilvania, where she edits, writes articles, translates, or writes video game dialogue. You can read more of her stories at alexwoodroe.com, or keep in touch on Twitter @AlexWoodroe. Her debut novel, *Whisperwood,* will be published by Flame Tree Press on July 11, 2023.

About the Introduction Author

Andrew F. Sullivan is the author of *The Marigold,* a novel about a city eating itself, and *The Handyman Method,* a novel co-written with Nick Cutter. His previous books include the novel *Waste,* and the short story collection, *All We Want is Everything,* both named *Globe & Mail* Best Books of the Year. Sullivan lives in Hamilton, Ontario.

About the Cover Artist

Oliver Jeavons (Olly) is a UK-based artist also known as *artofolly*. He works with many different medias and styles, and he is always pushing his creativity further. Comic book art, book cover art, and commissions of all types are included in his portfolio.

Permissions

Also Available or Coming Soon from Dark Matter INK

Human Monsters: A Horror Anthology
Edited by Sadie Hartmann & Ashley Saywers
ISBN 978-1-958598-00-9

Zero Dark Thirty: The 30 Darkest Stories from Dark Matter Magazine, 2021–'22
Edited by Rob Carroll
ISBN 978-1-958598-16-0

Linghun by Ai Jiang
ISBN 978-1-958598-02-3

Our Love Will Devour Us by R. L. Meza
ISBN 978-1-958598-17-7

The Vein by Stephanie Nelson
ISBN 978-1-958598-15-3

Haunted Reels: Stories from the Minds of Professional Filmmakers curated by David Lawson
ISBN 978-1-958598-13-9

Other Minds by Eliane Boey
ISBN 978-1-958598-19-1

Frost Bite by Angela Sylvaine
ISBN 978-1-958598-03-0

Monster Lairs: A Dark Fantasy Horror Anthology
Edited by Anna Madden
ISBN 978-1-958598-08-5

Chopping Spree by Angela Sylvaine
ISBN 978-1-958598-31-3

The Bleed by Stephen S. Schreffler
ISBN 978-1-958598-11-5

The Bones Beneath Paris by Kelsea Yu
ISBN 978-1-958598-12-2

Free Burn by Drew Huff
ISBN 978-1-958598-26-9

The House at the End of Lacelean Street
by Catherine McCarthy
ISBN 978-1-958598-23-8

The Off-Season: An Anthology of Coastal New Weird
Edited by Marissa van Uden
ISBN 978-1-958598-24-5

The Dead Spot: Stories of Lost Girls
by Angela Sylvaine
ISBN 978-1-958598-27-6

Voracious by Belicia Rhea
ISBN 978-1-958598-25-2

Available or Coming Soon from Dark Hart Books

All These Subtle Deceits by C. S. Humble
ISBN 978-1-958598-04-7

All the Prospect Around Us by C. S. Humble
ISBN 978-1-958598-05-4

Rootwork by Tracy Cross
ISBN 978-1-958598-01-6

Mosaic by Catherine McCarthy
ISBN 978-1-958598-06-1

Apparitions by Adam Pottle
ISBN 978-1-958598-18-4

I Can See Your Lies by Izzy Lee
ISBN 978-1-958598-28-3

CPSIA information can be obtained
at www.ICGtesting.com
Printed in the USA
JSHW032331170423
40459JS00003B/10

9 781958 598078